M000029280

HEAVEN'S SILHOUETTE

MELISSA LYNN HEROLD

HEAVEN'S SILHOUETTE

IYARRI CHRONICLES BOOK I

WISE INK CREATIVE PUBLISHING

MINNEAPOLIS

ISBN 13: 978-1-63489-264-3
LCCN: 2019907465

Printed in the United States of America
First Printing 2019

23 22 21 20 19   5 4 3 2 1

Book design by Patrick Maloney

Wise Ink
807 Broadway Street NE, Suite 46
Minneapolis, MN 55413
wiseink.com

For my husband, David,
who believed in me, and my writing, when I did not;
who understands what it's like to have entire worlds inside your head;
who patiently waited for years so he could discover this story in its finished form.
I promise not to read over your shoulder.

ONE

I FLED INTO THE POND with my hands clapped over my ears, but it didn't block out the shrill jeers of the other children or their footfalls pounding up behind me to the shoreline. The clear, sunlit shallows didn't hide my malformed feet.

"Freak!"

The word bounced off the rocks surrounding the pond. My tormentors wouldn't go in the water, as if whatever was wrong with me was catching. A stone struck the water next to me and I sputtered, wiping water and wet sand from my face. "Monster!" another called.

The next rock hit me in the chest; I cried out and crumpled into the water, cowering under my skinny arms. Stones battered the water and pelted my body like hail, red welts rising in their wake.

The rocks ceased, footsteps scattered. My mother's arms closed around me, and I sobbed as she lifted me from the shallows. I grasped my mother's skirt with my feet—three thick toes of equal width, the centermost longer—and hid them in the folds of fabric. God had made me, my feet, different, my mother said—as if that made it better. I pressed my face into her neck and curled my fingers around the flashing green pendant she wore, as though it were a protective talisman.

The memory played out, over and over, even though my eyes stayed trained on the painting before me. I curled my toes in my ankle boots until the leather pinched and balled my hands into fists, trying to shut out the jeers, the hate and fear in the voices of those children from long ago. If I ceded my thoughts to them, others would follow—two decades of similar encounters kicking against the back of my mind like invaders at the door.

I closed my eyes and breathed in the cool, filtered air of the gallery, chasing away the green, watery scent of the pond, the memory of bruises blossoming on my skin. When I opened my eyes, the painting that had conjured those memories filled my mind instead.

It was tall, narrow, and drew my gaze upward; the canvas hung high on the wall to reinforce the effect. Brushstrokes blurred unfamiliar, arcane-looking symbols into the background, undulating depths of blue swallowing their legibility. In the foreground stood a barefoot young man in jeans and a T-shirt, his figure rendered in translucent grays and blues. A second image overlaid the man: the bones of the face finer, skin pale golden-tan and luminous, and behind him, the shadowed suggestion of wings.

And yet it was none of those things that rooted me to the spot and pinched an icy knot in my stomach. My mother called me her wild Irish fae for my pale skin, willowy body, and wavy ginger hair, but neither faeries nor humans had feet like mine—the angelic man in the painting did, mirror-perfect and far beyond artistic coincidence or collective consciousness.

My eyes dropped to the information placard.

Angels Unseen
Stephan Keller
Oil on canvas

I wanted to talk to the artist and ask who, or what, his source was. Three-toed, winged creatures were not uncommon in art: harpies, sirens, Garuda. Any of them were a possible inspiration, but the explanation was unsatisfying and my stomach did not unknot. That the feet were attached to an angel and not a monster, too, was unusual. The eyes of the painted man looked heavenward to the lighter blues and silvers at the top of the canvas, while the angel looked downward, at me, his wings casting a shadow over his face. My focus shifted between the man and the winged version of the same man, trading wings for none and normal feet for those like my own.

"It's not often I see you so taken with a painting." The voice behind me was smooth, articulate, and wry.

I blinked, startled, but my lips curved in a smile as I turned to greet my friend and mentor. "Hello, Aamon." With his fashionable fitted sweater, understated scarf, and white-blond hair in a smooth ponytail, Aamon looked at home in the Minneapolis Institute of Art. And he was—a dozen or so years older than me, he was already a key patron, donor, and board member, his influence enough to usher me into a gallery job when I'd graduated college.

Aamon stood beside me and took in the canvas, pensive and critical. "Has it been well-received?" His accent, whose origin I'd never placed, added a musical stress to the occasional syllable.

"I think so; it's gotten a lot of traffic." An errant wave of hair escaped its twist and I tucked it behind my ear, wishing I could hide my thoughts of three-toed feet alongside it. I spoke, instead, of my admiration for the vertical effect, the colors, and the skillful execution of the shifting focus.

Aamon's high cheekbones and fine nose could have made him look haughty, but the way his skin creased around his eyes when he smiled was genuine. "A skilled deconstruction of the techniques used, and yet not one word about how it makes you feel."

I bit my lower lip as the desire to talk about it with Aamon built inside me. He, better than anyone, could help me suss out the tangled knot of emotions the painting evoked, but that also meant telling him about my feet, and Aamon loved beauty. Each time I'd told someone about my deformities, they'd reacted with disgust or pity; in either case, the relationship was irrevocably damaged, and I didn't want to risk anything changing my friendship with Aamon. "The feelings a piece invokes in each viewer are unique," I said, letting go of my desire to tell him with a sad smile. "And private."

Aamon was about three words from getting a better answer out of me when Jacob, my boss, hailed him with a wave of his hand. Aamon inclined his head in apology. "Another time, Aurelia. Enjoy your day."

My chest sank with a sigh, relieved I hadn't talked more than perhaps I should have, but disappointed, too, that the opportunity was gone.

As I looked back at the panting, a hand fell on my shoulder, my thoughts scattering like startled birds.

"Excuse me, miss?" I knew our regulars, and the man behind me wasn't one of them. Equal parts rugged and beautiful, his work-worn clothes were offset by his clean-shaven face.

"Can I help you?" I hoped it didn't show on my face how badly he'd surprised me.

"I need to contact the artist of this painting." His voice was edged with urgency, pale blue eyes flickering to *Angels Unseen* as he pushed one hand through dark blond hair. "Can you help me?"

Finally, I said, "The painting is a new addition, but I could check and see if the artist signed a release for his contact information."

"Actually, I'd be happy to answer any questions you had."

We both turned as a man interjected himself into our conversation. The new arrival was a short, middle-aged man in expensive but rumpled clothes, his smile bright and kind. The artist extended his hand to me. "Stephan Keller."

I shook his hand. "Aurelia Drake. Pleasure to meet you."

The blond man nodded. "Lucien Rohtin."

Shy by nature, I wanted to step away and try to talk to Stephan alone afterward, but the fear of missing out on the only chance I might get for information compelled the question from my lips. "Can you tell me about the angel? His feet are so unusual, I'd love to know why you chose to paint them that way."

Stephan smiled, appreciative of the question. "I saw him." Lucien and I traded a surprised glance, but Stephan seemed too absorbed in his own memories to notice it. "Last winter, I donated a painting to the Rivercrest Monastery for a charity auction. I dropped it off with the friars and on my way back to my car, I saw that angel standing on the edge of the bluff overlooking the river."

"He looked like that?" I asked, curious and skeptical. In my artistic studies there were hundreds of depictions of angels. Islamic pottery, where they wore Persian kaftans and had multicolored wings; Enochian-inspired woodcuts, where each angel had hundreds of wings that opened and closed to reveal ever-watching eyes; and cathedral ceilings depicting skies full of cute putti and white-robed seraphim with pale, serene faces. The winged man looming over us with inhuman feet and delicate features was none of those things. It looked like me.

"Yes, but I only caught a glimpse of him." Stephan took off his glasses and rubbed them with the untucked hem of his shirt. "When he saw me, he turned into a man, and when I looked again, he was gone."

Lucien folded his arms and frowned, but I leaned forward, enthralled. "What did you do?"

Stephan's hands fluttered with excitement. "I found a footprint—I hadn't imagined it. When I told the friars, though, they only said I should take it as a sign I was blessed." Stephan furrowed his brow, but his smile persisted. "I became a bit obsessed with researching what I'd seen and must have asked a hundred people about it. I did this painting hoping others who have seen similar might notice it."

Lucien raised two critical eyebrows and gestured to the painting. "Where did you get those symbols from?"

"They're Enochian, the language of angels." Stephan's response was too hurried, too fumbling to be the truth.

"Would you excuse us, please?" Lucien asked me.

I moved a polite distance away and feigned interest in other patrons, but not so far I couldn't hear Lucien and Stephan, though their voices were pitched low.

"Those symbols aren't Enochian." Lucien's tone was flat.

Stephan's excited demeanor returned. "You know what they are?"

Lucien adjusted his worn brown leather coat. "I know this is not the place to continue this conversation."

"Of course," Stephan stammered. "I'll get my jacket and meet you in the parking lot." He hurried toward the main entrance.

I took a half step after him, but second-guessing rooted me to the spot. What would I do, take off my shoes and show Stephan my feet? *Angels Unseen* was painted to get answers, but all it had done was give me a million more questions and a sense of unease.

"Stay away from him." Lucien brushed past me, the smell of his cologne as clear and icy as his warning.

Before I could respond, Lucien headed after Stephan, buttoning his coat as he went. I wondered what Lucien knew—perhaps the painting had worked as Stephan intended.

Angels Unseen was missing when I returned from my break, the white wall barren save for mounting hardware. Where had it gone? Panic raced in a current along my skin.

I hurried down a hallway, glancing into one back room after another until, in a gallery prep room, I found the work crew boxing it up. Jacob stood by the door, and I tried not to crinkle my nose at the clinging, stale smell of his cigarettes. "Why did they take the painting down?" I asked.

"Mr. Keller called and requested the painting be returned to him immediately," Jacob said, his expression pinched and voice terse.

"Is he coming to get it himself?" A hopeful note flitted in my words.

Jacob turned toward me, seeing opportunity in my interest. "I have other obligations this evening, and Mr. Keller will be here at nine o'clock. If you're willing to stay late and release the painting to him, it would reflect well on your next performance review." He gave me an insincere, yellow smile.

I agreed, grabbing onto the chance to talk to Stephan. As Jacob detailed the process of transferring the painting back to the artist, the work crew draped *Angels Unseen* with a heavy cloth, fit the painting into a box, and interred that inside a second, larger box lying open on the floor—it was going to take a hand cart to move. After Jacob left, I leaned against the wall and pressed my fingers to my temples. Whoever Stephan saw by the monastery was tangible enough to leave footprints, and I didn't have much time to gather the courage to ask him questions about my own anatomy that my mother had dodged for years.

I peered through the small window in the loading dock door into the dark autumn night. Beyond the yellow haze of the streetlights, the Minneapolis skyline stretched upward, skyscrapers piercing the midnight-blue sky.

Headlights sliced through the darkness as a hatchback towing a small trailer pulled into the loading area and backed up to the doors. Stephan got out and wheeled a handcart up the short ramp where I opened the door for him. "I have all the paperwork for the transfer," I said. "But if you had a second I wanted to ask—"

"I'm sorry, but I have to go." Stephan wiped his hands on his pants, seized the boxed painting, and hefted it onto the cart.

I wanted to press for answers, but his brush-off crumpled my determination. "I need to see an ID and have you sign these."

Stephan gave me his license and signed the paperwork without reading a word, then shoved everything into my hands.

"Mr. Keller?" He turned, and I held out his driver's license.

He took it without a "thank you" and wheeled the painting down the ramp. My hand lingered in the air as the resolve to force the conversation filled my chest and then receded in defeat.

The autumn air was crisp, but my fingers fell away from my half-buttoned coat. Stephan struggled with the handcart, his path a drunken squiggle toward the trailer. The boxed painting swayed, inches from tipping and smashing onto the concrete. I darted to Stephan and put two hands on the box, steadying it. "Here, let me help."

An engine roared in the darkness and a blue truck swung into the loading area, its headlights blinding. Lucien stepped out of the truck, reached under the back of his hip-length leather coat, and drew two black pistols. Bright beams of white light flashed on from under the barrels and cut through the gloom.

I flattened myself against the side of the trailer, icy fear sluicing over my skin and freezing a startled cry in my throat. A thunderous bang hit my ears and I cowered. Wooden splinters scattered around my feet—not a gunshot, but the box that held *Angels Unseen* crashing to the pavement.

Stephan crouched by the cracked wood. "No, no, no," he repeated as his hands fluttered over the splintered wooden corner.

"I told you not to come back for it," Lucien yelled.

Before Stephan could respond, a humanoid shape streaked from the sky and struck him like some lightless, falling star. I screamed, but didn't run, the artist in me staring, awestruck. Wings arched from its back like feathered scythes—Stephan's own painting had come to attack him.

TWO

THE WINGED CREATURE GRABBED Stephan by the front of his coat and slammed him into the side of the trailer next to me, so hard the metal thrummed against my back like thunder. Stephan's hand scrabbled at the angel's hardened leather gauntlet, but the creature didn't let go.

Stephan's attacker swung his lean, muscled arm and lamplight chased up the patterned swirling scars that decorated his luminous skin. A silver blade leapt out mid-swing, scything into Stephan's neck. I snapped my head to the side, sputtering as blood sprayed across my chest, my face, and up the wall of the trailer in a crimson arc. The monster dropped Stephan, hooked his hand into the front of my wool peacoat, and pulled his arm blade back to strike.

A gunshot boomed and, in a blur of dark wings, a winged woman wrenched her wingmate backward as his shoulder exploded into a spray of gore. The silvery blade whistled past me.

"Gephna." The woman snarled the word like an expletive as she hauled my attacker to his feet and clamped her hand over his ruined shoulder.

A third winged shadow alighted onto an awning over the door and unshouldered a compact, lethal-looking bow. It creaked as he drew the string backward and trained the arrowhead on me.

Hands seized my legs and I screamed, stomach lurching, as Stephan clawed his way up my body, blood pouring down his chin in a frothy, crimson sheet. An arrow punched between Stephan's shoulder blades and he jerked backward, pulling me a step forward. With a hitching cry, I wrenched myself out of Stephan's grasp; he crumpled to the ground at my feet as heavy footfalls pounded behind me.

In one motion, Lucien yanked me away from Stephan and shoved me toward the truck. "Get in."

The creature with the wounded shoulder then leapt and dove toward us, arm blades swinging in a silver arc. Lucien leaned to one side and twisted, capturing one of the monster's arms in the crook of his elbow—he swung the creature off balance, brought the gun under its chin, and fired.

The air bloomed with the smell of steam, sulfur, and hot metal. There was no great spray of blood this time, just small bits of flesh and a red mist that choked the air. The creature's body slumped to the ground, wings curling like dead leaves.

My breath shook and my legs threatened to buckle. Bare-chested, the monster's body was sinewy and muscled, slim and powerful. The hair on my neck prickled—his three-toed feet were perfect physical manifestations of the ones on Stephan's canvas, like my feet, but with hooked talons at the end of the toes and a dewclaw on each Achilles tendon.

"Go!" Lucien's order jolted me from my stupor.

I scrambled into the cab of the truck and shut the door as Lucien climbed in, wrenched the truck into gear, and sped out of the parking lot. I wiped my face with my fingers, Stephan's blood still warm on my hands. My stomach rolled and the heartbeat in my ears drowned out everything around me. Trembling, I squeezed my eyes shut, the impossibility of what I'd seen colliding with the reality of blood and blades and feathers.

We fled through city lights and the spaces of dark between them. Lucien drove with one pistol in hand, balanced at the top of the wheel, the flashlight mounted under the barrel clicked off. At some point, he slowed the truck, reached across me to the glove box, and handed me a stack of napkins. "Here. Are you all right?" The dash lights gave his face an amber cast in the darkness.

I took the napkins and ground them into my skin, scrubbing at the blood on my face and neck. The white paper came away dark and stained. I clenched the napkins in my hands and then loosened my grip, feeling empty and spent. "It's a lot to take in."

Lucien turned back to the road. "It is." The note of sympathy in his voice quelled some of my terror. He put a fresh magazine in his gun with a familiarity that made me go still.

"I only heard you shoot twice?" I asked, unsure why he was reloading.

"A full gun is better, just in case."

The centerline ticked by and my breath fogged the window next to me before evaporating. In the black reflection of the car window my eyes were dilated, my irises a thin steel band around wide, dark pupils. "Where are we going?"

"My place for now. I'll take you home once things have died down."

I should have been uneasy driving off to an armed stranger's house, but instead some of the tightness in my chest loosened. "Thank you for taking me with you. Stephan—" The way his hands clawed at me for help even as his throat gaped open like a toothless mouth—I shuddered and wrapped my arms around myself. "They killed him."

"At least we got you out of there." His gaze met mine in the reflection of the window. "I'm Lucien; your name's Aurelia, right?"

I nodded and wiped my bloody hands with the napkins. "You can call me Lia." The question hammering the back of my head escaped my lips in one tumble of words. "Were those things angels?"

Lucien shook his head with a snort. "Not angels, Iyarri. Keller knew what they were. When he put that painting out there for everyone to see, it was only a matter of time until they came for him."

Iyarri. I held the word in my mind as it crystalized into a meaning all its own, tempered with blades and feathers and blood.

Illumination gave way to stretches of darkness as we passed the edge of the sprawling Minneapolis suburbs and headed into farmland near Hanover. The roads were rough and full of potholes by the time Lucien turned down a winding blacktop driveway. A lone lamppost lit a mailbox, and a carved stone sign read *Rohtin Stonecutting & Masonry.* "You're a stone mason?"

He shrugged. "It pays the bills."

I had worked at the museum long enough to know stonework wasn't something someone did to pay the bills, and I wondered how a stonemason became someone who knew enough about Iyarri to be mercilessly efficient at killing them.

The driveway wound under thick trees that choked out the moonlight.

I twisted the bloody napkins in my hands and stared at Lucien's gun—I was at a strange man's house, in the middle of nowhere, and nobody knew where I was. I pressed my hand to one empty pocket and then the other. My phone . . . it was in my purse, and I hadn't brought it with me.

The trees gave way to a neat plot of open land, and a floodlight cast a wide circle of light from the top of a pole, illuminating a beautiful single-story house—gray brick, rust-colored stone accents, and a tall roof. The dark windows mirrored the night sky and the blacker reflections of trees.

Lucien got out of the truck, holstered his gun, and waited for me with a sympathetic expression. "Let's get you cleaned up." He opened the door to a mudroom, where we shed our shoes and he took my bloody coat. Lucien led the way into the house; without his coat, I could see the twin matte-black pistols in a holster tucked into the back of his jeans.

He turned on the lights to a bathroom. "You can wash up in here."

I thanked him and closed the door behind me. The feeling of Stephan's desperate, grasping hands on my coat, the keening whistle of the split blade as it'd streaked past my neck, the sulfur-steam smell of Lucien's gunfire—they rolled in from my mind's eye and crashed into me like a tidal wave. Suddenly hot and nauseous, I tossed the napkins in the trash, leaned my elbows on the sink, and covered my face with my blood-streaked, shaking hands. I took three deep breaths before I lowered my hands from my face and turned on the sink.

The mirror revealed hazy streaks of blood on my cheeks and a fine array of droplets I'd missed, as though someone had flicked a damp paintbrush and added cerise freckles to my skin. I washed my face and hands over and over, well past the point where they came clean, hoping that with the blood gone the world would suddenly go back to making sense.

It didn't.

My French twist had fallen and wild ginger waves tumbled to my waist. I straightened my clothes, smoothed my hair, took a steadying breath, and let myself out of the bathroom.

Lucien's kitchen was all silver metal and gray stone, and I found him pouring Scotch into a stemless, tulip-shaped Glencairn glass. He gave an inquiring tilt of the bottle. "Want some?"

The smarter thing was to decline, but I said, "A little." As he searched for a second glass, my gaze wandered.

I traced one stockinged foot over the tiles, each one embossed with weathered designs: a fleur-de-lis here, a cathedral rose there, a trinity knot a few tiles over. The house seemed spartan, with no knickknacks or paintings, but the art in Lucien's house was in the masonry itself. From the tiles, to the counter, to the brick arch over the stove, there seemed a story buried in each skillfully chosen and set stone. "Did you do all this stonework?"

"Yeah. Those are salvage pieces from old buildings, mostly churches. They were going to be thrown out, so I refinished them and used them here."

"You do beautiful work."

He pushed his hand back through his hair, his smile awkward but genuine. "Thank you." Lucien put the mate to the first glass on the counter and poured me a smaller measure than his. He pushed the glass over with his fingertips and lifted his eyes to mine. "Sure you're okay? You can say no."

My body teemed with nervous energy edged with exhaustion. I

leaned on the counter and wrapped both my hands around the glass. "I'm not sure yet." Too many questions crowded my brain, fighting with the terrible images of wings and blades and blood for my attention. I lifted the glass; it was smooth against my lips and the whisky caressed my throat with a comforting heat. "What's an Iyarri?" The question sounded naïve and stupid when I said it aloud.

Lucien glowered. "Winged murders. They're not divine, whatever they are. They bleed and die like anything else." That they had, but they had also moved with inhuman alacrity.

I cradled the glass in one hand and ran my fingertip around its rim with the other. "How did you know Stephan was in trouble? Or that the Iyarri would attack him?"

"I saw an Iyarri at the gallery this afternoon and knew things were going to get bad in a hurry."

"At the gallery?" I frowned at the impossibility; I'd walked every inch of that floor for hours, and tonight was the first time I had seen such creatures.

"At least one. They can make themselves appear human when they want to."

"What? That can't be possible," I pressed.

"You have to look at what's there rather than at what you think you see." He shrugged, searching for a way to explain it. "Most people don't really see things, especially in big places like the Cities. You glance over, you see what you expect to see, and you move on." He focused on me, gaze critical. "Iyarri use their ipuran to cover up what they are and let your mind fill in the blanks. You expect to see a human, so that's what you see. People walk right around the wings without realizing they took a few extra steps."

Perhaps like maneuvering past furniture in a dark but familiar room. "The Iyarri that attacked us didn't look human." Beautiful and monstrous all at once, with their immense wings, sharp claws, and luminous, pale-gold skin decorated with scars.

"They wanted us to see them. Seems they prefer that when they're trying to kill you." He picked up his glass and led the way to the living room. The fireplace, a carved expanse of pale stone, rose from the dark walnut floor to dominate the room. A sofa and love seat made an *L* in front of the hearth. Lucien turned on a light and we sat, him on the sofa, me on the love seat. "I told Stephan he should get out of town, but he didn't want to leave the painting. I don't know if it meant that much to him or someone paid a lot for it or what. He kept saying he could get it boxed and it'd only take a few minutes to pick up."

Those few minutes cost Stephan his life, and nearly mine as well. Apprehension coiled tight inside me, though the threat had passed. I finished my whisky with a grimace and set the empty glass on the coffee table.

Lucien took the holster from the small of his back, set it on the coffee table, and leaned back. "You realize you've seen them for what they are. If you hadn't known enough for them to justify wanting you dead before, you do now."

I sat, shell-shocked in the cratering realization that my life as I knew it was over.

He gestured to his holster. "I don't suppose you know how to use a gun?" His question was casual, as if he'd inquired if I preferred acrylic paints to oils.

"No." The word was a blunt statement of denial. This wasn't happening, there were no Iyarri, and I wasn't still in danger for having seen them. And yet the pair of black pistols rested on the table, two touchstones of cold reality.

"You should consider leaving the Cities. Maybe for good. They know where you work, and where you live won't be hard to find."

For good? I shied from the thought in an instant, visceral way. "My mom lives in Hastings. I could stay with her for a while but—" It was the last place I wanted to go given our complicated relationship, but I didn't have another choice.

Lucien got up with a nod and put our empty glasses in the sink.

"We've both had a long night. Why don't you stay here tonight, and you can go to your mom's tomorrow?"

I hesitated, wanting to be home where I would have a change of clothes, but Lucien was right: if the Iyarri went looking for me at my apartment, I'd be as dead as Stephan. "If it's not an imposition, could you take me to the gallery in the morning?"

"The gallery?" He edged the question with incredulity.

"My car is there, and I don't have my keys or phone. I must have dropped my purse in the parking lot."

He rasped his knuckles against his cheek in contemplation. "Should be safe enough, so long as it's during the day, I go with, and we don't stay long." He gathered a few blankets and a pillow and arranged them on the couch. "I hope it's okay. I don't really get much in the way of company."

I sat on the makeshift bed, sinking into the cool down blanket. "It's perfect, thank you."

Lucien gathered up his holster and pistols and turned off the lights.

"Lucien?" He paused and looked in my direction. "How did you find out about Iyarri?"

He turned and walked toward a door next to the fireplace. "In a way I would rather not have. Goodnight."

The sound of Stephan's blood spilled through my memory—the way it had spattered my face and I'd cowered, paralyzed with fear reminiscent of the lake, the rocks, the splashing water. Lucien understood—it was in the sympathetic way his brows drew together as he ushered me into the house, the offer of a drink and a safe place to stay. He knew I needed answers, needed to be told I wasn't crazy. Was his introduction to the Iyarri like mine? Somehow worse? The desire to know was overwhelming, and yet still not more than my depth of gratitude. Instead of pressing for answers I said, "Goodnight. And thank you."

"You're welcome." Lucien went into his bedroom and pushed the door closed behind him.

Wishing I had proper pajamas and not my blood-flecked work

uniform, I got into the makeshift bed. The blankets were cedar-scented and their bulk pressed down with a reassuring weight. I turned my face into the pillow and inhaled traces of Lucien's cologne, clear and icy-smelling. Nesting into the covers, I tried to let the whisky chase off thoughts of feathers and blades, of blood and death.

THREE

THE WIND LASHING THE trees outside woke me. I swam upward, through grogginess and the weight of heavy, unfamiliar blankets, until I broke the surface of realization. Lucien's house, that was where I was. Dreams of *Angels Unseen* and nightmares of Stephan's clutching, bloody hands had kept what sleep I'd gotten from being restful.

I listened for signs that Lucien was awake, but the house was still. Gray autumn sunlight shone through the windows, but also through the fireplace. Curious, I pushed the covers back and stood before the massive expanse of pale stone. Although the fireplace must have weighed an immense amount, the fluid way it was carved pulled my eyes upward, past trinity designs to the vaulted ceilings. The space meant to contain a fire was square; the surrounding stone carved into a trefoil arch. Without a back, it seemed more a gateway than a place to burn wood. Mindful of the ashes, I crouched, peered into the fireplace, and found myself looking into the room Lucien had retired to the night before.

Past the second hearth were a comfortable couch and a low table. On the far wall, between two narrow windows, was Lucien's bed, made and unoccupied. The rhythmic tapping of metal on stone broke the silence. I got to my feet and called, "Lucien?"

The cadence stopped. "I'm out here."

I followed the sound of his voice past the mudroom and out into his workshop. The air enveloped me, cool and smelling of stone and dust. Gargoyles perched on heavy shelves, crouched among tools and peered around pieces of damaged stone ornaments. Lucien stood at a large wooden table in the center of the room, a hammer in one hand and a chisel in the other. "Morning."

"Good morning." I picked up a stone chip from the table and rolled it between my fingertips. The edges were as wavy and sharp as a knapped arrowhead. "What are you working on?"

Two stones rested in front of him, one worn and cracked. Lucien ran his fingers over the rugged stone, exploring its edges. "Most of what I do is restoration work. I need to match the type of stone, and then replicate the style so whatever is being replaced looks like it hasn't been." He stopped talking, realizing my eyes weren't on the stone pieces, but the three scars on his forearms. They were pale, arcing lines of raised flesh, one so long it disappeared under the cuffed sleeve of his work shirt. Arcs like the one Stephan's blood made on the white trailer wall. My throat tightened but failed to snuff out my question before it escaped. "Are those from them?"

"Yes." He rubbed his hand over the scars on the opposite arm, and I fingered the stone flake. "They look worse than they are. The Laidrom, their warriors, keep their napta so sharp I barely felt them." The strange words were musical.

"Is that their language?"

He shrugged, though it seemed the answer was yes. "It's called Loagæth."

"An Iyarri taught you?"

Lucien shook his head, the set of his jaw tight. "No. A bishop thought he was teaching me an angelic tongue. Cost him his life, and nearly mine as well." He set his tools aside and dusted his hands off on his jeans, brushing off my questions, too. "Let's go inside and get some breakfast. You've got to be hungry; a half-shot of whisky isn't exactly dinner."

"I am hungry." I took a step and hesitated. "I don't eat meat, though. I hope that's not any trouble."

"No trouble at all."

I managed a grateful smile and followed him into the house. "Would you mind if I took a quick shower?" Despite washing Stephen's blood off my face and hands the night before, my hair was tacky in places and it made my skin crawl.

Lucien nodded in the direction of a door. "Go ahead. Should be towels in the closet."

"Thank you." I made my way to the bathroom. Inside, everything was sparse and neat; not so much as a comb left out on the sink. I turned on the shower, undressed, and dug my thick, muscled toes into the woolly bath mat. They split midway down the top of my feet, each toe long with working joints. The toenails grew in henna-colored and thick. If I let them grow out, would they curve into talons? I ran my thumb over the sunken, almond-shaped scar above my Achilles tendons where bony knots had once been—a birth deformity, my mother claimed. Over the years, she attributed other things to unnamed birth defects: my weak bones that often broke as a child, the total absence of hair on my arms and legs.

Water pattered on my body as I stepped into the shower and steam rolled up the glass door. The world felt as though I had my nose pressed to a painting, too close to pick out the right details and unable to discern what the larger picture was. One thing I did know was that it was best if Lucien didn't see my feet—I couldn't give him answers I didn't have.

By the time I got out of the shower, the air smelled of coffee, eggs, and buttered toast. Stomach grumbling, I toweled my hair and dressed in my rumpled clothes. I left the bathroom and found Lucien sitting at the breakfast nook, backlit by shafts of light that streaked through tall, arching Palladian windows. He reclined with one knee against the table and his chair tipped back as he read something on his phone. Lucien had changed into jeans and a black button-down that was untucked and cuffed to his elbows. Two plates of food were already on the table.

I sat cross-legged on the chair across from him; Lucien set his phone aside and nodded to my plate. "I hope breakfast is okay."

"It smells amazing, thank you." After a few bites I said, "Would you mind if I asked you some questions?" He raised a wary eyebrow, and I gestured to the ghost-white fireplace in the living room. "Can you tell me about that? It's beautiful and has to have a story."

His shoulders relaxed, and the tension faded from the bow of his lips. Fireplaces seemed an easier topic than Iyarri. "It was from an old church in Austin. The place was condemned after the foundation collapsed in a flood, so I got it for next to nothing." He smiled and added, "Well, nothing except the work to dig it out and haul it away. The relief used to be more elaborate, but the stone was damaged and I had to reface it. The other side is a similar fireplace taken from the same church. It was less damaged, though."

"Was the trefoil arch there when you started?" I asked.

Lucien answered all my questions with the patient joy of someone who loves having their work acknowledged but neither draws attention to it nor boasts.

"Seems a bit more than just something you do to pay the bills," I said with a knowing curve of my lips.

Color crept up his cheeks as he set his cup down and flashed an abashed smile. "Yeah, I suppose it's a bit more than that. And not often do I get to talk about it with someone who appreciates it. Do you sculpt or anything?"

"I have for classes, but mostly I draw and paint."

Lucien took my hand in his and lifted it into the light. "I should have guessed it wasn't sculpture; look at your hands."

It took me a moment to focus past the warmth of Lucien's hand on my own, but he was right: compared to his stone-worn hands and scuffed nails, mine were immaculate. I doted after my oval-shaped nails with glass nail files and smoothed my skin with salve, babying my hands both for the art they could produce and as a vanity to compensate for my feet. "Yeah, I suppose the worst they see is some paint thinner now and again."

"So it's not too much of a surprise I found you working at the gallery."

My smile faded and I pressed my lips together. "Do you think it's safe to go back? To the gallery, I mean?"

Lucien set our plates in the sink, the ghosted shapes of his pistols visible through the fabric of his untucked shirt. "Safe enough for you to go in, get your stuff, and leave. Iyarri aren't going to do anything to you in the middle of the day in public, but I'll come in with you."

"I'd like that," I said with a relieved smile. It evaporated a second later as I realized things were more complicated than just Iyarri. "What if the police are there? I dropped my purse in the middle of a murder scene."

Lucien paused, considering. "Unless they have a warrant for you, or intend on arresting you, which I doubt, they can't make you go with them. If your purse isn't there and you don't want to go to the police to get it, I'll take you right to your mom's and we can deal with it later. Assuming nothing goes wrong, though, you should be able to get your car and head to your mom's on your own."

"If I have to, I can tell the police what I saw, minus the Iyarri."

"Yeah—let's hope we don't have to tell them anything at all, though." We put our shoes on and he held my coat out for me. "I got the worst of the blood off, but the front is damp." The black wool hid any traces of blood, but as I shrugged the coat on and buttoned it up, I could smell it—iron with a rancid edge.

Lucien backed us out of the garage into the cold, gloomy day. A solid ceiling of clouds weighed low in the sky; skeletal tree branches tried to scratch through to sunlight. As we neared the Cities proper, the buildings grew taller and I asked, "How did you know about *Angels Unseen* in the first place? I didn't even know it was going to be displayed, and I work there."

Lucien chose his words with care. "I'm not the only one aware of Iyarri. There are a few of us; we trade tips and leads and stories. Most the time it isn't anything, but this time—with Stephan and his painting—it was." He frowned. "I haven't heard from most my contacts in months; it makes me worried they were found out and killed."

I sighed, shoulders drooping. "I wish Stephan would have listened to you."

"Yeah, I do too." Disappointment etched lines into his face, and he adjusted his holster. "At least you're alive."

My heart tightened at the despair in his voice, and I put my hand atop his arm. "I'm glad you were there."

His face softened, and some of the loneliness lifted when he smiled. "Me too."

We parked beside my car and walked toward the gallery, thoughts of Iyarri and the police crowding my mind. I stuffed my hands in my pockets and tightened them into nervous fists.

Lucien walked so close to me his sleeve brushed my shoulder. "It'll be okay."

I exhaled and nodded, some of the fluttering tension leaving my chest. Even though Lucien thought the odds of running into an Iyarri in the middle of the day were slim, I worried less with him beside me.

The interior of the gallery was strangely timeless—unchanged by Stephan's death and the attacking Iyarri. People milled in the lobby and I wove through them, headed toward the office doors.

"Excuse me, sir," a voice called from behind us. Lucien stopped, and I followed suit. A security guard walked up to Lucien and dropped her voice. "No guns are allowed on the premises." My throat tightened and heat flushed up the back of my neck. I glanced at the back of Lucien's coat; I was not able to see the guns, but the guard had.

Lucien spread his hands in a gesture of compliance. "I do have a permit to carry."

The guard shook her head. "No weapons are allowed, and I am asking you to leave."

My gaze darted between the two of them, not wanting to cause any sort of altercation, but not wanting to be without Lucien, either.

"Okay, I'll leave," he told the guard. He turned to me, expression reassuring. "I'll wait for you at the car."

"Thank you," I said as Lucien walked away toward the door. The guard trailed him until he passed through the doors and descended the stairs, out of my view.

I hurried into the main office and found Jacob shuffling through a stack of papers. "Ms. Drake!" The room smelled of cigarettes and a heavy dash of cologne. "I'm so glad to see you're okay. You no doubt heard about what happened last night."

"I did; it sounded horrible. It must have happened just after I left." I tried to smooth any telltale lines from my face. "Did anyone turn my purse in? I came to see if I forgot it here and to ask to take some time off."

"Not that I know of. As for time off, you haven't accrued—"

"I'm sure Aurelia has acquired whatever time off she needs," Aamon said. He stood near the back door to the office with his coat draped over one arm, perfectly put together and unconventionally striking. His accent became pronounced as he spoke, and Jacob hung on each musical word. "She's had quite the ordeal, and the proper thing to do would be to put her on paid leave until further notice."

Jacob let the papers in his hand drift to the desk, forgotten. "Of course. I'll put in the paperwork right away."

I stood, grateful and stunned, as Jacob turned and walked into his private office. Aamon lifted his tailored coat from his arm, my blood-smeared purse underneath. He offered it to me and winked. "Come; walk with me."

Questions and relief flooded me all at once. I took the purse from Aamon, the leather tacky, and tucked it under my arm. My coat was already bloodstained, more didn't matter. My queasy stomach disagreed with me. "Where did you get this?" I whispered as I fell in step beside him. I peeked inside my purse and found everything inside: my phone, my keys, my wallet. We turned down a dim corridor and walked across a Soribashi bridge; illuminated cases of Japanese calligraphy formed suspended walls on either side.

"From the police. We had a chat and they decided they didn't need to talk to you after all."

My steps slowed. I knew Aamon was wealthy and influential, but that extended to the police, too? And if he had my purse he knew I had seen everything. "Aamon . . . how?"

He smiled, the expression sublime. "I'm very convincing when I want to be, and I didn't want you tied up in that mess."

Questions and gratitude fought for prominence in my thoughts as the bridge ended at the edge of the Japanese Tea Garden. The teahouse was cut away to reveal paper walls and pale green mats. A bamboo ladle rested near a kintsukuroi cup, bright lines of gold gleaming where it repaired the broken pottery. Aamon gestured to a low stone bench as soft strains of Japanese music drifted around us. "Please sit."

I sat and he joined me, leaving a respectful distance between the two of us. Aamon and I had shared a thousand conversations, but this one already felt different, more intimate. He pushed his smooth, white-blond ponytail back over his shoulder and put one finger to his lips in contemplation. "*Gnay gi om sobam om g dooain omsomna, Linnia?*" The words rooted me like a spell and I stared, thunderstruck. Aamon's pale eyes searched my face.

"Loagæth." I guessed, exhaling the word.

Aamon's eyebrow arched and his faint smile became substantial. "Do you know what I asked you?" I shook my head. "And yet you both knew the name of the language and spoke it with an impeccable accent." I bit my lip and averted my eyes to the purification basin outside the teahouse. "I asked you if you knew that you have an Iyarri name."

An Iyarri name? The tea room became claustrophobic, the chiming music too loud. I stammered an explanation that didn't tie me to those winged creatures. "Aurelia means 'golden light' in Latin, and Liath, my middle name, is Irish for 'gray.'"

"Your name has a history much older than that. Would you like to hear it?" He lowered his voice. "And if not that, perhaps we could talk about your missing father?"

Thoughts crashed over me in a wave: the feet in *Angels Unseen*, my mother refusing to tell me so much as my father's name, the almond-shaped scars on my feet where Iyarri grew dewclaws. I stood, frozen, as each thought crystalized into a greater, unavoidable truth. I took two hurried steps toward the hallway. "Lucien is waiting for me and—"

Aamon's gentle voice stopped me. "Aurelia, you're trembling." I looked over my shoulder at him as he rose to his feet and walked to me; his knowing expression softened to one of sympathy. "Have I ever done wrong by you?"

"No." In fact, he'd helped me more than anyone. My mother had been vehemently against me going to college, but I'd gone. There, Aamon's interest in my art landed me substantial scholarships and a job. It wasn't Aamon that unnerved me, but the fact that questions I had long sought answers to might have answers I didn't want.

"This is not the place to finish this discussion. Why don't you come to my house so we can talk? Do you remember how to get there?"

I nodded; I knew the way from the dozens of gallery events Aamon hosted there.

"Good, I'll see you soon." Aamon gave me an acknowledging bow of his head and departed over the Japanese bridge.

I placed one hand on a bamboo fence and bowed my head until my forehead rested against it too. The world felt effervescent, so unlike the one I'd known a day ago. I drifted out to the parking garage, trying to be on the lookout for Iyarri, but the thought that Aamon knew of my father drew all my attention. What past did they share? Was that why Aamon helped me so much?

Lucien was leaning against a concrete pillar and pushed himself upright when he saw me. "There you are," he said. "Is everything okay? I was starting to worry."

I didn't want to lie, but I wasn't willing to go into Aamon and my father, either. "My boss put me on paid leave. I got my purse, too."

"Good." Lucien gestured to my car. "Get in and I'll give you my phone number." I obliged, not sure why he couldn't give me his phone number otherwise. Once the doors were closed he glanced about and, not seeing anyone, pulled one of his pistols out. "I want you to take this." I stilled and swallowed, uncertain. Lucien pointed to a small button on the side and a thumb switch. "That's the safety: the gun won't fire with it on. This turns on the flashlight." He opened the bottom, allowing the magazine to slide out. It was full, the bullets sitting inside like a neat row of tiny warheads. "There are eight bullets here and one already loaded in the chamber. Nine shots." He slid the magazine back into the gun with a scrape-click and held it out to me.

The matte black gun hung in the air—there was no point in refusing. Lucien wouldn't have offered it if he didn't think I needed it. I threaded my fingers between it and Lucien's hand, closing them around the cold metal. The gun was so big I needed to stretch my fingers to get them onto the trigger. I doubted I could pull it with one finger; I'd probably need two. When Lucien let go, the weight caused my hand to dip; I gripped the gun like a venomous snake, tight in my hand and away from my body. If Lucien thought my wariness stupid, he was polite enough not to say so.

I tucked it into my purse, not sure I could bring myself to pull the trigger, much less hit anything. "Do you have any extra bullets?"

Lucien shook his head. "I won't pretend you'll have the time to reload."

"Ah, I see." I lifted my phone from my purse. "I actually get your number too, right?"

He chuckled and took out his own phone. "Yes." After we exchanged numbers he said, "I suppose you should get going." He closed a reassuring hand over my shoulder. "We can meet up in a few days."

His eyes held mine, and my lips curved into a shy smile. "I would like that." It was for more than just protection; there was some sort of kindred bond born of sharing in the forbidden knowledge of Iyarri, having someone who would believe me when no one else would. I trusted him.

He got out of the car and jerked his head in the direction of the highway. "Go on. Lie low at your mom's, and I'll see you soon." He shut the car door and walked toward his truck.

I stole another glimpse of him in the rearview mirror and drove, not toward my mother's, but in the direction of Aamon's house—and hopefully, answers.

FOUR

AMON LIVED NEAR LAKE of the Isles, its serene waters lending a protected, natural view to the expensive homes nearby. His property was a peninsula on the north side of the lake, the stone house tucked into a private copse of ancient trees. The right side of the house was full of arched windows, showcasing a spiral staircase that climbed all three stories. I knocked on the door and Aamon answered. "There you are," he said. "Please come in."

I let Aamon take my coat, wary that he would notice the lingering aroma of blood as he stowed it in the foyer closet, but he seemed not to. The inside of the house was open and understated—decorated with warm wood, cool stone, and clean metal lines.

Aamon led me into the kitchen, took two glasses from a rack, and filled them with a clear, shimmering liquid from a frosted carafe. My artist's eye appreciated the smooth arc of the pour and the way he set the glass before me, but the sophistication did little to quell my nervous stomach. "Thank you."

"It's a unique infusion called pilzin." Aamon gestured to a sitting room off the kitchen. "Please, have a seat."

I sat on a slender love seat, him on a padded bench with rolled sides, a coffee table between us. My fingers smudged anxious lines in the condensation, and I drank the pilzin in small, nervous sips. It was dewy and thick and tasted like crisp juniper berries. I struggled with the morass of thoughts in my mind.

"Have you ever met your father?" Aamon asked the right question, as he'd done so often when I struggled to explain how a particular piece of art made me feel.

"No." The single syllable was heavy with history. I was my mother's only child—spoiled at best, cloistered at worst. For a time, I'd fantasized about meeting a mystery father, but that dream faded after years of my mother's stonewalling, all my questions met with dismissiveness and silence. Over time, the fantasy gave way to fear that my father's reaction to my deformities would be the same as everyone else's—disgust and pity. I had stopped asking about him years ago. "Do you know him?" I asked, my heart tearing between hope and dread.

"I know him." Aamon pressed the knuckle of his bent forefinger against his philtrum and watched for my reaction. "And I know you're not human."

My throat seized, and I forgot how to breathe.

"You are Linnia." His voice grew distant as my mind tried to pull me away from the truth. "Half-Iyarri, half-human, the product of what Iyarri call Doalin, the Unspeakable Sin. There are none living, save you."

I gaped, my lips half-forming one word, discarding it for another that I didn't speak, either. *Linnia*—the word became a vortex in my mind that drowned my other thoughts. Half-human, half-Iyarri. The truth resonated deep in my fragile bones.

Aamon leaned forward, his glass clasped in his hands. "You have three toes rather than five. Your night vision is superb. You weigh far less than you should for your height and your size. You can hear things most others cannot. Am I correct?"

I swallowed hard—Aamon's smile told me he already knew the answer to all his questions was yes. "Yes, but that doesn't mean . . ." My mind swam from one of my mother's excuses to the next: my birthweight was low because I'd been born early, my bones were light and weak because I hated drinking milk, the three-toed feet and bony deposits where Iyarri had dewclaws were a birth defect. Each one of her makeshift justifications capsized under the weight of the evidence that I wasn't human. My hands clenched, my identity shaken to its core.

Slowly, so as not to startle me, Aamon reached out with one hand and refilled my glass. "Drink. It will help calm you."

The glass shook in my hands, the pilzin rippling. "And you know this because you know my father. And you never told me?" My voice was equal parts heartbreak and accusation. That Aamon would not just keep something from me, but do it for years, caved my heart in.

Aamon made an apologetic spread of his hands. "I only meant to keep you safe, but now that you've seen Iyarri, there are standing orders to hunt and kill you. The . . . incident last night transformed your ignorance of what Iyarri are, and what you are, into a liability."

Feathered shadows gathered at the edges of my consciousness, and though I was in Aamon's spacious living room I felt boxed in, trapped. The Iyarri attack at the gallery was a bloody blur of blades and arrows, and I knew with panicked surety I would not survive another encounter with them. My mystery father resurfaced in my mind, and I latched onto thoughts of him, as hopeful as I'd been as a child that he would suddenly return and set things right. "If my father is an Iyarri, can't he help? I'm no threat to anyone. He could tell them that." The words sounded optimistic and naïve even to my own ears.

"Your father is a coward. He fled after he got your mother with child so the Iyarri wouldn't learn of his Doalin. No one has seen him since."

Aamon's words gutted me, piling heartbreak atop betrayal until I leaned forward, my elbows resting on my knees. I bowed my head, a veil of copper waves surrounding the glass in my hands, hope extinguished. I knew my childhood fantasy was just that, a fantasy, but I hadn't realized how hard I'd held onto it.

"Your father doesn't deserve you." Aamon's words were hard, but his tone softened them. "I've kept you safe in his spineless absence, and that will not change now."

I shook my head, unshed tears making the pilzin swim in my vision.

Aamon touched two fingers to the underside of my chin, his skin soft, dry, and feverishly hot. I blinked and froze, a gasp caught in my throat. Rather than the human hands I knew, Aamon had claws at the ends of his fingers, pale and glossy as white glass. Solid and sharp, light reflected along their curve in a clean arc.

A flush of adrenaline tingled through my body as Aamon tilted my head up—he was as frightful as he was breathtaking. Wings arched up and out of his back, an imperfect white, the color of sunlight on new-fallen snow. His skin was pale gold and radiant, the human white-blonde of his hair giving way to the same empyrean white as his wings.

I leapt to my feet and staggered away from Aamon, the sound of my glass of pilzin dashing to the floor punctuating my terrified cry. Fear permeated my skin, as cold as the pilzin soaking into Aamon's artful rug. My fists were balled, but pulled tight to a body too scared to run, or even defend itself.

Aamon's voice was low and reassuring. "It's still me, Aurelia."

My gaze darted from the spreading wet spot on the rug to Aamon's feet, three-toed and clawed, up the long, trailing feathers of his wings to, finally, his face. Aamon met my eyes and smiled, the expression familiar even though the green and amber within his irises were more vibrant than I'd ever seen.

His dark, vogue clothing contrasted with the celestial backdrop of wings, and the aperture of my realization expanded to his home; what I had mistaken as stylistic preferences were deliberate choices that made room for his wings. The walkways were wide and, except for the couch I occupied, none of the furniture possessed a back. It was subtle, but the allotments for wings were there.

Aamon's frown was solemn, his words contrite. "I didn't mean to scare you, but you had to know."

"Is there anything else you've kept from me?" I snatched the glass from the floor and set it on the table so hard the crystal thrummed.

He dipped his head in an apologetic gesture. "No. I'm telling you now because you have to know the truth if I'm going to keep you safe from the Laidrom." Aamon's great wings shifted, wafting the aroma of dry, white sandalwood wrapped in the warmer, deeper scent of amber. "Your father isn't here to keep you safe, but I am."

I shook my head, doubt and fear coiling tight around my ribs. Although Iyarri, Aamon didn't stand a chance against the frightening, battle-scarred warriors.

"I am an Aldaria, and my role is to hide the truth of what we are from humans, to see any evidence of Iyarri written off as angelic nonsense. I know the intricacies of both the human world and the Iyarri world, which lets me shield you from both Iyarri and other humans; it's why I brought you here to talk. Most Iyarri live at Idura, but as I spend much of my time interacting with the human world, I have this residence as well. You're quite safe here."

I didn't feel safe as I gazed at the Iyarri I had, until moments before, believed to be my human friend. "How long have you known what I am?" I demanded, wrapping my arms around myself.

"Since you were a child. While I never found out where your father went, I learned enough to lead me to you and your mother. Once I realized what you were, I knew I had to keep other Iyarri from discovering it, too."

"But they don't know I'm Linnia." My mind raced over the attack at the gallery, searching for anything that could have given me away.

"No. Right now they think you're a human who knows too much. If they thought you were Linnia, their efforts would redouble. Iyarri law demands your death in either case."

My face crumpled. How could being a Linnia be so bad that my life was forfeit?

Aamon leaned closer to me as he spoke. "Thousands of years ago, humans and Iyarri interacted often. Our society, the Elonu-Dohe, was more enlightened, but we helped the humans, taught them. Occasionally, children were born between the two races, and these too were tolerated for a time." Aamon's tone darkened. "But the humans who lived with the Iyarri demanded a seat on the Council of the Four Winds, and our greatest leaders convened to debate the matter. When the motion was ultimately denied, the humans who lived within our own walls rose up on the Night of Bloody Feathers, slaughtering half of each Saanir, the pairs that ruled Iyarri society. We killed them in retribution, withdrew our enlightened presence, and faded into mythos and religious imagery. The Aisaro, our code of laws, was amended: associating with humans was forbidden, procreating with one a capital crime. When I called your father a coward, that's why. He ran to keep Elonu-Dohe from finding out what he'd done and left you to risk discovery and death." Aamon took my human hand in his clawed ones, his touch reassuring. "I will not let that happen to you."

Before I could respond, a figure appeared on the balcony behind Aamon, her slender figure breaking the perfect mirror the Lake of Isles held up to the night sky.

She wore dark, wide-legged pants and a tailored tunic with wide sleeves, but despite the autumn evening wasn't wearing a coat. The woman opened the balcony doors with casual familiarity and blinked at me, surprised. A grin spread across her face, and she gave Aamon a slow clap. "I'll be damned—you found the plodder girl."

I took a step closer to Aamon—unsure of this strange, leanly muscled woman.

"Of course I did." Aamon nodded to the woman. "Aurelia, this is Tiahmani. You've already met, of course."

I opened my mouth to say I'd never seen her before, but stopped, unsure. Something was familiar about her: as dark and wild and dangerously beautiful as a thunderstorm. I could hear Lucien's voice in my head: *Look at what's really there rather than at what you think you see.* Tiahmani didn't appear much older than I was, but there were faint crow's feet at the corners of her jade-green eyes. Her hair tumbled past her shoulder blades, the sides twisted back and accented with wraps of silver and mahogany feathers. Below her left ear was a constellation of five freckles. As my gaze slid over each detail, her illusion shimmered.

I recoiled with a gasp. Her feet, which I swore were covered in boots moments before, were bare, with three toes and talons. Her face, while it had been pretty, was now striking, her tanned skin supernaturally radiant, as though she were dusted in pyrite bronzer. Behind her, two massive, coffee-colored wings blotted out the view of the lake. Like Aamon, two feathers trailed from the bases of her wings to her ankles, giving her swallow-tails.

"You," I stammered, "you were at the gallery." She had pulled the attacking Iyarri off me and caused his blade to miss.

"Aye." She flashed me an amused smile. "I wasn't sure you could get any paler, but you just did."

Aamon raised his eyebrows at me. "Your eye for detail pierced her ipuran. I'm impressed."

Tiahmani took a seat, lounging like a savannah predator. Under the wide sleeves of her shirt were her napta—sheathed, but no less worrying.

I eyed her blades. "Are you going to kill me?"

She shook her head, seeming put out. "No. Not unless Aamon changes his mind."

Aamon's face was the picture of feigned innocence. "And kill your niece? Why would you want to do such a thing?"

"My what?" she growled, her lush lips twisting into a cruel expression. "That," she pointed at me but spoke to Aamon, "has nothing to do with my brother. He never would have—" she sputtered, losing her words in disgust.

Aamon arched a white eyebrow. "Coupled with a human? Are you so sure?"

Tiahmani pulled me from the love seat by the front of my shirt, claws scratching my chest—she'd moved in a blur of speed and motion. I clamped my hands around her arm and tried to force her off but met the hardened leather of her gauntlet, just as Stephan had. Mewling with helpless panic, I twisted in her grip as she snapped her other arm, blade leaping out. The silver gleamed in the light, the split blade serrated at the bottom outside edges. She set the points under my chin.

They were like twin ice picks; with one thrust she could have sent the blade upward into my skull. "Tell me your father's name, you worthless human get," she snarled.

"I don't know it." The words came out in one terrified, quavering rush.

"Let her go." Aamon's voice was sharp.

Tiahmani dumped me back onto the cushions and stalked toward Aamon with a flare of dark wings that smelled of dragon's blood and ginger. "You had better be fucking with me."

I huddled against the back of the love seat, a line of sweat running down my spine. Every fiber in my body tensed to bolt past her and out the door, but I didn't dare draw Tiahmani's attention back to me.

Aamon raised his wings in a gleaming shield between me and Tiahmani. "Aurelia and her mother are why Cæl left."

Cæl. My father's name hung in the air before settling into all the places in my past where it belonged. Where he belonged and hadn't been.

Tiahmani's eyes were full of green hellfire. "How do you know that?"

"Knowing things is rather my business, wouldn't you agree?"

"You're wrong," she snapped. "You're wrong about all this. And you're going to get that thing out of the fucking house before I get back, or I'll kill it myself." In a storm of wings she left the way she'd come, out onto the balcony and into the night sky. Cold air and a few dried leaves blew into the room, and Aamon closed the sliding door behind her. If Tiahmani was my aunt, I dreaded what my father was like.

He held out his hand to me. "Are you all right?"

After a second of hesitation, I uncurled and allowed him to help me to my feet. There were angry pink scratches on my skin that the unbuttoned collar of my shirt didn't cover. My fingers shook as I closed my shirt up all the way. "It's quite safe here." I reiterated Aamon's words back to him, hurt and betrayed.

"I'm sorry." Aamon lowered his wings alongside the pitch of his voice. "I shouldn't have told her, or at least not like that."

I wrapped my arms around myself. "I think I should go."

Aamon began to protest, but acquiesced and retrieved my coat. "I understand. Catherine should be far enough away to limit your risk of discovery by the Elonu-Dohe. Perhaps she will be willing to tell you about Cæl, now."

He knew my mother's name and where she lived. Had he really kept my mother and me from being discovered by Iyarri all this time?

"I hope so." What I meant was *she'd better be.* After everything I'd gone through, she owed me the truth.

Aamon helped me into my coat and donned his ipuran, looking human again as he escorted me to my car. "Be safe. We'll be in touch."

FIVE

ÆL. I ROLLED THE name in my mind as I drove to my mother's. The road ran parallel to the Mississippi River, the waters as wide, as deep, and as turbulent as my thoughts. My chest grew tighter as I drove under sheltering weeping willows and parked in front of a small, European cottage-style house. The front door was unlocked; inside, it smelled of vanilla candles.

"Mom?" I called as set my purse on the counter and put the kettle on. Seemed we always put the kettle on before we fought. I pushed my hair back and pulled in a steadying breath. I didn't want an argument, but I did want answers.

A minute later the stairs creaked as my mother came downstairs. Catherine Drake was every bit as Celtic as she looked: pale skin, scattered freckles, and ginger hair gone darker with age. There were more twists of white in her curls since my last visit home. "I wasn't expecting you. Is everything okay?"

I straightened my neck and raised my eyes to hers, gray to green. "I think we're more than past the point where we need to have a talk about who my father is, and what the hell I am."

She took a nervous step toward the kettle before realizing it was already on. Part of me expected her to deny it, but she said, "I've been dreading this for a long time."

I braced both hands against the edge of the counter to hide the way they shook. "Were you ever going to tell me?" The edge of my question was sharp with accusation. First Aamon and now my mother. Did everyone know I wasn't human except me?

She shook her head. "No. Not if I didn't have to."

My words were instant and indignant. "How could you—"

"Lia," she cut me off, vexed. Her hand crept to the necklace she always wore, fingers curling around the pendant. "I will tell you what happened, as much of it as I know. But don't pretend you wouldn't have thought that I'd lost my mind if I had told you before this." I reached for the tea tray, but she brushed me off. "I need a moment. Go sit down and I'll finish the tea."

Heat flushed up my temples and I balled my fists, wanting to shout at her that she'd had twenty-five *years* to figure out how to tell me, but I turned on my heel and walked into the living room before the words escaped my throat. The screaming chasm between us was like the one after I'd moved out. My mother supported my art but had vehemently discouraged my going to college for it. When my passion had finally outstripped my uncertainty and fear of her disapproval, I had moved out and gone to school anyway. We hadn't talked for months.

The scrape of a metal tin opening and the clink of cups sounded brittle and tense. My mother arrived with the tray, set it on the coffee table, and poured us each a cup before she sank down on the far end of the couch. "How did you find out?" Her question was equal parts dread and relief.

She listened in silence as I told her about Mr. Keller and his painting, Lucien, and Jacob asking me to stay late. I got as far as Stephan loading the painting before I faltered, not sure how to say what happened next. I tightened my hands around my cup and blurted, "Iyarri killed him."

I expected some reaction from her, a gasp, clasping her hands together—*something*—but she sat stone-still, the only motion the steam twisting upward from her cup. My jaw tightened as I related Lucien rescuing me and my conversation with Aamon. I stopped, glared at her, and willed her to talk. I wanted her to volunteer one goddamn piece of information without me having to drag it out of her. Fearful I'd shatter the teacup in my hands, I set it down with a sharp sound. "I'm half-Iyarri. A Linnia." The lines on her face grew deeper with every word I spoke. "Tell me about Cæl. About what the hell I am," I demanded.

My mother balanced her cup on her knee. "I met Cæl when I was in college." My brows knit with surprise; I never knew she'd gone to college. I thought she'd worked in the floral shop just out of high school. She licked lips but didn't drink her tea.

"What did he look like?" I looked so much like my mother in coloration that there wasn't anything to attribute to Cæl—my gaze dropped to my boots—other than the obvious.

The faintest trace of a smile washed over her. "Handsome and serious, brown hair and hazel eyes." I mentally sketched the features onto Iyarri, with dark wings and long, sharp talons. Like Tiahmani.

"Did you know what he was?"

"No." The corners of her mouth pinched in a tight frown. "I knew him eight months or so before I realized I was pregnant and found out Cæl was Iyarri when you were born."

I sputtered. "But you had sex with him." That Aamon's true form had eluded me for years needled the back of my head.

She gave a dour, amused snort. "Obviously. He had a way of making himself look human, or of making me see him as human. I'm not sure which." She went to refill her cup, noticed it was still full, and lifted her hand from the teapot. "Your grandmother found my pregnancy test in the trash. When I refused to put you up for adoption, she disowned me. St. Anne's expelled me. I was twenty, pregnant, broke, and homeless."

"What did you do?" Some of the acidity in my tone gave way to curiosity and sympathy.

Her slender fingers twisted into the chain of her necklace. "Cæl said he'd support me, and you. I don't know where he got the money, but he had me in this house inside a week and made sure everything was in my name."

"And gave you that?" I asked nodding at the pendant.

My mother undid the clasp. The pendant dropped into her open hand, the chain cascading after it. "Yes." It rested there, familiar, and somehow foreign now that I knew its history. In the center was a smooth, gently pointed oval of green labradorite, its flashing surface streaked with black veins, like an ebony lightning strike down its center. The auroral stone was wrapped, lashed, and braided in silver wire that terminated to points at the top and bottom. A quartet of curling vines and silver leaves, three on one side, one on the other, held the labradorite in place. I turned my head, scrutinizing the silverwork anew—I had always pictured them as leaves, but perhaps they were meant to be feathers.

She traced her fingers over the stone. "Cæl wanted to know where the crucifix I always wore had gone. It was your great-grandmother's, and I'd worn it every day after she died." Catherine's tone went dark and bitter. "Your grandmother decided I was too sinful to be worthy of that crucifix and demanded it back. The night Cæl gave me this, I felt like everything was going to be okay." She heaved a great sigh and clasped the chain back around her neck.

"When did you find out what he was?" My demand for answers was tempered by sympathy and understanding.

Her gaze drifted far away. "Just before you were due. Cæl sat me down and told me he had something he needed to tell me. He made it sound like he had done something horrible, that people would be after him, and me for being with him. Cæl could have been a criminal and I wouldn't have cared. I was ready to forgive him anything, so long as he'd stay and we could be a family."

Learning what Aamon was had shaken me to my core, but for her to learn of my father after she'd fallen in love with him and was about to have his child? She'd already chosen him, and me, over her own mother's wishes. There was no taking that back. I knew none of it was my fault, and yet guilt tightened around my heart for the things I had said and done out of ignorance: accusing her of being overprotective, of not wanting me to succeed, of stifling me. Each one of those accusations must have hurt her deeply, and the one defense she had, the truth of why she did these things, she couldn't reveal. I folded my hands and pressed them to my lips, nodding for her to continue.

"Cæl told me what he was, and I laughed at him. I told him I'd already known he was an angel. He told me again, and I wouldn't have believed him at all if he didn't look so sad when he said it. He asked me if I would be willing to see him as . . . as he really was. Even when I said yes, I didn't believe it. I thought I did, but I didn't. When he changed from human into Iyarri, I screamed. I think I pushed him away, I don't remember. All we'd done and I'd never known. He tried to calm me down but my contractions started. We got to the hospital ten minutes before you were born."

Her green eyes lifted to me, and there was both heartbreak and the gleam of an accusation. "I kept hoping you would have been enough to make him stay, but I wasn't and you weren't either." The resentment in her tone was biting. "The last thing he told me was to keep you safe and never let anyone figure out what you were. I haven't heard from him since." My mother, the steadfast bastion of strength in my life, had never looked so sad, so alone.

"He never came back? Never called, wrote, nothing?" I felt betrayed on her behalf.

"No. Nothing." She shook her head and pushed one ginger and silver curl out of her face. "I did what he asked me to do; I kept you as safe as I could. I never tried to find anyone else because I couldn't risk them knowing about you. And all of it was for nothing." She looked older than she had a few moments ago, her face wan and haggard.

"It wasn't for nothing." My voice was soft, unconvincing.

It didn't seem she heard me, anyway. My mother gazed off into the dark, icy tears standing in her eyes. "He named you, you know. Liath was supposed to be your first name."

My lips parted in realization. She didn't call me Lia as a nickname for Aurelia, but as a way to use the name she'd picked for me instead. My mother had given up so much for Cæl, even the name she chose, hoping my father would stay. After he left she'd called me Lia, pronounced the same as the name she'd chosen and allowed to be demoted to my middle name. "Did you love him?" I asked the question gently.

"I loved part of him. The part of him I thought was human. It took me years to admit I really didn't know him, but I still wanted him to come back." She scrubbed her face with her sleeve. "He should have had to tell you this. Not me." Her words were tired and lonely.

I twisted a piece of my hair around my fingers, years of fiery resentment tempered with understanding. Her story explained so much more than just who my father was, it explained why my childhood had been equal parts joy and misery, why my mother would do anything for me but never let me do anything, and why she resented me throwing off her protective shackles as much as I resented her for putting them on in the first place. When the teasing at school became cruel, she'd homeschooled me. When I'd broken my arm falling out of a tree, she'd stopped letting me take risks. We did everything together, but I had no close friends; as we sat in her dark living room, the lines by her mouth drawn, I realized that she had nobody but me, either. My father's secret, my Iyarri heritage, walled us in together as much as it walled us off from everyone else.

She nodded upstairs, in the direction of my old room. "I think you should move home for a while." She caught the flicker of resistance on my face and chose her next words with care, knowing how hard I'd fought to have the small, normal life I'd forged for myself in the Cities. "Don't break your lease or quit. Just stay here until we know you're safe."

The tension left my shoulders and I acquiesced. "Okay." I stood and hugged her. "Thank you. And I'm sorry for being like that. I didn't understand."

"I'm sorry I couldn't tell you sooner." She picked up the tea tray, closing our discussion. "Goodnight."

"Goodnight, Mom." I gathered my purse from the kitchen and headed up the narrow, creaking stairs.

My bedroom was the same as it was seven years ago, the small space choked by my bed, a desk, and bookcases stuffed under the eaves. Most of my possessions were in Minneapolis, but the room was still cluttered with old paintings, clothes I hadn't worn in years, and other mementos from teenage years I didn't miss. If I was going to stay for any length of time, a lot of stuff was going in the basement, and I'd need some things from my apartment.

The small lamp on the nightstand filled the room with a warm, yellow glow, but it couldn't dispel the cool draft seeping past the old window frame. I opened my purse to get my phone, but stopped, my hand hovering above the dark, cold metal of Lucien's gun. A lot of good it had done when Tiahmani attacked me—she moved so fast I'd been in her claws before I'd realized she'd moved at all. I reached around the gun, picked up my phone, and set it charging.

I lay on the bed, fumbled one hand between the mattress and box spring, and slid out a battered sketchbook. Drawing poured the turmoil from my mind and captured it on the page with graphite. The texture of the paper was grounding, its temperature cool against my skin; I propped my head in my other hand.

My mind emptied onto the paper lines overlapping and extending before pulling together into a form. Pieces of *Angels Unseen* spilled out: the double faces, shadowy wings, and strange symbols. I pillowed my head on my arm and kept drawing, the rasp of pencil on the paper filling the silence.

Morning came with clear skies and bright shafts of sunlight, the cloud cover from the day before dissipating like the tension between me and my mother. Our relationship had been so strained for so long that the absence of umbrage was more noticeable than its presence. There was healing to do, but digging out the splinter of truth was enough for it to begin.

Over the weekend, I shuttled boxes into the basement, making my room habitable while my mother planted fall bulbs. After we'd cleaned up and eaten dinner, my mother and I relaxed, her reading and me sketching in the living room. There was no talk of Iyarri, just quiet evenings that we were both content to pretend were normal. Maybe moving home for a bit wouldn't be as bad as I feared.

On Sunday evening I called Lucien, hoping he would be willing to meet me at my apartment. I wanted a few things that would make staying with my mother tolerable—my laptop and clothes that fit. If Lucien's suspicions were right and the Iyarri could find my apartment, there was no safe way for me to go without him. I took out my phone, a warm, earnest desire to see him again glowing inside me.

"Hey, Lia." He answered with a smile in his voice. The sound of stone on metal rasped in the background. "I'm glad you made it to your mom's okay."

"Me too. I guess I'll be staying here for a while, but I do want to get a few things from my apartment. Could you meet me there? To get your gun if nothing else."

"For my gun, obviously." There a wry, inviting note to his voice that made me hope he wanted to see me for more reason than that. "Where's your apartment and what time should I be there?"

I gave him the address. "It should take me about an hour to get there."

"Okay, I'll see you then."

I pocketed my phone and hoped I could gain his trust enough for him to tell me his history with the Iyarri. Had they killed his family? His wife? A friend? He didn't wear a wedding ring, and everything about his house suggested he lived alone. I shook my head, knowing he'd have to offer up his past. He'd all but shut down when I'd asked about how he had learned about Iyarri, and I didn't want to damage the bond of trust building between the two of us.

Before I left, I double-checked that the gun was in my purse and went to say goodbye to my mother. She pulled me into a hug and said,

"Call to tell me you made it safely. And don't stay long." She gave me another hug. "I love you."

"I love you too." The words carried more sincerity than they had in a long time. She turned and headed back toward the house as I left for the Cities.

My hands clenched the steering wheel as the apartment building loomed in the skyline, all burgundy brick and white stone. Every shadow took the shape of wings, and I made sure my purse was open on the passenger's seat, the gun inside within easy reach. It was past dark when I pulled into the parking garage, but I didn't see Lucien's truck. I lingered as long as I dared, heart pounding as my eyes jumped from one patch of shadow to another. Caving to my own unease, I hurried into the lobby, thinking I might wait there. People milled about, and I stayed tucked in the doorway until I'd checked each one for an ipuran, hoping to see an Iyarri for what it was before it saw me—they all seemed human. Tense and wary, I twisted my fingers into the strap of my purse and hurried to the elevator. I'd be safer locked in my apartment than standing out in the open.

My apartment wasn't large, but after a night in my old room it was downright spacious; the front door opened into the kitchen, with the living room and balcony to the left. I locked the door behind me, put my keys on the counter, and sent a quick text to my mother letting her know I was there and safe. Midway through filling a backpack with clothes, someone knocked at the door.

"I'll be right there," I called to Lucien. I tightened my fingers around the lock and glanced out the peephole by habit.

The man on the other side of the door wasn't Lucien.

I jerked my hands off the door as though it were suddenly red-hot. Whoever it was had dark hair and wore a rough-spun coat.

Fear crowded my mind, but I focused on the jagged scar that began under one ear and curved down the side of his neck and tried to *see*. The Iyarri's ipuran rippled, revealing silver-gray, tattered wings. I stared, trembling. He raised his hand to knock again; his fingers ended in sharp claws, and a napta gauntlet peeked out from the sleeve of his coat. With a gasp, I jammed the deadbolt home and pushed myself away from the door.

A rustling sound came from the balcony, and I whirled toward it, a cry caught in my throat. Not blowing leaves—the sound of wings. I stilled like a doe in a thicket as the wingspan of the Iyarri blotted out the moonlight. He landed, reached for the door, and gave the handle a hard tug. It jolted, but didn't slide. I wrapped my arms around myself and backed deeper into my apartment, eyes darting from the balcony to the front door.

I was trapped.

SIX

I SNATCHED UP MY PHONE, my heartbeat hammering in my ears. The Iyarri on the balcony tugged the door again, this time harder, but the lock held. "Lucien, pick up the phone." My voice was tight and quiet.

It rang once, twice. I close my eyes and hoped. On the third ring, Lucien answered. "Hey, I—"

"They're here. There's one outside my door, and another on the balcony." My voice was a quivering whisper and under the phone, my hand was slick with sweat. "I don't know what to do."

"You're there already? Have they gotten in?" The fear in his words amplified my own.

"Not yet." From the balcony door came the sound of something striking glass. I flinched and swallowed a scream. "It's trying to break the balcony door."

"Do you have the gun?"

For a terrified second I thought my purse was in the car, but no, it was on the counter. "It's here, I have it." I pushed up the slouching sleeves of my sweater and pulled out the gun.

There was an undercurrent of worry in the forced calm of Lucien's voice. "I want you to go in your bedroom and lock the door. Brace it with a chair if you can."

A sound like ice creaking came from the balcony. I fled down the hall, shut the bedroom door behind me, and locked it. Putting the phone and gun aside, I jammed a chair under the doorknob and then scooped them back up. From the other side of the door came the sound of wood shuddering, echoed by the groan of the thick balcony glass. I cradled the phone to my head with one hand and slid down the wall until I was sitting on the floor in a puddle of blue moonlight. My voice was hoarse and quiet. "What do I do when they get in?"

The engine of Lucien's truck revved, nearly drowning out his voice. "Take a deep breath." I did; the exhale shook. "Good. Now, the Laidrom on the balcony is going to get through first. The Iyarri at the front door is there in case you run out. Okay?"

"Okay." The gun shook in my hands.

"Turn off the safety on the gun. Do you remember how to do that?"

My thumb left a glossy streak of sweat on the dull metal. "It's off." My voice was small, as though my heartbeat and the wind rushing past my window would drown it out. "How long will you be?"

The engine of his truck was loud and horns honked. "I don't know. Not long." Although Lucien's words were confident, his tone wasn't. I closed my eyes and held the gun tighter in two hands, my face crumpling. "Are you okay?"

"I'm afraid." Simple, hopeless, truthful.

"Just hang in there."

A crash splintered the silence as the balcony door gave out. Terror broke over my skin in a cold wave, and I jerked the gun upward with a gasp. "Lucien, he's inside." My voice was a smothered whisper. Lucien swore.

The bedroom door shuddered as the Iyarri slammed into it. A second strike against the door, and the composite wood cracked. "Lucien, I—"

My sentence ended in a scream as a napta blade punched through. I dropped the phone and held the gun with both shaking hands. Sweat ran in thin lines down my back and between my breasts.

The Iyarri stuck his arm through the hole in the door and grappled for the lock. I fired; the gun kicked back so hard it nearly hit me in the face. The smell of gunpowder and hot metal singed the air. The Iyarri pulled in a sharp, pained breath and retreated. There was tenuous stillness, and then the Iyarri charged in a rush of footsteps.

The door flew open and the broken chair ricocheted off the bed. The Iyarri consumed the entire doorway, wings like a ragged cloak splotched with blood. His head was half-shaved, the remaining hair a mass of plaits and woven beads and raised, patterned scars ran down his right arm. Napta extended out over each clawed fist and his dark eyes blazed with purpose and death.

I pulled the trigger. Once. Twice.

The doorframe splintered next to his head and blood erupted from his jaw. He staggered backward, then leapt atop me like a falcon pinning its prey to the earth.

My back slammed into the floor and the air heaved from my lungs. The arc of his strike was a silver swath in the moonlight, and I raised my arms to protect myself. The blade knocked my arms aside; there was no pain, just the sensation of my flesh opening and the blood welling forward. He knelt on top me, the talons of one foot biting into my shoulder, his opposite knee crushing down in center of my sternum. What little air I could get into my lungs came in a desperate gulp that lit a line of pain on my side. The Laidrom pulled his arm back and his strike streaked toward me like a falling star. With a wrenching sob, I jammed the gun between us and pulled the trigger.

The napta spiked into the carpet next to my head and the Iyarri crumpled on top of me, pinning the gun sideways between us. His forehead pressed into my shoulder, and blood dripped in hot spatters from his shattered jaw. I shrieked. The Iyarri turned his face toward mine, the reeking, bloody stench of his breath washing over my face. His clawed hand dragged its way up my shirt and opened like a thorny flower over my throat. His fingers wrapped around my neck, but there was no force behind his grip. With one great, hacking spray of blood, he went limp.

The Iyarri's blood soaked through my clothes, far hotter than

Stephan's had been. Sobbing, I tried to lift his body from mine, but his limbs, his wings, crushed around me. I squirmed out from under the dead weight and staggered to my feet. The Laidrom lay still, his glossy black wings splayed across the floor.

A tinny voice pierced my awareness, and I picked up the phone. "I'm here," I said, my voice a broken cry. Gun in hand, I peered down the hallway into the living room; shards of balcony door glass littered the carpet and reflected the night sky.

"Thank God." Lucien's voice buckled with relief. "Are you okay?"

"It's dead." I scrambled to the bathroom, locked myself inside, and backed up a few steps. It was depthless black, but I could see well enough. The bathroom was a long rectangle; the Iyarri would have to turn to his right before he'd see me.

"Are you hurt?"

It took his question to make me aware of pain through the panic. My forearms wore bloody red opera gloves. The fabric of my shirt was blotched and splattered, but I didn't know how much of it was mine. "Yes."

"How bad?"

"I don't know. There's a lot of blood." I paused, straining my ears to hear something, anything. "I don't hear the other one." I pulled some towels out of the cabinet and wrapped them around my arms, hissing as the fabric touched the raw edges of flesh. I slumped against the wall, cradling my arms against my body and the gun in my blood-coated hands.

The silence stretched out, thin and tense. Lucien spoke, his voice quiet: "You have five shots left." I was wounded; the other Iyarri was not. And that assumed there were only two Laidrom. The engine of Lucien's truck stopped and the sound of his door opening and closing boomed. "I'm in front of your building. I'll be there soon."

Wood splintered and the front door slammed open. I held my breath, listening. A second of silence; then footsteps crunched on broken glass. I whispered, "Lucien, it's in the house." The footsteps paused outside the door, the Laidrom no doubt looking at its fallen wingmate in the bedroom.

"I'm almost there."

Almost.

The second Laidrom slammed his shoulder into the bathroom door; it cracked under the first blow. The door sagged inward, and shadows of wings loomed on the other side. "Lucien . . ." I said his name as if there were something he could do from where he was, wherever he was. There was no answer.

I stood and leveled the gun toward the door, my blood-glossed fingers slipping over one another as they settled on the trigger. Blood slid down my arms toward my armpits.

In a smear of movement, the Iyarri broke open the door and turned, napta moving in a deadly sweep. I thumbed the switch, the beam of the gun's flashlight exploding into the Iyarri's face. He threw his hands up and I fired, and kept firing even after gun clicked empty.

The Laidrom staggered backward and tensed to leap at me—another gunshot boomed, and the Iyarri's face disappeared into a haze of red mist.

He collapsed onto the bathroom floor in between Lucien and me, the tangle of silver wings a feathered barricade between us. Brightness engulfed the bathroom—my eyes snapped closed and I brought my arms up over my face, just as the Iyarri had.

"Jesus, Lia." Lucien's voice made me jump, the stab of fear sliding to relief. I lowered my arms, queasy at all the blood—mine, and the expanding pool of it that spread from the pulpy void where the Iyarri's face had been; black in the shadows, it was vivid red under the bright light.

Lucien sat me on the floor, wrapped the already-sticky towels around my arms, and knotted them. Pain, white and hot, bloomed behind my eyes, but the towels held and the bleeding stemmed. Lucien took my gun from my hands, put a new magazine into it, and handed it back to me. "Stay here, there's at least one more."

He made to stand and I grabbed his arm, painting it with crimson. I wanted him to stay, but couldn't form the words to say so. Lucien closed one hand over mine. "I will be right back. I promise."

I let him go, slumping to the floor with my back against the wall, my forearms pressed against my thighs, the gun warm in my hands. My body swayed, rocked by waves that crashed red and terrified, then pulled back into thin, cold shock. I rolled my head to the side; droplets of blood shone like suspended rubies in the russet tangles of my hair.

The apartment was too still, too quiet. "Lucien?" Although I tried to call out to him, my voice was strangled and soft. I pocketed my phone and stood, swaying, bruised, and bleeding. Streaks of blood gleamed on the floor, broken and smeared by three-toed tracks and boot prints. The dead Iyarri lay between me and the bathroom door, the swallowtail feathers thick, silver ribbons in the spreading pool of blood. His skin was luminous; for all that the descriptions of angels failed to capture the ferocity of this fallen warrior, his skin was as illuminated and glorious as they said. That, though, faded to the drab shades of death as he bled out. I bit my lip and walked across the wings, feathers crunching under my boots.

Outside the bathroom, I stopped and stared at the Iyarri in the bedroom. His black, broadcloth pants were held with a wide belt of formed, hardened leather, embossed with intertwining designs of inlaid silver. His wing shifted, and I fired, sending a spray of blood and feathers up the white wall. He was dead, the motion a trick of shadow and terror.

Lucien rushed back to me, gun raised. He scanned for a threat and, not finding one, lowered the gun and laid a reassuring hand on my shoulder. "I'm going to move the bodies so no one else finds them. Then we're leaving."

He grabbed the foot of the nearest Iyarri and dragged it across the living room to the balcony. Bloody roses bloomed on the pale carpet in its wake. One at a time, Lucien threw the Iyarri over, the bodies falling four stories. I was thankful I couldn't hear the sound of them hitting the ground—just the sound of air rushing past their wings, and then nothing.

Lucien took the gun from me, holstered it next to its twin, and hurried me out of the apartment and into the elevator. My heart tightened as we descended past each floor, dreading that the elevator would stop to let someone else on. I shivered as everything washed back over me: the blood, the gunshots, the acrid smell of the Iyarri's breath. Dark wings closed over my consciousness, the rasp of feathers shifting past one another like a thousand knives sharpening. I crumpled around my aching shoulder, almost able to feel the piercing sensation of grasping talons all over again.

Lucien took me by the shoulders, hands and clothes smeared with blood from hefting the bodies over the railing. "Look at me." I did, tearing my mind's eye back to reality. His eyes were intense blue; usually they were much paler. "We're almost to the bottom floor. My truck is right out front, and I don't know where the last Laidrom is. We have to move quickly." I nodded, afraid I'd burst into tears if I tried to speak.

The elevator doors opened, and Lucien ushered me through the vacant lobby. Perhaps the sounds of gunshots and breaking glass had scared everyone into their apartments.

We got into Lucien's truck and sped to the other side of the building. Two warped, winged bodies lay sundered on the bloodstained ground. Lucien hurled them into the back of the truck—it rocked with the addition of each body, my stomach doing the same. Lucien climbed back in, and we fled from the fast-approaching wail of sirens.

SEVEN

I LIFTED MY TREMBLING HANDS to wipe the blood from my face, but my fingers were crimson-coated. Perhaps my sleeve, but no. My white sweater was so saturated with blood that it sagged and clung, my jeans blotched black with more of the same. How much of it was mine? Shaky and cold, I tucked my legs close to my body, curled up around the pain in my side, and pinned my lacerated arms between my chest and my thighs.

Lucien's face was drawn, his shoulders tight. "They might be waiting for us to show up at a hospital or trail us from there. And I don't think either of us wants to explain any of this to the cops." Lucien turned off the highway toward the country, the streetlights giving way to the quiet dark of farmland.

My head lolled against the cold glass of the window. I wanted to thank him. For showing up, for taking me out of there. Half-formed words shook with a shiver, and I closed my eyes, head swimming and body spent.

Lucien put a hand on knee and gave me a shake. "Hey." I blinked, head hazy. Lucien grabbed a half-bottle of soda from a cup holder and held it out to me. "Drink this. All of it. You need to get something in you to keep your blood pressure up."

I unscrewed the cap and managed some of the cold, flat cola.

A meteor strike impacted the roof of the truck, metal piercing through the steel into Lucien's left shoulder. I recoiled, throwing myself against my door with a cry. Lucien screamed—the truck swerved and skidded, throwing gravel at the edge of the road. The napta blade withdrew, and Lucien clapped his hand over the cut. Blood poured through his fingers and down the back of his leather coat.

"Lucien!" I made to sit up, move toward him, do something, but he pushed me deeper into the seat with his blood-coated hand.

"Stay down." Lucien unholstered one of his handguns and slammed the truck to a stop, throwing the Iyarri off with a screech of talons on metal. It hit the hood, rolled, and swept back into the air in a shadowy blur. In one motion, Lucien threw the door open, drew the second pistol, and got out of the truck, guns skyward. His shoulder bled freely, the brown leather going glossy and black. A winged shadow swept over him, circling once before it folded its wings and plunged. Two shots boomed; the Iyarri's body hit the ground in a spray of feathers and dirt. The sound of Lucien's gunshots echoed back.

Lucien dragged the body to the truck, and the vehicle rocked as Lucien dropped it in the back. My body swayed with it, seasick and light-headed. Lucien returned to the driver's side and swore, shedding his coat and rolling up the sleeve of his shirt so there was pressure on his wounded shoulder. He paused for a moment, eyes flitting closed. "God, I hope that's all of them." Lucien wiped his bloody hands off on his pants. "Either that's the last one or there's at least two more."

I shook my head, lips trembling too much to say the obvious: we wouldn't survive more.

Lucien holstered his guns and sped off, one hand on his lacerated shoulder, the other on the wheel. My vision swam, and before Lucien could shake me back to attention, I drifted into darkness.

The truck stopped at Lucien's house, jolting me awake. Lucien opened my door and caught me as I stumbled out. He leaned me against his side, and we took slow steps through the garage, leaving bloody footprints on the gray concrete. Inside the quiet dark of Lucien's house I felt safe, hidden. He sat me at the table in the breakfast nook. "I'll be right back." I nodded and pushed the heavy, matted mess of my hair back from my face and ran my thumb against the side of my forefinger. The blood on my hands was smooth and thick, like oil paint.

The light snapped on, bright spots danced in my vision, and the sound of the faucet roared like a waterfall. A large first aid kit clattered to the table. Hands still glistening from washing, Lucien set a bowl of warm water with a small stack of washcloths balanced beside it. He tucked a glass of lukewarm water into my hand and helped me raise it to my lips. "Here, drink this." It tasted sweet—he'd stirred sugar into it. When I set it aside, the glass was mottled with red fingerprints.

My heart hammered against my ribs, my breath coming light and fast—as though I were getting both too much air and not enough. Lucien moved his chair with a scrape so we faced one another, so close our knees touched. I stifled a cry at the sudden flash of pain as Lucien worked his fingers into the swollen knot holding the towel to my right arm. "I know, I know, I'm sorry," Lucien said, his brow furrowed. When he peeled it away, the terrycloth was so thick and stiff with blood it held the shape of my forearm. I scrutinized my arm, trying to see the wound through the blood as Lucien dipped a soft cloth in the bowl of water and daubed my skin, each press wet and warm. A trickle of water escaped and traced a clean path toward my elbow. The cuts made one angled slice when put together, starting at the elbow of one arm and ending at the wrist of the other. Once my arm was clean and dry, he sprayed it with cold, stinging antiseptic.

"This should have stitches, but these will have to do," Lucien said. His hands were deft and gentle as he used butterfly bandages to close the wounds with the quick precision of a sailor repairing a torn sail. My eyes trailed up his forearms, up the upraised lines of his scars. Defense wounds, like mine. The cuts on my arms disappeared under white gauze; Lucien stopped when both my arms were wrapped from wrist to elbow. I drank another mouthful of water and shivered, goose bumps spreading out across my skin. "How do you feel?" he asked.

It took me a second to find my voice. "Cold. Woozy." My ribs throbbed with each breath, and blood spattered both the edge of my chair and the tile below. "Lucien, my side." I tilted my head toward the pain.

He pressed a hand to my ribs and I shied away with a cry. His hand came back bright with fresh blood. "Christ." After a second of consideration he said, "Let's get you out of that sweater."

Lucien helped me slog the wet fabric over my head and discarded the sweater on the table in a ruined heap. The lace-trimmed tank top I wore underneath was mottled with red and blood-soaked on one side. Fresh bruises bloomed pink and purple on my shoulder. Lucien knelt on the floor next to my chair and rolled the side of my shirt up, exposing my side and my ribs. "The Laidrom knocked me down and pinned me." I tried to explain the hot line of pain on my side in that instant, but the words I wanted to say floated away from me. Temples pounding, I slumped forward, bracing my elbows on the table; the lights had a halo-like glow, and I blinked, trying to pull them back into focus.

The sensations of Lucien's hand pinching and pushing on my side registered through the haze, and I lifted my head. With all the fabric bunched up it I couldn't see the wound, but the stain across the top of Lucien's shirt was huge and wet. Blood ran in small rivulets down his arm, his shirt too saturated to hold more. "Your shoulder."

"I know." The words were tense, vexed. His hands were warm and dry against my clammy skin as he palpitated my ribs. "This went to the bone." Head throbbing, I braced my tender forearms on the table and hung my head as Lucien wiped my ribs clean, pulled the tissue closed with butterfly bandages, and taped a large patch of gauze over it.

When Lucien stood and finally turned his attention to his own injury, his complexion was ashen. He unbuttoned his shirt, a red Rorschach blot pressed onto his lean, muscled chest. Tossing the crumpled shirt on the table, he twisted, trying to see the wound. The lines of his body became an aching study in contrapposto, and I traced them with my eyes, wishing to do it with my fingers instead, to feel the soft skin and the resistance of muscle beneath it.

A gouge ran off the back of Lucien's shoulder and toward his spine in a painful comet. I slumped back in my chair and sighed in relief. "I thought for sure that had gone straight in."

"Good thing it didn't." His eyes focused far away, and I wondered what darker, horrible ways he imagined our encounter ending.

"Can I help?" I asked, not sure I could so much as stand.

He shook his head. "I want you to drink more water." He took up a wide roll of gauze and wrapped the cut, going over his shoulder and up under his armpit. Overtop, he wrapped a thick elastic bandage and moved his shoulder, testing to make sure the dressings would hold. Satisfied, he wiped off his hands, took my two in his, and helped me to my feet.

My breaths came shallow and light; within a few steps whiteness clouded my vision, and the world swayed under my feet. My body wavered and my pulse jumped, thudding in my ears; although Lucien spoke, the words were distant and warped.

I fell, but the impact of my body on the stone floor never came, just a floating sense of weightlessness; Lucien carried me, one arm under my knees, the other across my back. I drifted downward and settled onto something soft. When my vision cleared, I found myself lying on the couch, Lucien's drawn face hovering above me. He leaned so close, staring into my eyes, that for a delirious moment I thought he might kiss me. I traced my fingertips along the side of his jaw, but he pulled away from me. "Your pupils are way too wide—you've lost more blood than I thought. I'll be right back." My fingers lingered in the air where Lucien's face had been, memorizing it.

Lucien returned a minute later with a clean glass of water and a large, thick blanket. He helped me sit up and put the glass in my hands, holding them for a second to make sure I wouldn't drop it.

The water cleared my head. "Are they going to find us?"

He pressed his lips together, considering. "Laidrom hunt in odd numbers, and we got three. I think we're safe for the night."

As I stared into the wavering surface of the water, I could see the broken teeth of the Iyarri over me, feel the tallow-hot blood dropping from his shattered face onto my own. I closed my eyes, only to hear the split napta blade plunging into the carpet, the groaning glass, and splintering wood doors. Stress pressed down around me—the Laidrom's dead weight pressed down around me.

Dead by my hand. I had killed something. Someone. The thought raced through the cracks in my mind, chilling, expanding, and threatening to break my sanity to pieces. It shouldn't have happened. He should have left, not come at all. A piece of my innocence had dimmed and died beside the Laidrom.

My chest hitched once, twice, and two lines of hot tears burned my cheeks. Lucien lifted the glass from my hands and set it aside, then shook out the blanket and wrapped it around me, the fabric thick and soft over my thin camisole. I swallowed hard against hysteria, its tightness climbing inside my chest, wrapping and constricting. My pulse beat like a hummingbird trapped in my veins.

Lucien sat beside me and draped the rest of the blanket over his bare torso. "Shh . . . it's okay." In the darkness, I turned and buried my face in his shoulder. He didn't move for a moment, uncertain, and then folded me deeper into the blanket and held me against him.

Deep, shivering tremors radiated from my core, untouched by the blanket or Lucien's warm body against mine. A lifetime of Minnesota winters and I had never been so cold. Each tear took a bit of my strength with it. Lucien held me, one hand rubbing my back in slow circles, until the empty, shivering darkness of sleep overtook me.

I woke to warm light on my face, but it wasn't the dawn. Blue moonlight and orange firelight divided the room in contrasting hues, and shadows pressed in from the corners. Sensations registered one at a time—the weight of my blood-matted hair, the pillow supporting my head, the hand on my wrist.

Lucien was on the floor, slouched against the side of the couch—fast asleep, hair fallen forward, the longest pieces even with his finely-shaped lips. He held my wrist, two fingers on the inside of my arm and facing his wristwatch; he'd fallen asleep counting heartbeats. Lucien's nearness was comforting, the terrors of the night held back by the peace of his body touching mine—both of us alive and safe.

Gratitude swelled inside me—he'd risked so much to keep me safe, someone he barely knew. In the dark, huddled together in the wake of an Iyarri bloodbath, our growing closeness was as natural as two vines twining together for support. Careful not to wake him, I pillowed my head on his good shoulder and closed my eyes. The clear scent of his cologne cut through the metallic reek of drying blood, and I savored the even rhythm of our breath rising and falling in unison.

EIGHT

T HE SENSATION OF A warm, damp cloth moving in small sweeps against my face drew me to consciousness. The dried blood on my face was as stiff and flaky as dried paint, and my chest sank with a contented sigh to have it gone. A pause, then gentle arcs traced the contours of my cheeks. I turned my face toward the feeling and fluttered my eyes open.

Lucien paused, the red-stained washcloth in one hand. His complexion was better than the night before but there were dark smudges under his eyes and a weariness to his movements. He dipped a corner of the washcloth into a bowl of water, pressing it against the side to squeeze out the excess. As he returned to cleaning my face, he said in an appreciative and sweet tone, "Your eyes are gray. Don't see that often."

A flattered, shy smile crept across my lips. "How'd you sleep?"

"Better once I was sure you'd be okay." He wiped my forehead, where my hair was plastered to my skin with blood. The sun's feeble afternoon rays slanted through the windows, and the fire burned on in the hearth. "Are you hungry? Was thinking maybe we could get some food in you and then you could take a bath."

I nodded. When had I last eaten? A day ago?

"I'll get you something." Lucien propped me upright with pillows, then headed into the kitchen; he'd put a shirt on, a dark-colored button-down that he could ease over his bandaged shoulder. A few minutes later, the smell of cinnamon oatmeal piqued my stomach, and Lucien set a bowl on my lap.

"Thank you." My arms trembled lifting the spoon, and after a few ravenous bites my stomach rolled, trying to decide if it wanted the food or not. I slowed down but kept eating.

Lucien sank onto the love seat, the lines of his body rigid and stiff with pain. "How are you feeling?" he asked.

Weak, tired, sore. The nearness of my own death terrified me. "Overwhelmed."

A sad, understanding smile pulled at one corner of his mouth. "I can imagine." He rubbed at his shoulder. "Finish eating. I'll get a bath going for you and find something for you to wear while we wash your clothes." I wished for my backpack and the clothes I'd packed for my mother's, but we'd left it and my purse in my apartment.

"Okay, thank you." I finished my food, set the bowl aside, and pushed the blankets back with a wince of pain; the wound on my ribs made the smallest movements agonizing. As I eased my feet to the floor, I froze— my shoes were gone—but relief followed the heartbeat after. Lucien had left my socks on.

Lucien returned, sat on the coffee table, and gestured for my arms. "Should probably take that gauze off. We'll put fresh wrappings on after you're clean." He folded back the stiff sleeve of my shirt and unwrapped the gauze on my forearms, the dressings blemished with seeping reds and yellows. "If you can hold your shirt again, that'd help." He kept his tone unerringly neutral.

I rolled the side of the shirt up, and Lucien started to remove the gauze pad. "Ah," I said, squeezing my eyes shut as the tender skin around the gash lifted with the tape. He murmured an apology, adjusted the angle, and tried again. I was acutely aware of his touch, of the way he steadied the side of his hand against my ribs while his fingers worked to find the edges of the tape.

Lucien kept his eyes trained on his work as he spoke, his voice low. "I was afraid you were going into shock last night." The last piece of tape came free and he set the gauze pad aside. The marred surface mirrored the arc on my ribs, a rubbing done in blood. I lowered my shirt, and Lucien leaned back and met my eyes. "Not taking you to the ER was shit judgement on my part. I'm sorry."

I faltered at the bluntness and the concern in his voice. "Don't be sorry. It could have been worse if we'd gone." If the Iyarri had found us there.

"Yeah." His gaze drifted out the tall window next to us, the last bit of daylight burning out like a dying ember on the horizon.

I searched for the shadows of wings in between skiffs of clouds, and unease wound its way around my heart. I picked my phone up off the table and wiped off the blood. "I should let my mom know I'm okay," I murmured, thinking of how worried she must be.

Lucien frowned. "Maybe text her?"

"Yeah, that's probably best." She couldn't help me at this point, and the details of last night would upset her more. I sent, *Wanted to let you know I'm fine, but I'm not sure it's safe to call. I'll explain when I can.*

"Best turn off your phone, too, just to be safe."

I had no idea if Iyarri could find us that way, but if Lucien was concerned, I was willing to take him at his word. I turned off my phone and set it back on the table.

Lucien crouched and gestured for me to put an arm across his shoulders. "Come on, that bath should be about ready." He stood, lifting me with him. I sucked in my breath and buckled around my wounded side; my vision blotched white as a snowstorm. Lucien steadied me and said, "Yeah, ribs are miserable that way."

I took a half step toward the bathroom near the garage, as Lucien moved toward the master suite. "The other bathroom just has a shower. I don't think you should try standing too long." I changed directions and followed him.

Lucien's master suite was one large room—a sitting area sat to the left with the same fire burning in the sister hearth, Lucien's bed to the right.

Lucien pushed open the door to the bathroom, and the warm, damp air surrounded me in a vaporous embrace. Natural sandstone tile framed a deep oval tub three-quarters full of water—carved from a single gigantic rock, it was unfinished on the outside and polished smooth on the inside. Two towels and a small stack of folded clothes rested on the sink.

Lucien eased my arm from over his shoulder and said, "Call if you get light-headed. I'll stay within earshot just in case."

"Thank you, I will."

He left, closing the door behind him, and I crossed my arms and tried to lift my shirt, the motion arrested by a flash of pain. My left shoulder was mottled with bruises and an array of Laidrom talon marks, and even if my ribs could have tolerated the stretching, my arms protested the twisting.

The neckline of the camisole was elastic, and although wiggling it over my hips was painful, it was at least possible. Guilt lurched through me as I shed my socks. I felt like a thief, taking the compassion Lucien offered while keeping secrets from him. I dropped the crumpled socks to the floor and looked in the mirror, hoping the woman who lived there would have answers.

My hair was thick with bloody mats, and my skin was smeared with rust-colored swaths. The places Lucien had washed my face were clean and pale as a Noh mask in comparison. Tiny butterfly bandages held the edges of my lacerations together like little bridges over bloody rivers.

Weak and sore, my arms shook as I held onto both sides of the bathtub and eased myself down, hissing as the waterline rose over the arcing laceration on my side. The bath wasn't as warm as I would have liked, but I sank into it anyway. As I scrubbed my skin and washed my hair, my thoughts drifted to Lucien and me sleeping in front of the fire, my head on his shoulder, his face hovering so near to my own, the line of his jaw under my fingertips. He had sacrificed caring for himself to nurse my wounds instead; it showed in the way exhaustion dragged on him like a physical weight and how he held his wounded shoulder drawn tight to his body. It was a choice he made both willingly and with a depth of compassion that humbled me.

Each pale line of a scar gifted to Lucien by the Iyarri became a wound in my mind's eye, and my face crumpled as I pictured him trying to bandage all those bleeding cuts himself. I ached to return the favor, not because of a sense of debt but because I cared for him. The way my heart raced and the warm feeling that bloomed around it had nothing to do with blood loss. My future seemed a mess, I was Linnia, the Iyarri were hunting me, but whatever happened, I wanted it to include Lucien.

Eventually, the bath cooled past the point of comfort, and I let the orange-tinted water out of the tub. My head swam, and I knelt, water running past my knees to the drain, until I could get out on my own. Once clean and dry, I dressed in Lucien's clothes: a pair of black drawstring pants and a thick, thermal zip-up shirt. I put my own socks back on, hiding my feet. I needed to cuff the pants three times, and the shirt came halfway down my thighs, but too big or not, the clothes were dry, clean, and felt wonderful.

I gathered the rest of my clothes and found Lucien reclined on the small, comfortable-looking couch in front of the fireplace in his bedroom. The fire snapped and crackled, radiating light and warmth, and the windows framed a black and starless sky. He got to his feet and held out his hand for my clothes, shoulder tensing in pain. "I'll get these going and then we'll get your cuts wrapped back up." Glossy blotches marred his shirt over top of his bandaged shoulder.

I handed them over and nodded to the spreading bloodstain. "That bandage isn't holding."

"I can take care of it."

My face softened, and I touched his arm. "Or you can let me help you."

He hesitated, hand running over the bundle of clothes. "Okay. I'll be right back."

Lucien left and I moved near the fire, drawn to the warmth, just as my eyes were drawn upward to the Iyarri napta over the mantel.

There were half a dozen pairs hung in a fan with their split blades extended, the embossed detailing savage, arcane, and beautiful. The leather gauntlets varied from black to red, from green to brown; most were embossed with silver metal, but others had detailing wrought in copper, bronze, or gold. Perhaps the variations designated rank or were personalization. I counted the pairs of blades on the wall. There would be nine, now, after last night. That was a lot of times to face death and survive.

My eyes drifted to the mantel where strange sundries lay scattered: a bright silver spiral about the size of my little finger, a short petal-shaped dagger, and a handful of strange coins. Curious, I picked up the spiral and turned it in the firelight as Lucien returned, a bowl of water and clean washrags atop the first aid kit in his hands.

He set everything on the coffee table and nudged the box of butterfly bandages. "Good thing I have a bunch of these."

The spiral in my hands had a single, thin feather etched along its length. "What's this?"

"Some sort of hair decoration."

"It's lovely." I returned it to the mantle, amongst the blades and sundries. "Why do you keep them?"

Lucien's jaw tensed. "Because they're reminders that the truth is what you don't want to see. That beautiful things can still hurt you."

That they could.

I sat on the couch and gestured to the floor between my feet. "You're too tall for me to bandage the top of your shoulder standing."

Some of the wariness lifted from Lucien's brow. "I suppose I am." Lucien unbuttoned his shirt, eased it off, and discarded it on the table. A flush of warmth made my lips and fingertips tingle as firelight and shadow played over the planes and lines of his chest. I wrenched my attention back to Lucien's shoulder: the elastic bandage and the gauze underneath were dark with dried blood. He tried to unwind it himself, but stopped with a grimace of pain.

I lifted a teasing eyebrow. "I'm supposed to be helping, you know."

He gave me an abashed smile. "Yeah, you are." Lucien settled between my feet, the outsides of his arms against the insides of my calves. I settled my hand on his shoulder; it was muscled, his skin smooth. My fingers worked the little metal clips free from the dressing. The elasticity was choked out of the bandage, and it peeled away, stiff and flaking. The gauze beneath was worse, clogged with blood and stuck to Lucien's shoulder.

"Do you have enough light?" he asked.

"Yes." A human wouldn't have—I shoved the thought away, but it circled back, a reminder that I wasn't what Lucien believed me to be. Not wholly. I folded the washcloth into neat thirds, dipped it into the water, and daubed at the gauze, softening the blood. The more the gauze gave way, the more the tension in Lucien's shoulders dropped. As I worked, my eyes slid down the hollow of his spine to the holster he wore, the two pistols against the small of his back.

I didn't want to snuff out the small ember of openness kindling in our conversation and asked my question gently. "How did you find out about the Iyarri?"

Lucien stared into the flames, and time stretched out until I was sure he wouldn't answer. When he spoke, his voice was quiet. "I was raised by the Church after my parents died." He paused and rubbed one of his hands with the other. "They were Catholic missionaries in Sierra Leone. My parents taught the local people English, taught them about their faith." There was a small inflection on the word "their," not resentful or angry, but weighted with a note of despair. "They died when I was eleven. Best guess I have now is from typhoid fever, but whatever it was covered them in red blotches and burned them right up. My mother died first, then my father. I never caught it, whatever it was."

I cupped my free hand over his good shoulder. "I'm so sorry," I murmured.

He shook his head. "They buried my parents behind the church, if you want to call it that. It was a shack with a cross on the top. There was nowhere to send me, so the locals took care of me, fed me, but without a family I slept in the deserted church."

My eyebrows knit and my throat tightened picturing him young, afraid, and alone, forced to sleep on the floor of an abandoned building. "What did you do?" I asked.

"Someone got word back to the States, and they sent an older priest to bring me back. He took me to a monastery outside of Chicago. When I was older, they taught me stoneworking. There were a few old master stonemasons there, and they needed someone younger and stronger to help with the heavy work. I loved it there. The other masons told me I was doing God's work, and I believed that to my core."

The top layer of gauze lifted from those beneath it, and I kept daubing, careful not to pull Lucien's shoulder.

"After a few years, they asked if I would be interested in becoming a personal guard to some of the higher church officials. I thought it was an honor to prove myself to God by protecting His chosen. At twenty-two I was assigned to the protection of Bishop Saul, and I thought that both God and my parents would be proud." There was scorn in his voice, an undercurrent that ran through his tone like cold water in a warm stream.

"Here, lean back a little." I guided him by the shoulder until his back was against the edge of the couch between my legs. Lucien's body against mine was comforting, the closeness reassuring. I hoped it was for him as well.

"Bishop Saul often studied late into the night, but one time when I went to check on him, he wasn't speaking Latin—it was a language I didn't recognize."

"What did you do?" I asked as I lifted the gauze away entirely—the napta gash atop his shoulder was still oozing.

"Confronted him; I thought he was practicing the tongue of the devil. Instead, he told me he had discovered the language of angels. He went on about Enochian, how it was an erroneous and incomplete translation of the angelic language—" Lucien paused at my questioning hum and tried to explain. "Back in the sixteenth century, John Dee and Edward Kelley thought, or wanted people to think, they had been taught a celestial language by Enochian angels. Said the last person to speak it before them was Enoch himself. Bishop Saul believed he'd learned the true language of angels, Loagæth."

"Did you believe him?" I wiped the excess blood from his skin, tracing the contours of his body with the cloth.

Lucien rolled his wounded shoulder, testing the motion without the bandage. "Yeah, I did. Bishop Saul insisted on teaching me, and I was happy to learn. Something about the words he was practicing that night. He took it as a sign I had been guided to his study by an angelic hand and wanted me to be able to understand the angels when they chose to reveal themselves to me."

"Did they?" The disinfectant spray sputtered empty; there'd been just enough. The smell of woodsmoke from the fire obscured its medicinal odor.

Lucien watched the flames, as though the story replayed in them. "It was another two years before I met the Iyarri in the monastery library. There were two of them, and I was so blinded by faith I didn't even consider that they could be anything other than angels. When I fell to my knees, one tried to behead me."

I pulled the wound together with butterfly bandages. "What happened?"

Lucien pulled in his breath and tensed. "They killed Saul. I killed one of them and ran." There was so much more to that story; pain and betrayal so raw it bled through even without details. "Angels, divine beings, it was all bullshit. They were murderers. God was a joke, the Church nothing but lies. My parents died for a lie." His voice was punctuated with grief. "The Iyarri tainted everything I believed in, everything I was good at—every stone I had ever carved. So I ran."

"How did you start . . . well . . ." I gestured to the wall of napta.

Lucien regarded his grim keepsakes and frowned. "After I left, I changed my name, built this house, and was doing pretty well with my business." He ran his hand over the stubble on his face. "I was restoring the back steps of the Lutheran church on the other side of Minneapolis when I saw one. Hadn't seen an Iyarri in years, but I saw this one like I'd been trying to see through its ipuran the whole time. Perhaps I was looking for them and didn't know it. I have no idea. It walked right past me, so close its longest feathers dragged across my boot."

Spellbound and heartbroken, I wrapped clean gauze around his shoulder and taped it off.

"A few minutes later the Iyarri came back, dragging this girl with him. She screamed as she was taken out of the cloister, begging them not to let the angels take her. The humans had to think she was raving mad, but she knew them for what they were." Lucien's voice was low, his face drawn. He stood and rolled his shoulder. "Much better, thank you." He worked his shirt back on over the dressings; for a moment I feared he wouldn't continue, but he sat on the couch, so close our knees touched. "The Iyarri took her around the back of the building. I followed, tried to get to her, but he killed her with one napta strike."

I reached across the small space between us and took his hand in my own. His fingers tightened in mine.

"Before I realized what I was doing, I was on top of the Iyarri. I didn't have a gun, just a stone awl, but that was enough. I brought his body here and burned it. The girl I buried in an old cemetery. A few months later I went back and gave her a headstone." He dropped his gaze to our hands, his fingers threaded into my own, but he didn't take them away.

What did you say to such grief? I squeezed his hand. "I'm sorry."

He shook his head. "Don't be. It's better than living a lie." There was conviction in his words, but no happiness.

"You said you changed your name. What was it before?"

"Isaiah. Isaiah Eder."

"What would you like me to call you?"

"Lucien. I'm not Isaiah anymore." The finality in his tone was heartbreaking.

I tucked my hair behind my ear; the waves cascading over my ribs were starting to dry, lightening from a deep cinnamon to burnished copper. Though I knew Lucien's past had cost him everything, I was grateful he had been able to use those skills to keep the two of us alive. "Thank you for bringing me here and for keeping us safe."

Lucien sighed. "As safe as we can be, anyway. They've lost four Laidrom. If they find us, we won't live through it."

Tears pricked my eyes, and I looked away, not wanting Lucien to see how viscerally the thought of another attack frightened me. One tear escaped, spilling down my cheek before falling into the dark. Lucien's brow furrowed. His hand hesitated in front of my check for a second before he brushed the tear trail away with his thumb. "Don't cry, viruden. I'll do what I can," he murmured.

Exhausted and soul-weary, I shifted and leaned against Lucien's side. He wrapped one arm around me, and I leaned my head on his good shoulder, closing my eyes to keep in the tears. "Thank you."

NINE

THE HOUSE WAS QUIET come morning, the fire nothing more than dying fireflies in a bed of ash. I was curled on the small couch, alone, a blanket drawn over me. It had been so easy to drift away leaning on Lucien's shoulder, feeling the rise and fall of his chest against my body. I eased myself up, my ribs protesting the movement and my bruised shoulder stiff and aching. At least the bone-deep chill was gone. My clothes waited on the table in front of me, clean and folded. I gathered them to go change and looked about for Lucien.

Across the room, Lucien was sprawled across the top of his bed, fully dressed, holster still tucked into the back of his jeans. He slept, his good arm thrown over a pillow, half his face buried in it. The bed was between two windows, a heavy nightstand on one side. An alarm clock read nine o'clock in the morning.

I slipped out the door into the living room, hoping not to wake him as I went into the far bathroom to change clothes. My jeans were clean, but the camisole was slashed. I kept Lucien's shirt on instead, savoring its warmth and the way it smelled like him.

In the kitchen, I scooped coffee into the French press, set it brewing, took two steps toward the table, and stopped. It was awash in the remains of our panicked triage: the crumpled mass of our bloody shirts splayed across its surface, and pieces of bandages and tape were scattered like petals. Blood spatters marred the wood, the side of my chair, and the floor beneath it. I set the French press back on the counter, cleaned the table, and stacked its contents off to one side. As I dumped a bunch of bloody gauze into the trash, I spotted a duffle bag near the door to the garage. Easing myself to the floor, I parted the open zipper with my fingertips. Three pairs of gore-covered napta were piled inside.

Each pair was different in its design but unified by a coat of blood. I extracted one; the leather was still tacky, but fascination overrode the twist of revulsion. The formed leather gauntlets, the intricate lacing, and the metal framework holding the blade: all were forged with an equal eye to form and function. I followed the lacing with my eyes: hooks ran down one side of the leather, eyelets down the other. I turned the napta in my hands and tried to figure out how the blade slid forward.

The split blade was long and flat, like a katar, but thinner, finer, and serrated at the base. Etchings adorned either side of the split, the recesses coated in a patina of black. I traced my finger over the designs; they were nicked in places and the recesses were full of blood, likely mine. The Iyarri line work was reminiscent of Art Nouveau but pruned to simplicity. The fluid, refined shapes interwove like a melody smithed into metal.

From behind me Lucien said, "That coffee smells amazing." He walked over, rubbing his eyes with a smile, and focused on the napta in my hands. Lucien crouched beside me and pulled out the mate to the napta I held. "That pair is from the Iyarri you killed."

The Iyarri I killed. My brow furrowed. "What did you do with the bodies?"

"Threw them in the gully back there and covered them with brush. I'll burn them later; didn't want to risk others seeing the smoke."

His tone was callous and indifferent, feelings I couldn't bring myself to match. I rubbed my thumb on my forefinger and looked through the large windows in the breakfast nook. The brown autumn ground dropped off into the gully, but I didn't see Iyarri corpses or a concealing brush pile. Whatever rites Iyarri performed for their dead wouldn't take place; instead their more interesting trinkets would be added to Lucien's mantel, and their bodies turned to ash. The thought might have bothered me more if I wasn't certain they'd have showed Lucien's corpse, or my corpse, even less courtesy.

Lucien nodded to the napta from the Iyarri I had killed. "They're yours if you want them."

I glanced between him and the napta. "I'm not sure what I'd do with them."

"Keep them as a reminder, if nothing else."

A reminder that the truth isn't what you want it to be. That beautiful things can hurt you. They were not only beautiful pieces of functional art but also immutable pieces of my history. I turned the gauntlet in my hand. The leather on the inside, where the Iyarri's arm protected it from blood, was the rich brown of oak leaves. I bobbed the napta in my hands. "It's so light."

Lucien adjusted the lacing so there were loops of it on the eyelet side and slid his arm into the gauntlet. With his other hand, he slipped the loops over the hooks on the other side of the gauntlet and pulled the tail of the lacing, cinching the leather tight. "Thing is, Iyarri aren't any stronger than humans, maybe less so. They're just so fast it more than makes up for it. Whatever this metal is, they use it so they don't get tired swinging it."

"How do you make the blade come out?" I asked. Gory or not, I leaned close to the napta, curious.

He stood, stepped back a few paces, and tilted the blade so I could see. "You make a fist, then snap your arm, and the blade locks in place." With a flick of his arm, the napta lashed out like a viper strike. The edge of the blade was still rimmed in my blood. My fascination dimmed again to somberness, and I wrapped my arm around myself, pressing my palm to my wounded side.

"Ah." Lucien grimaced in pain, his hand closing over his wounded shoulder. He lifted it and his palm came away bright with blood. "Goddammit." His shirt grew dark and wet over the deepest part of his cut. He picked up a thick pad of gauze from the table and pressed it to his shoulder. "Stupid of me."

"You're undoing all my hard work," I teased, then gestured to his shoulder. "Can I help?"

He gave me a sideways smile. "I would love a cup of that coffee."

"I can do that." I put the mug in his good hand, sat on the counter, and waved his hand off the gauze. "Let me." I settled my hand on his shoulder, the side of my leg against his hip. I savored Lucien's company, his closeness, the way his seriousness broke when he smiled. Once I'd staunched the bleeding, I asked, "Do you want me to close it up again?"

Lucien gave his shoulder a tentative roll and frowned. "It needs stitches. It's too deep and moves too much to stay closed." He leaned against my side and took off the napta gauntlet, thinking.

"What if you took me to my mom's?" I offered. "She has to be worried sick, and I could stay there while you get your shoulder taken care of."

He frowned, unsure, but with one bad shoulder and me wounded too, his ability to keep one of us, much less both of us, safe was deeply diminished. "The Iyarri and the police are looking for you. I know you haven't seen the news, but with the blood, strange footprints, and feathers all over your apartment, it's been whipped up as some ritual attack. It's a giant mess."

I picked up my coffee cup and wrapped my hands around it, trying to ignore the wailing police sirens in my memory. I pictured the bloody mess and broken feathers we'd left behind. "They must think I'm dead," I said.

Heavy thoughts, full of uncertainty and despair, crowded in from the edges of my mind; I understood Lucien's loneliness, how his knowledge of Iyarri isolated him. "What am I going to do?" The words were urgent and hopeless.

"The police will have talked to your mom for sure. We can go there, but if there's any sign of the police or Iyarri, we'll keep driving and figure something else out." He put his coffee cup on the counter beside me. "If it's safe, I'll go get my shoulder patched up and then come back and get you." He tucked a stray ginger wave behind my ear; the way his fingers threaded through my hair made my skin tingle. "And then we'll figure something out." Our faces were level and his fingertips lingered, unwilling to leave the tumble of entropic waves. I reached out and ran my hand over the scruff on his cheek, tracing the contour of his cheekbone with my fingertips. His eyelashes flitted, but he stepped back, took my two hands in his, and helped me off the counter with a smile. "Come on. The sooner we leave the sooner we can come back." Even though I didn't have any more answers than I had a few seconds earlier, the uncertainty in my heart quelled at the idea of "we."

Lucien packed a bag with a small first aid kit, a gun smaller than his pistols, and some extra ammunition, then showed me how to reload the gun. After I'd practiced a few times, he stowed the gun in the bag and added in a pair of napta with deep brown leather, silver blades, and arcing accents. I gave them an inquiring tilt of the head. "Your napta. I cleaned them up for you." My brows pulled together in confusion, and he clarified, fumbling for a delicate way to say it and failing. "The ones from the Iyarri you killed."

I shouldered the bag, feeling less unsure about the macabre mementos than before. They were mine because I had survived their keen edges and my own terror, as much a persistent memory as the scars they'd leave on my skin. "Thank you."

We headed out into the bright, cold day. Frost covered the ground in a pale mantle, and sunlight glimmered, deceptively warm, across it. Lucien headed south toward my mother's, the road threading through the rolling, tree-covered bluffs.

When we arrived, the little white house was nestled like a dove between great willows and wrapped in a nest of my mother's gardens. No police cars or signs of Iyarri awaited us. Lucien parked on the road and walked me to the front door. I reached for the knob, but Lucien's voice stopped me. "Lia?"

I turned, and he put his hands on my shoulders, his face serious. "I meant what I said. I'll be back as soon as I get my shoulder patched up."

I smiled and put one of my hands atop his. "Okay. See you soon."

His eyes crinkled with a smile. "Be safe, viruden." He drew away. "Go on; I'll stay until you're inside."

I tried the door, surprised to find it locked. My keys were still in my ransacked apartment, so I rang the bell. A moment later my mother opened the door, her eyes red and puffy with dark smudges under them. Her hair was tied off in a days-old ponytail, her clothes sleep-rumpled. "Lia!" She pulled me into a fierce, crushing hug. Pain flared through my napta wounds, and I stifled an inhale of pain. "Oh my God, there you are." My mother hurried me inside, paying little attention to Lucien. He gave me a reassuring nod and closed the door between us.

She ushered me into the living room and sat me on the couch. "Here, come sit down—you're so pale." My heart sank at the sound of Lucien's truck starting, and I wished he'd stayed. My mother didn't so much as peer out the window or question how I'd arrived, fixated, instead, on a wrap of gauze sticking out of my sleeve. "You never came home. I saw the news, and then the police were here. I know it was them."

"The Iyarri were waiting for me," I said, cradling one wounded arm in the other.

"Aye, they were," Tiahmani said as she walked in from the kitchen. She looked human, but the long, wide, rectangular sleeves of her shirt didn't entirely conceal her napta.

Fear like ice water dumped into my veins. "What are you doing here?" I asked, my throat constricting my voice to a whisper.

A feline smile spread across Tiahmani's lips, as though she were a cat lapping up my terror. "You're coming with me."

I felt the color drain from my face.

"She's going to look after you," my mother said. Her eyes weren't just tired, they were unfocused and distant. "I've already packed some of your things." Her old backpack sat near the door.

There was no chance my mother would let a strange woman into the house and then suddenly decide the best thing was for me to go with her—not after I'd narrowly escaped an Iyarri attack with my life and returned home. I scrambled to find understanding amidst a sea of cold fear, all too aware of Tiahmani's claws, talons, and arm blades.

"You are going to spend a few days somewhere else. With relatives," Tiahmani said to my mother.

My mother shook her head, curls swaying, and blinked twice. "No, I should be with Lia."

"Mom, what's going on?" I pled as I gripped her arm.

Tiahmani took a deep breath before she spoke, an undercurrent of impatience barely in check. "Aurelia is coming with me. You are going to stay with relatives." Her voice demanded obedience, the same resonance I'd heard in Aamon's voice when he'd told Jacob to give me unpaid leave without question. The Iyarri's fist tightened—an unspoken threat. *Or else.* I didn't know where Tiahmani wanted to take me or why, but I knew with a core-deep surety she could kill both my mother and me with as much effort as it took for me to put a kettle on. Nervous, cold sweat stung my wounds, and I wished against all hope that Lucien would burst through the door and save us.

My mother rubbed at her temples, burdened with a sudden, excruciating headache. "But—"

The corners of Tiahmani's eyes gathered in concentration; her voice was a physical weight on my mother. "Go get your coat and leave."

There was no response from my mother, all her focus turned inward as she warred with her own thoughts. Tiahmani's hand flexed and the leather gauntlet of her napta creaked.

I scrambled in between the two of them, crouching in front of my mother and gripping her hands in mine. They were limp, unresponsive, and might stay that way if Tiahmani didn't get whatever she wanted.

Every heartbeat seemed a countdown to a swift, final napta strike. "Mom." She didn't even look at me; I shook her. "Mom, listen to me."

Focus crept back into her eyes as they met mine.

My exhale shook with relief. "Mom, you should go stay with Erin." I stole a glance over my shoulder; I didn't trust Tiahmani, but I would suffer the Laidrom's claws before I let her hurt my mother. Or Lucien. I was instantly grateful he wasn't there and ashamed that I wished he would put his life at risk for mine again.

Part of my mother's resolve broke off, like the edge of a cliff shattering into the sea. "Perhaps staying with Erin is best." She got to her feet, her hands slipping free of mine. "I'll get my coat." In a daze, she drifted toward the coat closet.

I got to my feet and spun to face Tiahmani in a single, desperate motion. "What did you—"

"Quiet." The sharpness in her tone silenced me. Tiahmani kicked the backpack. "If there's anything else you need, get it now." Not having a coat of my own, I grabbed an old coat of my mother's and eased it on, hands shaking too much to close the buttons.

My mother returned wearing her coat and carrying an overnight bag. She kissed my cheek. "Be safe. I love you." She said it as though she were going to the store, not leaving me alone, wounded, with an Iyarri.

I hugged her, my desperate embrace so tight the cuts on my arms threatened to split open again. I didn't want to leave her in whatever state Tiahmani had put her in, but I also needed her to be away and safe. "I will, Mom. I love you too." The words trembled, but my mother didn't notice as she left.

After she'd gone, Tiahmani escorted me outside and gave me a shove in the direction of a silver car parked midway down the street.

I fumbled with the backpack and Lucien's bag, dread stretching out like a thin line between me and my mother's house. The further away we got from it, the more the tension built inside me. "Where are we going?" I said, straining under the exertion of the bags and my own weak and wounded body. "And what did you do to her?"

Tiahmani unlocked the doors. "Get in." The car was sporty, and modified to accommodate an Iyarri. Both the front seats were tall and thin, two hand spans wide. Piercing her ipuran, I saw her wings were resting in the back of the car, the small, narrow seat back pressed between them. Neither Tiahmani nor I said another word, and I willed my mother to keep driving until she was safe at Erin's. Once we were out of Hastings and onto the highway, Tiahmani pulled her phone from her pocket and placed a call. "Got her," she said.

With my keen ears I could hear Aamon on the other end of the line. "Is Aurelia all right?" I sagged against the car door in relief.

"Messed up, but alive. She's favoring her arms and her side, all shaky, and lost some blood, too." The way her eyes narrowed gave me no doubt she'd be more than willing to finish the job the Laidrom started. "I'm going to lay low with her for a bit until I'm sure we're not being followed. Then I'll stash her someplace safe."

There was a contemplative silence before Aamon said, "That's likely best. I'll let Ikkar know of your assignment on my behalf. Has she mentioned what happened?" His voice was concerned, and I wished it was him there with me rather than Tiahmani.

"Not yet. Without knowing how the wind lies, I wasn't going to waste time getting her out of there. I was lucky enough the other Laidrom weren't there, or the police."

"Of course. Thank you, Tiahmani. Fair winds."

"And clear skies." She hung up, put her phone in her pocket, and turned her attention to the road.

When it became clear she wasn't going to say anything to me unless forced to, I asked, "You didn't tell Aamon where you're taking me?"

"He wouldn't want to know. Saves him having to lie about it."

I wiped my sweaty palms on my jeans. "What did you do to my mom with your voice? She never would have let me leave on her own."

She tilted her head, wary. "Interesting that you can hear the solpeth. Plodders can't." I looked at Tiahmani and she shrugged. "It makes us very convincing to humans. I can use it when I have to, but Aamon's much better at it." If that's what he'd used on Jacob, it was true. Aamon's suggestion had sounded conversational, save that Jacob never would have agreed to leave with pay under normal circumstances. "It was either use the solpeth on her or take you by force."

I gazed out the window, dread weighting my stomach. Although I knew being a Linnia wasn't my fault, my heart still ached as though I had wronged my mother. "Will she be okay?"

"If she does what I told her to." Tiahmani's tone was dismissive; my mother was at best an annoying obstacle, and at worst a defiler of Iyarri blood for her part in creating me.

The road slipped past us, dark and fluid as my thoughts. "Where are you taking me?" I asked.

Her fingers twisted into the reddish-brown feathers threaded into her hair. "To Cæl."

I gaped. "My father?"

"My brother." She corrected me through gritted teeth. "Cæl would never have . . ." Tiahmani shook her head and glared at the road ahead of her, her face darkening.

"Then why are you taking me to him?"

"Because if it is true and he's denied it this long, he'll keep denying it unless proof is standing right in front of him." Her grip tightened on the wheel. "I swear if he left us, left me, because of a plodder and a Linnia, I'll kill him myself."

TEN

"**D**OES CÆL KNOW I'M—we're—coming?" I asked.

"No."

The forest closed in around the road as the narrow strip of asphalt wound upward through the bluffs. Nightfall came early in late autumn; the trees overhead merged with the nocturnal sky. "Where are we?" My voice was small and scared.

"Somewhere with lots of good places to dump a body."

Clumps of brush crouched alongside the road, and my reflection in the dark window stared back at me. What would my father think of his bastard? A good portion of me was my mother—the red hair, the pale skin. I wasn't all my mother, though. Obvious Iyarri features aside, I was built like Tiahmani: fine nose, high cheekbones, and curves forsaken for a thinner, lighter stature. Our eyes were similar, too, the shape wide and upturned, the colors too saturated to be human.

The silver car scaled the river bluffs, and the snaking asphalt dissolved to gravel. Past the shoulder of the road, the earth sheared away to a dark crevasse of a valley. There were indeed lots of good places to dump a body. I fingered the zipper of the bag that held Lucien's gun. Tiahmani ignored me with surgical precision, pulled off the road, and parked in a larger, empty patch of gravel. There were spaces for maybe a dozen cars, but by the way undisturbed leaves and branches were strewn about, nobody had been there in weeks.

"Get out, follow me, and stay quiet," she said. I grabbed the bag with Lucien's gun. "Leave it," Tiahmani snapped. I hesitated, and she raised both her dark eyebrows at me. I dropped the handles of the bag and exited the car.

We followed the wide path of stones into the trees. The black river far below wound along the base of the bluffs, and in the distant dark the Cities glowed. After a while, the forest opened to a large, flat clearing with a tall, wrought-iron fence on the far side. The gate was closed with a wrap of chain and a lock, and bore a sign that read, *Closed for the season*. Beyond the fence was a grassy expanse with several stone buildings in a semicircle. "I'll have to lift you over," Tiahmani said.

I stepped back from her and the fence, not wanting to go into someplace I couldn't get out of. "Where are we?"

"A retreat. Cæl and I meet here sometimes. This time of year there are no humans, no Iyarri. Good enough?" I nodded, and she grabbed me by the waist, the hard leather of her gauntlets pressing into my stomach. "Squirm and I'll drop you." Her enormous, dark wings whipped the air, and we took off. Tiahmani's muscles bunched; my vision went white and I gasped as her arms slipped upward, gauntlet biting into my wounded ribs. My feet passed over the spikes atop the fence, and Tiahmani stopped beating her wings and glided to the ground.

She released me; I staggered forward, clutching my side. Pain and nausea swept over me in a wave, and blood seeped from the wound, the gauze warm and damp against my skin. Wind rattled through the tree branches; a loon gave a mournful cry, and the flock answered its lament. Tiahmani grabbed a fistful of my coat and pulled me forward so forcefully I stumbled.

The smaller buildings appeared to be cabins, all their windows dark. Tiahmani led me up the center of the clearing, where an imposing, larger, central building made of pale stone stood. She led me inside and let the door fall closed behind us. Tomblike stillness encompassed the great, arching space.

The massive room was divided by a rectangular reflecting pool, creating a watery corridor bordered by stone on the first floor and long balconies on the second. Everything was still. Even Tiahmani's voice was quiet when she spoke. "Stay here." She headed off into the shadows, leaving me alone.

The far wall was solid windows, a second moon floating in the tranquil water. I shifted my weight from one foot to the other and back again. What had Tiahmani told Cæl? What hadn't she told him? Unable to stay still, I walked along the pool's edge, my reflection a dark, ethereal twin.

A male voice, pitched low with longing and disbelief, broke the silence. "Catherine?" I whirled around, ears straining for the sound's origin, eyes searching for a figure in the darkness. A tall man stood on the walkway over the entrance. He said my mother's name again, this time softer. His human illusion disappeared, and massive wings blotted out the window behind him as he hooked one foot on the railing and pushed himself off. The Iyarri glided to the floor like a great bird of prey, the only sounds my heart hammering in my ears and his wings parting the air.

He landed not far away and walked toward me, talons rasping on the floor and wings folding with a susurrus whisper. Every nerve in my body screamed at me to run as the Iyarri approached me, each of his movements poised and deadly. It was his expression that softened my fear—questioning and longing and hopeful all at once. He appeared to be in his thirties; the planes of his face were strong, his eyes intelligent. His mahogany hair was pulled into a braid at the nape of his neck, but shorter strands fell level with his cheeks.

I tried to find my voice, but it failed me as he closed his clawed hands around my shoulders and turned me so my face was in the moonlight. My mother's name died on his lips, and his eyes clouded with confusion and surprise.

I swallowed around the tightness in my throat and shook my head. "No, not Catherine. Aurelia."

He scanned my features, seeing the ways in which my face was not like my mother's, but the strength of the resemblance reflected back in his pained expression. He took a half step back, and I caught him by one hand, my delicate fingers clasping his thicker, more powerful ones. My touch was light; he could have pulled free if he'd wanted, but he stopped, hand held in mine. "Don't leave," I said.

Cæl hesitated and then pulled me into a hug of both arms and wings, cocooning us in feathers that smelled of an ancient, sacred forest. I stilled, the embrace as frightening as it was comforting. He stepped back and held me by the shoulders, memorizing my face. "After all this time, I still imagined a little girl," he murmured.

Tiahmani emerged from the shadows at the edge of the pool and walked toward us, lips parted in disbelief. She scrutinized our reflection in the water. Family. It showed in the shape of our eyes and the bow of our lips. Tiahmani could have been my older sister were it not for my too-pale skin and earthbound body.

She glared at her brother and dashed one wing into the surface of the water. "How could you?" Her voice twisted with heartbreak. For a few seconds, only the lapping water and the enraged tremble in her breath broke the silence. "You left me for this?" She pointed one claw at me. "For a half-breed and a human? A human you didn't even stay with?" Her anguish was almost enough to crowd out the disgust in her voice.

Guilt carved deep lines on Cæl's face. My father's wings shifted as he chose his words, reddish hues undulating like the deepest flamed varnish on a violin. "I never wanted to leave you, noro." The Loagæth word was soft, endearing.

"You're supposed to be better than this." She scowled at me. "Than that." As if I'd had some say or hand in any of this. Tiahmani turned away, closing her wings around her like a second set of arms. She looked younger and lonely with her shoulders hunched and face downcast.

"You were all I had, and you left me because you were fucking a human?" The absolute disdain and otherness of the word hit me like a gut punch.

Cæl's brows knit with sympathy. "You were old enough, already a Laidrom. Aurelia was just born."

"When Aamon said she was yours, I didn't believe him." Tiahmani's voice dripped with venom. "I thought you'd never—"

"Aamon?" The edge to Cæl's voice made me take a step away from him.

Tiahmani barked a short, cruel laugh and crossed her arms over her stomach. "He said he's known about your Linnia since before she was born, since before you left. He let you rot in this bullshit self-imposed exile for nothing."

Cæl stood stunned, great wings like carved redwood. "What?"

"Aamon knew this whole time. He made sure nobody found out why you left, including me." Tiahmani spun to face him, hands clenched. "I had to find out about all this from him and not you, you fucking *coward*." The word echoed off the water, off the stone, the same way it echoed in my mind—Aamon had called Cæl a coward, too.

Cæl lowered his head to his hand and closed his eyes for a second before he spoke. "What do you want, Tiahmani? I have suffered my own shame and guilt. There is nothing you could heap on me now that I have not already done to myself." To hear him say it outright—that his relationship with my mother, that my existence, was something to be ashamed of—twisted my heart in my chest.

"I want you to come back." Tiahmani's words were quiet, as if saying them any louder was to hope too much.

He wanted to. The pause before his words hung heavy with longing. "I can't come back; it's a death sentence. Mine and theirs."

Impatience crept back into Tiahmani's voice. "Nobody knows, Cæl. No one."

"Nobody except Aamon. Do you think that's by chance? That this isn't a trap? If he didn't have some reason for his silence, he'd have been the first to kill Aurelia."

My thoughts came unmoored, and I cast about in waves of confusion and disbelief for an answer. "What? Aamon? Why would—"

Tiahmani ignored me and stalked toward Cæl. "If it's a trap, you're standing there with the bait. Get rid of her and the plodder and come home."

He shook his head, the lack of hesitation making me wonder how many times he had considered returning to my mother, to me, or to the Iyarri, always coming back to the conclusion—he had to stay away. "There is no place I could hide where they wouldn't be found, and if I go back there will be too many questions I can't answer, especially to an Ohlera."

"That isn't what I meant when I said get rid of them." Tiahmani snapped her arm at my throat, the click-whisper of her blade's release punctuating her words. Time expanded, the pull of my breath matching the rushing sound of the blade extending. In a blur, Cæl was between me and Tiahmani; there was the sound of metal on metal, of leather thudding into flesh, and Tiahmani hit the floor in a sprawl of feathers and limbs.

Cæl stood over her, his own napta extended, platinum-blue, in the moonlight. "That," he exhaled the word, "is the last time you raise a hand to my daughter." An icicle of sweat ran down my spine, and I pressed my palm over my heart, shaking and grateful for Cæl's intervention.

Tiahmani sat back on her heels and pushed her hair from her face, tears bright in her jade eyes. A brokenhearted, abandoned child peered through her warrior exterior. "That's your choice, then?" Her voice cracked.

Cæl's blade retracted into the straight sleeve of his coat; he held out a hand to help Tiahmani to her feet. "Noro, it isn't that simple."

She slapped his hand away, the sound echoing in the cavernous room. "It should be." She got to her feet and fled in a swirl of coffee-colored wings. Neither of us moved until the booming echo of the closing door behind her dissipated.

"There's no point talking to her until she's cooled down." Cæl turned toward me, the edges of his eyes creased with sympathy. "Everything Tiahmani said was true, but her pain makes her cruel and childish. Try not to take the things she says to heart—I made my decisions, and while they have caused hardship, I do not regret them, your mother, or you, Aurelia."

The constricting uncertainty around my heart eased, loosing emotions that tumbled about my chest. The warmth of relief, the sting of knowing he missed us but still had not returned, the clarity of realizing my father was still little more than a stranger. "You can call me Lia. Mom does," I offered, trying to bridge the gap of unfamiliarity between us.

"No," he said. "You have an Iyarri name; it will be used in full."

My steps slowed and I bit my lip. An Iyarri name he'd chosen over my mother's human one. But that also meant he thought I was worthy of an Iyarri name. "If you prefer—" I hesitated; the words "dad" and "father" were so strange on my lips I couldn't bring myself to say them.

"Essia is the Loagæth word for father. Perhaps that would be better." It seemed "father" was awkward for Cæl, too.

"Essia." I smiled as I said it; though the word was foreign, it felt natural. The father that inhabited my childhood dreams was human and trying to shoehorn Cæl into that spot felt unfair to both of us. Years of questions, of things I thought I'd say if I met him, fought to be spoken—*Where did you go? Why didn't you write, call, something?*—but what escaped my lips was, "You never came back to us."

"No, I didn't." He was silent for a moment, his expression fading to misery as he scanned my face. "I wanted to, though. More than you can imagine." The way he took in my features, paring the human from the Iyarri, made me self-conscious. "And I apologize for calling you by your mother's name. You look like her."

"I do, a little."

"More than just a little." Some of the dourness lifted from his voice. "My pasahasa grew up to be as beautiful as her mother." The Loagæth word was gentler-sounding, more musical than Cæl's English. He reached to where a piece of white gauze stuck out of the sleeve of my coat. "Did Tiahmani do this to you?"

"No, another Laidrom did."

"And you lived?" His tone carried a note of criticism. He seemed both grateful I was alive and aware that, had the Laidrom performed as he expected, I shouldn't have been.

"Apparently so." I smiled a bit.

He guided me toward the doors. "Come, let's sit."

We crossed the grassy courtyard to one of the cabins; its pale walls reflected starlight and spoke of solitude. The door was unlocked and, by the belted hip bags on the bed, Cæl had either a key or few reservations about breaking and entering.

The inside was small and spartan, but open enough that Cæl didn't struggle to maneuver with his wings. He closed the door and paused with one hand on it, speaking without turning around. "Pasahasa, how is Catherine?" There was so much dread in his voice. It asked a thousand other questions with it: *Has she forgiven me? Did she think of me? Is she happy?*

"She said she'd never stopped missing you."

He sighed, his great wings drooping with his shoulders. "I asked her not to speak of me. I thought it would make it harder on you to know something rather than nothing." He rubbed the back of his neck. "Has she . . ." He trailed off, unsure of how to ask the question written all over his face.

"No, she never found anyone else." The half-truth hung between us. She hadn't found anyone because she hadn't looked for fear of someone finding out about what I was.

The pain etched on his face mingled with relief. "I always wondered. I was unfair to her." Cæl cupped my chin in his hand, the thick claws resting on my face with a surprising amount of tenderness. "Thank you for coming to me."

I closed my hand over his. "Thank you for staying when I did."

He sat and gestured to the gauze. "May I see?" I shed my coat, sat on the edge of the bed, and eased up the sleeves of Lucien's oversized shirt. My skin broke out in goosebumps; the cabin was warmer than the air outside, but not by much.

Cæl unwound the gauze and set it aside, turning both my arms so he could see the gashes and the tiny butterfly bandages holding the edges together. "Who knows what you are?" Fear crept into his tone.

"Aamon said only he and Tiahmani know I'm a Linnia. The other Iyarri think I'm a human who knows about them." I told him as much as there was: Stephen Keller's death, Lucien saving me and taking me to my mom's. "And Tiahmani took me from there and brought me here to meet you."

My father pinched the bridge of his nose. "Aamon and a kiaisi. You have your aunt's knack for finding trouble."

"Kiaisi?"

"Iyarri-killer. Tell me Lucien doesn't know what you truly are."

I shook my head, my throat tight. "No."

"Keep it that way." He leaned back in his chair, steepled his fingers, and pressed them to his chin.

I tilted my head in question. "How do you know Aamon?"

"The better question is how you know him." Cæl's hazel eyes narrowed; like ancient moss, they were green in places and broken by flecks of black and brown.

"I asked first." I pressed my lips together and waited.

He rewrapped my arms, making several passes with the bandage before he spoke. "Aamon blames me for the death of his Semeroh, Siyah."

Aamon had never once mentioned Siyah; my mind played through every time I'd seen him. He was always by himself, never attended by a significant other or friend.

"I might have dealt the deathblow, but it was Aamon who killed her." Cæl scowled as he worked my sleeves back over my redressed arms and finished with a sharp tug. "That's Aamon's way, to let others take risks for him and die in his place. And why you shouldn't have anything to do with him."

"Aamon wouldn't hurt me," I said, incensed that my father presumed he knew my relationship with Aamon better than I did. If Aamon had intended to hurt me or my mother, there was no reason to wait so long. In the years I'd known him, he'd only ever been helpful. Aamon had noticed my art, gotten me scholarships, my job. He certainly hadn't had to personally ensure that an Iyarri attack hadn't gotten me in trouble with my boss, or the police. And he'd told me about my Iyarri heritage when neither of my parents had. Those weren't the things someone did if they intended harm.

"Directly? No, he doesn't have the stomach for it. Allow you to be harmed if it suits his goals? He would in a second." He nodded to my arms. "Is that the worst of it?"

"No." I pulled my hair over my shoulder and rolled my shirt up to reveal the bloody dressing and bruises blossoming across my side.

The flats of my father's claws pressed into the skin, palpating for the severity of the wounds. "This went to the bone."

I gritted my teeth, trying not to wince under the pressure. "I know." As he reapplied the bandage I asked, "What did Siyah do?"

"She trusted Aamon." He said it as though that alone were a capital crime. "Aamon loves human artwork, and Siyah learned about it from him. They especially loved anything depicting Iyarri. The things made by humans who have seen us truly."

Like *Angels Unseen*. Uneasiness tightened my stomach. How many other human artists shared Stephan's violent fate?

Cæl closed his hand into a loose fist and ran the pad of his thumb over the claws of his fingers. "To reveal what we are, what we truly are, to humans is against our laws; it was years before we discovered how badly Aamon and Siyah flouted them, hiding artwork and the humans who had created it."

My brow furrowed. He said this with such cruelty, treating Aamon and Siyah as monsters for not handing the humans over to death by Laidrom blade.

"When we finally caught them, it was worse than anyone suspected.

There was an entire trove of paintings and drawings they'd saved, but worst of all was that Siyah had sat for a human sculptor and let him carve her true form. And Aamon, whose very role is to conceal what we are, knew about it and hid it from us."

I inhaled and pressed my fingers to my lips, dreading the rest of the story.

"It was beyond even what Aamon could wiggle out of. Siyah contracted that sculpture without telling Aamon, and in the end that saved him. He argued to the Council of the Four Winds that his failure to report was because he felt the situation could be salvaged without death."

"Is that true? Could it have been?" My words tumbled out one after another.

"No." He said it with the finality of a book snapping closed. "Showing humans what we truly are is one of our highest crimes for a reason—they would descend upon us like a plague of rats if they knew we were real. Hiding in their mythology as angels and culling the ones that discover the truth is what keeps us protected. Siyah risked the lives of all Iyarri for a worthless sculpture. The Council of the Four Winds ordered all the art destroyed and sentenced her to death." Cæl closed his eyes and sighed, wings and shoulders sagging under the weight of the memory. "As Heeoa, it was my duty to carry out her sentence. And I did."

My lips parted in shock. "You were an executioner?"

He pushed his wide, raw-hemmed sleeves up past his napta gauntlets. Cæl's scarring surpassed that of other Laidrom, covering both arms, from the back of his hands all the way up his shoulders. Even more scarring adorned the small bit of his chest I could see through the V-shaped neckline of his tunic. "Laidrom are, among other things, the Elonu-Dohe's internal police. As Heeoa, I was the captain of the Laidrom at Idura. Siyah was well-loved, and Aamon should have had to endure the pain of killing her. But, better her death be on me than on the conscience of any of my Laidrom."

My heart wrung with sympathy on all sides.

Cæl let his sleeves fall over his napta. "If Aamon knew about you and

Catherine this long, but is only now revealing it, there's a reason." When I didn't respond, he held out his hand and I let him help me to my feet. "Come, let's go see if we can find Tiahmani." Cæl tidied the rumpled bed and, once sure all traces of our visit were gone, led us outside. The clear night air felt cold and brittle. There was no sign of Tiahmani, and once we reached the entrance of the retreat, we found the parking lot empty.

My father's expression teetered between annoyed and amused. "I think she means to complicate things by leaving you with me. Is there someplace you were going after this?"

"She said she was going to stash me somewhere, but not where."

Cæl rubbed his chin. "I think I know. She has a human residence she's maintained for years without other Iyarri knowing, hoping I'd agree to visit and stay there. It's worth a look, anyway." He gestured for me to follow and we walked to the edge of the clearing, where the bluff dropped off on the far side of the wrought iron fence. The stars and moon shimmered in the black waters of the Mississippi. Cæl smiled at me as the wind snapped my hair around my face and rippled the feathers of his wings. "What Tiahmani didn't count on is that I would like nothing more than a flight with my pasahasa."

My heart fluttered, both excited and nervous. "What if someone sees us?" We'd be flying right over parts of the city, and while it was night, the Cities were anything but dark.

Mindful of my ribs, Cæl wrapped one arm around my waist. "My ipuran will make anyone that sees us think they've seen a large bird." In one great push of his wings, he lifted us both so we stood on the top of the fence, nothing but air between us and a sheer drop down craggy rock to the river below. I sucked in my breath as my shoes skidded on the smooth metal surface that my father's toes gripped with ease. The long, swallowtail feathers of his wings lashed at our calves.

The cliffside was a jagged mass of stone and trees, and I grabbed Cæl's arms, my fingers twisting into his rough spun jacket. He held me tight, not painfully so, but enough that his arm wouldn't pull up onto my ribs. "Don't be afraid."

He jumped, and my throat closed down around a scream as we plummeted through the air, diving face-first toward the water. There was a great sound of rushing air and then the sound of Cæl's wings unfolding, catching the air. As one we lofted upward, and my heart lifted with us. The joy of flight was visceral, every inch of my body at home in the sky with the wind running its cool fingers through my hair. We passed the wavering reflection of the moon and Cæl glided, wheeling over the river, dipping so close that I leaned forward and skimmed my fingertips in the frigid, tingling water.

We soared higher, the river and its million glimmering lights getting smaller and smaller as we spiraled upward. There was nothing but the freezing air and the night sky. I stretched my arms out—the sky undid shackles I didn't know bound me—flight was weightless joy, a freedom I didn't know existed with my feet on the ground.

I could have flown with Cæl forever, but eventually he landed in a dark parking lot behind an old, brick building on the outskirts of St. Paul. Two stories tall and slender, it was wedged in between two shuttered warehouses. Cæl smiled, stretched his wings wide, and folded them down, a halo of moonlight around the feathers.

I swayed on my feet, fumbling for words that encompassed the exhilaration of flight. "Thank you," I managed, breathless.

Cæl's pushed the strands of hair that had escaped his wind-frayed braid out of his face and smiled at my joy. "You are welcome. Come, let's see if Tiahmani has locked us out on top of it."

ELEVEN

HE DOOR UNLATCHED WITH a *snick*, and my father kept himself in between me and the threshold as he pushed it inward. "Tiahmani?" he called.

The lights were on, but there was no answer. The interior of the building had been renovated into a loft: half the second floor carved away to make it open and airy. Crisp white walls contrasted the weathered hardwood floors and rough brickwork.

It reminded me of Aamon's house, not because of any sort of opulence, but because of the small indicators of Iyarri habitation—the backless furniture, the wider walkways. The loft was sparsely furnished, but peering around Cæl's wing I noticed my bags on the table.

"Noro?" he called as he closed the door behind us, taking care to sweep his longest feathers out of the way. He gestured for me to stay still and ascended to the open-edged loft. After a moment he returned. "We're alone."

The Loagæth word tickled my brain. "Noro is sister?"

He gestured, not satisfied with the translation. "It's more a term of endearment than a term of relation, although it is that, too."

"Do you think Tiahmani will come back tonight?" Not that I minded if she didn't.

"I'm not sure. Her anger takes a while to burn off."

"She was wasn't just angry, she was hurt," I corrected. It would have been easier, and was tempting, to write Tiahmani off as an abrasive bitch, but it would have been a partial truth at best. She used fury like a warrior's shield, but behind it her voice cracked, and her glare failed to hide the tears in her eyes. "Those are your feathers in her hair." It should have been a question, but I was so instantly certain that it came out as a statement.

"Aye, it's an Iyarri tradition to wear the feathers of those you miss, either in absence or in death."

"Why didn't you take me and mom with you when you left? Or Tiahmani, if not us?" I asked.

Cæl undid his coat. Made of earthy, hand-woven fabric, the large hood and wide sleeves were edged in needlework. "Because while a young human mother doesn't draw much attention, a young mother in the company of an Iyarri would. I knew other Iyarri were looking for me, and if they found me, they would have found you as well. As for Tiahmani, I was not going to risk her being implicated alongside me if I were caught. Still, there are few better at tracking than she is. It took her a while, but she found me."

"And you never told her why you left?" If Tiahmani had tirelessly tracked down her brother, I imagined she'd harried him endlessly about why he left, and more so, why he wouldn't return.

"No. That she reacted so badly to the truth isn't surprising." Cæl tugged at his ear—there was a triangular void missing from its lobe. "Tiahmani wasn't much older than you are when I left. The Laidrom became her family, and Ikkar took my place as Heeoa. I had hoped he would be the steady hand Tiahmani needed to help her temper her emotions, but it seems he wasn't."

"How old is she?"

"Fifty-eight. I'm one hundred and thirty-two." I blinked, my thoughts stopping as though the numbers were a solid wall in my brain. Tiahmani looked like my older sister, not old enough to be my mother. "Tiahmani was born late in our parents' life, and they passed away soon after I became Heeoa. She's been without immediate family for the last twenty-five years."

"Tiahmani said none of the Iyarri knew why you left. It didn't sound like you had to leave or stay away." It wasn't an accusation, but it was close.

A thought moved over his features like a passing cloud. "I did have to." I opened my mouth, but he waved one wing and continued. "My own weakness demanded it. I crossed every single line with Catherine that I promised myself I would never cross and knew if I stayed I'd never resist the temptation to see you or your mother." The corners of his eyes gathered as if he imagined how I'd changed in each year of his absence. A hint of a smile appeared. "Tiahmani is actually the reason I met your mother."

"I don't think you should ever tell her that." My tone was wry, and the unfamiliar distance between us closed with this new, shared secret.

He smiled, but it faded as he looked to the door. "Tiahmani, then, like now, ran off when angry. She'd been gone longer than normal and often went to Minnehaha Falls when she wanted space. I met Catherine while looking for Tiahmani."

"Mom didn't tell me how you met." I leaned forward, resting against the counter. My body was heavy; I tried not to show how sore and tired I was, lest Cæl stop talking.

"Catherine thought I was lost." His smile deepened, as though the memory were a ray of sunlight on his face. "I tried to brush her off, but she persisted, and we walked around the falls."

"You're probably lucky you didn't find Tiahmani."

"Aye, I was. Catherine obviously had my full attention. When she smiled, she smiled at me as a person, not at a Heeoa."

Person in the Iyarri sense, anyway. Resentment warmed my temples. In a way that Linnia obviously weren't. "The Iyarri women were interested in you because you were Heeoa?"

"There is only one Heeoa per stronghold, a handful of Vohim who act as lieutenants; the rest are Galearii like Tiahmani." He gave a dismissive shrug of his shoulders and wings. "I started to make excuses to see Catherine and, at some point, there was no denying it was much more than a passing interest." What small amount of happiness was in his expression evaporated. "When she told me she was with child, I knew staying risked your discovery and death. So, I ran away. And yet, here you are."

I wrapped my arm around my wounded ribs, pressing my hand against the bandage, and swayed on my feet. Cæl frowned at my pallor. "When's the last time you ate?"

Thinking back through the day was like walking through heavy fog, the details hard to make out. "This morning?" Maybe at Lucien's, but I couldn't remember for sure, or what I'd eaten if I had.

Cæl opened the refrigerator and found it bare. "Why don't you order something?" he suggested.

I reached into my pocket for my phone, realizing with an encompassing awkwardness that, though father and daughter, we didn't know the simplest things about one another—like our favorite foods. "Is Indian okay?" I asked.

"Yes. Order extra for me and Tiahmani, in case she turns up. Nothing with meat, please."

I paused, wondering if my preferences were more than choice. Even as a child I'd never had an appetite for anything more than a rare bit of fish. "Are Iyarri vegetarian?" I asked tentatively.

He shrugged. "Most of us don't eat meat, but we can if we have to. It's a novelty for those that enjoy it."

Cæl picked up my bags and carried them upstairs to the bedroom. After ordering enough saag paneer, aloo gobi, and naan for three people, I followed him, the sound of my boots echoing on the wooden steps. The upper floor of the loft was airy, with large windows and tall ceilings. I shed my mother's coat, tossed it on the bed beside the bags, and adjusted the gauze wrappings on my arms. My stomach tightened, but it was with thoughts of Lucien rather than hunger. He had to have been worried when he returned to my mother's to find us both gone.

I fingered the soft, raw edge of the gauze, missing his nearness and his gentle hands. "What does viruden mean?"

"Beautiful."

My lips parted in stunned surprise. "Oh."

"How much Loagæth do you understand?" Cæl's question was laced with hope.

"A few words; why?" I asked, curiosity piqued.

"Iyarri are born with an innate knowledge of spoken Loagæth. Reading and writing, however, require a teacher."

My hands stopped moving along the gauze as realization overtook me. "Mom said I spoke nothing but baby talk until I was three, then stopped talking at all until kindergarten. She told me I never called her Momma; I always made up words." Words she hated. I opened a bag on the bed and surveyed what clothes I had.

Cæl tilted his head. "Did you call her ahasa?"

Snippets of that day at the lake jumped back to my mind—this time the memory was as clear as the shallow water had been. The minnows shimmered and darted away from the splashing rocks. One stone struck me over the eye. "*Ahasa! Ahasa, oln z gna!*" I cried.

"Mother. Mother, make them stop," I murmured. Loagæth. I spoke it as a child. I reached through the recesses of my mind, the words like a song I'd known, but hadn't heard in so long I'd forgotten the lyrics. Wonder and hope fluttered in my stomach—perhaps I could reclaim a language that should have been mine. "Ahasa means 'mother,' doesn't it?"

"Yes, it does." He smiled. "Perhaps you didn't speak English right away because you already knew one language and didn't need another." I mused over the possibility while I opened the other bag. Lucien's gun rested at the top of the duffle; my father's eyes landed on it. I instantly regretted opening that bag and cringed before my father spoke a word. "That is not yours, I assume?"

"No, it's Lucien's."

"Typical of a kiaisi to use such a disgraceful weapon." He crossed his arms, the sleeves of his coat pulling up to reveal hardened leather gauntlets the color of dried blood.

"It kept me alive. He kept me alive." The way Lucien dispatched the Laidrom at the museum, the crack of gunshots and bloom of sulfur, was overlaid with the memory of my father moving in a blur of blades and feathers to save me from Tiahmani. My stomach coiled with nervous certainty; should the two ever meet, it would be a short, brutal encounter. I didn't know who would win and had no desire to find out.

Cæl's tone eased, though his wings continued to shift behind him, as though he paced while standing still. "And I take it the Iyarri he killed to save you weren't the first ones he's slain."

"No, they weren't," I said looking up at Cæl. "But one of them was the first one I've killed." I pulled one of the napta from the bag; Cæl took up the other, reading the markings in a way I could not. "You killed this Laidrom?"

"Yes." That gauntlet had been inches from my face—I could no more erase its markings from my mind than I could erase its scars in my flesh. The Laidrom's shattered jaw and blood-smeared teeth flashed through my mind.

Cæl put the gauntlet back in the bag. "His name was Mastho; he was a good warrior." I opened my mouth to apologize, but he waved it off. "Don't be sorry. If I had been there when he attacked you, I'd have killed him myself." Some other emotion flickered behind the surprise in his eyes, and Cæl paused before his next question. "What is this kiaisi to you that he calls you viruden?"

What was Lucien? My features softened at the memory of our fingers entwined in front of the fire; of the way he'd embraced me as I cried, overwhelmed by pain and fear; and of the tenderness with which he cleaned the dried blood from my face. I wasn't sure what we were, but by the warm glow in my chest, I knew what I wanted us to be.

My lack of a response and the wistful way my fingers trailed over the cuffs of Lucien's shirt seemed answer enough for my father. "I think it would be wise to put a stop to your relationship with him."

"That isn't your decision to make," I said, indignant at the way Cæl sidestepped his hypocrisy.

"And what do you think your kiaisi's reaction would be if he knew you were a Linnia?"

"He—" I stopped and shook my head, looking away. I wanted to believe it wouldn't matter, but it would; the certainty was a stone in my stomach.

Cæl's tone was gentle. "He's human."

"That didn't stop you," I snapped.

Anger flashed across his features, but then the expression eased. "It should have. When I showed your mother what I am she said she loved me, but her eyes told me the truth—fear, disgust, rejection. Nothing in the world has ever hurt me so much as that look."

"But she does love you." Or had, once.

"That look was not a lie. She loved me in spite of what I was, not *for* what I was." I furrowed my brow and twisted my fingers into the cuffs of Lucien's shirt. "All I ask is that you are careful. You are in love with a deadly man, and I worry what he could do to you if he took issue with your heritage."

"Lucien wouldn't hurt me," I said, my heartbeat skittering around the unease in my chest. But would he have helped me as much as he had? Or allowed himself to open up and share his pain? I hated that I knew the answer, and that it was something I couldn't change. "And I never said I loved him."

Cæl's eyes lifted from Lucien's gun to my face. "You didn't have to."

The sound of the door opening and closing downstairs saved me from our discussion. "Cæl?" Tiahmani called.

"We're here." My father gestured for me to follow him.

Downstairs, Tiahmani was waiting, hair wind-tossed. She shed her coat to a sleeveless shirt, and I stilled at bottom of the staircase, staring at the scarring on her right arm. A triskele scar swirled around her deltoid, and designs similar to the ones on her napta coursed down her arm, disappeared under her gauntlet, and reappeared on the back of her hand. Each scar was pale and upraised against her golden skin. Tiahmani tossed her coat onto the back of a chair and shot me a look that kept me from moving closer. She shifted her glare to her brother, but the corners of her eyes softened. "Noromi, we need to talk."

Some of the ready tension left Cæl's shoulders. "Aye, we do."

Tiahmani crossed her arms and leaned against the wall, folding her wings so the longest feathers crossed over the front of her shins.

Cæl gestured to me but spoke to his sister. "Why didn't you tell me you'd found Aurelia?"

"I wasn't sure you'd show up if I did," Tiahmani said. "And I'm surprised you're here. I thought for sure you'd have taken her and run." Cæl rubbed his face with one clawed hand. "You did consider it," Tiahmani accused.

Cæl's voice was a contemplative rumble. "I've considered coming back for her many times. But I can't take her yet, assuming she'd even want to come with. I need you to look after her."

The bolt of terror that shot through me was punctuated by Tiahmani's short, cynical bark of a laugh. "You are not possibly that fucking feather-brained. I brought her to you hoping you'd stay, not dump her on me to babysit."

"She's your niece," he reasoned. She flicked her wings once, annoyed. "Noro, please."

Tiahmani's shoulders dropped and she uncrossed her wings. "I want you to come home."

"I know," Cæl said, the words defeated. "But you're the only one I can trust."

Tiahmani chewed on her lower lip, and I took the last few steps down the stairs, unnoticed. "Fine. I'll keep an eye on her." She held up a clawed finger. "*If* you swear that when there's a way to come home, you take it. No more of this never shit."

Cæl stepped forward and held out his arm. "Done."

Tiahmani slammed her forearm against his, and the sound of their gauntlets striking one another echoed inside the loft. They gripped arms in a warrior's handshake, and Tiahmani beamed a warm smile up at her brother. I may not have wanted Tiahmani's protection, but it was better than her ire.

Three knocks rang out on the door, and I hurried to answer it, looking over my shoulder at the two Iyarri. Ipuran in place, they both appeared human. I collected the food and unloaded the takeout bags on the table.

My father pulled out the food and divided it for the three of us. The table was paired with backless stools, and Tiahmani sat with naan in her hands and a bottle of water clasped in her toes.

"Is it common for women to be Laidrom?" I asked, attempting polite conversation.

She ate another few bites of food without so much as acknowledging I'd spoken.

Cæl answered for her. "There are fewer women than men, but it is not uncommon. An Iyarri is simply judged on what they can or cannot do."

I traced my aunt and my father with an artist's eye. Though I had seen only a few Iyarri, Tiahmani the singular female, the lines of her body and my father's were much the same. In classical art, women were drawn with softer, curved lines and men with angles; were I to draw Iyarri, those rules would have still pertained, but to a diminished degree. Were Tiahmani human, with her small, high breasts and slender hips, her figure would have been called boyish; Cæl and the other males were lean and muscular, but not bulky. The extremes of voluptuousness and brawn fell away, leaving everyone lean and graceful.

After we finished eating, Cæl unhooked one foot from the rails of his stool and stood. "I'll need to go back to New York for a while."

"Already?" Tiahmani asked. The note of sadness in her question mirrored the drop of my stomach.

"Yes," he said. "Aurelia is safe enough for now, and I have preparations to make in case this all gets worse."

Tiahmani set her food aside. "I should go too, before I'm missed. I told Aamon I'd be back after I stashed Aurelia, and I don't want him finding out we saw you." She tossed me a key. "My car's outside. Use it until you get yours back."

"Thank you." I pocketed the key.

Cæl wrapped one hand around the top of Tiahmani's arm with brotherly tenderness. "Thank you for keeping an eye on Aurelia."

Tiahmani closed her hand over her brother's and smiled in spite of herself. "Yeah, well, I wasn't going to let her chase me off." She reached into one of the pouches on her wide leather belt. "Here." She held out a leather flask to Cæl.

He took it, turning it over in his hand. "I didn't think you'd still make good on the darignis."

"I'm angry at you, noromi, I don't hate you." She nodded to a linen sack under the table. "There's a small cask in there."

He hugged her fiercely, and she clung to him with such love and loss on her face that I wished Cæl would stay, for her as well as me. "Come on; I'll walk you outside."

She took a second flask from her belt pouch. "We can drink some of this. Can't have you breaking into what I brought you right away."

The two stepped out into the autumn night without so much as a word to me. I cleaned up the table and listened to their voices. I couldn't understand them, but the longer the lyrical and syllable-laden Iyarri words played through my ears, the more I thought I might be able to.

After the table was cleared, I called my mother, relieved to find her safe at Aunt Erin's, but the distant, happy chatter from her unnerved me—the effects of Tiahmani's solpeth hadn't faded, and she was completely confident in my safety. When I told her about the loft, she said, "I hope your new place isn't in your name."

"It isn't."

"Good. The police cleared your apartment as a crime scene, so I'm able to get some of your things. Is there anything you want from your apartment? I can have movers put the rest into storage for now."

I started off with practical things—clothes and my purse—but wound up asking, "Some of my art supplies. And my paintings. At least *The Little Mermaid*."

She laughed, and I pictured her shaking her head. "Leave the door to your new place unlocked, and I'll fit what I can in the car." I gave her the address.

The conversation sounded right, but felt wrong. She was behaving the opposite of my mother, concerned with things rather than the strange woman I'd left with. The change in her unsettled the food in my stomach.

Cæl returned and I gestured to the phone, offering it to him. He shook his head, but listened to my mother chatter about her day, able to hear both sides of the conversation from a few feet away, as I would be.

When I hung up the phone with a frown, Cæl asked, "Is everything okay?"

"She . . ." I gestured absently. "She's okay, but whatever Tiahmani did to her, Mom's not herself."

"Tiahmani mentioned she used her solpeth on Catherine. That Tiahmani is not particularly talented with it makes it . . . worse than it could have been."

"I'm not sure I understand."

"Done right, the solpeth sounds like normal conversation to a human, and they're happy to take the suggestions." I thought back to Aamon convincing Jacob to give me paid leave with only a few words. Cæl shrugged and continued, "Like any other discipline, the solpeth requires practice. Laidrom don't spend a lot of time on such things." It wasn't hard to gather what methods Laidrom preferred when dealing with humans. "The solpeth cannot force a human to hurt themselves, but it can persuade a human to put themselves into a situation where harm is likely. The more out of line a suggestion made with the solpeth is with what a human wants to do or believe, the more skill it takes. Catherine didn't want to let you go, and I imagine Tiahmani had to push pretty hard to make her agree to it."

I folded my arms. "And you're fine with her using the solpeth on Mom?"

He frowned. "I wish it hadn't been necessary, but I trust Tiahmani when she says it was the best option at the time."

"Mom won't stay like this, will she?" I asked, worry threading through my tone.

"The effects should fade on their own in a few weeks. Until then, it's best not to contradict what Tiahmani made Catherine believe." So, let her think I was safe, even if I wasn't. I frowned and rolled the ends of my hair in my fingers. A month ago it wouldn't have bothered me, but the dynamics of trust had changed in light of my mother being honest about what I was and why she'd raised me like she had. "And don't mention me," he added.

I shook my head, hurt on my mother's behalf. "You owe her better than that."

"I know." He wanted to talk to her—I could see it in his eyes—but there was also doubt there. Cæl wore the emotion like it was unfamiliar and physically uncomfortable. He pressed his lips together and shook his wings. "I should go. I wasn't anticipating a visit, and this changes everything. If Aamon has something in motion, I need to be ready." He gestured to my phone; I gave it to him and he entered his number. "Tiahmani promised to look after you until I return. I'll put her number in as well." He handed the phone back to me and smiled, although there was little cheer in it. "I am glad you let Tiahmani bring you to me, pasahasa. You were braver than I was." He slung Tiahmani's bag over his shoulder. "Be careful. And don't tell Aamon we met."

"Yes, essia."

The word made him smile. "Fair winds."

"And clear skies," I said, proud to know the right goodbye, but sad to see him go. Cæl put one clawed finger under my chin and stared at my face, memorizing it. Then, for the second time in my life, he left.

TWELVE

O NCE THE SOUND OF my father's wings merged with the night wind, I dialed Lucien's number. It rang twice before he answered. Unbidden, a soft smile broke across my lips. "Hello, Lucien."

There was surprise and relief in his voice. "Is everything okay? Where are you? Where is your mom?"

"My mom didn't think we should stay at her house in case the cops came. She's with relatives, but they'd ask too many questions, so I'm at a loft my aunt has but doesn't use. I was getting settled in." It might have been the truth, but it twisted my heart like a lie.

He exhaled in relief. "Good, I was worried when I didn't know where you'd gone."

"I know it's late, but I'd like to see you." My voice trailed off as I focused on the dark windows. If Tiahmani came back, if my father came back, it was better if Lucien wasn't with me. "Would you mind if I came over?" I was so spent, so weary, and his stone house in the woods was a sanctuary where we could simply be together.

His smile showed in his voice. "Of course you can."

"Do you need anything? I could stop on the way."

"Just you." There was an inviting lilt to his voice that chased away some of the fear and worry and discovery of the day.

Eager to be on my way, I changed into clean clothes and tossed the camisole with the cut down the side into the trash. I redressed my side, then changed into jeans, a fresh camisole, and a long, hooded green sweater that closed with big toggle buttons.

On the way to Lucien's house I drove with one arm, the other curled around my aching side, exhaustion bone-deep. The dark gathering of branches over Lucien's driveway was no longer menacing but protective and shielding.

Lucien had the garage door open for me, and I came inside with a gust of wet, cold November air. He was waiting for me. I smiled, suddenly bashful. "Hey."

His serious face softened as he looked down at me. "Hey to you, too." Lucien had shaved before I came over, face smooth and wrapped in the fresh, icy scent of his cologne. There was an artful imperfection to his face, the way it straddled the line between beautiful and rugged. I wanted to trace its lines with my fingers, pore over them in a study of my attraction to him, but no amount of graphite or clay could have captured the way his presence lifted my fear, or the way I found myself blushing when he smiled at me.

It was strange to be in so mundane a circumstance with him. Not fleeing for our lives, not bandaging Iyarri-inflicted wounds, not talking about guns or napta or Loagæth—just two people in a quiet house. It made the growing attraction between us impossible to brush aside. That I'd spent the day with my Iyarri aunt and father and couldn't mention it to Lucien gnawed at my conscience. "I have no idea what to say," I murmured.

He picked up both my hands in his, the soft skin of my hands molding into his calloused ones. He wasn't sure, either; thoughts ran behind the blue of his eyes, like water under an iced-over river. Lucien swept his thumbs back and forth over the backs of my hands and gave them a squeeze. "Say that you missed me."

I threaded my arms around his waist. My fingers brushed the holster and pistols at the small of his back as I hugged him and pressed my cheek against the base of his neck. "I missed you." *I think I love you.* A heartbeat fluttered against my skin, but I wasn't sure if it was his or mine.

He wrapped his good arm across my back and gave a contented sigh against my hair. Eventually, I unwound my arms from him. Under the shoulder of his worn, black button-down shirt was an upraised ridge of bandaging.

"How's it doing?" I asked.

"Forty-seven stitches." He waved off my apology before I started it. "You'd have more if you'd gotten stitched up. Besides, it'll feel better after a drink." He took down one of his tulip-shaped glasses and a bottle of amber whisky. "Do you want anything?"

"Just water, I think."

"Probably best for you anyway. You still look pale."

"To be fair, I always look pale."

"That is the worst pun ever."

I blinked as the words fell together and then laughed and bumped his good shoulder with mine.

"Careful, you'll make me spill," he teased as he led us to the sitting room in his suite. He set our glasses on the coffee table, undid his holster, and set his pistols beside the glasses. "I'm going to get some more wood from the garage."

I stood and asked, "Do you want help?"

"I'll be okay; just need to use my good arm." He tucked a wavy lock of red hair back behind my ear. "I'll be right back."

He turned for the door, and I moved closer to the fire, taking in the warmth as I lifted my eyes to the napta over the fireplace and then let them fall to the trinkets on the mantel. Now, it was harder to see the napta as weapons of faceless Iyarri; they made me picture Tiahmani and my father. I picked up the silver spiral and toyed with it. The moonlight chased up the rachis of the winding feather pattern in a quicksilver thread.

Lucien returned and unshouldered a broadcloth firewood carrier. He crouched in front of the fireplace, and soon enough fire popped and crackled within the pale stone. Lucien sat back on the couch with a controlled inhale, one hand over his bandaged shoulder. I sat beside him, my lips curving into a knowing smile. "Didn't need help?"

He picked up his glass and tipped a good part of the whisky down his throat with a grimace. "It pulled worse than I thought, even using the other arm."

I put a hand atop the bandage, his shirt the sort of softness that comes with hundreds of washes. "Did you tear your stitches?"

"No." He closed his hand over mine and smiled. "Not for lack of trying, though."

I shifted, tucking my legs under me so I sat cross-legged and sideways on the couch, the ends of my hair curling around my knees. He leaned forward until his leg pressed against my knees and took the spiral out of my fingers, eyes intense. "Here, let me show you." He slid the fingers of his other hand over my ear, fingertips warm against my scalp, and parted out a lock of hair as thick as my thumb. He held the silver coil steady and wound the lock of my hair through it until the waves contained in the sliver spiral were like something out of a medieval painting. When he released my hair, the lock swung like a pendulum. "It looks good on you, viruden; you should keep it."

Hearing him say that word made my heart flutter and my cheeks flush with warmth. "Are you going to tell me what that means?" My voice was scarcely louder than the fire. It didn't matter that I knew, I wanted to hear him say it.

There was an uncertainty in the way he paused before he spoke. "It means beautiful."

I murmured a thank-you and pressed my lips together, eyes searching his. His pupils had gone wide, the depths a tumult of emotions: doubt, hope, second guesses, and buried under it all, attraction that flickered like an icy fire. He cupped my cheek and leaned in, pausing when he was so close that his breath was warm on my face. I didn't; instead I put my hand on his thigh, slid forward, and kissed him.

It was a lick of flame to the tinder of our two hearts.

His lips were dry and soft, laced with the burning sweetness of Scotch. He cupped my face in his hand and kissed me back. The world closed to the touch of our lips, of my fingers sliding up his chest, of his hand twisting into my hair. Lucien's lips parted and the taste of woodsmoke and vanilla burned hotter against my mouth.

My heart pounded in my ears, pulse thrumming under every inch of my skin. There was no way to hide the way I trembled under his hands, but my desire was shot through with guilt. Lucien deserved to know who he was kissing, that the Iyarri spiral wound into my hair was far more fitting than he could have imagined. My lips parted and I hesitated; I wanted to kiss him again, but needed to tell him the truth just as badly.

Lucien read the uncertainty on my face and drew back with a restraining breath. He leaned against the armrest of the couch, perhaps meaning to give me space, but I shifted with him and settled against his chest. He threaded his arms around me and said, "I like you here, where I know you're safe."

I eased into his embrace, enjoying the way I could feel his voice when he spoke. My fingers lingered over the buttons of his shirt. "I like it here with you, too."

Lucien lowered his head so his cheek rested against my temple, the silence peaceful and filled with one another's presence. Eventually, the fire waned and my eyelids drooped.

"Hey." Lucien ran the back of his hand over my cheek. He nodded to the bedroom at the far side of the suite. "Why don't you lie down? Get some rest."

I got to my feet and pushed my hair from my face. "Are you sure?"

"Go on."

I took one of his hands in mine and ran my thumb over his palm. "Come with me."

He hesitated, emotions warring on his face.

"Stay with me, please." In the dark his eyes flickered like blue agate. "Nothing has to happen." Even if I wanted it to.

Some of the tension lifted from Lucien's face. "For a bit." We turned down the covers and puzzled our bodies together, fitting how our wounds allowed: him on his back, me tucked against his side and cradled in his good arm. It felt right, two broken halves making a whole.

The far-off rasp of metal on stone woke me—Lucien's side of the bed was empty. The day was gloomy and, judging by the frosty fairy wings pressed onto the glass, cold. I wrapped my arms around my knees, letting the kisses Lucien and I shared play through my mind. The silver spiral was still in my hair, and I wrapped my fingers around it with a smile.

I dressed and checked my phone. There was a text from Aamon: *I've something to share with you. Please come visit as soon as you're able.* I worried my lip with my teeth, wondering what Aamon wanted to show me, but there was a flutter of excitement in my stomach, too. If Lucien was working, I could go visit Aamon for a bit.

I went to Lucien's workshop, my stocking feet padding on the concrete. He was standing over the central table, a half-finished fleur forgotten in front of him. "Good morning," I said.

"Hey." Stone dust made white marks on the dark fabric of his clothes. His eyes were troubled, like the sea lashed lighter by a storm.

"Is everything okay?" My heart tightened against my ribs.

He nodded, then shook his head. "I don't know."

My hands went clammy and cold. Had he somehow found out what I was? "What's wrong?"

Lucien gripped the edge of his worktable with both hands and bowed his head, steadying himself before he spoke. "I shouldn't have kissed you last night."

I expected an accusation, a demand for the truth, but not that. "What? Why not?" That he regretted a kiss I cherished wrenched my stomach.

"I think you fell for an idea, not for me." We were only an arm's length away, but he'd forced a glacial chasm between us.

"You think that kiss was because you rescued me?" I tempered the indignation in my words, trying to understand. He was pushing me away, and if I pushed back, we'd only end up farther apart.

Lucien leaned against his worktable and ran his hair back from his face. The stone dust left it lighter in the wake of his hand. "Yes."

My expression crumpled with sympathy, and I slid my fingertips over his clenched, stone-worn hands. "Of course I'm grateful you saved me. I couldn't be anything else; but that isn't why I came back here last night, and it isn't why I'm here with you now."

He shook his head. "I . . . it isn't that simple. I won't ever be safe from them. Anyone with me won't be safe, either."

It sounded like a reason, an excuse, he'd used to deny himself relationships before. I pushed myself up and sat on the edge of the worktable, my fingers still lingering on his. "It's a risk already shared."

He took a step away but didn't take his hand from mine. Lines of doubt lingered on his face. "Lia, I don't know what you're looking for, but I'm not the type of person you marry and have kids with. I'm just not." The ache in his voice betrayed how badly he wished he was.

Any child of mine wouldn't be human. The realization swirled and settled uneasily in my gut. I pulled Lucien back toward me and squeezed his hands. "I know what I want. I want you."

We stayed in the monastic stillness of the workshop, hands clasped between us until, slowly, Lucien's fingers traced over one of my hands, memorizing the lines, the curves. He turned my hand, his thumb rubbing in smooth circles on the inside of my wrist. His voice was subdued, the tension in it gone, but doubt remained. "I don't know what you think you see in me, but you don't owe me anything."

I cupped his cheek with my other hand, the stubble rough and soft at the same time, like a cat's tongue. His eyes flitted closed; his hands slid into my back pockets as I leaned against his chest and brought my lips to his.

Lucien drew me against him so the inside of my thighs pressed against his hips and my butt teetered on the edge of the counter. My body softened and twined against his, desire flushing along my skin and gathering where we touched. I tilted my head, tasting him, fingers threading between the buttons of his shirt, seeking the skin beneath it. His heartbeat raced under my fingertips and my pulse thudded in my ears—half the blood hammering under my skin Iyarri.

I tried to banish the thought, selfishly not wanting my Linnia heritage between us—perhaps I was truly my father's daughter, not willing to shatter what Lucien and I shared with the truth. I pulled back, my breath shaking. "Does that," I ran my fingertips over his lower lip, "feel like I owed it to you?"

"No, it doesn't." He kissed my fingers and slid his hands out of my pockets, resting them atop my thighs. It was a small comfort that not all the hesitation was mine—Lucien had rebuilt his entire world one brick at a time, and he needed that slowness, that security with us too.

Disappointment and relief warred in my heart. I didn't want to stop, every inch of my aching body wanted not to stop, but the farther we went, the sooner he'd discover I was Linnia—the fragile love between us couldn't weather that. Not yet. For now, it was enough that the distance between us had closed, that he knew I wanted him and why.

Lucien leaned back and held my chin between his thumb and forefinger. "I have to pick up some tools and tell my clients I can't finish these jobs until my shoulder's healed. I might be gone a while, but you're welcome to stay here."

I nearly said yes, but wondered what Aamon wanted to share with me. Instead, I slid off the counter and dusted off my jeans. "My mom said she was able to get some of my stuff. I think I'll go check on a few things, then call you later tonight." It wasn't a lie, but the heavy coil around my stomach told me it might as well have been one.

Lucien walked me to the car and stole one last kiss goodbye. I opened the door and then paused. "Lucien?" He tilted his head in question. "Last night? I kissed you."

He smiled and tugged the lock of hair with the spiral on it. "I know. Be careful, viruden."

A fitting warning, being that I was going to visit an Iyarri.

THIRTEEN

HIS TIME, AS AAMON led me through his house, I was better able to appreciate his abundant art collection. There were paintings and textiles, fine works of pottery, and carved stone, each displayed in a way that looked effortless, but I knew wasn't.

"It's good to see you well," Aamon said as he poured pilzin for the two of us, then gave an inquiring tilt of the head to Tiahmani. She was packing her hip bags on the counter and waved off his offer. Aamon handed me my glass. "Are you doing anything for Thanksgiving?" His penchant for human small talk was something Tiahmani and my father had either no ability or no interest in mastering.

Tiahmani blinked in confusion. "Oh, the plodder holiday."

I followed Aamon into the sitting room, fussing with my cuffs. "No, not really." I fumbled through a non-answer before asking, "What kind of holidays do Iyarri celebrate?"

"Iyarri do not believe in manifestations of the divine, and so our holidays focus on specific events in our history, venerate Iyarri of note, and celebrate different facets of our society. In the summer there is Micali, the Fête of Hands, which focuses on physical achievements. This is presided over by the Laidrom and is often . . ." He paused and searched for a word. "Boisterous."

Tiahmani snorted. "We can't even stand when it's over."

131

Aamon sat and gestured for me to sit on the chaise across from him. "Over the five longest nights of the year, we have Nalvage, the Fête of Remembrance. Two and a half days of darkness, two and a half days of candlelight. We reflect on what separates us from the human world and are mindful of those who have sacrificed to maintain that position."

Tiahmani shook her wings, disinterested. "I have to go. Fair winds."

"And clear skies," Aamon said. After she'd gone, he leaned forward, forearms on his knees, shedding the discussion of Iyarri holidays. "How are you doing? Tiahmani mentioned you were wounded by the Laidrom and rescued by a kiaisi." His face softened, concerned.

I pushed up the sleeves of my sweater and turned my arms so Aamon could see the bandages.

His expression turned serious. "And does this kiaisi know what you are? What you truly are?"

My brow furrowed and I shook my head. "No, he doesn't. I haven't been able to tell him."

Something in my face, the vexed angle of my brows or my downcast eyes, gave Aamon pause before he spoke again, face solemn. "He's more than a kiaisi to you, I take it?"

"Yes. Lucien and I, we—" I stopped talking, not sure how to put the rest of what was between Lucien and me into words.

Aamon's face became solemn. "Your kiaisi is not the only risk you take. The police are searching for you. The Laidrom will not stop hunting you. You know too much, and as long as you appear more human than Iyarri that will not change. While Lucien has protected you thus far, you are both balanced on the vane's edge of life and death."

My shoulders slouched, unable to hold the weight of my despair and crushing guilt. It wasn't just my life I risked, it was Lucien's too. The thought of the Iyarri finding him was a giant sinkhole in my chest. The edges eroded further still with the mortified knowledge that I was a liability Lucien would never have taken on if he knew the truth.

Aamon tilted his head, pensive, and then held out one clawed hand to me. "Come; walk with me. There are new pieces in the gallery." The words and gesture were familiar, the claws on his hands less so. I placed my hand in his; Aamon lifted me to my feet as though I were a lady accepting a dance.

As we ascended the great, wrapping staircase, the two long feathers trailing from the base of Aamon's wings swept behind his heels. Though they reminded me of a swallow's tail at a distance, the feathers were not narrow and pointed, but broadened to tapered ovals at the ends. I took care not to step on them.

I'd been to Aamon's private gallery a time or two before, when he hosted parties exclusively for wealthy museum patrons. As he unlocked an arched set of steel filigree and glass double doors, I walked around a pedestal in the center of the circular landing; atop it sat a small-scale replica of Canova's *Amor and Psyche*. Their entwined, pale marble bodies captivated me in a way they hadn't before: Psyche reclined into Eros, her arms wrapped backward, the nakedness of her stone flesh covered by a swath of cloth and Eros's arm. My steps slowed; a line from their tale circled the base.

> *Why should you wish to behold me? Have you any doubt of*
> *my love? If you saw me, perhaps you would fear me, perhaps*
> *adore me, but all I ask of you is to love me.*

Eros embraced Psyche, but his wings were spread, ready to leave her. And indeed he had abandoned her when she disobeyed him and opened her eyes to see what he truly was: not a vile serpent-creature, but a beautiful winged man.

"Aurelia?" Aamon's voice was low and polite, drawing my attention from one pair of white wings to another. I tucked a stray ginger wave behind my ear and met him at the doors.

Aamon's gallery encompassed the entire third floor of the house. It was a great, rectangular hallway that wrapped the entire perimeter of the floor, its length notched with inlets and small rooms. We walked through it, but none of the pieces were either new or noteworthy enough for Aamon to comment on. At the midpoint, he paused in front of a great mirror set into a recess in the wall, slid his fingertips behind the frame, and pressed something with a click. The mirror, backed with a heavy steel door, swung open; Aamon bowed his head and gestured for me to step aside. I hesitated, uncertainty barring the threshold, but Aamon's smile promised some wonderful secret on the other side.

White steel and whiter stone shouldn't have been so light, so airy. The room was an atrium-like gallery, the pale walls crowned with an extended pyramid skylight. I drifted from one piece of art to another, each step I took echoing in the still room. Each piece featured angels; I turned in a slow circle, slowly realizing that no, each piece was Iyarri.

I stilled; *Angels Unseen* stretched up the wall like a late afternoon shadow. "How did you get that?" I asked, voice hushed with uneasy wonder.

Aamon walked to my side, smoothing his pale hair back over his shoulders as he gave *Angels Unseen* an appreciative smile. "The Laidrom recovered it. Iyarri love art, it is woven into everything we create, but as this was painted by human hands, it must stay here, in the human world."

"That's why you were at the gallery that night? To see it?"

"Aye." He lifted his eyes and took in the expansive canvas with appreciation. "After Mr. Keller asked enough questions about Iyarri to catch my ear, I contacted him and arranged for the painting's display." The corner of his lips turned up in a subtle, very Aamon expression.

Realization steeped into me. "You wanted me to see it."

Aamon looked at me over his shoulder and smiled. "Your reaction was everything I hoped for." His expression darkened. "The Elonu-Dohe have no interest in human art. I can only conclude Stephan made so many inquiries that another Iyarri picked up on what he'd done and sent the Laidrom after him before I could intervene. They took the painting, meaning to destroy it, but others helped me squirrel it out of Idura. Now, it can reside here, where it is safe and appreciated." He turned, feathers sliding against my ankles. "Come, I have something else to show you."

At the far end of the gallery, in a tall, arched alcove, was a statue of an Iyarri woman—body, wings and arms twisting upward into a shaft of light. Her long hair and stola dress cascaded over her body with all the fluidity of water, and her eyes were twin moons of pale stone. Aamon's expression softened into something wistful and mournful. He bowed his head, and my heart contracted with sympathy.

Aamon lifted one hand and traced his fingers down the statue's wings, his touch reverent and light. Faded scorch marks and ghostly cracks had been painstakingly restored, but the damage was impossible to wholly mend. "Siyah and I were Semeroh." The word hung in the air until Aamon realized I didn't know it. "Semeroh are mates of spirit and passion. Sometimes it transcends into the physical, but in the case of Siyah and I, we were brought together purely by a shared passion for human art." He paused, seeming to make sure he had control of his voice before he continued. "It cost her life at your father's hands."

I swallowed, my heart in my throat. None of the blame was mine, and yet Aamon's pain alone compelled me to apologize. "I'm so sorry."

"You have nothing to be sorry for." Aamon turned from Siyah to me. "You are the first and only one I have ever thought might be worthy of her place." Pride glowed in my chest. "But you are also Linnia, and right now your Iyarri blood is a curse." The feeling dimmed, swallowed by the darkness of reality. I cast a grim gaze at the statue. He was right—as a Linnia, there would never be safety or true respite for me in the human world. Aamon lifted a small, weathered book from a nearby shelf and handed it to me. It was old, the pages thick and yellowed, the leather cover so worn it whispered like silk in my hands. "It doesn't have to be."

For a second there was nothing but my heart beating in my chest. "How?" I asked, the word a single exhale of hope and wonder. The book in my hands had a title, but I wasn't able to decipher the symbols.

Aamon translated it for me. "*Rituals of the Nephilim.*" I turned the ancient pages with care—the ink long since faded to translucence on brittle paper. "Humans called Linnia *Nephilim*, and a long time ago, Iyarri also used that term. That changed when the humans murdered half of each of our Saanir, our ruling pairs, on the Night of Bloody Feathers. When contact with humans became forbidden, we changed the name to children born of such unions to Linnia, literally 'beasts.' Before then, half-breeds were uncommon, but not reviled. With this ritual, they were given wings and the Elonu-Dohe welcomed the survivors as Iyarri."

My fingers whispered over my shoulder blade, its surface flat. Empty. Wistfully, I imagined wings, how the soft feathers and powerful muscles would feel.

Aamon nodded to the book in my hands. "Now, only half the ritual is performed. Wings are conjured forth from the bodies of Linnia as punishment, rending their bodies asunder as a death sentence." He paused, looking for the right words. "If the ritual is done in full, Linnia can survive summoning of their wings. I have Iadnah, Iyarri skilled in ritual and healing, willing to help. We believe that, if you were prepared and we were ready to care for you afterward, you could gain wings and survive. It's been done before, after all."

The rays through the skylight shifted, the play of light and shadow on the statue's face making Siyah seem to move her lips in a hushed smile. "And this would make me Iyarri, not Linnia?"

"Had you but wings, yes, you would be Iyarri."

I could be Iyarri, but I couldn't be made human. Given the choice between the two, would I be wholly human if I could? A month ago, I would have said yes, instantly, undoubtedly, but now there were only pieces of my human self I cherished. "What about my hands?" I held one out, the fingers long and slender, the nails oval-shaped and clear. They trembled. Iyarri hands were thicker, stronger, but I wouldn't trade anything in the world for the artistic dexterity my own fingers had.

Aamon took my human hand in his clawed ones. "Your hands would stay as they are."

My father's words echoed in my mind: *I would like nothing more than a flight with my pasahasa.* Perhaps wings were mine by birthright. If they were not, how could they be summoned from my back? Wings made of muscle, bone, and feathers couldn't be called from nothing.

But my feelings for Lucien, the bond growing between us, were just as rare. He understood me, and I him, in a way that lifted away years of loneliness and vulnerability. My human fingertips pressed into the cover of the Iyarri book. I fumbled for words, not sure how to describe my tangled heart. Aamon stayed quiet and thoughts undulated in my mind. I looked through the open door to the statue of Eros and Psyche, and in their forms I saw Lucien and me. "I can't." My voice broke with frustration. The happiness I shared with Lucien was real, tangible, but tenuous, and becoming Iyarri wasn't a decision I could take back. "At least not yet."

Aamon stood beside me, lending his comforting presence. "Does the ritual frighten you?"

I shook my head. "No." In truth, it did, but I could overcome that.

Aamon followed my eyes to the marble figures. "Your kiaisi, then, is what holds you back?"

"He and I—" I tried to put words to what was between us. "There's something there I've never had before. I want to give it time, and I want to do it right." I needed to muster the courage to tell Lucien what I was, and give him the chance to accept it. He deserved the choice my mother hadn't been given truth enough to make.

"He cannot protect you from the Laidrom or hide you from the police forever. That is not, however, the only thing to consider. You have so many other Iyarri qualities; it would not surprise me at all to find you have our lifespan as well. Three times a human's. Even if your relationship proves viable, you may well outlive him by two centuries. Can you bear him watching you stay as you are while he fades? Wings or not, what you are will become obvious to him with time."

I chewed on my lower lip. Even if Lucien accepted me as I was, a Linnia, how much harder would it be to maintain that acceptance through the years?

"I don't tell you these things to scare you, only to help you make the right decision."

Any optimism in my heart withered away to a gray and barren wasteland. Finally, I said, "I can't accept your offer, Aamon, at least not right now. I'll tell Lucien the truth and hope he understands."

A moment of silence stretched out. "You must love him a great deal to forego so much."

Eager to escape my own decision, I turned toward the staircase. "I think I should go."

Aamon cupped one wing around me, the feathers smelling of white sandalwood and amber. "If you wish." We stepped back onto the landing, and as Aamon closed the gallery behind us, my eyes fell back onto the entwined figures of Eros and Psyche. I stared at the tiny statue, turning the base to view it in the round, reading the inscription over and over. Would Lucien stay with me once his eyes were opened? He had promised not to leave me, but that promise was to a human.

I stood, gaze lingering on the statue. "Could I have this? Would you mind?"

"Of course, but what for?"

I ran one finger up the longest pinion of Eros's wing. "Art speaks where words fail."

Aamon paused for a moment, considering my words. "Yes it does. Let me get a box for it." After the statue was boxed, Aamon escorted me to the foyer and helped me into my coat. He opened the door for me. "My offer still stands if you change your mind."

I held the box containing the statue tight to my chest. "Thank you, Aamon. Goodnight."

A swath of cartons awaited me at Tiahmani's loft, so many boxes of my things it was a wonder they all fit in my mother's car. In the stillness of the strange loft filled with familiar belongings, I felt unmoored, like a boat being pulled out to sea by lapping waves. I set the box on the table and picked my way through my possessions, finding clothes, my nail polish bin, and art supplies, but the comfort and sense of happiness I anticipated in these familiar things did not come. Perhaps they were too out of place, or perhaps I was.

I pressed one hand to my side, the gash in my ribs pulling as I crouched and opened another box. One of my gallery shirts rested on top, clean and white. It was something I'd worn daily, but was now an artifact from a life I didn't miss as much as I thought I should. I lifted my fingers from the crisp fabric and twisted them around Lucien's Iyarri spiral wound in my hair. My eyes fell on the box with the statue inside, and I took out a sketchbook.

Without even taking out the statue, I formed the nearly-touching faces of Psyche and Eros in long and light graphite strokes across the paper. When the page was full, I turned it over—this time a female form rising, kneeling, back naked, her hair pulled over her shoulder. I shaded in the shadows along the curve of her spine and beneath her shoulder blades. A human back, the great expanse of skin unbroken by wings. I closed the sketchbook, folded my arms atop it, and put my head down, gathering my resolve. A few seconds later I took up my phone and called Lucien.

Our conversation became lost in my tumbling thoughts of what I would say and how I would say it. Lucien asked, "Is everything okay?"

My fingers tightened around the pencil in my other hand. *I need to tell you something.* "I just want to see you."

"I'm actually not too far away. Let me finish things up at this site, then I'll come get you."

"Thank you." My hand throbbed—I looked down to find my pencil broken, the splintered ends biting into the skin of my palm.

FOURTEEN

OUTSIDE THE WINDOW A lone crow pecked at the ground under a gray and cloudy sky. The wind stirred naked branches and a storm cloud of other crows descended, hopping as they squabbled. There were seven of them, plump and sleek. Remembering a rhyme my mother taught me as a child I murmured, "One for sorrow, two for mirth, three for a wedding, four for a birth, five for silver, six for gold, seven for a secret not to be told." The first crow grabbed his prize in his beak and took off, the others following in a roiling mass of black wings.

Seven for a secret not to be told. I tightened my toes in my boots and fingered the silver spiral on the end of my braid, knowing Lucien deserved the truth, even if it risked losing what was between us. My thoughts circled back to the Eros and Psyche statue, the two pale stone figures intertwined. I would not repeat my father's mistake. I'd give Lucien the statue and the story, and we would talk. But I didn't know which to dread more: a long conversation or a short one.

By the time Lucien arrived, night had fallen, and it was all I could do to lock the tumult of emotions churning in me behind a smile. As I let him in, he leaned over and kissed under my earlobe. "I like your hair like that. It shows off your neck."

Heat flushed upward from where his lips had touched me up to my cheeks. "Thank you." My skin tingled even after he'd lifted his lips away. I'd changed into a cream sweater with a wide neckline that clung to the tops of my shoulders and had put my hair up in a twist, save for the accent braid wrapped in my spiral.

Lucien lifted his gaze; I followed it to a painting propped against the far wall. The Priestess of Delphi scryed in the flames of a fire, her craggy face illuminated in oranges and golds. In the fire before her, tiny people acted out a scene of pain, suffering, and loss. "Is that yours?"

I nodded from the Priestess to another stack of paintings not far away. "They're all mine."

He picked up one of my hands and kissed it, then my cheek. "Soft hands or not, they do pretty amazing work."

My lips curved into a smile as I ran the flats of my palms up his chest. He put his hands on my hips and slid his fingers through my belt loops. I stood on my toes and kissed him, enjoying the tenderness of it.

When we parted, I shrugged on my coat and picked up the box containing the statue. Lucien gave it an inquiring tilt of the head. "What's with the box?"

"Something for you." My heart raced and my hands tightened around the box, but I couldn't either make myself open it or extend my arms and give it to him. "For later," I fumbled. It felt wrong, telling him such a personal truth in such a strange place. I ached for the intimacy of his house, the two of us curled in front of the fire.

"You shouldn't have gotten me anything," he protested as he opened the door and we headed toward his truck.

As he started the engine, I held up the silver spiral on the end of my braid. Lucien made a dismissive sound, but he was smiling. The night was cold, and I held my hands in front of the vents, the black box with the statue resting between my feet. There was a pleasant familiarity in the way the glowing skyline of Cities faded to dark skies and the highway dwindled to a narrow strip of asphalt between bare trees.

The headlights illuminated our way, and Lucien's hand rested on the inner curve of my thigh. I closed my eyes and leaned my head against his shoulder. Lucien kissed the top of my head and gave my leg a squeeze. "I'm falling in love with you." The words were simple, truthful.

My heart swelled and hit cold walls of worry and guilt, and I was keenly aware of the statue resting between my feet in its black box. *I love you.* My lips parted, the words dancing on them.

A sharp crack broke the silence, and the sound of breaking glass followed. The windshield exploded into spiderwebs, and flecks of glass pelted me. Lucien screamed and turned away from me, toward his window. The truck veered; an arrow, long and dark, protruded under Lucien's left collarbone, pinning him to the seat. Shadows, winged and blacker than the night itself, flashed in front of the crescent moon.

"Lucien!" I grabbed the wheel and centered the truck in the lane, heart hammering. Another arrow punched through the windshield and flashed between us, burying itself in the back seat.

Wrenching his shoulder, Lucien pulled the arrow free of the seat, but it still extended a hand span past his back, and thrice that out in front of him. He closed one hand over the arrow and snapped it off; Lucien didn't scream, but the cords in his neck stood out and his breath was ragged. The sky was a thunderstorm of wings and darkness. Lucien threw the fletched end of the arrow to the floor and took the wheel back.

They found us. The thought pounded in my head with every panicked heartbeat. *They found us, they found us.* I leaned forward, put my sweaty hands on the dash; above us a dozen winged forms gathered. "There's so many," I whispered. The truck leapt forward, headlights slicing down the dark road. Lucien tightened his jaw, drew one of his guns, and drove with a bloody hand clenched around it.

An Iyarri hit the roof of the truck like a comet, and Lucien wrenched the wheel. Talons scraped on metal, and a dark, winged form tumbled off the top of the truck.

In a flash of feathers and napta, an Iyarri swooped down in front of Lucien's truck, wings spread out wide and bow drawn. Lucien's gun boomed. The Iyarri wheeled out of control.

Time stopped, Lucien swerved. I shrieked and threw my hands in front of my face as the Iyarri crashed through the windshield and the truck careened off the road.

The sound was like an ancient set of steel jaws closing, the twisting metal groaning deep. The impact snapped my body against the seatbelt, and my head struck the passenger-side window. My vision bloomed red, then black.

Darkness and silence reigned absolute, but slowly, sounds registered: the patter of blood, the sodden slap of wet feathers, the crunch of broken glass. I opened my eyes, but they closed like lead curtains, and I had to force them open again. The Iyarri in the windshield struggled, half inside and half outside the truck, pale hair streaked with blood. Her wings were shattered, the delicate bones bristling out through the feathered skin like porcupine quills. Blood poured down the dashboard, the lower portion of the windshield buried in her stomach. Thick, dark-colored organs oozed out of the wound; the smell of her blood choked the air in the truck.

Beside me, Lucien groaned, dazed. He wore a half-mask of blood that welled from a gash over his eyebrow. I unbuckled my seatbelt and tried to speak, but terror pinched my throat like a vice. Leaning across the center console, I touched his face "Lucien!" I managed his name. "Lucien, are you okay?" His eyes rolled as he fought for consciousness.

The dying Iyarri's ivory wings shuddered in pain and shock, but she clawed toward Lucien, lips working wordlessly around a dribble of blood.

My hand came down on Lucien's gun, tossed between us. I flattened myself against the seat, pointed the gun at the Iyarri, and squeezed the trigger. Nothing happened. Panic hit me, wiping out everything except a clear, desperate sense of finality. The Laidrom drew her blade back, aligning the angle of her strike with Lucien. I thumbed off the safety and pulled the trigger again.

The gun erupted in my hands—the Iyarri's body jerked once, crumpled forward, and went still.

Lucien cracked his eyes open, put one hand to his forehead, and took the gun in the other. "We need to get out of here." He spat blood and focused on me, eyes bright with pain. "They're waiting for us to run. Stay under the trees." I nodded and gripped the door handle, then turned back and kissed Lucien, tasting blood. Our eyes met, storm cloud–gray irises to icy blue, before I flung open the passenger side door and leapt out, pulling him with me.

Our boots hit the cold ground and Lucien yelled, "Run!" I sprinted from the tree line into the woods. Lucien turned, both guns aimed heavenward, twin beams of white light slicing through the darkness. Each muzzle flashed, and a winged body fell from the sky. He caught up to me and we ran deeper, the trees closing in around us.

A Laidrom plunged from above, grabbed me, and lifted me into the air in a single raptor strike. Lucien's gun roared, and blood and flecks of bone sprayed my face. All sounds ceased save for a high whine in my ears. The Iyarri and I tumbled to the ground in a tangle of limbs and feathers.

Instantly I was back in my apartment, crushed under the body of the dying Iyarri, his jaw dripping scalding blood onto my face. I screamed and thrashed like a trapped animal beneath the weight. Gunfire barked and another Laidrom fell from the heavens, slamming into the ground with a spray of chilled earth and pine needles. Lucien pulled me free and we fled through the darkness.

There were too many Iyarri—we were going to die.

An arrow whistled past me. Lucien screamed, stumbled, and fell, the arrow through his calf. I crouched next to him, the smell of blood and damp earth overwhelming, dizzying. Lucien's face was ashen, his exhale frosting as it left his lips.

I put his arm around my shoulder, my wounded arms and side lighting up with hot arcs of pain as I helped Lucien stagger to his feet. We took two fumbling, running steps before a Laidrom slammed into me from behind and lifted me from the ground, a second diving for Lucien from the front. The ground spiraled away in a dizzying twirl of stars above and trees below. A bullet exploded through the Iyarri's wing, and she dropped me. I screamed, free-falling, the wind whipping my face as I tumbled. My body jolted as I was caught by another Laidrom, my breath heaving from my body with the impact. His body strained as we ascended to the sky, his wings pumping with a colossal effort.

I couldn't see Lucien save for the piercing beams of white light from his guns and the muzzle flashes in the dark. I screamed his name, my throat feeling like it would tear from the force.

The gunfire stopped. The beams of light went out.

I screamed Lucien's name again. My captor's wings were a black storm around me, whipping my hair around my face, the long strands sticking to my blood-spattered cheeks. "Let me go!" I yelled.

My captor brought the flat of his napta against the side of my head, and my world exploded into white stars and darkness.

It was a strange sensation, to wake to flying. My captor's wings pulsed like a heartbeat, strong and rhythmic, his arm locked around my waist. I opened my eyes and tried to focus. Pain twisted from each temple: the Laidrom had struck one side of my head, the window of Lucien's truck the other. I tried to move but my arms were pinned tight to my sides. I shivered in the endless November night.

Lucien. Hopelessness pressed down on me, as dark and enveloping as the nocturnal sky. I hung my head. Pain, bright and white, bloomed behind my eyes, and I nearly lost consciousness again. From behind my ear came the Iyarri's voice: "Stay still." His unfamiliar voice was a rich tenor, the English made ariose by his Loagæth accent. I cringed and tried to make myself smaller in his grasp, bleakly wondering who he was and where he was taking me. And for what purpose? Had the Iyarri wanted me dead, I would have been. My stomach twisted. Did they, somehow, know what I was?

The sound of other wings registered, too far to the sides and behind for me to see. A flutter of hope registered in my chest. Perhaps they were carrying Lucien. The sensation ceased with the quiet abruptness of a butterfly dying. Perhaps they were carrying Lucien's corpse.

The black sky loomed above me, and the ground far below was dotted with lights as we skirted the Cities. The Cathedral of St. Paul sat atop its hill, radiating pale amber and gold light. Far ahead of us, other Laidrom carried bodies in slings, outpacing my captor and our escort.

We flew away from the city and followed the dark thread of the river. Buildings relinquished the landscape to bluffs and trees, bright city lights to starlight, and the sounds of the city to the roar of the river. Far atop a precipice in the distance, pinpricks of light winked from the crouching stone form of the Rivercrest Monastery. My captor wheeled toward a cliff with a tilt of his wings, seemingly bent on dashing us into the rough limestone face. I swallowed a cry as, at the last possible instant, he dipped beneath a ledge and up again into a stone cavern. His wings flared as he set us down, then settled behind him like a dark cloak.

I pressed my hand to my head, woozy and unused to standing after the bobbing sensation of flight, but the Laidrom kept me upright.

Four other Iyarri touched down around us, like a murder of crows landing. I broke out of the Laidrom's hold and turned, desperate to see Lucien, but none of the Iyarri had him. I squeezed my eyes shut, possibilities racing through my mind: Lucien was in one of the slings ahead of us, he'd gotten away, or the Iyarri had left him to die, riddled with arrows, alone, in the dark. Torn between desperate hope and futile despair, I didn't resist when my captor closed one hand over my shoulder and led us down a sloping tunnel.

No one spoke; the sound of my boots scraped and echoed on the stone floor, clumsy and loud compared to the bare feet of the Iyarri. Their wings surrounded me with menacing shadows and, as we walked, the silver spiral on the end of my braid bounced off my ribs. I caught it in my fingers and closed my hand around it, sick with dread but still daring to hope. The Laidrom had taken me alive; perhaps they'd bring Lucien too. If he'd let them.

The passage split and branched until we came to a dead end. The female Iyarri came alongside my captor and asked something in Loagæth. My captor set his lips in a thin line and gave a flick of his wings. Whatever he said, his response was grim, uncertain.

The female Laidrom opened the wall before us, the stone sliding away with a grinding, scraping sound to reveal a great cavern in the heart of the bluff. It loomed so high I could not see the farthest reaches of it; the bottom filled with a great subterranean lake.

The far wall was nothing wrought by human hands; full of carved arches, airy windows, and delicate balconies, each fragile turn of the architecture pronounced its otherworldliness. Carved from the natural stone of the bluff, every inch of it was polished to a higher gloss, deep veins of white and black running through the warm gray and tan.

The other Laidrom took to the air, leaving me alone with my abductor. He was all the colors of midnight in an autumn forest—black hair and dark wings flecked with terracotta. The sole footpath to the other side of the cavern was a thin stone isthmus that terminated at imposing double doors. My captor shoved me toward it and I stumbled, head throbbing. There were no sides to the bridge, no rails, and I lacked wings to catch me if I fell toward the water far below.

I took small steps, hobbled by equal parts fear and awe. Above us, the roof of the cavern shifted with captured aurora borealis and the lake reflected the sublime illumination. Light shone from windows and alcoves in the fortress, and all around us Iyarri flitted through the cavern like swallows, soaring from one part to the next. Aamon said most Iyarri lived at Idura; I wondered if that's where I was, or if captives went someplace else.

The narrow stone path broadened to a landing, and we passed through the carved doors into an enormous hall. Three Iyarri statues stood in high alcoves, one brandishing napta, another holding a tome, the third with a human kneeling before him.

A few Iyarri gathered in tight, curious bundles of wings and stared as my captor marched me through the halls. In the distance, someone wept. The smell of unguents and salves, of alcohol and clean linens, registered before we reached an infirmary. Several beds were tucked into stone alcoves, a few of them occupied by wounded Laidrom. One slouched against the wall, her wing sagging and splattered with crimson. A solemn male Iyarri held a flask to her lips—he seemed too young to handle so much blood with such stalwartness. Another Laidrom lay on his back, a bloody, saturated bandage cinched around his abdomen, and a third groaned under the ministrations of an Iyarri with bright blue wings and copper-gold hair.

My stomach lurched with horror and guilt, and although I wrenched my eyes away, it neither quelled the weeping nor banished the coppery stench of blood. It was easy to hate the Iyarri as faceless monsters in the night, but their agony made me wish them whole again.

The last Iyarri was not wounded, but dead. He lay sprawled on one of the beds, discarded bandages and abandoned supplies scattered around him. A female Laidrom clung to his chest. "Essia, essia . . ." She sobbed the word over and over. Her brown wings shuddered as she clasped one of her father's hands and pushed blood-soaked hair back from his face. I covered my mouth with both hands, stifling a cry of horror—from what was *left* of his face. Half of it was shattered, one eye socket empty and open to the void where the side of his head had been.

My captor stilled, expression eclipsed with sadness. The blue-winged Iyarri turned and came near us, wiping his bloody hands on a woven cloth. "Miketh," he greeted my armed escort with a bow of his head and a tip of the top joint of his wings. Even amongst this bloodshed, there was a serenity to the healer's face that stripped years from it.

"Irel," Miketh addressed the healer, rubbing his anguished face with his hand. I didn't understand the words that followed, but they were heavy with grief and loss.

A snarl of Loagæth erupted from the grieving Iyarri. Head still bowed, she glared at me, lips curled and quivering with rage. Her brown eyes were flecked with red, as though she'd gotten blood in them and all the tears in the world could not wash them clean. I took a hurried step backward and raised my empty hands.

The healer reached a placating hand for her shoulder. "Væries," he said her name, trying to calm her.

She struck Irel away with a wing and came across the room in a streak of grief and blades. Miketh shoved me behind him and blocked Væries's blow, her napta blade striking the hardened leather of his gaunt-let. I flattened myself against the wall as Væries screamed at Miketh for his interference. Fear sapped the strength from my legs; I would have slumped to the floor had Miketh not pinned me between his back and the stone wall. The bow and quiver slung between his wings pressed against my chest, arrows bristling in my face.

With strength surpassing her size, Væries shoved Miketh sideways. Her claws lashed out, grabbed a fistful of fabric at my side, and jerked me toward her. I slammed into Miketh's wing as he dropped it to stop her from pulling me forward. I struggled against Væries's unrelenting attempt to drag me out, my face pressed into Miketh's feathers, Væries's claws hooked into my sweater.

Finally, Irel pulled Væries away. She pointed to the dead Iyarri, cursing me in Loagæth, the words a mournful howl of anguish and rage.

Miketh pushed me out the infirmary door and shoved it closed behind us, waiting in case Væries followed. When she did not, the tension in his shoulders eased and he gestured for me to follow him. I wrapped my arm around my throbbing side and drifted after him, wondering where he was taking me and why, but afraid to ask.

Miketh opened a door and gestured me into a small room with a stool and a high counter. Stone shelves held bottles and jars of all man-ner—some clear glass, others opaque clay stopped with cork. Miketh turned and closed the door. His wings were tri-toned and patterned like a kestrel's; the feathers near the base of his wings were spiced orange flecked with black. Farther down his wings, the feathers became dappled gray, the longest feathers sable black rimmed in white.

He pointed to the stool, the claw on the end of his finger black and glossy as obsidian. "Sit."

I sat, gripping onto the sides of the stool to hide the way my body swayed and my hands shook. My head pounded and my stomach lurched, threatening to relieve itself of its contents.

In the light, I could better see Miketh's face. It was proud and fiercely handsome—high cheekbones, the cupid's bow of his lips angled and full. His glare, however, was as sharp as his blades. "How badly are you injured?" His Loagæth accent was so thick it took me the measure of several heartbeats to realize he'd spoken in English.

The side of my sweater was red and wet, the mending tissue torn asunder by Væries's claws. A trickle of blood ran from one nostril; I wiped it away with my sleeve. "Why do you care, Laidrom?"

Miketh's eyes, amber as harvest moons, narrowed to firelit slits. "Speak our language again, human, and I'll tear your tongue from your head."

He reached toward my face with his clawed hands, and I cringed backward. Organic, patterned scars swirled down both arms and up the sides of his neck, the finest details terminating under his ears. Miketh paused and took my chin in his hand, his deadly-sharp claws pressed against my face as he turned my head so he could see my eyes in the light. Sourceless illumination streamed from the ceiling, as though the stone itself were made of sunlight. Miketh inspected the sides of my head and the bloody gash along my ribs, then pulled me off the chair by the shoulder. "You're fine. Come with me."

I stopped short of the threshold, my body refusing to move closer.

Miketh turned on me, his voice an impatient snarl. "What?"

"Are you going to kill me?" I asked, my voice a trembling whisper.

"No." He walked through the door and looked over his shoulder to make sure I was following. "If anyone has the satisfaction of your death once we're done with you, it will be Væries." My temples throbbed and

I cradled one hand to my head, the other to my bloody side, as I shadowed Miketh through the winding stone halls. At each intersection I cast anxious glances about, fearful, hopeful, and desperate for any sign of Lucien, but only found either empty hallways or curious Iyarri.

Eventually, Miketh opened a heavy door and pushed me inside. I stumbled into an Iyarri with wings like knives of snow: Aamon.

I recoiled a half step, the tiny flame of relief snuffed out before it could sputter to life—no recognition, just a frown that made his fine features sharp and cruel. My lips half formed a plea, a question, but fearful of what might have caused such a change in him, the words escaped me. I stepped backward, but Miketh's hand closed over my shoulder and held me still, claws pricking in warning. Aamon addressed Miketh, his Loagæth curt.

The two exchanged words, but the pain radiating from where my head had struck the window was so severe I couldn't pay attention. White spots, muzzle flashes in the dark, flickered in my vision.

The door closed, signaling Miketh's departure. Aamon reached past me, locked it, and turned to me, the lines of his face softening. "Are you all right?" he asked in English.

No words made it past my lips, just a terrified, pain-filled exhale. Aamon opened his arms and I crumpled against him. "We were attacked, and . . ." My voice broke and I sobbed, my head pounding.

"Shhh. I know. I made it so you were captured rather than killed. It was all I could do."

The room twirled, and I balled my hands into fists so tight my nails bit into my palms. Desperation swelled and receded in my chest with every breath. Finally I managed to whisper, "What about Lucien?" I squeezed my eyes shut until Aamon answered, stretched tight between hope and dread.

Aamon pushed my bloody, wind-matted hair back from my face. "They haven't brought him yet, so far as I know. I bartered for your lives under the pretense that you may have useful information."

Tenuous relief trickled through me. If Lucien was still alive, they'd bring him here. "Where am I?" I asked.

Aamon sat me in one of the chairs that surrounded the small table. "At Idura. How badly are you hurt?"

I managed a garbled litany of my injuries, my fingers hovering over the side of my head.

Aamon's wings snapped open and closed once. "Laidrom." His voice matched the scowl of disgust on his face. "Come with me, we need to get you hidden before one of them decides to try to avenge Ikkar."

Væries's red-speckled hate flickered in my memory, and I wrapped my arms around myself. Fear smothered my voice to a whisper. "But haven't they heard us talking?" Even with the thick walls, any Iyarri in earshot could hear everything we said.

"This room is for gatherings of the highest confidentiality; no one has heard us." Aamon paused at the door. "If anyone questions us, act the part of my prisoner and stay silent." He opened the door and led the way through twisting hallways and stone arches.

Neither Aamon nor I spoke, and I kept my eyes downcast, on the three borders of needlework holding the raw hem of his clothes. Something about seeing Aamon without his expensive, fashionable human clothes sent tendrils of unease down my spine. The robe he wore was regal in its simplicity—the unbleached linen was fitted through the chest with a mandarin collar and then flared in panels from the waist over wide-legged pants. I licked my wind-chapped lips. I *knew* Aamon wasn't human, that his beautiful house and stunning art gallery were a facet of his surface-self, but the realization cut cold and deep. His compassion and distress over my injuries, the knowledge that to him I was Aurelia and not some nameless human, took the edge off my terror, but the fact remained—here, in this strange stone refuge, Aamon was fully Iyarri.

We passed fewer and fewer Iyarri as we walked deeper into the sanctum, until we seemed alone in an area of Idura abandoned to disuse. Aamon unlocked an arched wooden door and led me inside.

The cell was crowded with a cot, a chair, and a small, low table. There was a bathroom, but it was scarcely big enough for the sink and a stone box with a hole in the top that I assumed was a toilet. I wondered about other human prisoners before me and how many, if any, were left alive.

Aamon put his hand back on the doorknob. "I can't stay. Ikkar's death may cause me to be preoccupied for some time."

"Where is Tiahmani?"

"I'm not sure. She wasn't involved in this mess, so she's safe. Try to rest. I'll be back when I can." As Aamon left, a lock scraped home.

The world contracted to the thudding of my own heartbeat against my temples and the dampness of my bloody sweater against my side. Too taxed by exhaustion, pain, and despair, I curled in the corner where the bed met the wall. The room was tomblike, trapping me in with silence and my desperate hope that, somehow, Lucien was still alive.

FIFTEEN

C
LAWS, DEFT AND GENTLE, parted the hair at the side of my head and stirred me to consciousness. "Aamon, I'm no healer." Tiahmani's voice sounded drained. "He hit her pretty hard; that's all I can tell you. Well, that and what you *don't* do when people get cracked in the head is leave them alone and let them fall asleep."

I struggled out from under Tiahmani's hands and sat up, my head throbbing. She was kneeling next to the cot, eyes red and puffy, dry tear-lines on her cheeks. "Is everything okay?" I asked.

She stood with a swish of dark wings. "No. Your damnable kiaisi murdered five of my wingmates." Pain and rage twisted her voice, and she turned away.

"What about Lucien?" My voice cracked with desperation. *Please let him be alive.*

Aamon sat beside me on the narrow bed. "The Laidrom killed him." His voice was low with sympathy and frustration.

My soul shattered, pieces of it raining into the empty cavern of my chest. I clasped my hands together and crumpled over them, my consciousness cratering to numbness edged with panic. I tried to say something, but grief and guilt twisted my throat until all that came out was a strangled cry of anguish. Hot lines of tears stung my wind-burnt face. Why hadn't I stopped any of this when I could have?

155

Aamon hugged me to his side with one arm and layered the embrace with a wing that smelled of sandalwood and amber. I managed a single choked question. "Can I see him?"

Aamon shook his head. "There's no way I could take you there without attracting attention, and even if I could, it isn't something you should see."

A tear dropped from my cheek onto my jeans. Aamon tightened his wing around me. "I'm sorry. He wouldn't be taken alive." Of course, Lucien had chosen death over capture. My headache bloomed anew; I squeezed my eyes shut and pressed the heels of my hands into my temples.

Tiahmani turned back around and tightened the laces on her napta so hard her skin rose between them. She spoke to Aamon: "Tell Miketh to send me to Lilnon."

"Now?" Aamon stood, his feathers brushing my knees.

"Maroch needs to know our Heeoa is dead. Væries is in no state to give orders, and Miketh is our only other Vohim. If you ask Miketh to send me, he will."

Aamon put his hands on the sides of her arms. "Someone else can send a message. Why do you—"

She snapped her arms and wings open in one motion, knocking Aamon away. "Because I can't stay here." Her voice broke and fresh tears coursed down her cheeks. "Did you see Væries? That is all Laidrom right now. How did they know where Aurelia was, and how did they not know about the kiaisi?" When answers didn't come, she bowed her head, face crumpled. This time, when Aamon put his hands on her cheeks and lowered his forehead to hers, she didn't resist. She closed her hand over his. "Please send me away." The torment in her voice made my throat tighten in sympathy.

"Go pack, then. I'll talk to Miketh."

She dredged up a heartbroken, grateful smile before she fled. Aamon gave my shoulder a reassuring touch and then followed her, leaving me alone with my pounding head and aching heart.

There was a lamp in the room, but I left it dark. A set of strange chimes hung in one corner, a spiral of metal tubes with a stone shard in the center. The stone never swayed, never struck the metal, but every so often it flashed and the chimes played a melody; each time it was different. Above me, the ceiling undulated deep indanthrene blue, the night sky spellcast onto the stone. My body ached from the impact of the accident, my face was tearstained, and my hands were covered with blood, but at least I had a body that could be filthy and feel pain.

The chill of the stone room seeped through my skin to my core. I wept, shivering, for Lucien, picturing the arrows bristling from his body and the napta slices that would never mend. There would never be a grave to kneel at. No flowers to leave, no last touches to a cold brow. Anger flared in my chest, directionless and desperate. I cursed the Iyarri, Lucien's past that had driven him to hate them so, and my parents for making me what I was. My body contracted with a sob so deep I couldn't let it out. Most of all, I hated my own weakness for not telling Lucien what I was and dragging him down with me.

Hours later, the shifting lights in the ceiling brightened to something dawn-like. I pictured my mother looking out the front window with one hand clutched around her Iyarri necklace in worry. I fumbled my phone out of my pocket; the screen was an unreadable spiderweb of cracks, and nothing happened when I tried to turn it on. I set it aside, tucked my knees to my chest, and rested my head atop them, feeling stupid and hopeless. There was nothing she could do, even if my phone worked and a signal could penetrate a mountain of stone.

The lock to my room scraped open with a rasp of metal on stone, jolting me to attention. I tensed, fearing Miketh or another Laidrom, and slouched with relief as Aamon entered, a bowl of steaming amaranth porridge and a cup of pilzin in his hands. "I'm sorry I was kept so long."

Despite the grief draining me and worry harrying me, I was happy to see Aamon. The familiarity of his voice, of his presence, quelled some of the teeming fear inside me. He set the porridge on my thighs, the stoneware bowl heavy and warm. Famished, I tried a spoonful. The porridge had a nutty, earthy flavor that settled the nausea in my stomach and a comforting, wholesome warmth that chased off some of the oppressive chill.

Aamon let me eat before he took up conversation again. "I wish I had better news to bring you, but I think it's best to be direct; I doubt my ability to keep you safe." I struggled to breathe, my chest suddenly constricted by a corset laced tight with fear. "Lucien killed Ikkar, the Laidrom Heeoa. There is a great cry for retribution, and the only person left for them to exact it from is you."

"Can you get me out of here?" I whispered, my hands tightening around the silver spiral in my hair.

Aamon shook his head. "Even if I managed to sneak you out of Idura, where would you go that the Laidrom would not find you?" He was right, and yet my thoughts darted one way and then the next like a mouse running between the paws of a cat, looking for a way to escape. "They want you dead because they think you are a human who knows too much. An Iyarri knowing about other Iyarri, however, is no sin." Aamon's voice was soft. "I have not rescinded my offer of wings. If you were willing to accept my help, I would see it done."

Doubt pushed in on my mind like a wall of thunderclouds rolling in. "They hate me for what they think I am, and you said being a Linnia was worse. Wings aren't going to change that."

Aamon crouched down so our faces were level, his expression creased with sympathetic understanding. "This is not giving you wings. This is making you Iyarri. From what the Iadnah tell me, the only thing that won't change is your hands, and you wanted to keep those anyway."

I twisted the spiraled lock of hair in my fingers. My throat tightened and my eyes pricked with tears at the thought of Lucien dying, bleeding out on the cold ground, alone. It felt like betraying him to survive by choosing to become the thing he hated. "I don't know, Aamon."

Aamon took the stool across from me, frowning at the bloody Iyarri handprints on my sweater. "How many times have you narrowly escaped death now? Three? You won't survive the next time they find you. And they will. I can only do so much for so long."

If I'd told Lucien sooner, he'd have left me and would still be alive. Why was I so weak and selfish? I hung my head and wrapped my arms around myself. "I wish I had told him what I am."

"For all you know, telling him would have put you here, at this same impasse." His voice was low and understanding.

I scrubbed my cheeks with my sleeve. "I know." Knowing, however, did nothing to stop regret from twisting my insides together.

Aamon reached to put a hand on my knee, and I stiffened. He paused, his hand in the air. "You've never looked at me that way before—as though you're afraid of me. Not even when I first showed you what I was."

I twisted my fingers into the cream fibers of the sweater. "I'm sorry. I—"

He took up my hand. Aamon's fingers were much hotter than a human's, but there was no sweat on his palms; the skin was soft and dry. "Have I ever hurt you?"

My ginger waves glimmered in the ambient light as I shook my head. "No." And he'd saved me instead of leaving me to discovery and death when he could have. I knew that, but what else hadn't he told me? "I feel like I don't even know you."

"The first time I found you in the gallery studio covered in paint—do you remember it?" he asked, claws shining like moonstone against my skin.

A smile ghosted my lips. A few years ago, I'd been trying to finish my rendition of *The Little Mermaid*. The mermaid had been given a choice, to pierce her love's heart with a blade and spill his blood on her feet to undo the sea witch's spell or let him lie sleeping with his new wife and know she would dissolve into sea foam at dawn's first light. She chose to let her prince live on.

The painting was full of murky predawn greens and grays, the mermaid splayed out on the rocky shoreline, her tail trailing into the water, hair running in pale blonde rivers between the stones. She clutched the dagger she'd been unable to wield at her chest, the first golden rays of the sun illuminating the two trails of tears down her face. Her tail had already started to dissolve; the edges of the fin lost to the lapping waves, small strings of sea spray washing her away.

Aamon found me slouched on a stool in front of the painting, exhausted and unhappy with it. "You sat next to me and gave me a cup of coffee," I said. Aamon was smiling. "And you asked why I was so unhappy with such a beautiful piece."

"And then what?"

"And then we talked about it, and you just . . . you understood. And we were able to figure out how to make it better." That painting was my favorite, not only because I loved the result, but because Aamon came and kept me company whenever he was at the gallery and I was in the studio. He understood that art was the pulse of my veins in my body, and he matched it in such an all-consuming way that I knew it was genuine.

"You, much like your mermaid, have a choice as to what you become." He squeezed my hand. "And I am here for you now, like I was when you despaired then."

A tear dropped from my cheek to our hands. For me to do nothing, to choose to do nothing, as the mermaid had, was to choose death. And unlike the mermaid, my prince was gone; there was no danger of hurting him. Aamon's offer glowed in front of me like the first rays of dawn over dark water.

Aamon gave my hand another squeeze, pulling me from my thoughts. "Will you let me help you?"

The ritual was no guarantee, Aamon was clear on that, but it was the difference between dying swimming for shore and giving up and sinking underneath the waves without a fight. As a wingless Linnia, I was as good as dead; with wings, I'd be Iyarri. I'd be spared. "Yes." The word began in sadness and ended in resolve.

"Good. I'll let Nesah, Sofiel, and Irel know immediately."

"So soon?" My decision hadn't even settled in my mind.

"There are preparations to make. Time is short; I'm going to see if any of them are able to see you. Remember, the ritualists, the Iadnah, are much more interested in their magic than the human world. You'll have to forgive any peculiarities." Without waiting for me to respond, he left and locked the door behind him.

Aamon returned and gave me a reassuring smile before ushering two Iyarri women inside. They were nymph-like, slightly built, with hair and wings the color of spun gold and wide, vivid eyes. He gestured to the older one and introduced her in English: "Aurelia, this is Sofiel." Sofiel took in each of my features, sifting the human from the Iyarri. "And this," he said, putting one hand on the elbow of the younger Iyarri, "is Nesah; they're sisters and have been curious to meet you." I nodded, but couldn't find words; surrounded by wings, I felt small and naked.

"Stars and feathers, a living Linnia," Nesah murmured in wonder, pressing her hand to her lips. The sisters' hands were tattooed a brilliant Prussian blue—the color solid on the thumb and forefinger, with voids of Iyarri designs, similar to the scars of the Laidrom but smaller and more intricate. The blue markings wrapped up their up their arms like azure incense smoke given form and disappeared under the long sleeves of the Iadnah robes. There was irony in a creature as breathtaking as Nesah blinking at me in disbelief.

Sofiel focused on my human hands, pensive and critical. She untucked a folded square of linen from under her arm and held it out to me. "Change into this, please." Her English was lilting and musical, but not hard to understand.

I took the clothes and froze—with the path to the bathroom choked by wings there was no place to change but in front of them. Nesah looked at me expectantly and Sofiel frowned, confused as to the delay. "Here?" I asked. Aamon nodded and gave a sympathetic knit of his brows before he turned around. Color flushed to my cheeks and tears pricked my eyes with a rush of timidity.

My boots and socks went first, the stone cool beneath my bare feet. Nesah's clawed fingers gestured to my bandages, and she said something to her sister in Loagæth. I undid my pants and then sloughed off my sweater, wincing where the fibers stuck to the marred bandage on my side. When I reached for the robe, Sofiel said, "All your clothes." Her tone was gentle and understanding, but I still cringed around a pang of self-consciousness. The air in Idura was cool; goosebumps raced over my skin and my nipples contracted to hard points as I shed my bra and panties.

I stepped into the robe and eased my arms through the sleeves. The back had a swath of fabric that pinned up between wings, but it was undone and left my back bare to my Venus dimples; I couldn't twist my wounded torso enough to fasten the clasps myself. "Let me see your back," Sofiel said. Her hand, feverishly hot, closed over my shoulder and eased me down until I knelt on the edge of the bed. Sofiel leaned close, her feathers smelling of herbs and incense. The tips of her claws pricked my skin as she walked one hand down the side of my spine, pinky over thumb, like a living cartographer's sextant. I gathered my bloody sweater to my chest for warmth and comfort.

Aamon's voice was low. "When can the ritual be performed? I would rather not delay."

"At nightfall," answered Nesah. "The others will be gathered for Ikkar's burning rites."

I took a breath to steady my quickening pulse, but I didn't know if my heart beat faster from hope or fear. "How will it happen?" I asked.

Sofiel spread her hands over my shoulder blades, thumbs on my spine. She spoke slowly, putting the final preparations together in her mind: "There will be three of us there."

"Aamon will be the third?" I asked, my voice small. I trusted Aamon and wanted someone I knew to be there.

Nesah shook her head and explained. "Only Iadnah may enter the ritual chambers."

"I will be there as soon as I'm allowed to be," Aamon reassured me, or tried to, but my insecurity was not so easily dispelled.

Sofiel closed the back of my robe, stood, and steepled her blue-tattooed hands in contemplation. "There will be two overlapping rituals." She paused and frowned. "In this case, there will be three Iadnah. There will be two Sondn, Sofiel and me, to summon your wings, and Irel, a Li'iansa, a healer, to tend you after our ritual culminates. Five would be preferable, but our circle of trust is small." They worked in odd numbers, the same way the Laidrom hunted. I tucked my bare calves under me and put my back to the wall as she considered her plan for a moment. "That will work. I'll send Irel to begin preparations." Sofiel turned and spoke to me over her shoulder, her wings sweeping the floor. "Rest well. You'll need all your strength for this."

Aamon stood to escort them out, and as Nesah followed she smiled and squeezed my hand, seeming to say, *I hope you make it.*

Evening came, the chimes in the corner sang, and someone knocked at the door. Aamon closed a reassuring hand over my shoulder before he opened the door and stepped aside for Irel. The healer and I locked eyes, surprised. "This is not the first time you two have seen one another," Aamon said.

I shook my head. It was Irel who had helped keep me safe in the infirmary. His wings were sails of helio blue, the feathers under the topmost joint a bright marigold that matched the color of his loosely braided hair. "She was with Miketh when he came to see if Ikkar survived." Like the other two Iadnah, Irel's English was proper, textbook.

Irel gave me a monastic bow of the head. He carried a tray laden with a teapot, a cup, and an amber bottle. "It is my pleasure to help you today." His eyes were the same startling azure as his wings, and bright lines like veins of gold ore ran through his irises.

"Irel, do you need me here, or can I see to other preparations for tonight?" Aamon asked.

The ritualist shook his head. "You may go. Aurelia and I will be fine."

Aamon gave me a reassuring nod. "Trust Irel," he said as he closed the door behind him.

Irel set the tray on the low table, and I picked up the amber bottle. "What's this?" The timbre of my voice shook; by the way Irel's expression grew concerned, he had not missed it.

"The ritual is a connection between your body and the minds of the ritualists. The tincture will open that channel." My gaze fell to the dark bottle in my hands. Irel's wings rippled behind him, a shifting summer sky. "You are not sure of this."

I shook my head, my heart wringing like a wet rag. "How can I be?"

Irel spread his hands. "You do not need surety so much as conviction in the face of doubt. Uncertainty can manifest as subconscious resistance. That could . . . complicate . . . the ritual without proper precautions." Complicate, destroy. My pulse skittered even though Irel had chosen one word over the other. "The tincture will relax your body and numb the pain, but it will also cloud your mind and keep you from resisting. So, before we begin, are you sure you're ready to do this?"

Shoving my doubt deep inside, I replied, "Yes."

He nodded and reached for the bottle on the table. His hands were dyed and patterned the same way as Sofiel and Nesah's. I hadn't noticed before in the infirmary—they'd been covered in blood. Whatever Iyarri healing entailed, it was more than magic words. There had been blood and bandages and bottles with strange contents. "Are you sure this will work?"

Irel stayed his hand and leaned back, away from the bottle on the table. "The ritual of wings will work, but no one in living memory has tried to heal a Linnia. Iyarri, despite looking somewhat human, are not, and do not respond well to human medicinal treatments. I am also here to explore where you fall on the balance between human and Iyarri so I can adjust accordingly."

I mulled over the way I straddled that divide. My three-toed feet, the ability to see in the dark, how I could hear things humans could not, the way I was light for my size and had broken so many bones as a child; all these counterbalanced my human hands, my paler skin, and the more generous swells to my hips and breasts.

Irel's eyes trailed from my human hands to where a piece of gauze tufted out of the cuff of my robe. "You are injured? May I see?"

Mindful of the cuts, I unwound the gauze from my arms and adjusted the robe so one of the wing-slits was over the napta cut on my ribs. Irel tilted his head, pensive and meditative, as he examined the napta wounds. "Here." He gestured for me to move and took the blanket off the bed. "Sit down again." I did so, and he sat opposite me, both of us cross-legged so our knees met in the center of the bed, his wings spilling over the footboard. Irel wrapped the blanket around my shoulders, its weight enveloping me. A sigh of relief and comfort escaped my lips, and I held the blanket closed with one hand, feeling warmer and less vulnerable. "Better, yes?" Irel asked with a smile.

The corners of my lips softened into a grateful smile. "Yes, thank you."

He stretched his wings over his head, brilliant as a bird of paradise, and wrapped them forward so they settled in a great, feathered circle around me. His wings smelled like clean linens and herbs, and inside them it was so warm it chased the chill from my fingertips and bare toes. Some of the tension lifted from my shoulders; some of the fear melted away from my heart. "The bodies of Iyarri are more easily affected by magic. Sondn, like Nesah and Sofiel, are trained in arts like summoning our tattoos onto our flesh, turning an Iyarri into a Naphal, or cremating our bodies into ash. But if their magic can give a Linnia wings, mine should be able to heal one too. May I have one of your arms?" he asked.

I threaded it out of the blanket and gave it to him. Irel turned it so the napta slice faced upward. The edges of the laceration were pink banks around a dry, scabbed riverbed, the butterfly bandages wrinkled and stained.

"Let's see how hard you are to heal." His expression was kind and his hands gentle where they cupped my arm. "There will be some sensation, but no pain." Irel shifted to a language reminiscent of Loagæth, but ancient and songlike. Not having to fumble with English, his voice was rich and resonant. Inside the circle of his wings the air became thick and charged with energy, closing us off from the rest of the world. Irel's chant was low, as soothing and repetitive as a lapping bath. The warmth of his blue-dyed hands wove into me, seeking the injuries. My eyes fluttered in relief as my headache lifted, and around the lacerations, the edges of my flesh thrummed, not painful, but skirting the edge like a deep massage.

The butterfly bandages curled, wilted, and dropped from my arm like petals from a dying flower. I tingled, not in discomfort, but with surprise as the pink skin faded to cream and pushed out scabs that fell onto the bed between us.

I looked from Irel to my arm, my lips half-parted in awe. A thin, upraised white scar remained—like the ones on Lucien's forearms. Irel touched his fingertips to my other arm. "Go on, look." It, too, was healed, and when I ran my hand over my ribs—there were no bruises, no blood, only mended flesh and the smooth arc of a scar. Irel's smile reflected a quiet joy in my astounded expression. "You're not nearly as human as you appear. I think we'll be just fine." His quiet confidence chased away some of the fear, and gratitude blossomed in its wake. Warm and without pain, the weak, pulsing sensation of hope became a steadier glow in my heart.

Irel poured a cup of tea, the steam curling upward in the chilly room. He undid the glass stopper on the bottle and measured out a spoonful of rum-colored, acrid-smelling syrup into the cup. Irel blended the contents with the spoon; bits of ground herbs swirled within. "Drink the whole cup at once."

The clay was warm in my hands, simply patterned with a single feather that coiled like an ammonite and unfurled around the rim. Wishing I knew a prayer in Loagæth, I drank the potent liquid. The loamy tincture clung to the walls of my throat, and I gagged trying to swallow it. I squeezed my eyes shut and forced it down, but the swampy flavor lingered. "Ugh." My stomach heaved. "That's awful."

Irel chuckled. "I imagine so." Without pause he prepared a second cup. "I am not sure how many cups it will take until you start drift in and out of awareness. If you hear me chant, I am attuning to you."

I drank the second cup. And a third. With each cup the bitterness increased, but my body protested less. The chimes overhead played, but their melody was far away and distorted. When I set the empty cup down I paused, rubbing my thumb across the pads of each finger, examining the sensation. It was like I was frostbitten, but without pain.

After the fourth cup, I found myself laying on the cot, my body detached from my mind. Irel settled his hand on my arm, his touch as gentle and as practiced as any human doctor's. He spoke, but his words were evanescent and their meanings eluded me. Irel's fingertips touched my forehead and my skin thrummed. Though persistent, it was not uncomfortable. Above me, the luminescence of the ceiling waned toward darkness.

"Irel," I asked, my mind clouding and my voice a mumble, "does it bother you?"

"Does what bother me?" he asked, peering into my half-lidded eyes.

"Me. What I am. Becoming you." I tried to catch the image of what my wings might look like in my mind and hold it, but it slipped away.

There was a pause and his hand shifted so his whole palm lay across my forehead. "No. Helping you realize yourself does not bother me."

I knew the draughts given to me near the end were potent, burning, and bitter, but couldn't taste them. Irel pulled the hood of the robe up so it covered most my face, then gathered me in his arms. I was aware of my cheek against the fine fabric of Irel's robe, the smell of tinctures, and how in this moment, I couldn't have asked for the ritual to stop if I'd wanted to.

SIXTEEN

IREL CARRIED ME THROUGH the hushed, twisting passages of Idura until a large set of white stone doors etched with blue, swirling patterns filled my vision. Irel did not knock, but the doors scraped open. The dim room warped in and out of focus, but smelled of incense and wet stone. Pillars loomed like sentinels, and still water divided one half of the room from the other. A swish of feathers and fabric registered to my left, and then Sofiel spoke. "Take her through the cleansing pool."

The healer shifted me in his arms and we descended, one step at a time, the warm, damp air pressing from under me as water wicked into my robes. There was no doubt, no fear, no hope, nothing but my body caught between awareness and detachment and the enveloping sensation of submersion. The water rose to my neck, over my mouth, and lapped at my nostrils, but I didn't lift my head from Irel's shoulder. Steam and incense smoke curled around me, shapes appearing and disappearing: an arctic fox, a coiling dragon, a woman in a full, swirling skirt. Irel walked up the steps on the far side of the pool, and the drag of my wet robes pulled me from the cloudscape.

Nesah waited for us, and though her lips moved, the sounds wouldn't become words. The sopping weight of my robes slouched downward and then disappeared. Golden feathers haloed the edges of my vision as Nesah cupped her wings around me and drew shapes in the air over my body. My flesh prickled with each word she spoke. Nesah turned and pushed open an arched door of ancient wood, put one hand on my upper arm, and gave it a squeeze of reassurance. The sensation registered an eternity later, radiating and tingling.

The circular room past the doors drifted and shimmered—only the air shifting over my skin made me aware that we weren't underwater. Tall, arching windows cast rippling light onto the labradorite floor, its surface aflame with shifting hues. A stone table—an altar—dominated the center of the room.

Irel laid me on my stomach atop the altar, the blue and gold of his wings a softer extension of the labradorite around us. The air was charged, full of energy, the stone cool and grounding beneath my naked body. A bowl filled with liquid sat on a pedestal to one side, and as my head swam it faded into the flickering hues.

An aureate eclipse broke overhead as each of the ritualists spread their wings, the tips of their feathers touching. Sofiel spoke, syllables reverberating through the chamber, rising and falling—a spell made song. Irel and Nesah repeated the chant back to her, their voices twining, echoing, rising and falling in unison. The air teemed with energy, and the colors in the stone floor undulated with the voices of the Iadnah.

Sofiel spread her hands over the labradorite bowl and, without breaking her mantra, dipped one blue index finger into the bowl. She traced a line of slick, heavy oil down either side of my spine, stopping where the small of my back curved upward to my buttocks. The heat of the oil sunk through my muscles and into my bones. The thrumming energy in the air followed it, delving into my core and unfurling my mind, body, and consciousness one petal at a time—stretching each to the farthest reaches of my awareness. The blue stone around me became the sea, became swaths of sapphire velvet, became the night sky.

Nesah's voice, higher and clearer, joined her sister's. Each beat of their chant pushed into the lines of oil like seeds into a furrow. They sprouted and forced roots of energy downward, twisting and branching into my flesh. Sofiel's fingertips pressed against my back, distorting the clean lines of oil into symbols and patterns. The roots became briars that twined around my spine and pushed thorns into my bones.

My heartbeat thrummed against the inside of my ribs, sweat coursed down my skin, and a tight, horrible pressure built in my back. The furtive smell of incense laid a heavy curtain back over my senses but didn't deaden the lucid coldness of fear. I willed my hands to move, watching them more than feeling them grip the edge of the altar.

My body expanded and strained under Sofiel's touch. I bowed my forehead to the cool stone and closed my eyes, but hot tears escaped and slid over my cheeks. As she lifted her hands from my back, Sofiel's voice shifted, the rhythm changed, and the words rolled together. There was the soft swish of her fingertips in the bowl of oil, and she swept her hands down my back, wiping the symbols away. I twisted, peering over my shoulder, and went still, panic beating against the confines of my mind. Upraised bony ridges ran parallel to my spine and to my hips, and Sofiel's fingers ran over every crest and hollow. Every inch of my skin was too tight, too small, and too thin.

My vision swam, and the pain gnawed through whatever protection the herbal tinctures offered. Sofiel redrew the symbols, her touch crooked on the warped canvas of my back. Her chanting increased, and with each wiping of the oil, with each drawing of new symbols, the ridges under my skin grew. I latched my hands onto the edge of the table and tried to drag myself out from Sofiel's touch, from the syllables that drummed my body like hail. Nesah and Irel's hands clamped onto my sweat-slicked body and bore down, pinning me in place.

The things growing in my back convulsed under the muscle and skin binding them, slamming me into the stone. I couldn't breathe, the expanding pressure too much for my lungs to counter. A single, startling thought pierced through the herbal draughts and the pain: this ritual was nothing more than it had always been—a punishment and torturous execution.

I plead for it to stop, but my words came as pained mewlings punctuated by heaving gulps. My body rent itself asunder, stretching and pulling itself in ways it was never intended to contort. One of my ribs snapped under the pressure, and I curled and uncurled, contracted and released in pain. There were flashes of light and darkness, and somewhere, from a great distance, I could hear myself shrieking.

Irel's voice joined in, his chant slower and soothing, a measured underscore to the sisters' higher voices. The chant came to a crescendo, and my flesh gave way with the sound of a sail ripping in the wind. The pain tore me from my own body, and my vision went white as the pressure released in a rain of blood and gore.

Nesah screamed, but Irel kept chanting, his wings cupped around my body in a circle. His magic dug into my back and wrenched the caverns in my flesh closed. Blood, tallow-hot, coursed down my neck, over my face, and into my mouth. It ran off the altar and drowned the shifting hues in the floor. Bits of skin and tissue clung to my hair, quivering. The things that sprung from my back slapped against the stone: they were not wings, but deformed swaths of tissue and bone. My throat peeled with a screech, and I cowered under them. Their leathery surface was crumpled and featherless, the pale skin covered in a sickly placenta with dark, pulsing veins. They trembled as the rest of my body did, like the legs of a newborn fawn. Deformed, naked, misshapen things—when the abyss of unconsciousness yawned open before me, black rimmed with a glowing halo of candlelight gold, I threw myself through it and wished for death.

Somewhere, on the edges of my perception, I was aware of my body being lifted and moved. Faces passed in front of my eyes, blurred and distant. Sofiel's and Nesah's, both pale with hollow cheeks; Aamon's, his white wings behind him like two arches of holy light. Irel's voice was there, still chanting, although now the notes were drained and empty. My flesh still pulled, knitting and threading itself together, but the sensation was weak and slow. Every cell in my body ebbed with pain, and the edges of my vision pulsed red.

There was the touch of warm water and soft cloths as the blood was cleaned from my skin, from the things that should have been wings. I pictured Lucien wiping the blood from my face in the gray sunlight. My eyes fought to stay closed, but pain hooked its claws into my body and dragged me back to full consciousness.

Sofiel dressed me in a robe, one limb at a time, like an infant. She sat me up, leaned me forward onto Nesah for support, and pinned a wide swath of blue cloth to the shoulders of my robe. They tucked the mis-shapen flaps of flesh into it, pinning it closed and hiding the wings from sight. The raw, new tissue screamed at their gentle hands, and I writhed against Nesah. She shushed me, stroking my damp and tangled hair.

The remains of the herbal draught rode through my system, height-ened by blood loss and exhaustion. Sofiel touched my brow—her fin-gers should have been burning hot, but felt cool. I wanted to speak, but I had neither the words nor the strength to find them.

Aamon lifted me into his arms. He smiled, but deep lines of worry swallowed his otherwise reassuring expression. The ritual doors closed behind us.

The halls of Idura were dark and quiet, the strange ceiling not yet brightening with dawn. Aamon hurried through ascending staircases and dark hallways. Lines of Iyarri statues faced one another, and we passed between them. As Aamon unlocked a door, one of the statues along the wall moved, eyes glittering in the dark. I tried to focus, to pull shadowy shape into substance. The door groaned as Aamon opened it with his back, fighting against the wind. The statue moved again, wings closing.

Icy air screamed by in a gale across the top of the bluff, snapping the thin fabric of the robe I wore. I turned my face toward Aamon's chest, but the sensation of cold did not come. I could feel the chill of the wind on my skin, but it didn't reduce me to shivers. The night was a black, cloudless expanse, and the lights of the Cities made them seem afire.

A gust of winter air did not wholly swallow my cry of pain as Aamon took to the sky, jostling my body as his great wings pulled us skyward. Aamon's heart beat against my cheek, a mirror to the rhythm of his wings, and I collapsed again into the void of unconsciousness.

I wished for Irel's bitter-tasting herbal tincture. I would have drunk gallons of it, foul murkiness and all, to numb the pain. My body ached and throbbed though I lay still. A tender hand descended on my brow. Irel's voice chanted over me. All the aching tissue in my body went weightless, and I shed some of my misery. Under Irel's touch, I stilled and found sleep once again.

Eventually, I surfaced to consciousness and stayed there. Trading one uncomfortable position for another, I tried to roll from my side to my stomach, arrested by the dragging weight on my back. I bit my lip and squeezed my closed eyes tighter. Flashes of the ritual appeared behind my eyelids: the smell of my own blood, the sound of my screams, and the deformed appendages closing around me. Whatever I had become, it wasn't Iyarri. I hunkered, still and terrified. What had I done to myself? How could Aamon have been so wrong?

Unable to will myself back to unconsciousness, I lifted my head. I lay cupped within a large, scooped wooden oval, the center filled with a thick cushion bordered with pillows: a huge, shallow nest. A Tiffany lamp on a nearby nightstand illuminated the room, the sky outside the windows dark. Strange bed aside, I was in an otherwise human bedroom. Irel slept in a chair not far away, tattooed hands clasped in his lap and his helio blue wings crossed in front of him in a makeshift feathered blanket. I teetered on my hands and knees, unbalanced by the weight on my back, and peered at the ritual-conjured flesh. Oceans of pinned blue cloth filled my vision, but my mind's eye was crowded by memories of blood, pulsing veins, and gore.

A great cavern of regret yawned open in my heart, excavated by pain, by uncertainty, by loss. Why had I ever thought this better than death? Exhausted and shattered, I crumpled back onto the cushions and wept. My shoulders shook and my stomach heaved with disgust, acrid bile climbing my throat. What had I done to myself? Why hadn't they cut them off? Why hadn't Irel granted me the mercy of death?

Irel laid his hand on my shoulder. He spoke in Loagæth, his tone reassuring and soft. The words became less elusive, but he switched to English anyway. "Hush, Aurelia. It's over." It was over, irreversibly over. How could Irel comfort me after he saw those featherless monstrosities? "Why don't you try getting up? I can help you."

My vision warped as Irel sat me on the edge of the strange Iyarri bed, moving my legs for me until my three-toed feet dangled over a silk Isfahan rug. The thick, henna-colored toenails had grown into arcing talons. Every bruised muscle of my body ached, and I gripped the edge of the bed, head hanging, vision blurring. I tried to speak, but my voice was a hoarse whisper, stale from disuse. I tried again. "Where am I?"

"Aamon's human residence." Irel crouched on the floor in front of me. Exhaustion dulled the lapis lazuli of his eyes. "You are not sick from injury but fear. Once we remove the uncertainty, you can heal." His words chilled me—crystalizing every terrible memory of the things on my back into reality. What else had changed? What was left of what I had been?

Lucien's spiral flashed, still tangled in my hair. My head spun, my stomach tightened. Irel took my human hands in his clawed ones. I sighed in relief; the slender fingers had not sprouted thick, curved claws. "Come."

Irel eased me to my feet, and I shook my head. My legs were trembling too much to support me. He gave me a few seconds to gather myself and then walked with me across the room. The talons on my feet dug into the rug when I tried to walk heel to toe; mimicking Irel, I lifted my heels, rocked my weight to the balls of my feet, and picked my toes up with each step. A thin, gossamer thread of happiness wound its way through me: for the first time my feet felt and looked natural.

An oval mirror slid into my peripheral vision and I stopped short, my feet and my eyes both unwilling to go closer. My lungs stretched too full, and my heart pattered under the strain of them. Inch by inch, I lifted my eyes to the reflective glass.

The blue-swaddled appendages loomed behind me in an oppressive backdrop. My skin was still fair, but it now held the same radiant glow as an Iyarri's, illuminated from within like a candle set behind a porcelain mask. My face was still not quite human, not quite Iyarri.

Irel laid a hand on one of the seams. "Should I begin?"

I searched the lines of his face for some tell of what lay under those heavy folds of blue cloth, but there was nothing but patient compassion. "I think so," I lied. My eyes dropped to the foot of the mirror, dread a cold stone in my stomach. I couldn't watch.

Irel removed pin after pin. The fabric hung down as he opened it, and translucent, chitinous tubes, all cracked along one side, fell to the floor around our feet. Visions of the naked, crumpled, bloody things under the cloth licked at the edges of my memory. Linen whispered as Irel slid the cloth trappings away and let them fall to the floor. I pulled a deep breath, filling my chest with air. I released it; the sound threatened tears. "Look when you are ready," Irel said.

I lifted my eyes and gasped, staggering back from the mirror. My wings arched upward in a brilliant copper display, no longer hunkered like naked beasts, but something both delicate and powerful. Relief cascaded through me, sweeping away the nausea and doubt with such force I swayed on my feet. My wings flared, instinctually keeping me balanced.

Afraid it would dissolve into an illusion at my touch, I took one wing in my hands and wrapped it around my body. The feathers under my fingertips were smooth and soft, the structure underneath lean and muscled. While I slept, the compressed bones had unfurled to their proper proportions the same way the crumpled wings of a monarch expand after their confinement in the chrysalis. In places, some of the pinions were still pushing their way out of the flesh and into the world, sheathed in the stiff casings that littered the floor. Tentatively, I pulled one of them away. The casing slid upward with a rasp, and a bright feather unfurled in its place. I ran it between my fingers with an enraptured smile, memorizing its texture: the supple outer edge, the stiff rachis, the softness that balanced its strength. Each plume was burnished copper, the edges of the feathers lighter, sharpened to a golden edge. There must have been thousands of feathers, and each and every one was part of me.

Irel pressed his bent index finger to his lips, his smile contemplative and proud. "Stars and feathers, a winged Linnia."

SEVENTEEN

Wings, *my wings*, were so *big*. Laughing in relief, I willed them to unfold. The new muscles bunched and protested, but the wings unfurled like a sail filling with wind, the full wingspan three times my height. Not ready for the extent of their size or the power those pained muscles held, I lost my footing. I'd been reborn, shaky and unsound in my own body. Irel steadied me and the wings refolded of their own accord, the muscles too weak to hold them open.

The two longest swallowtail feathers brushed against my calves; I gathered one up and wrapped it around my body. Long and supple, it ended in a pointed oval. At the widest point, a golden teardrop rested in the swath of copper.

"Unalah." Irel nodded to the feather in my hands. "Eye-spots and ocellate markings are the epitome of Iyarri beauty. Yours are particularly lovely." His expression faded to concern. "There is more you should see." He picked up a hand mirror from atop a dresser, gave it to me, and turned me around so my back was to the large mirror. Irel undid the center piece of my robe. I focused past the coppery expanse of wings and let out a wordless, whispered cry. Irel had healed my back, but had not been able to make it whole again.

The golden scars that leapt from the bases of my wings were mirrored lightning strikes. The tattered masses of sunken scar tissue exploded outward into a hundred scars, some wider, others finer, arcing across my spine, up the back of my neck, and down to my Venus dimples. The scars were already sunken and glossy against the pallor of my skin, but they shone golden, as if Irel's magic had healed into the flesh. "I am sorry," Irel said. "There was so little flesh to work with."

My throat tightened and my eyes blurred with tears as the joy of my wings cratered into a despair as shattered as my back. I lowered the wavering mirror, but the image persisted in the dark places of my mind. Irel took the mirror with one hand and braced me with the other. "Let's return you to the tianta. You've gone pale." He walked me back and sat me on the edge of the Iyarri bed. I collapsed forward, my elbows on my knees, face buried in my hands. A wave of clarity crashed over me, my toes curled tight against my feet as I cowered from the thought, unwilling to confront it, but my own flesh and bones made it unescapable—this body, this winged and scarred body, was immutably mine.

Of course there were scars, why wouldn't there have been? Aamon mentioned I would need healing, and I hadn't expected the Iadnah to conjure my wings out of the ether, but the way they'd grown under my skin and tore their way out like feral animals . . . the scent of hot blood on cold stone surfaced from my memory, curdling my stomach with nausea.

Human hands, Iyarri feet, Linnia scars. What was I?

Voices called back from the corners of my mind. *Freak. Monster.* My thoughts edged toward Lucien and what he would have thought of me—if the Iyarri hadn't murdered him. I swooned, my vision white.

Irel sat beside me, pressed my shoulder to his, and wrapped one wing around me, the feathered expanse long enough to get around my body and wings in a way his arm alone could not. "Your body is still trying to adjust to its new self," Irel said. "You lost so much blood, and the addition of your wings demands more than you started with. The weakness should fade in time." The weakness would, but the scars would not. I took a shaking breath, then another, and another, until the sound of running water registered in my ears.

Irel guided me to my feet. "Come. I've drawn a bath for you. Being clean will make you feel better."

My skin itched with dried sweat and tears. "I don't think I can." I had barely managed a bath at Lucien's, and I hadn't had new limbs to contend with on top of blood loss and weakness.

"I will be there to help you."

My lips parted to protest, to form some excuse or another, but what was there to say? There was not an inch of my naked body Irel had not already seen and pieced back together.

He helped me walk to an adjacent bathroom, and thick, damp air closed around my exposed skin. Travertine and soft lights surrounded a large tub carved from pale stone. With the back of my gown undone and mirrors on every wall, my scarred back was in front of me at every turn. The sound of gore raining on the labradorite floors beat inside my mind like the sky opening with a downpour. The ginger gleam of feathers in my peripheral vision did not diminish the memory of the naked, bloody flaps of flesh crumpling over me.

"Aurelia." Irel's voice drew me back. How many times had he repeated my name? My arms were wrapped tight around myself, and I unwound them. Irel eased the robe forward off my shoulders and let the fabric fall to a puddle around my feet. I braced my arms on either side of the tub and stepped inside; the water closed around my foot, sliding up the three toes and over my calf. Irel lowered me, supporting my weight. I folded forward over my knees, my wings draped over the edges of the tub, bright feathers splayed like copper blades.

Light and shadow played across the water and memories flooded into me. Of Lucien's bloody kiss, of the way he'd threaded the silver spiral into my hair, of the rise and fall of his chest against my then-perfect back.

Irel knelt by the bathtub, reached off to one side, and settled a red Japanese clay teacup into my hands. It was hotter than the bathwater, the cup full of fragrant tea. Cracks of gold ran through the clay; the cup had been broken and repaired with smooth, gleaming metal, a sister to the way Irel's magic repaired my back with radiant, golden scars. Irel scooped water from the bath with a small bowl and poured it down the riverbed of scars on my back. "When something has suffered damage, it has a history. That history is unique and makes the piece more beautiful for having been broken."

My not-quite-me reflection wavered in the surface of the tea. "Do you really believe that?" I whispered.

"I do." If the words were anyone else's I might have thought them a comforting lie, but Irel's serene sincerity was guileless. "I believe each living thing works toward its end, whatever that may be." His sleeves were cuffed, the blue tattoos coiling up his arms. Irel picked up a loofah and dipped it into the water, wringing it out with one hand before rubbing it on my back. He removed the filth from my skin, the sponge gliding in gentle arcs. "It is not my place determine what the proper course of the journey is, or allow it to end prematurely, even when others might think it is broken beyond repair. I have been given what appears to be a talent for healing those in need of aid. It is not my place to decide who deserves those skills, only to administer them so someone may continue onto whatever destination is meant for them." He nodded to the kintsukuroi cup. "I would no sooner have turned you, a Linnia, away than I would have an Iyarri. I only regret not being able to do better than see your skin crudely knit back together; but your scars are as unique as your wings. They are two adjacent chapters in a history that is yours alone."

His words quieted the tumult of emotions inside me. "What day is it?" I asked.

"December fifteenth. Well, the wee hours of the sixteenth."

"Already?" Three weeks asleep felt like I'd been gone a few moments and a few months all at once.

"Aye, we've kept you asleep so you could mend." He took the empty cup from my hands, the contrast of the red and gold clay bright against his blue skin. Irel set the cup aside and gestured to the spiral tangled in my hair.

"Let me," I said as I unwound the length of metal and held it in my two hands like a candle at a vigil.

Irel tilted my head back and poured water over my head, wetting my hair. His hands disappeared for a moment and then returned with cool gel that smelled of crisp herbs. He worked it into the long mass of damp, ginger waves. Fat drops of warm lather fell onto my shoulders, distorting the clean lines of Irel's reflection with suds. Like my father, Aamon, and Miketh, Irel's cheeks and jaw were smooth, not growing so much as stubble. I tightened my hand around the silver spiral, wishing for the rasp of Lucien's cheek against my hand.

The crushing, guilty loss of Lucien, the elation of wings, the devastation of my ruined back: the highs and lows made my head spin, and not even the rinses Irel poured over me cleared it. Finally, Irel helped me stand on my unstable legs, dried me off, and helped me into a clean robe.

He combed my tangled hair, humming a foreign, soothing song. I sectioned out the same lock of hair Lucien had and wrapped the spiral around it while Irel plaited the rest of my hair. I closed my hand over the spiral. If I could mourn Lucien in no other way but to wear that token of his love, then that would be what I did.

Irel put me back in the scooped bed and spoke in Loagæth. My mind almost caught the words, but they flitted like a butterfly just out of a child's grasp. He made an apologetic gesture and asked in English, "Are you hungry?"

"I am hungry, but can you keep talking to me in Loagæth?" Irel tilted his head in question. "The more I hear Loagæth, I feel like I might understand it."

He mused. "That would be possible, wouldn't it?" He said something else in the Iyarri tongue, no trace of the bookish, formal tone that marred his English. I shook my head, not understanding, but my mind tingled. Irel translated for me. "I'll get you something. Rest until then."

After he'd gone, I pulled one of my wings across my body. They were strange, but felt right; perhaps they should have been mine all along. I slid my fingers into one of the chitinous shells ensconcing an emerging feather and broke it from the coppery plume. I freed a second feather, and then a third. Slowly, the aperture of my world closed, and each opening of my eyes took more effort than the last. Still, my fingers worked on, freeing one feather at a time.

Aamon was leaning on the doorframe to the room when I woke. He was dressed in an Iyarri robe, pale gold with detailing around the raw edges. It was simple, elegant, and lordly, the effect reinforced by his neat ponytail and white wings. His face held a pensive expression I'd seen a thousand times before: the quiet appreciation of a piece of compelling art.

Irel's chair was empty, but Aamon helped me out of the tianta, then held me out from him at the shoulders. "Let me look at you," he murmured. His hazel eyes took in the expanse of my wings; he turned me so I was facing the oval mirror. "Look at you: perfect. Amazing and absolutely perfect."

Perfect—the word hung in my mind. I didn't think I'd ever heard that particular word used to describe me. It settled over me like an unfamiliar garment, but not one I wanted to take off. The pair of us looked wholly Iyarri in our strange garb and arching wings—it made my reflection feel foreign, as though someone else stared back from the face holding my eyes. What joy I'd found in Aamon's words waned with my strength. "Haven't you seen my back?" That shattered landscape of flesh and skin was far from perfect, and I worried he'd find me too flawed to be Iyarri.

"I have." Aamon smoothed his hands over my shoulders. "Every other Iyarri was given wings by birth, all the same. Just as in art, what determines the value of a piece is its uniqueness, its rarity. You are the sui generis of all Iyarri." His voice dropped to a gentle, concerned tone. "How are you feeling?"

"Sore and weak, but better than yesterday." I gave an awkward smile. "And hungry. Irel was going to bring me something last night, but I fell asleep."

"Let's go downstairs and I can make you something. I'm sure getting out of this room would be nice."

I agreed, even if I couldn't remember most of the time he spoke of. Aamon helped me down the stairs and onto a padded bench in the living room, then brought me a bowl of thick soup, dense bread, and a cup of tea.

A few ravenous bites in, I made myself slow down. "Where's Irel?"

Aamon sat across from me, early morning light casting a warmth to his wings like dawn on white clouds. "Resting. The ritual taxed him, and he's been taking care of you ever since. Though I do have to return to Idura, I am able to spare a few hours while he sleeps."

The Iyarri statues Aamon and I passed on the way out of Idura stood in the dark recesses of my memory. "Did anyone see us?" Drugged and teetering on the edge of consciousness, the statue's movement may well have been a trick of the light, though my gut told me it hadn't been.

"No. The ritual chambers are soundproof, so there was nothing to be heard, and no one saw anything." His face went grim, but then he smiled again. "But there is no need for secrecy any longer. You are Iyarri."

Pride swelled in me, and an eagerness to show my father my wings kindled alongside it. As for my mother—my heart tightened in my chest. "I should call my mom. I'm sure she's worried."

"If you were to call her, do you think you'd be able to not tell her?" Aamon asked. After considering for a moment, I shook my head. "Some things are best done in person," he said. "I'll take you to her house myself once you're sound."

"That might be best." Much as I wanted to soothe her worry, my father's words echoed through my thoughts. *She said she loved me, but her eyes told me the truth—fear, disgust, rejection. Nothing in the world has ever hurt me so much as that look.* There wasn't enough strength in my mind, my heart, or my body to weather her heartbreak. At least not yet.

I twisted my fingers around a feather, hating my selfish thoughts when I knew her anguish would be a thousand times worse.

Under Irel's endless patience, I relearned both my body and my long-lost Loagæth. Fragments of the Iyarri language returned to me, each word like a firefly in the dark. A familiar Loagæth word would pulse in my mind, and I'd chase after it. Oftentimes the word eluded me and faded back into the forgotten recesses of my mind. Sometimes, though, I caught a word and would hold it in my mind, as carefully as I'd cupped my hands around a firefly as a child. In time, I was able to respond to Irel in Loagæth, albeit in simple, fumbling fragments.

We stood in the open expanse of Aamon's gallery, one of Irel's hands on my spine, the other on my shoulder as I opened my wings, held them spread as long as I could, and folded them back down. Irel's smile was tranquil, and his marigold hair gleamed in the lamplight. "This is encouraging. Your body already knows what to do; it just has to relearn what it has never needed to use."

Footsteps approached, and Irel and I both turned toward the sound. Aamon arrived and gave us a quick bow, more a flicker of wings than anything. He set a bundle wrapped in fibrous paper on a nearby chair and said, "Irel, Sofiel said you're needed at Idura."

Irel kept his hands on my wing, reluctant to go. "Did she say what she needed?" he asked.

Aamon shook his head. "Just that it was Iadnah business."

"I'll gather my things. Thank you for bringing Sofiel's message." When Irel was ready to go he touched one of my wings, the blue of his hand a contrast to the copper-gold feathers. "I'll see you soon. Take care and don't push yourself."

"I won't."

"Good." He spoke to Aamon: "Call me if you have concerns. Fair winds."

"And clear skies." Aamon nodded as Irel headed up the wrought iron stairs to the roof. "Aurelia." Aamon held out the package he'd brought. "I've brought you a gift."

I undid a single length of ribbon and the paper folded open like a lotus flower, a square of white cloth in the center. I lifted it with tentative hands, the fabric spilling downward. The Iyarri dress had a scooping neckline, and delicate lacing pulled the sides in. The skirt was long and elegant, and the sleeves fitted to the elbows before ending in split bells. "It's beautiful. Thank you so much."

"You're welcome. I would have come sooner, but it's the first night of Nalvage and I had obligations to see to before I could leave."

"That means Idura is dark tonight?" I ran my fingers over the fabric, thinking of the five-day celebration of darkness and light.

"For tonight and tomorrow night, yes. After that, it's candlelit."

"It sounds beautiful."

"It is. It's the reason for your gift."

I lowered the dress in my hands. "What?"

"Nalvage is the perfect time to welcome you, and your father, into Iyarri society. We'll be meeting him shortly."

EIGHTEEN

"**M**Y FATHER?" I ASKED, excited and nervous at the prospect all at once.

Aamon bowed his head to Siyah's statue, his hands clasped into a tight knot behind his back. Grief clouded his eyes, but his voice was steady when he spoke. "Cæl broke the Iyarri laws enshrined in the Aisaro, but he still has more he could give to the Elonu-Dohe."

I pressed my lips together, not wanting to draw attention to Aamon's sorrow, but asked my question anyway. "How can you look at her like that and say you want my father to come back?"

Aamon turned and held one hand out to me with a smile. "Because I saw you made Iyarri while he cowered in exile. For every second of the rest of his life at Idura, he will have to live knowing I was there for you when he was not, that he can only return because of me."

Perfect forgiveness was likely beyond either Aamon or my father, but if my becoming Iyarri was enough for a tentative truce, that would be enough for me. "Tonight, though?" My wings quivered with nervous energy, excited at the possibility of being welcomed to Idura. I bit the inside of my cheek, remembering the way Miketh had held my face in his claws. *Speak our language again, human, and I'll tear your tongue from your head.* My wings pressed tighter against my back. "I'm still weak, and Irel said—"

"Irel will, at worst, be pleasantly surprised. He's fond of you." Aamon nodded to the dress in my human hands. "Why don't you get dressed, and come downstairs when you're ready? We have time before we need to leave."

I wanted to see my father, wanted to have the future I'd suffered for. Aamon had said becoming an Iyarri removed the punishment of being a Linnia; perhaps Cæl's transgression of fathering one could be pardoned too? I wasn't sure what life the two of us could have at Idura, but I wanted to find out. For the first time since the Iyarri had torn away my mundane life, optimism lit up my future in a way it never had when I thought I was human.

All my life I'd felt alone, awkward, and apart, not knowing how to fit in and afraid of how people would turn on me if they saw my feet. My three-toed feet made me a freak, a monster in the human world, and there was no magic ritual to dispel my abnormalities and tear down the walls my mother had built around me to keep me safe. Yearning pressed the confines of my heart outward. Amongst the Iyarri, though, I could belong, could experience a freedom that wasn't and never would have been possible in the human world.

In my room, I unplaited my hair and worked myself into the dress. I left my hair down, save for one lock at my temple, braided and secured with Lucien's hair spiral. Iyarri dress, Iyarri hair ornament, Iyarri wings, and even Iyarri feet. Lucien's spiral felt heavier—each sacrifice I'd made, willing and unwilling, added to its weight.

When I returned, Aamon was standing in front of the sliding glass doors overlooking the balcony. Outside, the clouds were heavy and the earth aglow with new-fallen snow. Aamon gestured for me to come and stand beside him. I walked forward, bumped one wing into the coffee table, and apologized.

Aamon chuckled. "Don't be sorry. Fitting that your first trip as an Iyarri is on such a beautiful night."

Flakes spiraled down from the sky, thick and fluffy. I bunched my toes up. "What should I do about my feet?"

Aamon pulled the balcony door open—frigid December air spilled over the floor and across my bare toes like ice water. I tensed, feeling the sensation of cold, but then relaxed, realizing that it was muted to a tingle. "You seem to have gained several Iyarri attributes, our higher temperature among them. The cold shouldn't bother you, although without an ipuran, your wings are obviously a concern." Aamon smiled, amused. "Though since it is Christmas, should anyone see you, we can write you off as a Christmas angel and my solpeth can take care of any problems."

We got into his car and wound our way through the Cities, the way to Idura less direct than I expected. I was grateful Aamon hadn't opted to fly. The distance, from what I could piece together, was great. My body was still bruised bone-deep; the journey would have been painful for me and trying for him.

"Did you tell my father about my wings?"

"And ruin the surprise?" Aamon's smile was subtle and knowing.

"I didn't think anyone knew where he was."

"Tiahmani did." I arched both my eyebrows in question and he explained. "I've never been able to pinpoint where your father ran off to, but I suspected she'd known for a good while. I suspected correctly, and she's eager for her brother to be accepted back."

When the car stopped, I was surprised to see the Cathedral of St. Paul. "Why are we here?"

"To meet Cæl. He wouldn't agree to meet at Idura, so I offered this instead."

It was still snowing as Aamon helped me out of the car. The tiny white flakes danced downward and laced bare branches and wrought iron with white. My bare feet left strange three-toed tracks, but wind and snow blurred them.

The windows of the cathedral were aglow, and from inside radiated the soft harmony of many voices singing. "Midnight Mass," I said.

"Yes." Aamon paused at a low, wrought iron fence that sectioned off a snowy parcel of land to the side of the cathedral. I followed his gaze up to the copper dome of the cathedral, the stained glass windows shining. "The view of a candlelit Midnight Mass from above is something to behold. May I show it to you?" I smiled, intrigued; if Aamon thought the view was worth seeing, it likely was. Aamon stood between my wings, clasped his arms around my waist, and pulled us into the sky. Even the short ascension made my bruised body scream, gravity pulling me down as Aamon carried me upward.

I exhaled in relief as Aamon set me on the narrow sill of a stained glass window; without my Iyarri feet, there would have been no way to stay on the small strip of stone. Aamon stood behind me and helped me balance, his feet curling around the edge of an even thinner run of granite.

Up so high, the wind gusted, catching my wings. Aamon steadied me and nodded to the window. "Look." I cupped my hands around my face and leaned closer.

High in the dome hung the glass Star of Bethlehem, bathing the church in golden light. The nave below was dim, but candelabras lit the altar with the wavering flicker of candlelight, and tiny reading lamps dotted the pews. People filled every seat in the colossal building and even more stood in the back. Poinsettias flowed from the altar in great swaths of red, and wreaths of evergreen adorned the walls.

A figure entered from the far side of the cathedral. My breath frosted on the window; I wiped it away with my hand and peered closer. The man was tall, blond, and wore a dark coat. The details of his face were blurred by the dim light, the stained glass, and the immense distance, but my hands gripped the stone and I pressed my face closer to the window all the same. Lucien—it had to be, but it couldn't be. Heart hammering with hope and dread, I watched as the man passed the pews, away from the front of the church, and stopped before a wrought iron stand filled with prayer candles. My heart a knot in my throat, I watched as he lit one of the candles, set the match aside, and bowed his head. His prayer complete, he neither made the sign of the cross nor put money into the tithe box, only turned and walked out of the cathedral. No, it couldn't be Lucien, but how badly I wished it were.

"Aamon." My father's voice rang across the icy sky. He descended from above us and hovered nearby, great wings tossing snowflakes around him.

Aamon turned, his white wings a curtain between me and my father. "Cæl, you decided to join us." Aamon's tone was inviting, but the sardonic, cruel edge to it made me uneasy.

"Where's Aurelia?" Cæl demanded.

In one motion Aamon lowered his wings and gestured to me. "Here, as I promised."

Cæl's confusion collapsed into stark realization. "Aurelia." My father's wings faltered for a single beat. "With wings?"

Aamon smiled, and I fumbled for words. "Are you okay?" Cæl asked.

"I'm—" The wind gusted, catching in my wings and threatening to sweep me off the icy stone. I scrambled, grabbing onto Aamon's arm with one hand and pressing the other to the stained-glass window—it was a sheet of ice under my palm. There were no handholds, just glass, sheer stone, and Aamon.

My father rushed forward, one hand extended toward me, but Aamon held up his hand. "That's close enough," he warned.

Cæl stopped. "Are you okay?" he repeated.

"I'm okay." I didn't feel so and likely didn't look it: my hair wind-tossed, my body unsteady and in danger of falling. The height made my stomach churn.

My father glared at Aamon. "What did you do to her?"

"Isn't she exquisite? You abandoned her, and I made her so much more than a half-breed pretending to be human." This time when Aamon looked at me, I didn't feel flattered or appreciated; I felt like an object he'd carved to suit his own desires. Desires that had little to do with my own. I cringed back, trying to move away from him, but there was only the ledge I stood on and open, empty air.

"I didn't abandon—just let me take her." The desperation in my father's eyes poured icy adrenaline into my veins, made my pulse jump.

Whatever Aamon had told him, had told me, wasn't true. We weren't going to Idura for a welcoming into Iyarri society. My thoughts careened inside my head like swallows gone mad, unable to put together why I was there or what Aamon intended.

"I am not giving her back to you so you can reduce her to a freak in exile." Aamon cast me an appreciative glance before returning his attention to Cæl. The ground was far below us, the distance full of eddies of blown snow; maybe I could glide to safety. The thought vanished with another gust of wind; I couldn't even hold my wings open in a still room, they'd never support me in the air.

"Aamon," my father pled, "I'll leave forever, whatever you want. Just don't hurt her."

Aamon's smile was as cold and beautiful as the snow in the sky. "But I have what I want. You, here, to see her as the angelic muse I've crafted her into." He turned to me and took me by both shoulders—pressed my back against the glass, far above the thousand people far below. "And you, here, to teach your father how it feels to lose something priceless."

Realization froze me as still as the stone form of Aamon's Semeroh. *You are the first and only one I have ever thought might be worthy of her place.* Not her place in life, but in death, as a tool of revenge against my father. I grabbed onto Aamon's forearms, twisting the fabric of his shirt in my hands. "Aamon, no, please."

Aamon hesitated, holding me in his hands as the mermaid held the blade over her prince's heart. Some of the victorious vengeance lifted from his features and his eyebrows drew together. "Siyah always reminded me that art requires sacrifice."

My palm left a sweaty streak against the icy glass. "No, it doesn't." My words shook. "Art requires courage."

The scrape of leather on metal must have been lost to the wind. Suddenly, blood erupted from Aamon's wing, the point of a silver blade shining in the wound. Hot droplets spattered my face, and Aamon screamed, his hands clenching my shoulders. Cæl rushed toward us, a blur of dark feathers and blades, and, with a flare of wings, Aamon thrust me backward through the stained-glass window.

NINETEEN

THOUSANDS OF PAINSTAKINGLY CUT pieces of glass rained down with me. I screamed and twisted, covering my face with my arms. My muscles bunched, and I tried to force my wings open, but they were too weak, too new. A sea of people below me pulled in their breath at once, and the warm air of the cathedral rushed past me. I closed my eyes, accepting the candlelit glass and snowflakes glittering in the air around me as the last thing I'd see.

When the impact came, it was not the stone floor that slammed into me, but another body. Tiahmani seized me in her arms as we hurtled toward the ground. She landed and buckled to one side as her leg bent with a wet snap; clenching her teeth, she kept running. The stunned congregation rose to their feet, a tide swelling, as Tiahmani fled under the great balcony that held the organ and through the marble narthex.

My wings flapped wildly, but they didn't stop Tiahmani from shoving open the front doors. We burst into the colder air outside. Voices, excited and astonished, neared.

"Give her to me. Hurry." My father's voice. Tiahmani dumped me into Cæl's arms, their wings thundering as they lifted off the ground and into the sky.

Shaking, I clung to Cæl and pressed my face into his neck. Still, the sensation of falling came over and over again, the twirling dread knowing that any second the impact could come. Cæl's pulse hammered beneath his skin, and his arms crushed down around me as if he felt it too. Within a few seconds, we were deep inside the snowing clouds, my father and Tiahmani somehow able to navigate through.

All at once, the adrenaline drained away and left me empty, shaky, and nauseous. The flight was short, but by the time we descended my skin and my clothes were damp with condensation. Far below us, and several blocks away from the cathedral, was Tiahmani's car. She landed gingerly, left foot curled off the ground. Cæl set me beside her. My whole body trembled and swayed, fine red cuts from the glass bright against my skin and marring the white of the dress. My voice broke around the threat of tears. "Aamon—"

My father cut me off, his voice directed at Tiahmani like a booming clap of thundersnow. "Take her to Catherine. Now."

Tiahmani's mouth worked wordlessly for a second before she managed to say, "I'll take her to—"

"No." Cæl's voice hit her as though he'd slapped her. It was the voice of a commander, a Heeoa, and it brooked no protest. "Take her to Catherine, and keep them safe until I get there."

Tiahmani leaned against the side of the car, face contorted in pain, her ankle wrenched out of line with rest of her leg. "And where are you going?"

"After Aamon." Cæl's wings pulled him into the air with such force that the air swirled my hair around my face.

Tiahmani scowled. "Get in the car before someone sees you."

As we drove away, my mind raced, tripping and stumbling over my tangled thoughts. Aamon's triumphant smile at Cæl's terror and desperation, the way his eyes had held me like a precious statuette, but most of all what he'd said—*And you, here, to teach your father how it feels to lose something priceless*. I wept, confused and terrified at how close I'd come to death.

Tiahmani slammed her hand into the dash and yelled, "Gephna, why does Cæl always have to be right?" Her face was stricken and her accent was thick, the words torn between Loagæth and English. The car accelerated onto the highway; moments of silence passed, with only the sounds of the snow under the tires, the steady flick of the windshield wipers, and my quiet sobs to fill them.

"If Cæl catches Aamon, he's going to kill him." Tiahmani glanced from the road to me. "I can't believe Aamon did that." She shook her head at my wings. "Or that." Swearing, she bit her knuckle. "Fuck me, yes I can. Why would you let Aamon take you to the cathedral?"

"I didn't. He said we were going to Idura."

"What? Why?" she asked, dumbfounded.

My words were measured as I tried to find where the puzzle pieces fit together. "He said tonight I'd be introduced as an Iyarri and . . ." Tiahmani's face twisted with disbelief and contempt—I stopped talking.

She glared at the flakes streaking toward the windshield. "You're a Linnia and, wings or not, you're no Iyarri. And you're sure as hell never going to be accepted by the Elonu-Dohe. They'll kill you."

I swallowed and turned toward the black landscape outside my window, hope imploding into a great pit of despair around my heart. And Aamon knew. Worse, he'd planned on it. The depth of his betrayal flayed me so deeply that I wrapped my arms around myself as his words played through my mind: *Siyah always reminded me that art requires sacrifice.* My stomach rolled, and I pressed my forehead to the cold glass. Aamon had given me wings so my father could watch my death as helplessly as Aamon once watched Siyah's execution—*to teach your father how it feels to lose something priceless.* And to do that, Aamon dangled everything my father could have wanted in front of him—his daughter so achingly close to Iyarri, the possibility of returning home—and smashed them both to pieces. Flecks of glass shimmered in my hair as I lifted my head.

Aamon's plan ended with my death—the realization dawned bleak and clear. He'd given no thought to how I'd survive and in what world—because I wasn't meant to have survived.

Despair and loneliness stretched out all around me like a cold, black sea, my Linnia body an island in the center. Too human for the Iyarri, too monstrous for the human world. The things I'd thought of as deformities—my feet, my brittle bones—were so insignificant, so easy to hide. Now, I couldn't even pretend to be human if I wanted to. A thousand small pleasures, a walk in a gallery, a quiet afternoon reading in a café, a shopping trip with my mother, lay sacrificed on the altar of wings.

Fear lapped higher, the bleak waves shrinking my future even more—what would happen if I were found, captured by humans? Images of sterile laboratories and cold cages made me shiver. There was no Iyarri stronghold to shelter in, no place in the human world where the Iyarri wouldn't find me. Discovery by either meant death.

Fresh tears stung the shallow cuts on my cheeks. I wished to take it all back.

The windows of my mother's house were dark when we pulled up. Tiahmani parked in the driveway, opened the car door, and swung both her legs out, hesitating before putting weight on her broken ankle. When she did, she swore and fell back onto the seat. Before I could offer her help, she grabbed the sides of the door once again and pulled herself out of the car, into the air. She touched down with one foot onto the front porch, and I slogged through the snow after her.

Tiahmani gave me a critical glare. "So, are you going to put an ipuran up, or are we waltzing in there like this and hoping your mom doesn't faint when she sees you?"

"I can't." In truth, I'd never tried. Irel had planned on working on it with me, but we hadn't gotten the chance. Doubt pressed in around me—perhaps Linnia couldn't do it at all.

"Great." She lifted the hem of her pants to her knee and I cringed. Tiahmani's golden skin was a screaming mess of reds and purples, her foot cocked at the ankle, the delicate joint swollen to twice the size of the other. Tiahmani took the flask from her belt; when she opened it the scorching scent of mulled spices, fire, and ash bloomed out. She drained the entire thing, melted snow running from her hair down her neck as she gulped. She returned the drained flask to her belt and gestured to the door. "Well?"

I reached for the doorknob, but my hand hovered over it, stilled by dread. Tiahmani reached past me and tried the door. It was unlocked and swung into the dark foyer, chased by a swirl of snow. "Mom? It's me," I called.

Catherine hurried down the stairs in her nightgown, barefoot. "Oh, thank God, I was so worried when I couldn't get a hold of you and I—"

Her face went white. Fear, disgust, rejection; all the things my father said he'd seen in her eyes were there, each a shamrock that grew together into one field of pain and loss. "Oh, my Lord, what did they do to you?" My mother crossed the room and laid one hand on my shoulder, the other cupping my face. She looked ill at the sight of my wings, staring at them like they were some sort of parasite and not a part of me.

Part of my heart broke off under the weight of her grief, crumbling under a torrent of shame and regret. Exhausted and overwhelmed, I released a shaky breath. "I'm sorry."

Tiahmani maneuvered her wings through the doorway and eased the door closed, cutting off the spill of cold air.

My mother's face did not recover its color and her lips trembled. "You," she said to Tiahmani as she gathered me to her and pulled me a few steps away. "You took Lia. You made me think you were human." Catherine shook her head as though it were hard for her to remember. She closed her hand over her pendant, the green stone and swirling silver giving her focus. "You said you were going to look after her."

Tiahmani leaned against the wall, her broken foot curled inches over the tile. She closed her eyes, gathering strength and patience. "I did," she said through clenched teeth.

"You said you were going to look after her," my mother repeated, her voice hardening as the lingering effects of Tiahmani's solpeth broke. "And I was right," her voice shook with righteous indignation. "I never should have let you take Lia." My mother's hand became a fist, clutching the side of my ruined dress. "What did you do to her?" she demanded, voice low and desperate. When no answer came she screamed her question again: "What did you do to her?!" Anguished tears spilled down her cheeks.

I cringed away from them both, head spinning.

Tiahmani flared her wings and limped a step closer, voice full of disdain. "What did I do to her? You're the reason she's Linnia. If it weren't for you, maybe those wings wouldn't be fucking useless."

"Useless?" My mother dropped the word like a dish to the floor.

Useless. In my mind, wings and flight were one. That I could have wings and never fly, that they were and would never be anything more than a freakishly beautiful decoration—the thought was a single thread woven into the tangle of panic in my chest. I pulled on it, trying to unravel it, but this only drew the knot of anxiety tighter. Irel had never mentioned the possibility and said strength would come in time—but what if it never did?

I stared at rug in the foyer, desperate to avoid my mother's face. "They're weak and new," I said, not sure of who needed convincing more, me or my mother. The fibers in the carpet twirled together in my vision. I closed my eyes and dug the heels of my palms into them.

The door opened, and I lowered my hands in time to see my father let himself in. His ponytail was undone, and his snow-dampened hair fell around his shoulders. What little color remained in my mother's cheeks evaporated. Cæl gave her a long, uncertain look. "Hello, Catherine," he said.

My mother wiped her cheeks and pressed her hand to her side to hide the way it shook. "Hello, Cæl."

He hesitated, but then in two large steps crossed the room and pulled her into an embrace both fierce and gentle, his wings dwarfing her. She wrapped her arms around him and pressed her cheek against his chest. After a minute she stepped back, her eyes bright with tears. "Of all the times I wished for you to come back, I'm glad you're here now."

Cæl pushed my mother's hair back from her face. "We can't stay. Get dressed and pack a few things, Catherine. We're going someplace safe."

Relief smoothed some of the creases of tension in her face. For once, she didn't have to face uncertainty alone. "I'll hurry," she said as she went upstairs.

Cæl ignored Tiahmani's disapproving glare and gestured to her leg, his face softening. "How is your foot?"

"My ankle's busted. I'll have to go back to Idura and have it healed."

My father's voice was understanding, but wary. "Be careful. We can't be sure what backlash this has caused, or what other plans Aamon may have for Aurelia, or for you."

At the mention of Aamon's name, Tiahmani reached behind her brother and pulled a short knife from the back of his belt, the blade still covered in Aamon's blood. She turned it over, her face grim, solemn, and betrayed. "You didn't kill him?"

He took his blade back and sheathed it. "No, I lingered too long after you caught Aurelia to find him. I recovered my okada and came here. I imagine Aamon's escape bothers you less than it should."

"He deserves to be brought to justice, not run through by a deserter Heeoa." Their eyes locked, but it was Tiahmani who looked away from her brother's accusatory glare. "Aamon told Aurelia if she had wings she'd be Iyarri. That they'd accept her."

Cæl's expression was tactical and contemplative. "Winged Linnia haven't been accepted as Iyarri for eons. But they were, at one point." He turned to me. "Tell me what other lies he fed you, pasahasa."

I wrapped my arms and wings around myself and related what was becoming an overwhelming tale. I spoke of Aamon's initial offer of wings. "After Miketh brought me to Idura, Aamon said the Iyarri would kill me without wings, but they'd accept me with them." My voice was small, uncertain in the face of my own naïveté. "So, I agreed."

Cæl's face was as cold and motionless as one of the angels carved above the cathedral's door, but his wings folded and unfolded like dark shadows behind him. "How did you not know that he was planning any of this?" he asked Tiahmani, words frigid.

Tiahmani folded her arms. "Gephna, Cæl, I didn't know!"

It all played over in my mind: the icy stained glass against my back, the resolute grief in Aamon's eyes. My voice was quiet, but everyone fell silent when I spoke. "He did it for Siyah. Aamon said Siyah believed all art required sacrifice, and that I was there to teach Cæl how it felt to lose something priceless."

Cæl swore and pinched the bridge of his nose.

"Why did you rush him?" I asked. "Aamon was listening to me. He might not have pushed me."

My father scowled. "If he went through all this, he was going to put you through that window one way or another. You came through it as Aamon intended, some heavenly being cast toward earth." I frowned, unsure. Aamon intended that, yes, but he'd hesitated, and for a second seemed to see me as Aurelia and not as some piece of angelic art. My wings sagged, despondent. Maybe I just wanted to wanted to believe that.

"I'm going back to Idura," Tiahmani said. Cæl stared at her, stone-faced. "What? You think I'm joining your little family expedition? I have a broken ankle, and all of Idura will be talking about what happened tonight. Do you want to know what they're saying or not?"

Cæl reconsidered. "That is probably best. Will you take the car?"

"No. I'll fly." She slung her arm across her brother's shoulders as he walked her toward the door. "The Laidrom will have my back. They dislike Aamon anyway and will be glad to hear I'm done with him." Hate and betrayal bled into her voice. "He didn't just throw your Linnia through that window to kill her. That was your death sentence, too, noromi. Fuck him."

Cæl helped his sister out the front door. "Thank you for saving Aurelia."

Tiahmani nodded. "Be safe, I'll join you as soon as I can. Fair winds."

"And clear skies, noro."

The door closed and my father walked back to me, worry in his face. "Pasahasa?" He pulled me to my feet, his wings cupped forward into a circle of dark-colored feathers. "If Aamon hadn't tricked you into this, I would celebrate your transformation."

"Even though I'm not Iyarri?" My throat tightened around the words, crushing the hope out of them and making them hard to say.

His claws sifted through my copper feathers, and his features softened. "They are Iyarri wings, and if you have them, they were meant to be yours."

I sighed, relieved. Cæl's hand tightened on my tender, weak wing, his expression determined and contemplative all at once. "If there is any chance you can fly, I'll see that you can. Those napta from the Laidrom you killed, are they still at Tiahmani's loft?"

"They should be." If Aamon hadn't found out about it and sent Laidrom there already.

"We'll stop there. Get what you can here, just in case." I turned toward the stairs but paused at his question: "Can you muster an ipuran?" I shook my head. "Hopefully that, too, will come in time, otherwise Aamon will have made you whole and damned you all at once. We have to be able to survive in the human world."

Dread boxed in around me—what if I had suffered so much for wings that might not fly and couldn't be hidden? I turned with a shake of feathers, but it didn't chase off my dour thoughts. "I'll go pack."

I'd ascended the stairs in my mother's house a million times, but now they were too narrow, the passage claustrophobic as my wings scraped the walls and dragged on the stairs behind me. The clothes in my room were ones I'd already passed twice over, and few of the options would work with the wings. Other things found their way into the remaining space in my old backpack: a sketchbook, my battered pencil case, and an airy scarf patterned with the mottled garden hues of *Le Bassin Aux Nymphéas*. I paused partway down the stairs, aware of my parents' voices in the sunroom. One of the doors was open, and in its reflection I could see my mother on the couch, Cæl using the coffee table as a bench. They sat facing one another, leaning forward and clasping hands over my mother's packed bags. They were silhouetted by a small lamp behind them. My father's claws stroked the back of my mother's pale hand, and I wondered whether their sharpness made her uneasy.

"I have a house in New York, big enough for the three of us," Cæl said.

My mother bowed her head, her copper and silver curls brushing her shoulders. "Will they find us?"

Cæl stayed silent for a contemplative moment. "They might. But it's the safest place we can be."

"You've been there all this time? In New York?" Her soft voice carried the undertone of an accusation.

"Yes." His wings sagged, heavy with regret. "The longer I was away, the harder coming back was."

"And you couldn't have asked me this twenty-five years ago?"

"I'm asking you now. You have no idea how much I regret waiting this long to see you again."

"Oh, I might have some idea." Her voice was wry, and he shook his head and smiled. "What do you think of Lia?" she asked.

"She looks a lot like you." He paused, uncertain. "When I first saw Aurelia, I thought she *was* you."

My mother chuckled. "If only. Time hasn't been as kind to me as it has been to you. You're not any older."

Carefully, as if he feared she might pull away, Cæl unclasped one of his hands and touched my mother's silvering curls. "You're as beautiful as the day I left."

"Considering I'd just given birth when you left, I'm not sure if that's a compliment."

My father laughed and, for a moment, I saw a bit of how they might have been years ago. "You've always been beautiful. Aurelia got a lot of that."

"She got a lot of you too. And more lately." The joking tone faded from her voice, and my father's face sobered. "Will she be okay?"

"I think so."

"She's more Iyarri than human, now." I tightened my hand around the railing, hating the heartbreak in her voice.

"She's still your daughter and she needs you." Cæl put one hand on my mother's shoulder. "Will you come to New York with me?"

"If I said no, that I'm staying here, would you take Lia with you?" *And leave me alone and in danger?* was the unspoken ending to the question.

There was a pause filled with the shifting sound of his wings. "I don't know."

"Yes you do, Cæl, it's written all over your face."

"I don't want to separate you two."

"But you would." I swallowed hard, thinking the same thing. "To keep her safe, I think you would." There was a heartbroken note in her voice.

Cæl shouldered one of my mother's bags and held out his hand to her. "Please, Catherine."

I stepped onto the landing and opened the front door. With a resolve I wasn't sure I possessed until I heard my own voice, I said, "The three of us need to go now, together."

TWENTY

THE BRITTLE SOUND OF my mother's weeping woke me, her cries echoing off the high ceilings and driftwood-gray floors of Cæl's house. I heard the comforting resonance of my father's voice, but her heartbroken sobs went on.

I stifled a groan as I pulled myself out of the tianta, body still stiff from the long, cramped drive. My bare feet whispered over the wood floors as I stole to the door and opened it enough to peer through. Two curved, padded benches flanked a circular coffee table in the center of the great room. My mother sat tucked against Cæl's side, one of his great wings cupped across her back. Her face was in her hands, and her Iyarri pendant hung downward, flashing green as it shook with her shoulders. "Her back is ruined," she sobbed. "Those scars . . ."

I covered my mouth with my hand and leaned against the doorframe, sagging under the weight of her heartbreak and my guilt. Soft feathers brushed the luminous scars around my wings. I clutched my dress to my chest with one hand and reached over my shoulder with the other: the back was undone, the center piece peeled away, my skin left bare. My fingertips traced the scars that threaded up the base of my neck.

"She is not ruined, Catherine."

"You saw her back. And she can't even hide her"—she stumbled around the word *wings*—"how she looks now."

Cæl smoothed her hair. "Perhaps she can learn. There are many things we don't know, but if you give up on her now she may not try at all."

She steadied her voice and wiped her face with her sleeve. "I haven't given up on her."

"I know." He lifted his eyes to me, the set of his jaw resolute. "I'll do whatever I can to make sure she flies so those scars aren't in vain."

My mother gave him a weak smile and put her hand on his knee. "I'm going to head to bed. It's late." She stood, walked into the den, and pushed the door closed behind her. I retreated into my room, grateful she hadn't seen me.

Cæl knocked and entered a few moments later. "She's not staying with you?" I asked, tracing the smooth wood of the tianta with the pads of my toes.

Uncertainty moved across the shadows of his face. "Most our time together was spent with Catherine assuming I was human. We've never been together for this long with the truth between us. It's best to take things slow."

As I child, I'd wondered if the divide between my parents was because of me, because of my deformities. I found myself, as an adult, wondering similar, dark thoughts.

Something must have shown on my face, because Cæl tipped his wings in acknowledgement. "I wish I had better words of comfort for you, but I don't. What was done at this point cannot be undone. Don't let it destroy you."

"Don't you mean ruin me?" My tone was bitter. A thousand hopeless thoughts twisted my mind—I couldn't fly, couldn't hide my wings, couldn't live in either the human world or the Iyarri one. Lucien was dead, and Aamon had betrayed me for his chance at revenge. What was left to ruin?

Cæl ignored my comment and closed the back of my robe for me. "I did not say what I did to Catherine to make her feel better. I believe you can fly, but I worry that if we wait to strengthen your wings they may never hold you. I want to train you in Capmiali, like you were a Laidrom apprentice learning our fighting style."

I hesitated, nervous. The most physically demanding thing I had ever done in my entire life was yoga, and I'd stopped after the studio implemented a no-socks policy. I wanted to try Capmiali, but the fear of failure wilted my budding eagerness.

A smile pulled at the corner of his lips as Cæl bent and picked up Lucien's bag from where it lay in a pile of backpacks and duffle bags.

"Where did you get that?" I asked.

"From Tiahmani's loft. We stopped while you slept." He extracted the napta and leveled his gaze to mine. "You swear you killed the Iyarri who bore these arms?" For a beat he was again Heeoa, commander.

"I swear; I killed him." The words came unwavering: I was neither proud nor regretful to have ended the Laidrom's life.

He touched the napta in my lap. "There are two ways to earn the right to bear Laidrom arms. One is to pass initiation, the other is to kill a blooded Laidrom in combat." He set the other bladed gauntlet in my hands. "These are yours to bear."

A kernel of excitement sprouted amongst uncertainty. I was looking forward to learning to move with the grace and speed of Tiahmani. "When will we start?"

"In the morning. Capmiali training is done in Loagæth. You mentioned it's been coming back to you; hopefully this will accelerate the process." He closed one massive, clawed hand over my slender shoulder, and I felt a fundamental shift in our relationship. It was in the way he looked at me, at my wings, his love tempered with some unspoken expectation. "Get some rest; you'll need it." He turned toward the door. "Goodnight, pasahasa."

"Goodnight, essia." After he departed I took my sketchbook from one of my bags and sank into the cushions in the curved tianta, my mind too full to return to sleep. I wished for a proper, heavy blanket to curl up in, but Iyarri used their wings as blankets. The house stilled to sanctuary-like silence as Cæl settled down to sleep in his room. Even the design of my father's house reminded me of a temple: gray and square with a large, slanting roof topped by a cupola.

I opened the sketchbook to the first blank page, hovering the tip of the graphite above the smooth surface. Once I touched the pencil to the paper, there was movement and release. The wordless tumult of hopelessness, of despair, lashed across the page in a thunderstorm of blacks, whites, and grays. A barren landscape full of naked trees with gnarled branches reached to scratch the sky, the heavens above dark with clouds. In the foreground, symbols from *Angels Unseen* were etched into the rain-pummeled sand, washing away with each raindrop. And in the center a rippling puddle gathered—in it a single white feather, cupped upward like a boat on a stormy sea.

"Again." My father boomed the Loagæth word. Sweat ran down my face. Oi biah, the first stance. I bit my lip, trying to keep my wings steady as I mimicked him: left arm at my side, bent at the elbow, forearm parallel to the floor, palm up; the right arm crossed in front of the chest, palm to the floor. Toes splayed, balanced.

Sunlight streamed into the great room, and I focused on my father. He trained shirtless and in wide-legged, raw-hemmed Laidrom pants, the scars on his naturally hairless arms and torso more lustrous than even his skin. The largest triskele patterns on his deltoids spiraled in on themselves and ended in stylized feathers reminiscent of talons or scorpion's stingers.

"Second stance." Cæl's voice was critical, commanding. I rocked forward on my toes, stepped forward with my other foot, and swept my right arm outward in a forward strike. I arched my wings out and upward, fighting for balance; the overexerted muscles were rubbery, and my feathers shook like dead leaves on a winter branch. Arms leaden, I clenched my jaw and struggled through the pose. Cæl's voice struck like a whip. "Third." I followed his movements: a sweeping turn that used one wing to block an invisible assailant, the left arm following through with a strike.

Cæl watched me out of the corner of his eye as I completed the stance. "Fourth." Gritting my teeth against the shaking in my overworked wings, I stepped forward, crossed my arms in a block, and side-stepped with a sweeping motion that required me to lean back impossibly far for a human body. I cupped my wings forward to balance the pose, but one of my wings buckled and dipped lower, and I stumbled backward, breaking the form.

My father stepped out of the fourth position and said, "Again. Oi biah." His face was hard, his mouth a grim line.

My shoulders sagged and my arms, too heavy for me to lift, hung at my sides. "I can't," I said in English.

"In Loagæth," he barked.

"I can't," I repeated in Loagæth, the words breathless and pleading.

"Yes, you can."

"Then I won't." I glared at him, exhausted and frayed. He was wrong. I wasn't strong enough to do what he and Tiahmani did so effortlessly.

"Yes, you will. Again. Oi biah."

"Cæl." My mother's voice was soft, but we both turned to see her standing at the edge of the great room. "Let her rest. You've been at this for three hours already." Her face was soft with sympathy, but she searched for her daughter in my strange body.

"Her wings need to gain strength."

My mother stared down her scarred Heeoa, her eyes like green fairy-fire. "You're pushing her too hard."

"No, I'm not." He turned toward me, his wings blocking my mother, and switched back to Loagæth. "Again. Oi biah." The lines of Cæl's face were unyielding, and as hot sweat trickled down my skin my spark of defiance dimmed to resentment and obedience. There would be no arguing, begging, or yelling my way past the orders of a Heeoa.

Giving my wings a shake, I dragged my body back into the first stance. "Oi biah."

My father and I flowed through Capmiali for the better part of another hour before he declared the session over. "You're doing well," he said.

I clenched my toes until the talons dug into the hardwood floor. "Thank you." The words came clipped and hollow.

"Go shower. Afterward, I'll show you how to clean your wings." My feathers were dull with sweat, the copper color muted from travel.

My father's bathroom was dominated by a large shower and a deep oval tub that could have sat four people, or one Iyarri, wings and all. I wanted a bath, but couldn't muster the effort—the prospect of filling the tub may as well have been scaling a mountainside. Instead, I wrenched on the hot water in the shower and sank into a puddle of spent muscles on the tile. Water pummeled my body; I flopped my wings away from my back, the staccato of droplets painful and wonderful all at once. The water drained into my scars and turned in tiny, coursing rivers over the sensitive skin. While the sweat rinsed from my skin, the water beaded off my feathers and they regained none of their former luster. I lay there in the drumming water, mind empty and body limp until the hot liquid became warm, became cool. Muscles quivering in protest, I got my hands under me and pushed up, but my arms buckled and I flopped back down, feathers slapping around me. It took three tries for me to haul myself back to my feet. Even those ached, the arches sore and toes wanting to curl.

Once dressed, I found my father waiting for me in the great room. He'd returned the curved benches and the coffee table to their normal places and spread a thin leather chamois over the tabletop. On top of the chamois sat a few folded cloths and several clear bottles of oil. Smaller, darker vials sat nearby, each topped with a black cap. I eased myself down until I sat by his side, letting my wings fall behind the bench. He handed me a heavy amber bottle and took off the lid. "Hold that still while I pour." My resentment cooled and I obliged, curious how bottles of oil were supposed to clean anything.

Cæl filled it three-quarters full with a thick, clear oil, and added a bit of a second oil the color of oxidized honey. When he was done he capped it and gave it a shake. "Add any of those plant essences for scent." I uncapped each of the vials and breathed in—each vaporous and potent, but natural and clean-smelling. I tinkered, adding a few drops of one essence and a few drops of another until the aroma of green moors, nighttime dew, and vanilla wafted out of the bottle.

Cæl picked up a cobalt bottle and uncapped the lid, a familiar woodsy smell escaping. I realized this cleansing oil made his wings smell as they did, giving them a signature scent of ancient woodlands, just as Tiahmani's smelled of dragon's blood and ginger, or Aamon's of white sandalwood and amber.

With a quick, practiced motion, he settled a corner of the soft cloth over the mouth of the bottle and tipped it forward and back, dampening the fabric.

I mimicked him, pulling my wing forward and stroking the feathers with the cloth in small diagonals that followed the lay of the feathers. The oil on the cloth was not enough to leave the feathers greasy or damp, but polished them to a soft shine. He sifted through his feathers, working each one from the base of the quill down the blade. Emulating his motions, I stroked my own feathers with the sweet-scented oil. The feathers regained their copper luster, the edges brighter gold and the teardrops in my unalah gleaming. Preening proved as repetitive and soothing as brushing my hair before bed, and beneath the feathers, my skin felt moisturized. We worked in silence until my father, taking pity on my slowness, set aside his oil and cloth and helped me.

While I cleaned the front of my wings, he worked on the back, his fingers deft and efficient. It was comforting, and some of the weariness lifted from my fatigued muscles. When we finished, I smoothed the traces of oil on my hands over my hair—both my tresses and my wings shone, glossy and bright.

That night, I found my father at the kitchen table, Mastho's napta deconstructed in front of him. A sleeve of metal tools sat unfolded nearby, and pieces of leather and lacing scattered the surface. Cæl had removed the blades from the gauntlets and the metal gleamed under the lamplight. I made a cup of tea and sat across from him, entranced by the artful ingenuity of the weapon. The napta was as fascinating in pieces as it was a whole. Iyarri craftsmanship blended aesthetics and functionality, with few concessions to either one or the other. I traced one finger over the metal inlaid in the gauntlet, feeling the perfection of its flow, its proportions.

"You were angry with me," my father said without looking up. "You have never taken such a tone with me as you did today while we trained."

Unable to bring myself to lie and say no, I said, "You didn't believe me when I said I couldn't do more."

"Because you could, and you did."

As the revelation settled on me, I lifted the teacup to my lips and blew, dissipating the steam. "You think I lied to you?"

"No, but I don't think you have any idea what you are capable of. You limit yourself to what a human should be able to do." He caught my eyes, his words both encouragement and challenge. "You can be as graceful, and as deadly, as any full-blooded Iyarri if you let yourself realize it."

Pride swelled within me—he thought I could do even what I doubted—but the joy in his confidence waned when I pictured the way my mother watched: strange forms with an unfamiliar body. "It bothers Mom." I picked up a stray scrap of leather and fingered its smooth surfaces and rough edges. "That look you told me she gave you when you showed her what you are? She gave me that look, too."

"Catherine spent a long time pretending you were something you were not." *Human.* The word hung unspoken between us. "You have to realize her biggest fear is the one I instilled in her—that because of what you are, you could be hunted. The further away you get from human, the more danger she sees. She is afraid, and she has every right to be, but in time, she will accept how you are now." He picked up one of the gauntlets. "Hold out your left arm for me." Cæl draped the leather over my arm; the gauntlet was too large, and he marked the overage with a piece of white chalk.

His love for me was different now that I was winged, as were his expectations. My mother had been able to pretend her daughter was human for twenty-five years, and now that my father had me, more specifically a winged version of me, he wanted an Iyarri daughter. "We'll train more tomorrow?" I asked, the question laced with dread. I wasn't sure I'd be able to get my body out of bed, much less do Capmiali come dawn.

"Yes." He flattened the leather of the gauntlet in front of him and used a short, sharp blade to trim the excess off. "I am not doing this to you to be cruel."

"I understand." His fear of me being winged but flightless was written all over his face. Perhaps there was nothing worse for an Iyarri. The golden kintsukuroi scars that gleamed in my mended back were a high price to pay to remain earth-bound.

Our conversation faded into silence, and I watched him work with an artist's patient fascination. Cæl used a flat metal hook to seat the airy metal frame holding the blade into the top of the gauntlet. He checked the leather against my arm, then punched holes into it. Along one side, he set metal eyelets; down the other, hooks. Cæl wove a length of supple leather cord through the eyelets, leaving loops between each one and a short length at the end. It allowed the gauntlet to be put on with one hand, the loops of cord fastened to the opposing hooks, and the whole thing to be pulled tight in a matter of seconds.

When he switched to the right-hand gauntlet I caught his eye and raised my eyebrows, hopeful. "Explain to me what you're doing? In Loagæth?"

Some of the tension was chased off his features by the ghost of a smile. When he spoke again it was in the Iyarri language, and I understood. "Of course, pasahasa."

TWENTY-ONE

WINTER HERSELF SEEMED DETERMINED to help hide us. Day after day passed where thick clouds choked out the sunlight and dumped so much snow that Cæl's house was buried to the bottoms of the windows. My mother's touch appeared across Cæl's house in ways that made it more like home—a vase of holly and calla lilies on the dining room table, a soft throw for the benches in the great room. Cæl and my mother often retired to the den at night to read; sometimes I joined them with my sketchbook, but more often I sat on one of the stone benches in the snow-covered garden behind the house and practiced my ipuran. I was not immune to the cold, as I first thought. My tolerance for it was higher—I didn't need so much as a coat until it was well below freezing, but eventually I'd start to shiver, all the faster if I was snow-dampened.

Cæl's house was deep in the upper regions of New York—there wasn't a single streetlight, just acres of trees and hills and sky. I exhaled a plume of vapor and settled onto one of the stone benches.

The spiral twined in my hair flashed in the moonlight, leading me down the dimly lit corridors of my mind where a not-quite human girl and a kiaisi sat in front of a fire. Self-consciousness, dread, and the shame of kept secrets seeped into my stomach. I shook my wings and scattered the memory and the imperfect ipuran before it coalesced into an illusion. Better, perhaps, to try to lay the ipuran atop my Iyarri form, like restoring a painting. I ran my human fingers over the knife's-edge of a feather, the edge of the vane rippling, and closed my eyes again.

In the darkness behind my eyelids, I painted myself with the slender human feet I wished for a thousand times growing up—petite with five perfectly tapering toes. Snowflakes brushed my cheeks and I squeezed my eyes tighter. The cracked and shattered landscape of my back I made smooth and whole. I erased my wings, muted my radiant skin, and reduced my irises from polished pewter to dull granite.

The image of human me became solid in my mind. The longer I pictured it, though, the more it took on its own form, separate from the Linnia body I had inhabited all my life. The illusion settled over me like a second, airy skin. I peeked through parted lashes, wary I'd chased off my progress by looking. My wings were still there, crossed over three-toed feet with the henna-colored talons. And yet the airy feeling of the ipuran remained.

I eased myself off the bench and stepped onto the cold bricks. The ipuran wavered and I paused to steady it, then reached for the French doors leading into the great room. Firelight flickered in the den. As I passed through the threshold, my mother looked up from her book, and it slipped closed, her place lost. A knot formed in my throat and I went still, the pride in my accomplishment swept away by a torrent of guilt.

Hope. It eclipsed my mother's entire face—to her, I was human, right down to my bare feet. My father followed her gaze, surprise crossing his face before it faded to pride and relief. My mother stood and walked around me, avoiding my wings even though she couldn't see them. She stopped in front of me, scrutinizing, but not as hard as I knew she could. She didn't *want* to see through the ipuran. I was deceiving her, betraying her, and she, in her heart of hearts, preferred that lie. Unexpected resentment surged inside me, shaking my concentration.

"Focus, pasahasa," Cæl said, but my ipuran dissipated like a breath of warm air evaporating from a cold window.

My true form surfaced, and my mother took a half step backward, her hopeful expression swallowed by disappointment and grief. "Very nice, sweetheart," she said as she returned to the couch, picked up her book, and leafed for her place with a schooled, flat expression.

The distance between us expanded, until the space from where I stood to where she sat seemed a thousand miles. My heart contracted with anguish even as my temples thrummed with anger. I didn't expect her to prefer me with wings and gleaming scars and claws, but to see how badly she wished those parts of me gone so plainly on her face . . . "That's all you have to say?" My words were both an accusation and a plea for reason. Hot tears stung the edges of my eyes. For her to ignore that I was as good as dead without an ipuran, to not even be the smallest bit relieved that I could feign humanity if I needed to—my thoughts broke down into white blotches of rage.

My mother snapped her book closed and gave me an icy, even stare. "I'm glad you can pretend to be human." She said it without an ounce of happiness, and a twist of bitterness on *pretend*.

"What choice do I have?" I yelled, hands clenching into shaking fists. In an instant it was every argument we'd ever had all over again—my fury and heartache colliding with her sorrow and cold resentment. The only thing missing was that neither of us had put the kettle on.

If my mother said anything, it was lost to the crack of my wings closing, the sound as loud and sharp as a wet sheet snapping in the wind. I spun on my heel and fled firelight for the winter garden and solitary stone bench. Tucking my knees to my chest, I wrapped my arms and wings back around me and tried to keep the sob knotted in my chest from escaping.

Fuck her. The thought came in on a tidal swell of anger and receded with a pull of guilt and realization. Her life was a cage of consequences for choices she'd made because of Cæl's ipuran. Right up until the night I was born, each decision she'd made—to love my father, to have sex with him, to suffer her mother disowning her rather than give me up—was built on Cæl deceiving her into thinking he was human. She had sacrificed her education and her own mother's approval for her lover and a child she'd already named Liath. In one puff of an ipuran she'd learned the child growing inside her wasn't even human.

A shooting star flashed across the sky, disappearing over the tops of the bare, black tree line. I pressed my lips together and ruffled my wings, settling the ipuran back over me with a sigh.

She was wary of how much I'd changed—it rested like a stone at the bottom of the deep green pools of her eyes. Though a lot had happened to me, I was in the center of my transformation; my mother, an outsider, was only able to watch as I became more and more Iyarri.

Behind me, the door to the great room clicked open; I kept my concentration on my ipuran and pretended not to hear it, half-hoping it was my mother coming to make amends.

A snowy missile exploded off my feathers and spilled in a glittering cascade down my wing. Not far away, Cæl was packing a second snowball. "You kept your concentration. Good job, pasahasa." My shock faded to gratitude; he appreciated my progress in a way my mother could not. Cæl's smile grew and he threw the snowball, overhand and hard. I swept my wings to the side and got to my feet in the same motion, the snowball streaking past me. I grinned, scooped up some of my own ammunition, and caught him on the shoulder. He rushed me with a double handful of snow. My laughter rang out over the icy landscape as I dashed through the garden, giddy with the newfound grace and speed at which I moved. Cæl caught up to me and dumped snow on my head in a tingling shower that took my ipuran with it.

"How nice to find you enjoying yourself, noromi." Tiahmani's voice was as cold as the starlight overhead. Cæl and I looked up and found her perched on the edge of the roof like a gargoyle. She opened her wings and glided to the ground.

"Tiahmani." He walked toward her, shaking the snow from his wings.

She stood stone-faced. "I've had a long day, so whenever you're done out here, why don't you come inside so we can talk." While Tiahmani never lost her Iyarri poise, her movements were weary as she turned toward the house, no sign of her limp. We followed her inside; she unbuckled her belt and hip bags, sat at the kitchen table, and dumped her bags at her feet.

Cæl poured her a hot cup of coffee and set it in front of her. She wrapped both clawed hands around it. "I missed you, too."

Cæl's annoyance softened into concern. "How are things at Idura?" My mother stepped into the doorway, brows laced with confusion. Cæl repeated himself in English for her.

"Nobody knows—" Tiahmani began.

"In English, noro, please." He nodded to my mother.

Tiahmani glared at him and pulled her wings tight, but complied. "Nobody knows Aurelia is yours, or that Aamon was behind what happened at the cathedral. Anyone who knows she's a Linnia has kept their mouth shut." I thought about Nesah and how sweet and concerned she was; I doubted she'd bear the burden of secrecy well. "There is an investigation to see who tried to reveal us to the plodders. Aamon was appointed head of that committee."

My father shook his head. "He was appointed, or did he appoint himself?"

"Does it matter?" she snapped.

Cæl shook his head. "Did he say why he did it?"

"You know why he did it, Cæl. He got to fuck you over without breaking the Aisaro. Even if he is caught, I can't imagine there'd be much of a punishment."

My mother interrupted. "No punishment? For trying to kill Lia?"

Tiahmani's tone was like acid. "No. Because of you, Aurelia is a Linnia and—"

Cæl cut her off. "Enough, Tiahmani." Tiahmani's glare should have withered my mother, but Catherine met it, unflinching. My father continued, "With Ohlera presiding over the rule of law, the Aisaro has no spirit of the law, only the letter. Aurelia, being a Linnia, is not an Iyarri. The rules that govern us do not apply to her, save ordering her killed for the crime of being Linnia." Cæl turned back to his sister. "Has Aamon told anyone I was there?"

"No. He's smarter than that." Tiahmani refolded her wings and drank her coffee. "If everyone is chasing an invisible enemy, there's less focus on him."

"If what he did isn't against your laws, then why won't he admit what happened?" My mother asked.

Cæl tried to explain. "Aamon, as an Aldaria, is supposed to use the myth of angels to divert attention from us, not direct it toward us. Considering Aamon's high standing in the Elonu-Dohe, his actions would be frowned upon at worst, but that's still something he'd prefer to avoid."

Dread muted my voice. "So, then what? We hide forever?"

Cæl's expression was grim. "Only an Ohlera, an Iyarri law-speaker, could spare your life. Or mine, or your mother's. And that will not happen." He sighed and refilled Tiahmani's cup. "Does anyone know you came to New York?"

She leaned against Cæl's side. "No. I was careful, and Aamon is tied up with his 'investigation.'" She paused. "He's not stupid, though. He'll assume I ran to you."

Just then, there was the nearly inaudible sound of compressing snow on the roof—Tiahmani and my father looked at one another, tensing.

Catherine managed to say, "What is—" before my father grabbed her in one hand and me in the other and shoved us toward my room.

"Stay there and be silent," he whispered. His eyes were intense, and his movements quick and deft as he crossed the great room, looking at the moonlit cupola before he headed into his bedroom. Seconds later he came back out, lacing his napta with frightening precision, his hands a blur of motion over the deep red leather. In practiced coordination, Tiahmani rushed out the front door and my father out the back.

Something heavy struck the roof and rolled toward the back of the house. I turned just in time to see two winged bodies freefall over the eaves and to the ground in a cascade of broken icicles. My father flared his wings, righting himself, and landed on his feet and one hand. His assailant rolled as soon as he hit the ground, clearing the range of my father's napta in a flurry of white snow. There was no squaring off or sizing one another up, only motion. My mother stilled at the devastating speed with which the two Iyarri moved. Cæl leapt toward his attacker, bringing napta blades down in a flashing, starlit arc. The other Iyarri crossed his own napta, caught the blow, and directed it aside.

The intruder called out in Loagæth, "Heeoa, stop. I did not come here to fight you."

My father paused, napta poised. "Why are you here, Miketh, if not to die?"

Miketh, my captor. I stilled, remembering his crushing grasp on me as we'd flown to Idura, leaving Lucien to die in the dark.

Miketh snapped his blades back and slowly unwound the swath of cloth wrapped over his nose, regarding Cæl as an apparition. He saluted, bowing from the waist, crossing his gauntlets over his chest and fanning his wings out parallel to the icy ground.

Cæl regarded him with an even look. "Don't bow to me, Miketh. I am no longer your Heeoa."

Miketh straightened, shaking the snow from his kestrel-colored wings and folding them into place. "Then I will call you it freely, out of respect and not obligation."

A shadow of wings flickered as Tiahmani wheeled overhead and settled on the snowy ground beside Cæl. She clasped forearms with Miketh. "You bastard, I thought Aamon had sent someone to follow me."

Miketh's smile was droll. "He did. Aamon asked me."

Tiahmani's gleeful expression evaporated, and they headed inside.

I translated for my mother, who retreated deeper into the darkened bedroom. "We shouldn't be seen," she whispered.

The Iyarri came inside a moment later. Miketh's bow gleamed in his grasp, as exotic and frightening as he was. The string was black and woven back and forth between the limbs of the bow, making it look like a five-string harp. The claws at the ends of his fingers were just as dark, and I put my hand to my cheek, remembering the way they'd pricked my skin as he'd threatened to tear out my tongue. Nevertheless, I edged back out into the short hallway so I could see into the great room. Miketh set his things at his feet, and his eyes flicked to the hallway where I stood. I suppressed a shiver. He was as fearsome as I remembered, his shoulder-blade-length hair partially braided and tied off with leather and metal trappings.

"Why are you here?" my father asked Miketh.

The colors of Miketh's wings shifted under the lamplight. At the ends of his black unalah were blotches of orange rimmed in gray like unblinking, searching eyes. "Aamon asked me to follow Tiahmani and see where she went, who she's associating with."

"That was all?"

"Yes, Heeoa." He paused for a moment. "I don't trust Aamon. I don't know if he expected me to delegate his request, but I saw to this myself because things with him haven't added up for a while. Not since the night the kiaisi killed Ikkar and I brought that plodder girl to Aamon." Even though I could hear him clearly I leaned forward, heart pattering. "When I checked up on it, Aamon said they'd gotten the information they wanted from the girl, Tiahmani had killed her at Aamon's request, and then gone to Lilnon. The next night I see Aamon carrying the plodder girl out all wrapped in blue cloth. She wasn't dead—she looked right at me."

A memory, hazy through pain and drugs, surfaced. Miketh had been the moving Iyarri statue I saw as Aamon carried me out of Idura.

Miketh shook his head. "And then this 'angel' crashes through a window in front of a thousand people, but nobody can find her. The same night, Aamon shows up with a bloody wing and Tiahmani with a broken ankle. Irel and Hataan weren't even done with Tiahmani when Aamon asked me to have her followed. The last thing I expected was to find she'd come to you." His voice was laced with the faintest traces of both hope and disappointment. For a Laidrom, I imagined there were no acceptable reasons a Heeoa might leave their post save, perhaps, death.

"Ask it, Miketh. Your question is plain on your face." My father's voice was flat, calm.

"Have you been here the whole time? What kept you from returning?" He turned to Tiahmani. "How long have you known he was here?"

Cæl's voice was somber. "What I would tell you is a death sentence to myself and those that matter much to me. Do you want to bear the weight of the truth?"

Miketh nodded, and I watched a droplet of melted snow run down the edge of a long black feather and fall to the floor. "I accept the weight of your secret as my own, Heeoa."

Cæl regarded his Vohim for a moment before he called to me. "Come here, Aurelia."

My heart pounded and I tried to step forward, but fear froze my limbs and they wouldn't move. I took a deep breath—Cæl wouldn't let anything happen to me. Willing myself forward, I walked to my father's side, talons clicking on the wood floor. Miketh evaluated me the same way I'd imagine he would a tactical plan. "You've met my daughter before," Cæl said.

"Your daughter?" Miketh shook his head. "No, I don't think I . . ." He stopped when his eyes fell on my hands. Human hands, with delicate, tapering fingers and smooth, pale ovals for fingernails. His confusion deepened when he saw my bare Iyarri feet.

"I don't imagine you have many human captives that speak Loagæth," I said with a soft, knowing smile.

Recognition surfaced across his features before he gave a single, dis-concerted shake of his head. "No, I do not."

My father glanced over his shoulder and said, "Catherine?" She walked to Cæl's other side, features taut and wary. "Catherine is Aurelia's mother."

There was a flicker of revulsion as Miketh looked from his exalted Heeoa, to my mother, to me. Although Miketh followed his Heeoa to

English, his melodic Loagæth accent was so heavy it nearly turned the English into song. "This still does not explain the sudden appearance of her wings. She was a plodder when I caught her."

Cæl put a hand on my arm. "Explain to Miketh what happened to you?"

I settled onto the bench beside my father, uneasy under the dissecting way Miketh weighed each of my changes since he last saw me: the luminosity of my eyes, the pallor of my skin, and, of course, my wings. His gaze settled on my hands, the one strange feature in what would otherwise pass as an Iyarri body. The story was long, and while I told it my mother shrunk back toward Cæl's room, away from Miketh's scrutinizing gaze.

When I was finished, Miketh's expression was clouded. "You're who Aamon is looking for," he murmured. "Here he has all of Idura trying to find this 'angel' who came too close to revealing what we are, and he knew the whole time." Miketh sighed and flexed his wings before settling them against his back. The fierce Vohim looked at Tiahmani. "You knew he manipulated our orders the night we attacked the kiaisi? That he made it so Cæl's daughter was to be captured rather than killed?"

Tiahmani clenched her coffee cup in her hands. "Yes, I knew that much."

Miketh's face was intense. "Did you know Aamon initiated the orders for that attack in the first place?"

My hands fluttered to my face, betrayal choking out my words. Aamon hadn't tried to save me and Lucien, he'd ordered my capture. My face crumpled. He'd ordered Lucien's death.

Tiahmani's face went paper white. "No . . ."

Miketh's eyes were on Cæl, glinting distant and dangerous as firelight in a dark forest, and his words were measured. "We lost many Laidrom that night, Ikkar not least among them. Aamon knows Cæl's daughter is Linnia, and if he were found, would have to answer for that and for his desertion." In a rush of bristling, dark wings, Miketh stood, his shadow swallowing me and Cæl. "And that's why he wanted me to follow Tiahmani, so I'd find you and bring you back."

TWENTY-TWO

ADRENALINE FROZE ME IN place like a dove in the shadow of a hawk. The leather of Miketh's gauntlet creaked, and I tensed, waiting for the cold line of his blade to part my skin.

Clawed hands closed over my shoulders, but they were my father's, strong but gentle. Cæl eased me back and stood, placing himself in between Miketh and me. They stood eye-to-eye; Miketh took in my father's unflinching expression, looking for something he seemed unable to find. "Do you want to do this?" my father asked. "Take me to Idura and certain death?"

Miketh swallowed and shook his head. "It doesn't matter what I want. You deserted the Laidrom, committed Doalin, have a Linnia daughter." His gaze fell to me, but his expression wasn't fierce as it had been a moment ago—he was vexed. It cut tense lines in the smoothness of his face and put a bleak edge on his voice.

Tiahmani put a hand on Miketh's gauntlet, her expression understanding. "You realize Aamon asked you to follow me because he knew that seeing Cæl would be hell for you both, right?"

It was true. Cæl and Miketh wore mirrored expressions of pain and loss. The shame on Cæl's face reflected the disappointment on Miketh's. Miketh rubbed his face with his hand and lifted his face to the moonlight streaming from the cupola. "You were there," I said, drawing

Miketh's attention. "You saw Aamon carry me out of Idura after the ritual." He nodded reluctantly. "Why would he have taken me out that way if he didn't have anything to hide? If you didn't suspect he was up to something, why would you have been following him through a vacant section of Idura?"

Miketh's wings sagged. "His crimes don't excuse Cæl's." But there was no conviction in his words.

Cæl tilted his head in consideration. "No, they don't, but you once offered me a life boon." Miketh straightened, surprised, and gestured for him to continue. "I will consider that debt honored in full if you help me find a way to bring Aamon to justice. If you choose to turn us in after that, then that is still your choice."

Miketh's wings opened and closed with uncertainty, feathers whispering against one another. Tiahmani got to her feet and tugged at her sleeves. "It's late and this is a lot of bullshit to take in. Why don't you sleep on it?" She jerked her head to the door. "There's a guest loft over the garage, and I can show you where it is if you're ready to turn in. We both had a long flight."

Miketh stood for a moment more before he shouldered his satchel and bow. "Aye, perhaps more discussion is best held until tomorrow."

Tiahmani held open the door for Cæl. "Walk us outside?"

My father flicked his wings in acknowledgement. "Of course."

The three Laidrom stepped outside and I retired to my room, wondering if I was excluded from the discussion because I was not Laidrom or because I wasn't Iyarri.

The sun was out the next morning, casting hazy orange hues across the pale landscape. When I emerged from my room, I found Cæl in the kitchen looking out over the frozen garden, the shadow of his wings stretching across the driftwood-gray floor. I paused in the doorway, not sure if I should disturb him. His stillness made him seem far away. My father did not turn from the window, but said, "Miketh and I will be going out to talk."

I tilted my head in question and he switched to Loagæth. "Catherine makes Miketh nervous. He is acutely uncomfortable discussing Iyarri matters around her." He sighed. "As he should be. He is not so bothered by you, though. Although I doubt he thinks of you as Iyarri, he seems to think you are something more than Linnia."

I wrapped my arms around myself and twisted my hands into the fabric over my ribs. "Did he say if he was taking us back? Or reporting us?"

"No, not yet. Miketh's first loyalty has always been to the Elonu-Dohe and the Laidrom; he values his honor more than his life. He has to decide if helping us and risking his honor is worth a life boon."

Nervous tension coiled through me. Could Cæl defend me and my mother, or even himself, against Miketh if he needed to? "What was the life boon for?" I whispered, trying to gauge the weight of Miketh's debt to my father.

"That is not for me to say."

There was a knock at the front door and Cæl opened it for Miketh. I'd never seen him with an ipuran before; it struggled to mask his Iyarri traits. It hid his wings and the scars on his arms and reduced the unnatural radiance of his skin, but his eyes were unchanged, fiery Baltic amber. Miketh gave me a nod and I returned it, fussing with the spiral in my hair.

My father paused at the door and said to me, "I am unsure when we will be back. Let Catherine know when she wakes." The terse set of his lips spoke more: *Tell her not to worry.*

They left and the house fell silent. They day was bright, wisps of cloud skiffs trailing across the sky through the windows in the cupola. My wings rustled behind me, yearning to be in the air. I closed my eyes, poised my body, and started the Capmiali stances. When training with my father, I moved in a fluid dance of napta and feathers, but on my own I went slower, focusing on balance, breathing, and my wings. My toes splayed in ways that would have caused pain months ago—my foot bent in half, allowing me to move on the balls of my feet and my toes. I was faster this way, better balanced than I was on flat feet. There was joy in the now-familiar movements.

My reverie was interrupted by the front door opening. Tiahmani sat on one of the benches and lowered her face into her hands. Her skin was pale, tinged with green, and her hands trembled. I rushed to her side. "Tiahmani? Are you okay?" She didn't seem to hear me, and I laid my hand on her shoulder and repeated myself in Loagæth.

She lurched to her feet and rushed to the bathroom. The door slammed and Tiahmani started retching.

My mother came out of the den, dressed and squinting at the sunlight. "I heard the door and . . ." She gestured toward the occupied bathroom in question.

"Tiahmani," I said simply.

When my aunt came back into the great room, her face was ashen and stark within the frame of her dark hair.

My mother moved to put a hand on Tiahmani's scarred arm but changed her mind. "Why don't you sit down for a bit?"

Tiahmani opened her mouth to protest, but then said, "For a while. I came for something to settle my stomach." Tiahmani made herself tea and, as it steeped, sat atop one of the high stools with her hands in her hair. She eyed her tea and groaned. "I'm thirsty enough to spit feathers, and I still don't think I should drink that."

"Are you going to be okay?" I asked. "Should we call Cæl?"

She shook her head, the motion making her color worse. "No, I'm just tired and stressed."

My mother and I exchanged a fleeting look. Neither one of us believed her, but my mother knew something I did not. Catherine's voice was gentle, not patronizing. "Is there anything I can get you? Crackers?"

At the mention of food, Tiahmani's color shifted from exhausted white to green and she took a deep, steadying breath. "No, but thank you." She managed a sip of tea and put her head on her folded arms. I ached with sympathy, wanting to do something to help her, but also knew she hated me and my mother seeing her vulnerable. Though Tiahmani didn't lift her head, she said, "I should go before Cæl gets back. I'm in no mood for another one of his lectures."

Catherine opened a can of ginger ale and set it in front of her. "Start with that, and I'll put some things together for you to take to the guest house."

Though I expected her to protest, Tiahmani kept her head in her arms and nodded. Catherine found a bag and filled it with a sleeve of saltine crackers, a few packets of plain oatmeal, and more ginger ale. Without warning, Tiahmani clapped a hand over her mouth and rushed again for the bathroom. When she returned a few minutes later she said, "I'm going to go."

My mother shouldered the bag of food. "I'll bring this." Tiahmani could barely carry herself, but my mother was smart enough not to say it. I watched them go, thinking of all the times my mother had babied me when I'd been home sick from school. Tiahmani might enjoy it, if she let herself.

Cæl and Miketh returned soon after. My father shed his ipuran as one would a coat, slipping it off, but Miketh hurled his away, his true form snapping into view with a startling ferocity. Cæl noticed my mother's shoes were gone from the foyer. "Where's Catherine?"

"Tiahmani came over this morning but she was sick, so Mom took her back to the guest house."

He frowned. "I'm going to check on them." Cæl departed; I left Miketh in the great room and went to the kitchen to brew a cup of tea.

"I should have realized you weren't human when I captured you. You didn't weigh enough," Miketh said. I turned around to find him standing inside the kitchen, arms folded across his chest. His attempt to engage me in conversation was polite, but I knew how sharp those claws were and how merciless he could be.

I sat on the corner of one of the benches and balanced my teacup on my knee. "I'm sure you'd have still hit me in the head and threatened to tear my tongue out."

One corner of his mouth twitched in amusement, but he didn't apologize. "Are you sure the kiaisi was human?" he asked.

I ran my fingers over the silver spiral in my hair. "Why?" The question was critical and defensive.

"He didn't fight like a human. It made me wonder if perhaps he was a Linnia, like yourself."

I could imagine Lucien's disgust at being called a Linnia, but for all his loathing, Miketh's observations would still hold true. The gunfire he'd rained down brought so many Laidrom to the black emptiness of death. I shook my head, the pitch of my voice dropping. "Lucien was human." I took a sip and cradled the cup in one hand. The jasmine tea was sweet and soft-tasting, but the tightness in my chest didn't unknot.

Miketh scanned my wings, eyes lingering on the teardrop shapes in the unalah. He nodded to my hands. "Didn't they finish?" I furrowed my brow, unsure what he was asking. "Your hands, they didn't change."

I hesitated—that I preferred my human hands wouldn't sit well with Miketh, and trying to justify it would be pointless. "You'd be better off asking one of the Iadnah, there's a lot I don't remember."

"The Iadnah are a bunch of bookish shut-ins; they'd tell me it was none of my business." He shrugged his wings. "Worst case, you're going to tell me the same."

I lifted my head, challenging him. "Worst case, I'm going to ask you what the life boon from my father was—"

A bang scattered my thoughts, and Miketh turned, spreading his wings to block the entry to the kitchen, napta readied. My father came into the house like a hurricane, wings bristling. Before my lips could form a question, Tiahmani threw open the door and slammed it behind her with as much force as her brother had. Her eyes were like green hellfire, and though her complexion was still blanched, there were bright splotches of color high on her cheeks. "How dare you, Cæl, of all people, tell me to take responsibility for my actions. This is what responsibility looks like. I'm not going back."

He turned on her, wings flaring. "You can't do this to your child. An Iyarri baby belongs with the Elonu-Dohe."

I covered my mouth with my hand as my stomach dropped.

TWENTY-THREE

MIKETH'S FACE DIDN'T MIRROR my stunned expression; he watched the siblings, his body tense and wary.

Tiahmani balled her fists. "What? You're going to tell me I can't keep a child from the same society you abandoned?"

Cæl's voice was fearsome. "Do you think I wanted exile? Wanted to leave everything I had? I didn't have a choice."

"Don't paint yourself up as some martyr. You ran to save your own ass."

"It doesn't matter. Your child is Iyarri; it belongs with the Elonu-Dohe."

I twisted my fingers into my sleeves. Her child was Iyarri—it belonged, while he, and I, did not. Cæl hadn't meant the emphasis on those words, but they echoed in the cavern around my heart.

Tiahmani scowled at her brother. "I never thought I'd hear you telling me to go running back to Aamon with his kid." There was a cruel, taunting edge to her voice.

Miketh's jaw tightened. Cæl's voice was like a thunderclap. "You always said you weren't—"

"I lied, Cæl. Look at you! Do you blame me?"

"You weren't using a contraceptive ritual?" he snapped, exasperated.

"Of course I was. And who the fuck are you to lecture me on birth control?"

237

"Don't use my mistakes to defend your actions!"

Tiahmani rolled her eyes and her head in the same motion. "Gephna, you're such a fucking hypocrite. Do you think if I go back and they find out Aamon and I are Nuam that he'll face justice? You chose exile, I can too."

"Exile is a living death." The pain in his voice carved through me. Life in exile was all I had—for me, there was no going back to either the human or the Iyarri world.

"None of this was supposed to happen; it wasn't ever supposed to be anything serious." The anger in Tiahmani's voice buckled into desperation.

"You are going to need help. Pregnancy is near the wind enough; you can't give birth to a child without Iadnah there."

"If I go back they're going to want to know where you are, and when they find out, they'll kill you." Tiahmani talked faster, her tone frantic, desperate. "We can stay here and you could raise the baby; you missed out on raising Aurelia and—"

"No. That's nonsense." His words slammed down like a gate.

"Why won't you help me?" she cried.

Cæl threw his arms and wings open in a mirrored gesture of frustration. "What can I possibly do? You want me to hide you here and risk you and your child dying?"

She scrambled for words. "You could go back and help me bring Aamon to some sort of justice. If he were found a traitor and punished before they knew I was pregnant, they couldn't spare Aamon because of it."

Cæl scoffed. "It'd take an Ohlera to rule on what Aamon's done. Do you think I would so much as get a word in about Aamon before she ordered me killed?"

Tiahmani turned for the door, her wings flaring, defiant. "Then I won't stay here with you, either."

Cæl caught her by one wrist. His voice was gentle, pleading, "Noro, stop. We'll figure something out, but you cannot do this on your own."

Tiahmani turned on him, lashing out with one hand as she tried to pull her other arm free. Her voice was twisted by heartbreak. "Let me go!"

Cæl caught her other hand and held her two wrists together.

She struggled, her wings beating against her brother and whipping up a gale of wind. I jumped back as a lamp shattered across the floor.

Though Cæl closed his eyes and turned his head, he did not release his hold on Tiahmani. She fought harder, trying to pull her hands away, her talons digging pale trenches in the wood floor. He whispered calming words to her and, slowly, she ceased to struggle. Sinking to her knees, her wrists still held fast between Cæl's hands, she bowed her head and let loose sobs that made her wings shake. "How can you let me twist in the wind like this? You hate Aamon."

Cæl knelt by Tiahmani and circled her in his arms and his wings. "But I do not hate you, and I do not hate your child." Tiahmani let her brother hold her while she wept. "I'll help you, noro, I promise."

Miketh put his hand on my shoulder and jerked his head toward the back garden. I followed him out the French doors into the snow-laden yard. Even with the doors shut behind us, Tiahmani's sobs carried on the crisp air.

Miketh didn't bother brushing snow off a bench, preferring instead to perch on it with his long toes locked around the edge. I picked up a withered stick and made absent-minded lines in the snow. "Is Tiahmani in danger?" I asked.

"Yes." Miketh stared off into the bleak winter landscape, the sadness in his eyes so instant, so raw, and so complete I knew he hadn't meant for me to see it. "Tiahmani," his words came evenly, "would be safest with other Iyarri. There are many risks with Iyarri pregnancy—even ending one—and while she is as fearless as they come, this isn't something she can fight and defeat. She needs help."

I tilted my head in question.

He shifted his wings, searching for words. "Iyarri are built for flight first and all other things second. We have finer bones, and our women have narrower birthing passages. And wings make for a bulky baby. Premature Iyarri babies seldom live, but full-term ones are difficult to birth even in the best of circumstances. To stay here and try to have her child without help is . . . perilous. If she had Iadnah help, she would be safer, no matter what she chose to do about the pregnancy. Iyarri fertility has been declining for generations. Tiahmani is willing to shoulder the risk because Iyarri children are so rare, and she knows there are many others who would be all too happy to raise her child if she doesn't want to. Tiahmani is strong, but let's hope she comes to her senses and goes back."

Heartsick for Tiahmani, I wished she didn't have to choose between her baby and her brother. I threw my stick in the snow, turned from Miketh, and walked toward the house.

"Aurelia."

I paused at the sound of his voice but did not turn. "This changes things, and I need time to think. Tell Cæl I'll be back later tonight." I nodded, and Miketh took off, wings beating the air and then fading into the whisper of blowing snow.

My father sat alone on one of the curved benches in the great room, gaze distant, hands clasped, elbows on his knees. There were red, angry scratches on his forearms. "Essia?"

He bowed his head, voice burdened with stress and uncertainty. "Tiahmani is resting in my room." He lifted his head and realized I was alone. "Where is Miketh?" I relayed Miketh's message and Cæl's hands tightened. "Whatever decision he comes back with will be final."

The sun sank below the treeline and quiet settled on the house, but Miketh didn't return. Trying to quell my nervousness, I stretched out on the benches in the great room and cleaned my wings. Flat on my stomach with my knees bent and feet up, I wrapped one wing around the front of the bench, spreading out the feathers like a gleaming sienna fan across the floor.

Cæl emerged from the den and gestured to my wings. "How do they feel today?"

I smoothed the oil-damped cloth over the plumes, the aroma of crushed Irish gardens, vanilla, and nighttime dew filling the air. "Better. Rested." The relaxed Capmiali earlier hadn't taxed my wings; they felt stronger, more controlled.

"Good. If things go well tonight, I want you to try flying tomorrow." He said it with so little fanfare I almost missed it.

"Really?" I sat up and pushed the neck of my slouching sweater back onto my shoulder. My heart fluttered with fear, excitement, and desire.

"Yes. Do some stretching tonight, but nothing else. I want you to save your strength."

Two booming knocks came from the front door, and I tensed as Miketh let himself in. He unslung his bow and quiver and set them next to the door, shaking new snow from his wings.

Miketh clasped Cæl's forearm. "Heeoa." Turning to me, his eyes settled on my hand—the way I held the cloth, how the long, delicate fingers functioned. He snapped his attention back to my face and flicked his wings. "Aurelia."

I folded the cloth in my hands, not sure what to make of either his curiosity or the thoughts moving behind his schooled expressions. My heartbeat quickened. Perhaps I was not the monstrosity he expected a Linnia to be, or perhaps his respect for my father was enough to gain his allegiance. My words were calmer than I felt. "Hello, Miketh."

Cæl gestured to the benches; the Laidrom settled across from one another, with me at the bench bridging the two, floating in the current of unease that flowed between the two of them. My brow furrowed; I wasn't sure if I should stay, but didn't want to draw attention to myself by leaving. Instead, I added oil to the cloth, twisted my wing around to reach the pin feathers, and listened.

Miketh's sigh broke the stillness. "Heeoa, this isn't easy for me. I can't live with the dishonor of not demanding you face justice." His hand became a fist and my body tensed, fearful he'd unsheathe his napta. "But I can't live with your death on my conscience, either." Miketh gestured to me. "Or hers."

I sighed, the trembling exhale audible.

Miketh clasped one taloned foot around his opposite ankle. "Aamon needs to answer for what he's done, too. For the Laidrom that died because of his deceptions. But Tiahmani was right—if Saan-Eleéth knows they're fertile, it might buy him lenience he doesn't deserve." Frightening as Miketh was, I empathized with the way the choice he needed to make tore him apart.

My father nodded. "I agree with you, and while the decision is still yours, I have a solution to offer."

Relief broke across Miketh's face. "What's that?"

"Saan-Eleéth resides at Lilnon, a stronghold not overly far from here. I can't expect her to listen to me after twenty-five years' desertion. But she'll listen to you." Miketh leaned forward, interested. "To repay the blood boon, I'm asking you to go to her and request audience for me. If she grants it, I'll tell her what I've done and what Aamon's done. So long as Tiahmani stays here and neither of us mentions her pregnancy, it can't influence Saan-Eleéth's decision." I stilled, the whisper of chamois over feathers ceasing as uncertainty gripped me—I was missing from this entire idea, but I bit back my questions.

Silence threaded through the darkness, and Miketh sifted through it before he spoke. "Then you trade your life for Tiahmani's." *And mine.* If Iyarri law couldn't pardon my father, there was little hope for me. I clenched the cloth in my hand, heartbroken and fearful that Cæl had given up, that his only concerns were Tiahmani, her child, and seeing Aamon brought to justice.

My father's voice was contemplative and even. "There is a chance my word is still worth something and Saan-Eleéth will listen to what I have to say. I have hidden far too long, and my cowardice has taken its toll on many. Tiahmani has a long life ahead of her, and I want to make sure I've done everything I can for her and her child."

Tiahmani emerged from the kitchen, her hands wrapped around her stomach. "You would really do that for me?" she asked, her dark brows pulled together in humble relief.

"Aye, for you and Aurelia." The jealous emptiness that stretched across my heart was arrested by my father's addition.

Miketh made room for Tiahmani beside him. "Saan-Eleéth will want to know the reason for your desertion."

"Yes, she will." Cæl answered.

"And when she asks after Aurelia?" Miketh pressed. "You're too near the wind on this; both your lives will be forfeit."

"Perhaps not." Cæl said it in a contemplative, calculating way. Tiahmani and I exchanged a hopeful look.

"What?" Miketh leaned forward, resting his forearms on his knees. "How?"

My father's voice was slow, deliberate. "I am no Aldaria, but I am well-versed in the punishments for my crimes. I think I know how to make Saan-Eleéth see reason." Cæl sighed, his wings and shoulders sagging. "I am tired of living in fear, in shame. If bringing Aamon to justice is the most I can do to set some things right, then that is what I must do. Will you seek an audience for me or not?" my father asked.

"Yes, Heeoa, I will."

Tiahmani squeezed Miketh's arm. "Thank you."

Cæl nodded in appreciation. "Good. Then our debt is settled. I want you to leave tomorrow."

Miketh stood to go but spoke, his tone hopeful. "Heeoa, one more question." There was a pause as Miketh chose his words. "If it all works out and Aamon is sentenced, Tiahmani is willing to return, and you and Aurelia are pardoned, would you come back to us?"

Cæl was quiet for a contemplative moment. "I am not one for optimism, but yes, I would consider it, if they'd have both me and Aurelia."

TWENTY-FOUR

ALL AROUND US, THE wind whispered promises. The air up high was thinner, colder, and invigorating. Cæl carried me over the treetops of the great forest behind his house, and it was everything I could do to keep my wings tucked when the wind begged me to open them. My feathers tingled with a desire for flight so consuming I could almost ignore the sick undercurrent of doubt beneath it.

An abandoned fire tower stood like a lone sentinel over the treetops, and my father wheeled and descended until we landed on the square roof. I left tracks in the thin layer of windswept snow as I walked to the edge, locking my thick toes onto the corner of the roof. The winter forest was so far below me that the clouds overhead felt closer than the tiny dotting of evergreens.

Cæl pointed to a white swath cut from the base of the fire tower through the forest. "I think this way is best—there's fewer trees and a pretty clear path through them."

The wind gusted and the tower swayed beneath us, wood creaking. My toes gripped the edge of the roof so hard they ached. "Isn't this a little high?" I asked. I might have been winged, but the ground was far away and my nerves screamed with very human fears about crashing into it.

Cæl peered over the edge with me. "You're gliding today. You'll need the height."

I wasn't sure I needed quite that much height. A hawk circled nearby, still not half as far up as we were. My fingers wrapped tight around Cæl's arm, the brick red fabric of his shirt worn and comforting to touch. I wished for a harness, something to catch me if I fell, but there was nothing between me and the frozen ground far below. My fingernails bit into my palm, the pain unable to chase away the grisly image of the Laidrom in Lucien's windshield—her shattered wings, the bloody bones bristling out of the feathers. My bones were just as light and just as fragile.

Cæl stepped behind me and off to one side, his voice drawing me back to attention. "Now, when you take off, you'll need to feel for the air currents." He paused, looking for words to describe what Iyarri were gifted by instinct. "When you're standing still, the air rushes past you. In the air it becomes something to go with, to ride atop of. The currents will be thicker, and there will be with voids without lift beneath them. When you feel one, tilt your wings to ride atop the air current."

"Or I'll drop like a stone."

Despite my attempt at a joke, Cæl didn't smile. "Yes. Are you ready?"

"That's all the instructions you have?" My tone was incredulous.

"Yes. Your body will know what to do." But the way his eyebrows drew together betrayed him. He *hoped* my body would know what to do.

I stared over the precipice and swallowed. Cæl put his hand on my shoulder. "Keep a clear mind. I'll go first. Watch, and once I'm back in the air, you can go."

Cæl stepped off the edge of the roof, his wings opening wide to scoop the air. They didn't flap; instead he kept them wide, gliding like a great bird of prey toward the ground. He landed, taking a single running step before he lofted himself back into the air, circled around the tower, and hovered over the void I was about to jump into. "Are you ready?"

I wasn't, but I nodded, not trusting my voice. Fear clutched my insides, and I wrapped my wings and arms around myself. The tops of the evergreens were pointed, the deciduous trees' branches like bare, grasping hands. The earth was so far down, too far.

"Open your wings," Cæl called.

They stayed clamped closed to my body, unready and uncertain. I wanted to beg off, words tightening in my throat. Maybe another day. I wasn't ready. I wasn't strong enough. My lips parted, but no sound came; the words I wanted to speak were afraid too.

Cæl barked his order again. I inhaled, steadying myself, and opened my wings. My wingspan felt so much larger now that there was all the space under heaven to unfurl them. The copper gleamed in the sunlight, a bright contrast to the deeper, richer tones in my father's wings. I hesitated at the edge of the tower roof, mouth dry, bright strands of hair lashing against my cheeks. *Jump*, I willed myself, but not a muscle in my body twitched.

The wind gusted, rushing over the treetops like a charging bull, slamming headlong into my wings. I staggered backward with a gasp, the edge of the roof behind me a crouching, looming presence. My toes grappled for the frigid shingles, clawing the air for a second that spanned forever. Dry, glittering snow swirled around me, the warm sunlight giving the snowflakes a candlelight glow. I screamed as I went over the edge of the tower. For a second I was back at the cathedral, helpless as a baby bird, winged but only able to fall.

Cæl yelled my name as I tumbled toward the earth. His voice echoed, far away. My wings steepled over me, pointed toward the sun, as bright as the stained-glass Star of Bethlehem at Christmas. The wind screamed, victorious. With a cry of desperate exertion, I snapped my wings open to my sides, but the wind caught one wing and spun me like a child's toy. My vision melted into a twirling mass of white light and smears of gray trees and blue sky.

I slammed back-first into the snowdrift at the base of the tower, a spray of white erupting around me. My vision went black, the whole world went still.

An eternity later, my shaking exhale broke the hushed silence of deep snow. I opened my eyes, blinking away snowflakes that fell from my lashes and melted on my cheeks. The sky overhead was the purest blue, the clouds so white they seared my vision. My body rested at the bottom of a snow angel sunk two feet deep, trembling but whole.

Wings flashed overhead and my father leaned over me, his face silhouetted against the sky. "Pasahasa? Aurelia?" I tried to sit up, but he put one hand on my collarbone. "Stay still. Does anything feel broken?" With minute movements, I tested each of my limbs, my neck, then shook my head as tension dissipated from my body. "Are you sure?" he asked.

"Yes," I said, struggling to sit up. Cæl helped me to my feet and I swayed, sore and shaking. Adrenaline chilled me in a way the snow could not. My father checked my eyes and flexed my wings over and over until, finally, I said, "Essia, I'm okay."

"It appears as much." Relieved, he turned his face toward the sky and then helped me to my feet. "Come, let's try again."

I shook my head, mustering my refusal before I could find words to voice it. "I don't think I should." My voice wavered.

He gathered me up and carried me back to the top of the tower. "You are shaken, but uninjured. The worst thing you can do is let fear take root. Best to rip it out now." Cæl shoved off the roof, leaving me alone.

High up again, I hesitated at the edge of the tower roof. My stomach rolled and my vision spun.

Cæl called from the sky nearby. "Go ahead. I'm here to catch you."

Air slipped around me, not a gusting wind, but a cool, welcoming caress. My wings opened, still eager where I was fearful. Perhaps they knew better than I what they were capable of. I handed myself over to hope and jumped.

I fell, the white ground rushing at me, but then, instinctively, my wings beat, pulling me upward in the air. The copper feathers flashed in the cold sunlight and surged heavenward, my blood pumping faster. My fear evaporated in the sun. The wings were powerful, no, *I* was powerful, in a way I had never been with my feet on the ground. The sky stretched out overhead, and delirious with relief, with freedom, I rushed toward the clouds like an animal released back to the wild. *I could fly.* The realization was heady, exhilarating, the wind its own potent liquor.

One wingbeat over another I climbed toward the blinding burst of sunlight in the sky. I broke through an air current, the cold air lifting me and carrying me. The wind ran like glacial water through my hair and a thousand beads of cold moisture gathered on my skin, a glittering mantle gifted by the heavens.

My wings faltered, not beating fast enough, hard enough, to keep me in the air. I gasped and strained, desperate not to stop my skyward ascent, but the long muscles in my wings quivered and my back burned as gravity dragged me downward, greedy and eager to keep me earthbound. Unable to flap my wings more, I held them open and glided downward, away from the sun, away from the sky. Leaving that blue, empyrean plane enveloped me with a homesickness I hadn't felt, even when my human life was pulled away from me.

Cæl followed above me, his silhouette like a hawk. The ground below shimmered white, the rippling shadow of my wings getting larger as I descended. My heart hammered as the air slipped past me, cold and thin and too fast to control.

As I coasted below the treetops Cæl said, "Tilt them back, but don't—"

Before he could finish his instructions, I'd tilted them too far. The air slammed headlong into the open faces of my wings and I lost my uplift. Before I could fall, Cæl grabbed one of my arms with both his feet. I expected criticism, but instead he was smiling, the expression genuine and broad, full of relief and pride. "You did it. You didn't just glide, you flew. All you need is more strength." His wings beat, whirling the snow around us in sparkling eddies until my feet touched the snow.

Breathless, my heart bursting, I threw my arms around my father. *I can fly.* The words wouldn't come, smothered by joy so great I could have dissipated into sunlight.

We arrived home damp with sweat and snow. My mother looked up from her book when we came through the door. "How did it go?" she asked.

"I'm learning." I wanted to say so much more. How the sky broke a homesickness I didn't know I had, the freedom, the joy in spite of the pain. But I couldn't. It would make her feel like more of an outsider, more afraid I was abandoning everything she had taught me about being human.

I filled the kettle and went back to my mother in the study; she was curled at one end of the couch. "Would you like some tea?" I asked. "And some company?"

She smiled. "Of course I would."

I filled two cups and tucked my sketchbook and pencils under one arm.

She smiled and took the cup I offered. I sat with her on the couch, leaning against the armrest with my wings draped off the end. We settled into our old roles; before I'd gone to college, she and I would often sit together, me drawing, her reading.

After a while, my father came to the study and leaned against the door, watching my mother and me. Catherine smiled. "I'm sure we can make room for one more."

Cæl gestured for us not to move, but did come closer, looking over my shoulder at my drawing. The page was filled with sketches of Iyarri, one after the other, each more refined than the last as I sought to perfect drawing wings and feathers. I turned the page and started over, a female form and the rough outlines of wings taking shape. With a few more pencil strokes I summoned shadow, depth, and dimension. My father raised his eyebrows at Catherine, surprised and impressed.

My mother gave an amused snort. "She's always been talented, especially if it was all over the walls in permanent marker." I hid my smile in my sketchbook.

When I finished the drawing, I wished them goodnight and closed myself in my room, wondering if it would work out between them. They cared for one another, but the distance between them hadn't closed with our time in New York. There were small things—a touch on the shoulder, a smile of shared understanding, the way my father's defenses eased around her—but nothing passionate or romantic. Perhaps they were stifling it; perhaps the ashes were too cold for anything to be rekindled. My father appeared older than me, but only by ten or fifteen years. Meanwhile, my mother's hair was graying and the lines on her face deepening, and the wider the gulf of changes between her and my father became, the more my hope for their relationship dimmed. If we were doomed to exile, who else did they have but one another?

I sat on the edge of the tianta and closed my hand over Lucien's spiral, my heart resting heavy in my chest. During the day it was easy to focus on training, on flight, on our plans ahead, but at night sorrow and loneliness crowded out the distractions. Lucien had understood me in a way no one else had, and perhaps no one else ever would. I wanted to be grateful for our time together, but instead my insides were gnawed by heartsickness and dogged by guilt.

Skies have mercy, I missed him.

Flight used more than my back and wings; it took every part of my body to maneuver in the air, and when I woke, every one of those parts was sore. I groaned, grateful Cæl had let me sleep in, as I rolled onto my back and let my wings hang off the edges of the tianta. Their weight stretched the muscles anchoring them to my back—they ran parallel to my spine, and curved around my ribs. I flexed my toes and arched my back, the ache horrible and empowering all at once. My slender artist's body was strong enough to *fly*.

When I left my room, the benches in the living room were pushed to its edges; Tiahmani lounged on one of them, her color restored.

"How are you feeling?" I asked.

"Fine." She grimaced. "Although I think I'll be sick to death of that question before long."

"You're awake, good," Cæl chimed in from the kitchen. "Your mother is out shopping; get your napta, we'll train before she gets back." His expression hardened. How much did his upcoming audience with Eleéth weigh on his mind?

I changed into yoga pants and a cream-colored tank top. As with the other times we'd trained together, Cæl wore his wide-legged pants, his napta, and the Heeoa scarring that covered his back, chest, and arms.

We began with the first stance, our arms, legs, and wings poised but relaxed, but as I moved to the second stance, my arms and legs burned. I willed grace into them, hoping the session would be brief, knowing my flight-taxed body would begin to falter. After completing the first dozen stances, my father nodded to my gauntlets. "You earned those blades, it's time you learned how to use them."

I traced the metal inlays of one gauntlet with my fingers. I'd worn them during Capmiali so my arms would acclimate to the weight, but I had yet to unsheathe the blades in training. Any other day I might have been excited, but today I was as weary and clumsy as I'd ever been, and the last thing I wanted was to work with the honed napta blades. The ease with which the fine edges of the metal had dipped into my flesh made me shiver, and I didn't need more scars. Out of the corner of my eye I saw Tiahmani cross her napta-clad arms over her chest and lean against the wall, taking an interest in our sessions for the first time.

Cæl cleared his throat, drawing my attention back to him. "To expose the blade requires that you mind its clearance, especially to your body. The blade needs to be able to extend to its full length in one motion so it locks in place. Go through the first three stances, and at the end of the first stance, snap your arm to expose your right blade. Then release the second blade on the third stance. Like this." As he extended his right arm outward in a sweeping motion, the deadly split blade leapt from the gauntlet. He pivoted and brought his left arm up in a block, the second napta lashing outward, turning the defensive move into an offensive one.

Focusing, I turned and extended my right arm with a snap to the movement, sending the blade leaping outward. As I moved to complete the pivot and left-arm block, I faltered. I couldn't extend the second napta and keep an eye on the first. I had too many limbs moving in too many directions, and the blades made my arms ungainly. The split metal blades flashed cold and sharp in the light, but I wove them past my body, completing the forms.

When I finished, Cæl frowned. "You're afraid of your own blades."

"Of course I am. They're sharp."

His arm moved in a blur of motion—a second later blood trickled from my bicep. The tip of his blade was rimmed in red.

"You cut me!" I cried, the indignity stinging far more than the cut.

Tiahmani snorted in amusement.

Cæl sheathed his blade and grabbed my wrist, preventing me from covering the wound with my hand. "Did that hurt?" His voice would have made a legion of Laidrom cringe.

Rage burned away my fear and I tried to pull my arm away, but his fist was vicelike. Blood traced down to my elbow in a thin line and dripped onto the floor. "Let me go!" I twisted my arm, but he didn't release me.

"Compose yourself," Cæl snapped. Tiahmani frowned at his tone. I stilled, tamping down my resentment and anger with reality—there was no way I was going to physically wrest myself from his grasp.

Cæl asked again, "Did it hurt?" I shook my head. "You cannot be afraid of your blades. Or mine. Sometimes you have to take a strike so you can deliver a better one."

He released his clawed fingers from around my wrist, and I instinctively put pressure on the wound. Looking at my father and the many thin, upraised lines crossing his body, perhaps it was a human instinct. A warm droplet of blood landed on my foot.

"Retract your blades."

"How?" I asked. Under the blade there was a thin strap of leather that tucked out of the way when the blade was retracted. The worn leather rested across my palm, and allowed easy control of the blade, but there didn't seem to be a button or lever for retracting the metal.

"Use the strap to push the blade forward until it unlocks, and then let go." I did so, and when I released the strap, the blade snapped back onto the gauntlet in a blur of silver. "Good, now do the stances with blade extensions again."

I wove through the stances, napta glinting in the pale afternoon light as it shone through the cupola. My shoulders and wings drooped; it felt like I hauled my fatigued limbs through water. I pulled the blade through the fifth stance without enough clearance, and it sliced both the thin fabric of my shirt and the tender flesh at the dip of my waist. I stifled a cry and bent to examine my wound.

Cæl turned on me, his voice a snarl of frustration. "Why won't you focus?"

"I am." I clamped my hand over my side, exhausted and desperate for some shred of sympathy.

"You're not. You can do better than this. I expect better than this."

Tears, instant and ashamed, jumped to my eyes.

Tiahmani got up and stood so close to her brother that he stepped aside and let her take his place. "She's not getting it the way you're explaining it, Cæl. Move."

He stood steadfast. "You're in no condition—"

"I'm pregnant, not an invalid. Besides, what do you know about pregnancy?" Her expression dared him to answer.

"I know all pregnant Laidrom stop training at five months and are grounded at six months."

"So, the extent of your knowledge on pregnancy is Laidrom policy." She gestured to her stomach. "Do I look like I'm five months along?"

Cæl shook his head and moved, but stood nearby, skeptical. Tiahmani stood with her back to Cæl and raised two encouraging eyebrows at me. A moment of shared understanding, of sympathy, warmed the space between us. Perhaps she, better than anyone, knew how it felt to fall short of Cæl's expectations. "This is what you should be doing." She flowed through the stances, her tumble of dark hair and gleaming skin a symphony of contrasts in motion—I mentally sketched the lines of her limbs. She stopped and centered herself again. "This is what you're doing instead."

Even from oi biah, her movements were hindered. As Tiahmani turned, pivoting into the second stance, I mentally flipped back and forth between the pages in my mind. Her feet were closer together, elbows splayed out rather than close to her sides and ready to drive forward. The differences cost her in balance, reach, and blade clearance.

"I understand," I said as I sunk into oi biah. This time, Tiahmani and I moved like a mirrored image and I felt grounded, wings and blades pivoting around the center of my balance. Gratitude swelled in my chest; Tiahmani might have saved my life for her brother, but she still stood against him for me.

When we finished, Tiahmani turned and flashed a grin at Cæl. "Rusty, brother? I suppose it has been forever since you've done anything meaningful with Capmiali."

My father's body whirled, his arm scything toward Tiahmani. I scrambled backward with a cry of surprise. Tiahmani reacted with a virtuoso display of reflexes, catching his blade in the arcing strike of hers, deflecting his blow. She grinned; there was a faint smile on my father's lips as well. "Like I said, rusty," Tiahmani teased.

Cæl made to sweep Tiahmani's leg out from under her, but she executed a neat flip, knocking him away with her wing. I flattened against the wall, heart pounding, but safely out of the way. They sparred, each move countered as they used wings and arms and legs in an intricate dance of blows. Tiahmani made a lethal-looking lunge at Cæl; he sidestepped, locked up her arm and shoulder, and dropped her to the floor.

She went down on her butt and sat there, surprised, until Cæl offered her a hand to help her up. As he pulled her to her feet she said, "Okay, maybe not that rusty."

"Now, if you're done, I'd like to finish with Aurelia."

She flicked her wings. "I'll join." And so I gained a second, if unexpected, teacher. Tiahmani flitted in and out of my lessons, jumping in when she wanted and then out again when the repetition bored her.

After we finished, I sat down and unlaced my napta. They were tacky in places, the blood on the edge of my blade dull. My father sat beside me, applied a stinging salve to my wounds, and covered them with small bandages. "Throw that shirt in the trash before your mother gets home and then meet me in the kitchen. I'll take care of the floor." There were matte smears on the glossy wood, with partial three-toed prints scattered through them like autumn leaves.

After I changed clothes, I held the bloody shirt over the garbage can, guilt making me hesitate. I hated hiding things from my mother, but what was there to say? I stuffed the shirt under some trash, my chest falling with a sigh.

When I met Cæl at the kitchen room table, his Heeoa gauntlets were laid out beside mine, as well as two hardened leather pouches. Inside each was a vial of oil, a circular container of balm, a leather chamois, a strangely-shaped whetstone, and a metal tool that was hooked on one end and flat on the other. With the same precision he used when reconstructing my napta, he showed me how to take the blade off the gauntlet, first using the small hooked end of the tool to release the tension and the flat side to pop the blade free. I wiped the blade free of blood, oiled it, and rubbed the gauntlet with balm. I polished until each tiny metal detail on the gauntlet was shining, and then stopped and stared at my hand.

My oval-shaped nails, usually obsessively manicured and buffed to a glass-smooth finish, were scuffed and chipped. Once, I would have hurried for a nail file and cuticle oil, but instead I turned my attention back to my napta, rubbing the metal blade until it gleamed.

TWENTY-FIVE

THE NIGHT MIKETH RETURNED was bitterly cold. Outside, tree branches snapped under the weight of oceans of wet snow and freezing rain. I was in front of the fireplace, struggling to read a book on Capmiali philosophy. While my spoken Loagæth neared fluent, reading and writing came slowly. Tiahmani was lying on the couch with a cup of ginger tea, helping me. "It could be worse. Cæl could have you copying passages, too," she teased.

Before I could respond, there were three loud knocks on the door. My father crossed the great room while Tiahmani and I exchanged a look. Cæl let Miketh in, his cheeks ruddy from the cold and his tri-colored wings so wet the orange and gray hues matched the black. Cæl closed the door behind him and they clasped forearms. "I bring word from Saan-Eleéth."

My father put a hand on Miketh's shoulder. "You've had what looks to be a miserable flight."

"Aye, it was." He unshouldered his bow and quiver, exhausted.

Cæl nodded to his bedroom. "Her message can wait. Go dry off and change."

"Thank you, Heeoa."

When Miketh returned, we gathered in the study. Tiahmani perched on a chair; I settled near her feet while my mother stood behind Cæl like a quiet shadow. Miketh warmed himself by the fire, his obsidian claws reflecting the orange light. "How did things go with Saan-Eleéth?" Cæl asked.

Miketh stretched his wings and let them settle, the shadows a deeper pantomime to his movements. "There is not much to tell, Heeoa. When I arrived at Lilnon, I was given quarters; the wait for an audience was, as you expected, several days. Saan-Eleéth is a woman of few words, and my audience was brief." He opened his flask, and I caught a whiff of scorched spices and alcohol as he took a sip.

Cæl frowned. "And what did she say when you told her who requested an audience?"

"That she found my loyalty admirable, if not somewhat misplaced. She stared at me, then wrote her missive." He shook his head as if to rid himself of the memory. "I am glad to be done with her."

"That is all she said?"

"That is all, Heeoa, other than to bid me to give you this." He took a pale piece of marbled parchment from a pouch on the side of his belt. It was still dry and folded with an unusual intricacy, the places where the corners came together sealed with shimmering viridian wax, a single feather pressed in the center in place of a seal. In the firelight, the tiny plume waned from black to purple to gold.

My father held the letter in his hands like a captured dove before he hooked one claw under the seal and cracked the letter open. The color drained from his face as he read aloud, translating to English.

Cæl,

When you disappeared years ago, I wondered if you would return. Something has forced your hand—bring me whatever that was. Your audience is one week from today.

Until the skies fall,

Saanire Eleéth Ohlera

Cæl lowered the letter to his lap and lifted his eyes to me.

"No." My mother set her teacup on the windowsill with a harsh clink. "Absolutely not." She walked around the couch and stood in front of the door. "I won't let you take her." Desperation twisted her words.

"Catherine," Cæl's voice was low in warning. "I have given up much for you; do not ask for what's left of my honor on top of it."

"I am not debating this with you," she snapped.

"No, you aren't." My father's icy tone stilled everyone in the room.

My mother's hands trembled with rage, but my father's expression was as even and unyielding as stone. Without another word, she turned on her heel and left the room. Cæl ignored her, turning back to Miketh and Tiahmani. "I'd like you two to stay here with Catherine while Aurelia and I go to Lilnon."

Miketh nodded, but Tiahmani protested. "Let us come with you."

"And risk Saan-Eleéth finding out you are with child?" Tiahmani huffed, but crossed her arms over her stomach and acquiesced.

From the direction of my bedroom came the thump of a suitcase hitting the bed. "She's packing," I said to Cæl, dreading a confrontation in front of the other Iyarri.

His face was impassive as he crossed the great room. "I'll talk to her."

I stole a nervous glance sideways at Miketh; he was staring at the feather pressed into the broken sealing wax, deep in thought. I picked up the fire poker and rearranged the burning logs in the fireplace. "Tell me about Eleéth?" I asked.

Amber fire motes swirled upward into the flue as Miketh stood. "Saan-Eleéth," he corrected. Trepidation built inside me. If I couldn't even remember to use her title, there were a thousand ways to earn her ire and hurt my already slim odds of survival. "Her title designates her as half a Saanir, a ruling pair."

"I've only heard of Saan-Eleéth as the lawspeaker."

Miketh crouched beside me, toes splayed and wings cupped for balance. They made a private, feathered wall around us that smelled of oakmoss and leather. He rubbed either side of his mouth with his thumb and forefinger. "A proper Saanir is an Ohlera and a Rior, a lawspeaker and an empath. Their gifts make the two halves of rulership: the Ohlera truth and justice, the Rior insight and mercy." Contempt turned his rich voice cruel, and he threw a bit of stray bark into the fire, making it flare brighter. "We haven't had one in over two thousand years, not since the kiaisi murdered the Rior on the Night of Bloody Feathers." Kiaisi, once the word for humans who lived within Iyarri walls, its meaning turned to Iyarri-killer in one blood-drenched night. The same night that had reduced Nephilim to Linnia, to 'beasts.'

"Can't they appoint more Rior?"

"No. They are born like any other Iyarri, but without other Rior to train them they go mad when their powers manifest." He turned his arm and closed one hand over his gauntlet, expression forlorn. "They're put down as a mercy."

The heat of the fire washed over my face, stoking the feverish, uneasy feeling inside me. There was no insight or clemency in Iyarri rulership, only the letter of the law. I cast about for a way Cæl and I might find a more sympathetic ear. "Perhaps there's someone else he could plead our case to, then—"

Miketh cut me off with a shake of his head, making the two small feathers tied into his plaits sway—both pale gold, one dappled with gray. Who did he miss? "Ohlera are rare; there are maybe a dozen or so on this continent, and Saan-Eleéth is by far the closest. Cæl has to go before her if he wants an audience."

"Are they like a line of royalty?"

Miketh tilted his head in surprise. I bit my lip and fussed with the fire, feeling stupid for not knowing. If my father's Vohim thought me simple-minded, he kept it out of his voice when he answered. "Ohlera attain the position by birth, but one Ohlera rarely gives birth to another."

I scoffed, but it was a shield more than anything. If birth elevated an Ohlera to rule, maybe the Iyarri would have a harder time than I thought reconciling my Linnia nature with my new wings. "How do you know who is an Ohlera and who isn't?"

"Physically, they're the only Iyarri that have feathers growing in their hair." Miketh stole at glance at Eleéth's letter on the table as if it could overhear him. "More importantly, her ohleræ, her power, allows her to discern truth from a lie without error."

Worry sapped the conviction from my words. "My father doesn't lie. He's going to Saan-Eleéth to tell her the truth, that's the entire point."

Miketh's already sober expression deepened. "Cæl has to be careful with which truths he tells."

Doubt and futility compressed the space around my heart. There was no taking back Cæl's request. I sighed, the sound despondent. Silence filled the space between us.

Miketh's wings rustled as though he might stand, but instead he shifted to better look at me. "Your father is training you with napta." His voice lilted with a question.

"Yes." I said the word slowly, wary of Miketh's reaction.

"I noticed your arm." Our gazes intersected on the cut from Cæl's napta. The wound was a red line so thin my mother hadn't noticed. I rubbed my hand over it as it prickled.

Miketh rocked forward so he was perched on his toes, then leaned closer to me. I'd not been so near to him since he'd captured me. His Laidrom scarring threaded up the sides of his neck, and metal cuffs accented his ears. My eyes flickered to his napta, his sharp claws, and his questioning, critical expression. "And by what right do you bear napta?"

I steadied my nerves and lifted my chin. "I killed a Laidrom."

He raised one dark eyebrow, the arch broken by the thin line of a scar. "Did you now?" His gaze moved to my shoulder, bare where the Laidrom all bore the same scarred design.

"Cæl said his name was Mastho and altered his napta for my arms."

The incredulity in Miketh's expression buckled to surprise, but then became a devious smile. He pushed up his sleeves, revealing the green and black leather of his napta gauntlets. "If that's true, any Laidrom can challenge you to the Circle of Blades." His eyes glinted, amused and cruel. "Single combat, first blood."

My skin went cold, and my lips parted in shock.

Miketh snorted and the corners of his full, angled lips turned up in a smile. "Cæl left that part out, did he?" I stammered, unable to find a response—had he ever.

"Miketh, you're so knackered you'd be spent after three swings," Tiahmani said as she leaned against the doorframe of the study. Inwardly I scoffed; I wouldn't last one strike in combat with Miketh, much less three. She nodded toward the door. "I'm going to go to the guest loft and get some sleep. You look like you could use some rest, too."

"Aye, I could." Miketh gestured to the fine napta cut on my arm and smiled. "Congratulations." He stood, the circle of his wings breaking, and a rush of cool air brushed my skin.

My parents returned, their features heavy and drained. They weren't talking, but they weren't angry. Without Miketh and Tiahmani to scrutinize, I imagined my father had been gentler with her.

My mother put her hand on my shoulder, the fingers of her other hand knotted into the chain of her necklace. She took a deep, steadying breath before she let the pendant fall, flashing, against her sternum. "Everything will be okay," she said, voice wavering. "And when all this is done with we'll have a lot less to worry about. Be careful."

"I will," I said, hugging her. "I love you."

"I love you too, sweetheart." She released me and turned for the bathroom to wash the drying tear lines from her face.

Cæl turned to me. "Gather the things you absolutely must have. We're only taking my hip bags, and I'll need to add a few things. We leave at first light tomorrow."

Thoughts, as dark and shifting as the feather pressed into Eleéth's missive, crowded in from the shadowy places of my mind. The night Cæl asked Miketh to beg an audience, he seemed, if not confident, then at least cautiously optimistic that he could go before her with some chance of mercy. But tonight, when he opened Eleéth's letter, the color had drained from his face. My first trip on wing might easily be my last.

The sky was still black and dotted with stars when Cæl and I stepped outside, the world held in the embrace of predawn winter. The snowy landscape stretched from us to the horizon, where the weak, orange glow of impending sunrise backlit a skyline of trees. A breeze rustled my feathers and clothes and I shivered, not from cold, but from nervous anticipation. The natural fiber of my Iyarri tunic scooped low on my shoulders, the sleeves narrow at the shoulder but ending wide enough to cover my napta. A richly embroidered belt held the tunic in at my waist; I fingered its raw hem, heart skittering at the prospect of going to Lilnon. Cæl smiled at me, and I wondered if I could pass for an aspiring Laidrom in Tiahmani's clothes, with an Iyarri spiral twisted into my hair and napta on my arms.

I stretched my wings, keen to be on our way. "How far away is Lilnon?"

Cæl adjusted the hip pouches on his belt and checked his okada—the two blades crossed at the back of it. Okada meant "mercy," and I thought it a strange name for a blade. "Lilnon is in a northern part of the state, near the Canadian border. We'll get there after nightfall."

Realization stuck me and I swallowed. "That's hundreds of miles from here." My elation evaporated into worry—my wings were nowhere near strong enough.

"I know. You'll fly as far as you can, then I'll carry you until you've recovered your strength." He tightened the chest strap that held his bow and quiver to his back.

"Those won't be needed, right?" I asked, hoping the weapons were expected Laidrom attire and Cæl wasn't anticipating some sort of altercation.

"I hope not." Cæl opened his wings.

My stomach twisted with unease, but I checked the lacing on my napta and took to the air.

The flight stretched out, as endless as the sky. The further we journeyed north, the less I saw of human civilization. The occasional farm or hunting cabin gave way to a forest: untouched, untamed wilderness dotted with lakes and divided by rivers. The evergreen trees were capped in white; the leafless, deciduous trees had snarled brambles for branches. The same thoughts spun circles in my mind, one anxious idea chasing another. What if I couldn't remember the right word for something? What if we needed our napta? I was worthless in a fight against Laidrom. Would Cæl fight at all if we were sentenced to die? My father's wings beat steadily while he carried me, like a great heartbeat. I pressed the side of my face against him, taking solace in the rhythm. It never faltered, despite the distance and the extra weight Cæl carried.

Night fell and, far in the distance, the black waters of Lake Ontario appeared. Cæl set us on a cliff, the shale awash in glittering, dry snow. The cliff was different than the light-colored limestone bluffs in Minnesota—the stone darker, sharper, and eroded to a thousand jagged steps. I stretched my limbs and peered over the precipice. A great, scooped valley awash in evergreens protected a still lake and a looming stone promontory. Cæl walked to my side and turned his gaze to the towering protrusion of stone in the lake. "You'll fly the rest of the way. There's a good tailwind."

"That's Lilnon?" I asked. I was eager for our journey to be over, but terrified at the same time.

"Yes." He nodded to my sleeves. "Keep your hands hidden and speak as little as possible."

Anxiousness pierced through me. "Is something wrong with my Loagæth?"

"No, but there are many things you do not know about Iyarri society, and your ignorance might give you away." He put a reassuring hand on my shoulder and squeezed. "Follow my lead."

Cold wind gusted, but it was at our backs and made the glide into the valley easy. A steep cliff pierced the lake, craggy and unclimbable. As we neared and dropped lower in the sky, I could see windows, wide balconies, and doors flanked with pillars all carved into the stone, pinpricks of reflected light wavering on the surface of the water.

I stiffened, my wings faltering in fear for a single beat as winged silhouettes emerged from the sky and flanked us. In the pale starlight, the napta on the Laidrom's arms glinted. My heart fluttered and my mouth went dry, but my father flew onward, scarcely acknowledging our armed escort. Projecting a calm I did not feel, I followed Cæl as we flew closer to the carved cliff face. The Laidrom split, three moving ahead of us, three behind us, guiding us in. We descended toward an outcropping with a domed roof, an open hole in the center glowing golden in the azure-black night.

The Laidrom ahead of us folded their wings and dropped inside. My father followed, but I balked in the air as terror struck me—I couldn't make it. The hole was too small, I was flying too fast, and the drop was too sharp. Behind me, the wings of the Laidrom beat like approaching war drums. Stifling a cry, I centered myself over the oculus, pinched my wings against my body, and fell.

I hit the stone floor and pitched forward, slamming onto my hands and one knee, unalah slapping down behind me. My wings splayed in a desperate bid for balance, one of them striking a Laidrom. She glared at me as I scrambled to my feet and pushed my hair out of my face with one pale, human hand. Heat thrummed in my temples and nauseous fear rolled my stomach. They had to have noticed. My hand was wrong, my skin too pale—so many things betrayed me as Linnia.

I folded my hands into my sleeves and pressed against Cæl as the Laidrom landed around us, walked to the edges of the room, and waited. I stared at the floor, the tile wrapping around itself toward the walls as dizzying as my thoughts. Overhead, the moon gleamed like a sickle through the oculus. The ceiling undulated with dim, magical light, tossing a ring of our shadows at our feet. No one spoke; there was the rasp of talons on the stone floor and the small sounds of feathers folding against one another. Everything smelled like Iyarri: incense, feathers, stone, and herbs.

A thin Aldaria entered from the heavy, dark wood door on one side of the room. His robes were rust-colored, trimmed in black, and embellished with needlework; the Iyarri, by contrast, was plain, with a severe face and muted wings. "Who seeks safe haven at Lilnon?" he asked.

My father's voice boomed resonant. "Cæl Heeoa and his daughter Aurelia."

"I have records for you, Cæl, but none for Aurelia." My body tensed and I eyed the Laidrom, fearing the next words would be an order to attack. "At whose request should she be admitted?"

"Saan-Eleéth's."

The Iyarri in front of us raised an eyebrow and gave a curt sniff. "Come with me."

I released the breath I'd been holding in a measured exhale, trying not to betray my nervousness. The drab Iyarri led us through the door and into a cavernous corridor wide enough to let two Iyarri walk wing-to-wing, high enough to allow for flight. A chorus of voices echoed from far away—many Iyarri were gathered together somewhere. Halfway down the hall, our guide stopped at a door and gestured us inside. "Please wait here while I check your admittance." Cæl thanked him, and the door closed behind us.

Two backless benches sat on either side of a low, round table, on which stood a carafe and a few upside-down glasses. There were no windows, only pale, tan-colored stone walls that gave way to an arching alcove on one side. Uneasy, I turned in a slow circle and murmured, "What is this place?"

My father unbuckled his hip bags and sat, finally allowing his wings to sag, spent from the flight. "This is where we wait."

I turned over two of the cups and poured pilzin into them. Handing one to my father, I sipped the crisp liquid and traced my fingers over the cup. A feather pattern unfurled at the base of the cup and continued around it. Simple, functional, beautiful, and perfectly rendered.

Looking around the room, each object from the room itself to the furniture bore the earmarks of Iyarri craftsmanship: the perfect balance of form and function embellished with clean lines and knotwork that furled and unwound as though it had grown that way.

Cæl, though fatigued, was relaxed enough to lean back in his raw-edged tunic and enjoy his drink. I wondered if he felt more like a Heeoa here, more like he belonged. I fingered the hem of my sleeves, wishing I felt like anything other than an imposter in an unconvincing disguise.

There came a polite knock on the door, and the drab Iyarri pushed it open. "Saan-Eleéth has cleared your admittance. Please come with me to your rooms." Cæl picked up his hip bags, and we followed once again.

Although the corridor branched and intersected with many others, our guide wove through the maze without hesitating. We passed other Iyarri, and though I cringed inside under their passing glances, they seemed uninterested in me. As we approached the next archway, the hum of Loagæth grew louder. The side of our path opened to a ledge and I took a few steps closer, wanting to see the source of the voices. My bare feet stumbled to a stop, and I stared in awe, lips parting and wings going limp in surprise. The entire center of the bluff had been hollowed out into a massive, spiraling bazaar—the Roman market of Trajan wrapped upward upon itself a dozen times over.

The cylindrical void loomed upward two stories above us and yawned another ten stories down, the walls dotted with a thousand arched windows and doors. I drifted forward, putting one hand on a column, and leaned over the edge, my long, windblown tumble of ginger waves falling over my shoulder and swinging in the air as I drank in the spectacle. A wrapping, stepped ledge allowed walking, but many Iyarri soared from one stall to the next, their wings flashing among suspended, glowing orbs of light.

In the center of the vast cavern hung a set of time-telling chimes, each metal tube big enough around to fit my arm in, and longer than my wingspan. In the center dangled a great, carved crystal. Each time it flashed a chime answered it, filling the air with both light and music. The Iyarri made something as simple as telling the time captivating.

Iyarri filled the market like birds in an exotic aviary. Some wore casual tunics and robes; others I identified as Iadnah with their blue-patterned hands or the Laidrom with weapons and scars on display. Among them, the Aldaria stood out pure and unaltered—no jewelry or visible body modifications, only subtle needlework bordering their tunics. I wanted to draw them all, capture the thousand details commonplace to them, but mesmerizing to me.

Cæl closed his hand over mine and lifted it from the wall. "Come." Lilnon seemed larger, grander than Idura with many more Iyarri inside its walls.

We passed a library, two Laidrom sparring in a ring of their wing-mates, and Iyarri with their hair in complex, artful plaits and twits. Had any human, or even half-human, ever seen such a thing? The hallways narrowed, becoming quieter, until our guide stopped in front of a door and handed my father a key. "This will be your room. Please accept the hospitality of Saan-Eleéth until your audience."

The quarters were carved from pale stone in a way that could have felt cloistering but was, instead, open and relaxing. The walls and floor were all the natural, subtle colors of a riverbed; overhead hung smaller chimes that toned each hour with its own melody. The central sitting room held two soft benches and a table, and off the back were two bedrooms with an adjoining bathroom.

Cæl ushered me inside; once the heavy wooden door had closed, he said, "I have half a mind to reprimand you for staring like a gape-mouthed human." He paused, his face softening. "But, perhaps, your wonder is warranted."

"It's amazing." My whole body felt light with elation. "Did you miss it?" Though Cæl had lived at Idura, he was obviously no stranger to Lilnon.

His smile faded into a tumult of emotions I struggled to read. "Aye, I did. More than I realized."

TWENTY-SIX

HUNGER AND UNEASE FOUGHT in my stomach the next morning as I dressed in the same pants, embroidered belt, and natural fiber tunic from the day before—to travel light enough, we only had the clothes we'd worn and needed to purchase more. "Should I wear my napta?" I asked as I adjusted the neckline of my tunic so it scooped low on my shoulders and slouched my sleeves enough to hide my hands. "Am I supposed to be a Laidrom?"

"No." Cæl turned, scrutinizing me. "And no." Crestfallen, I stopped reaching for my napta and let my arms drop to my sides.

He rubbed the earlobe with the triangular notch in it. "The Laidrom, Aldaria, and Iadnah are the three specialized groups that comprise the ternion. Each has three ranks—four if you count their novitiates, the Aaiom. Admittance to one of them takes years of preparation you shouldn't pretend to have. If anyone asks, you are an Akarinu painter."

"So, part of a guild?" I crossed my wings behind me, annoyed at my own ignorance and fearful of the danger it put us in.

"Yes, in a way. Akarinu are the backbone of Iyarri society. They are our merchants, educators, artisans, farmers, and architects." He handed me a set of bronze cuff bracelets with stylized brushes and swirls of pigment in a lighter metal. Cæl helped me close them over my forearms and ankles. "These are worn by Akarinu painters. You are artistically

269

talented, more so than many Iyarri. It's fitting." Pride warmed the smile we shared. "Come," he said, as he shouldered a sturdy, woven satchel. "Let's get something to eat."

We walked to the market and entered a curved room with carts full of food near the door. A balcony on the far side of the room opened to the market cavern, places to sit scattered in between. Bowls of spiced grains, fire-roasted fruit rolled in cinnamon, creamy dips, and fresh bread spoiled me for choice. For once, the lack of meat was the norm rather than the exception.

"Where does all this come from?" I whispered as we gathered our food and sat at a secluded table at the edge of a balcony.

"I'll show you later, pasahasa." We were midway up the market cavern, and a thousand Iyarri dined, shopped, and soared all around us.

Not far away, two male Aldaria leaned against one another as they shared breakfast, smiling and talking in low voices. A group of Iyarri children flew past the balcony, giggling as they dipped and soared in unison like a murmuration of starlings. The sliver of envy in my heart was crowded out by how happy they were. The freedom, the friendship among them was more than I had as a child, or still had as an adult. Two Iadnah met near the door, and while they each gave a bow of the head and wings to the other, the one with less blue tattooing on his arms bowed lower.

"Aurelia," Cæl said with a wry smile as he nodded to my untouched breakfast. His meal already finished, Cæl leaned back, cup in hand and eyes distant, as though the hum of a thousand Loagæth voices were the sweetest song in all the world.

Above us were shops and stalls with a million curious sundries on display, including tamed birds and sugar gliders in place of cats and dogs. From the levels below us came the ringing of a hammer on metal, the wooden clatter of looms, and the wet, slippery sound of pottery being shaped. Music filtered upward, resonant hand drums with a woodwind melody lilting over top. I was so distracted, it was a miracle I finished my breakfast at all.

"Essia?" I pushed my empty dishes away. Cæl turned his attention to me, and I fumbled through my question, afraid he'd say no and think me stupid for asking. I gestured to the market shops overhead. "Can we?" I bit my lip and waited for him to tell me he would take me back to our rooms and would purchase what we needed alone.

"I think that's best," he said. "Stay close." My face broke into a smile.

We walked the spiraling ledge upward, my chest tightening as we neared a group of Iyarri clumped in the middle of the path. What if I did something wrong, or didn't do something I should? But they smiled at us and gave affable nods—both a bow of the head and a tip of the wings. Tentative, I returned the gesture. Some of the tension left my shoulders and wings and I brightened, realizing that, save for my hands, I was not so strange here. While all Iyarri had luminous, golden-tan skin, some, like Aamon, were lighter, others darker. My Irish skin was pale, but not freakishly so. Perhaps Iyarri did the same thing as humans—they glanced at me, saw the Iyarri they expected, and moved on.

There were a million items in the market: clothing, jewelry, furnishings, books, weapons, and art. I lingered over the jewelry, taken with the novelty of finally seeing other items like my mother's pendant. In my mind it was always the pinnacle of beauty—the stone shone like a shaft of sunlight in a green forest captured by silver vines and feathers. Here, in this strange, spiraling stone market, I found its lost sisters. Subtle and intricate, Iyarri designs captured fluid motion with neither too much nor too little detail; all the artistic concepts I always valued distilled into one perfect form. It flowed through everything—trinkets and architecture, clothing and weapons alike. I wanted to master the Iyarri style, elaborate on it, and make it my own.

Cæl let me linger over one item after another, and after several stalls, I realized none of the market goods were necessities. Artisan foods, yes, but we hadn't paid for breakfast earlier. There was clothing for sale, but none of it was specific to the ternion—no Laidrom gauntlets, Iadnah ritual components, or Aldaria tunics. Not a single Iyarri seemed poor or in need, but the nuances of their economy and society eluded me.

I picked up a traveling belt like my father's in my sleeve-covered hands. Made from pale doeskin leather, the belt clasped in the front and had a pouch over each hip. Each could have held a sketchbook with room to spare for my other, smaller, items.

"Try it on," the Iyarri behind the counter said. A little younger than me, she smiled and flicked her chickadee-patterned wings. "Go ahead, it'll look lovely on you." A sleek flying squirrel peeked out from behind her thick black braid, its oil-drop eyes wide and curious. I suppressed what might have been a very un-Iyarri exclamation at its cuteness as it snuffled the Akarinu's earlobe and then blinked at me.

Setting down the belt, I held out my hands, sleeves making a nest in my palms. I nodded to the flying squirrel. "Can I hold it?"

The animal was gone in a flash of gray-brown. The Iyarri giggled. "She's shy. And nocturnal, so maybe you'd have better luck trying again at night." There was an alluring lilt to her voice.

Cæl picked up the belt with one hand and held out several strange coins with the other. "We'll take this," he said, completing the transaction and ushering me away with a thank-you and an amused smile.

I looked back over my shoulder at the Iyarri. The flying squirrel was back on her shoulder; she gave it a kiss and winked at me. I blushed and smiled back.

Spoiled for choice, I eventually selected a few tunics and flowing pants. To this, Cæl added a rich, blood-red robe. Soon, his large woven satchel was bulging.

We ascended the great, spiraling market, passing through the booths selling scented oil for wings and bowls of powdered incense. An Iyarri woman stepped out of a salon, a tumble of black Botticelli curls cascading between her cardinal-red wings. There were captivating eye spots of black and gray at the ends of her unalah. She caught me staring and called to me, "Such pretty hair deserves better treatment, wouldn't you think?" Iyarri grew their hair long, but often wore it in updos, twists, and plaits to keep it out of the way of their wings. My hair tumbled past my waist and was pretty enough—if one found chaos pretty.

Trying not to seem over-eager, I twined my fingers into the ends of my waves. "Can I?" I asked Cæl.

He rubbed his knuckles against his cheek and directed the woman. "Style it into something elegant."

The Iyarri guided me onto a stool and took Lucien's hair spiral out of my hair. She turned it over in her hands, admiring it, and set it on her tray. The spiral rested among familiar tools—scissors and combs—but there were unfamiliar items, too: a bone hook, little pots of oils and creams, and strips of leather.

She slid her clawed fingers through the tumble of copper waves. I stiffened, expecting them to scratch my scalp or snag the snarls in my hair, but she was deft and gentle as she worked out the tangles, then swept the sides up, splitting each side into tiny rope braids. These she pinned to the back of my head, letting the twists tumble down my back, save one. The last rope braid, from behind my left ear, she left down; she put Lucien's spiral back in place, the bright metal flashing against my ribs. For the length she rubbed a sweet-smelling cream between her palms and smoothed it through my hair, defining the waves into pulled-out curls. The red-winged Iyarri turned toward my father and inclined her head. "Much better, yes?"

I appraised my reflection in the mirror and found myself more Iyarri than moments ago. Cæl nodded in approval. "Aye, she's lovely." His compliment stoked my heart until it glowed.

Leaving the salon, Cæl and I threaded our way through other Iyarri and back through the halls. They thought I was Iyarri, and I *felt* Iyarri with my swaying wings, woven clothes, styled hair, and belted hip pouches. I was so enamored with the feeling that it took the roar of water to make me realize we hadn't gone back toward our rooms. Curious, but not able to ask where we were going, I hurried and fell into step beside my father. Like Idura, Lilnon had areas that seemed to have fallen into disuse, as if the population of Iyarri inside its walls had once been greater. We wound lower, deeper into the bluff; the stone around us grew damp and the sound of water rolled like channeled thunder.

Cæl opened a huge, groaning door of wet wood. I took two steps forward into tender, cool grass and paused, struck by wonder—behind the doors was an entire lush valley, growing green and vibrant under an enchanted stone ceiling that shone like sunlight. Terraces wrapped the walls in a great spiral and a stone channel of water followed it, irrigating stalks of amaranth, wild rice, and legumes. An aqueduct emptied from the ceiling into the channels, misting the cavern with prismatic droplets of moisture. Akarinu flitted from one height to another, harvesting with hand sickles and tossing their spoils into large fabric satchels.

I inhaled, the air heavy with the scents of flowers, herbs, water, and greens. Pale mushrooms dotted the shadows and added an earthy undertone to the aroma.

Cæl leaned on the edge of a great stone trough. Behind him, unglazed amphora vases bobbed in the flowing water, full of watercress, chicory, and herbs. The water echoing in the cavern must have been enough to drown out our voices from eavesdroppers, but Cæl still gestured me closer before he spoke. "This is the Glade. Each stronghold has one. Almost everything a stronghold needs is grown here." He smiled at my awestruck expression.

Fruit trees grew in the circular copse in the center, the spaces between them studded with apiaries. Golden, fuzzy bees flashed in the light, droning from medicinal herbs to tubs sprouting with fennel and ginger. I wandered through the Glade, my fingers trailing over the bobbing heads of flowers. "It reminds me of Mom's garden." A pang of home-sickness struck me, and Cæl's expression became wistful.

Every year, my mother transformed her yard into an ever-changing botanical fireworks display. Perennials burst through the earth and bloomed one right after the other. In the spring the yard was pink, purple, and white with impatiens, lilac, and echinacea. In the summer it warmed to yellow and blue with meadow bright, lilies, and irises. Autumn was an orchestra of reds, golds, and oranges with daylilies, poppies, love-lies-bleeding, and mums. Her garden didn't even stop blooming at sundown. At night, moonvine, angel's trumpet, and evening primrose bathed the whole yard in an effervescent perfume.

I wished she were here with me in this everblooming garden; the yearning wilting into a pained realization—she never would be. Whatever Iyarri life I might have, my mother would never share in its wonders.

Cæl and I returned to our rooms, more spent than either of us expected. I sunk into one of the deep beds with a sketchbook and captured the details of the day in graphite.

Sometime in the night Cæl shook me awake. "Get some clean clothes. We're going to the baths."

Overhead, the ceiling undulated with blues and blacks. "It's the middle of the night."

"I know. Keep your back to the wall and your hands hidden."

Cæl led us past the lower levels of the market and down an endless flight of stairs, until we were closer to the base of the bluff. I hoped the water wasn't straight from the lake. There'd been ice on it the night we'd arrived, and Iyarri-blooded or not, I was not getting into freezing water. We stopped outside the baths. "Be quick and do not to draw attention to yourself. Generally, women stay to the right, men to the left." Cæl pushed open a mammoth set of double doors and a puff of warm air escaped. "Those that care to mingle do so in the center of the water."

I stopped mid-step, dread seizing my limbs and throttling my voice to a whisper. "You mean there aren't separate baths for men and women?" The idea of bathing with strangers, and my father? My stomach clenched into a fist, and I clutched the clean robe to my chest. I couldn't even remember the last time I'd seen my mother naked.

"No." His tone was mild, but his expression held a warning: this was neither the time nor the place for this discussion, and my human modesty would be as obvious as my hands and my glowing, golden scars. He put a hand on my shoulder. "Come on." I didn't move.

An Iyarri passed us with a curious tilt of her head. Trembling, I gripped the bundle of clean clothes tight and walked forward. Inside the baths, burning sconces lined the walls and cast dancing light over a large pool of deep blue-green water. Overhead, the ceiling glimmered with aquatic colors and shafts of light, like looking at the surface of the water from a great depth. Steaming water poured into the pool from a tall, gravity-fed aqueduct. Dried lavender buds bobbed atop the water, but the relaxing aroma did nothing to calm my nerves or settle my stomach. There were not many Iyarri at so late an hour, but a few lounged naked in the water, talking. Bowls, full of whipped soaps and scrubs, lined the edge of the pool, and stone steps disappeared into the water, the far end of the pool deep enough to swim in.

Cæl walked off to the far side of the baths. I looked at my feet and hurried to an isolated space at the opposite end. My cheeks on fire, I undressed and slid into the water. I kept my scarred back to one of the pillars supporting the domed ceiling and my hands beneath the surface. My wings dragged under the water; were I not nauseous with stress, I might have fanned them out and enjoyed the sensation.

Two Iyarri exited the water, one male and one female, and I couldn't help but steal a fleeting look. Laidrom scarring was familiar to me, but I hadn't seen the full markings of the Iadnah in person before. The blue covered her thumbs and forefingers, a folded circle wrapping around the opposite side of her hands all full of arcane, patterned voids. The blue continued past her wrists, breaking into swirling arcane symbols that coursed up her arms, terminating in a draped circle of blue symbols that scooped over her collarbones and skimmed above the bases of her wings. The man with her was Aldaria, and in a sea of tattooed, scarred, and decorated Iyarri, his unaltered flesh glowed. Aamon's skin would have been much the same, a perfect envelope for someone capable of such subterfuge and cruelty.

I scrubbed myself clean, toweled off, and changed into one of my new robes. Cæl was waiting for me outside the doors, but an Iyarri I didn't know reached him first. "Stars and feathers, I'd written you off as dead. It's good to see you again, Cæl."

My father clasped forearms with the other Iyarri. "pir-Maroch, it is good to see you." Maroch was a broad, grizzled man with tattered snowy-owl wings. His Heeoa scarring matched my father's, but Maroch's continued to a fearsome half-mask over what otherwise would have been a gentle and dignified face.

Maroch waved off the formalities and clapped Cæl on the shoulder. "So, tell me, where've you been? It's been a long time." His white hair was braided into an upraised, five-strand braid that ran from forehead to shoulders and was tied off with a tight wrap of leather.

My father gestured me toward them, and I tried not to stare at the scarred side of Maroch's face. Maroch raised two eyebrows at Cæl and grinned. "That's what kept you away? Can't say I blame you, but isn't she a little young?"

My father cleared his throat. "Aurelia is my daughter."

Maroch laughed—loud and roaring as a Viking in his hall. "Well then, you have been busy. Come on, let's go drink and you can catch me up on your exploits."

Cæl smiled, and I could see how much he liked this Laidrom. "I would, but—"

Maroch made a dismissive motion with his hand. "Don't make me pull rank on you. I have a full flask of darignis, and half of it is yours."

My father chuckled. "Let me see Aurelia to our rooms, and I'll come down."

"Why not bring her with?"

The napta cut on my arm tingled, and Miketh's voice surfaced in my memory. *And now any Laidrom can challenge you to a Circle of Blades.* Realization jolted through me and unease rippled in its wake—Cæl was considering bringing me with. I fumbled for words, wanting to come up with some excuse, but I also didn't want to say anything in embarrassing front of Maroch.

"Let us drop some things off and we'll come down," Cæl said.

Maroch put one massive clawed hand on my shoulder. "It is my honor to meet the daughter of an old wingmate." He turned toward Cæl. "I'll go find that flask. Don't make me come looking for you." He walked away, his dappled white wings like an emperor's cape.

My father smiled. "Well, that was unexpected." Unexpected, but not unwanted. Cæl walked toward our chambers, and I hurried to catch up to him. "If anyone offers you darignis, don't drink it. The name means *hellfire*—you'll have no tolerance for it."

I crinkled my nose at the idea. It must have been the stuff Tiahmani and Miketh favored as well—every time they opened their flasks, a choking cloud of mulled spices, fire, and ash wafted out. Tentatively I said, "I don't want to go, essia." I hurried an explanation, my voice timid and small. "Miketh figured out I'd earned napta and said anyone could challenge me to them."

Cæl let us into our rooms and rubbed his thumb and forefinger over the nick in his earlobe. "Technically you'd need this before anyone could challenge you"—he gestured to the triskele on his shoulder—"but if you don't want to go, you don't have to."

I sighed in relief, some of the tightness lifting from my chest. "What does the scarring on Maroch's face mean?"

"That he is the Laidrom advisor to Saan-Eleéth. All Laidrom answering to her also answer to him. As such, you should address him as pir-Maroch."

"Saan-Eleéth has advisors?" I asked, curious. Miketh hadn't mentioned that the other night.

"Since the Saanir splintered, the Ohlera are attended by five advisors. Just as each stronghold is ruled by a Council of the Four Winds, Saan-Eleéth has one advisor from each division of the ternion and two from the Akarinu." He pulled a package from his satchel and handed it to me. "I will not be gone long. Not as long as Maroch would like, anyway."

"What's this?"

"It's for you." Inside the brown wrapping paper were several books on Iyarri artistic techniques including drawing, painting, and sculpture. Cæl couldn't hide his smile. "I saw you looking at them."

I set the books down and hugged him, inhaling the scent of an ancient, sacred forest. "Thank you, essia."

He hugged me back. "You are most welcome, pasahasa. Stay here, and don't open the door for anyone."

The morning of our audience with Eleéth, Cæl and I practiced our entrance and presentation. There wasn't enough room in our chambers to spread our wings properly, but by the end of it, our movements matched. The preparation should have made me less nervous, but instead it stirred up anxiousness and doubt.

As the hour of our audience neared, I dressed in the deep red robe and tied and retied my belt while Cæl finished getting ready. He went shirtless, showing the rank of Heeoa across the skin of his chest and both arms. He added his molded leather belt and his napta, the deep red leather polished until it shone like blood-drenched rubies. With a speed that defied the complexity of the task, his thick, clawed fingers recreated the wide five-strand braid Maroch wore. "Is that the style Heeoa wear?" I asked.

He inclined his head as a yes, and took in my appearance. "Here." He reached forward and adjusted my belt so the drape was uniform and stepped back. "Do not speak to Saan-Eleéth unless she asks you a direct question. If she does so, answer politely, succinctly, and honestly. If her advisors are there, make sure to address them with pir- and then their name."

"I understand."

"And no matter what happens, be strong. Strength and honor are two respected Iyarri qualities."

I bit my lip and, after a second of hesitation, followed him out the door. I hoped I was Iyarri enough.

TWENTY-SEVEN

W|E DESCENDED INTO THE stone depths of Lilnon and stopped in front of a great set of double doors inlaid with bloodstone. The tiles beneath our feet were the same stone, the deep green luster spattered with red. Though we made no sound and did not knock, a female voice from the other side of the door called, "Enter, Cæl, Heeoa and protector."

The ceiling of the stone room arched overhead—mottled gray stone layered with undulating white light, as if the hall were carved from the heart of a thunderstorm. Tapestries edged in swaying feathers hung along the walls and Laidrom armed with napta and tall spears filled the spaces in between. I took a deep breath, the scent of incense filling my lungs. The air shook as it left my trembling lips.

We walked to the center of the room and stopped where the path widened before Eleéth's dais. In unison, Cæl and I knelt on one knee, bowed our heads, and spread our wings wide and parallel to the floor. After a few seconds, we both stood and folded our wings behind us. In a voice that could have made a whole complement of Laidrom stand to attention, my father said, "I thank you for your audience, Saanire Eleéth Ohlera."

"You are most welcome." Her voice was serene but tempered with a noble fortitude.

I lifted my eyes to Eleéth and froze, stunned.

She was aurora borealis distilled into a woman's form with wings made of the night sky. Her lips curved and her amethyst eyes glinted—she was as deadly, if not deadlier, than any Laidrom. Hers was not a smile of welcome; it whispered of power. With a rustle like velvet curtains, she unfurled her wings, feathers black, but glimmering with purples and gold and greens. "I'm pleased you brought her with you, though what relevance she has remains to be seen." Her voice lingered in my ears even after she stopped speaking. She sat on a bench, her wings easing around her like the full gown of a courtly lady. "Your audience is granted, Heeoa. Speak your piece."

My father stood straight-backed, his voice confident. "I have come to speak to you about a breach of the Aisaro. I trust you have heard about the incident at Idura, with the angel that fell through the cathedral dome at Christmas Mass."

Eleéth nodded. Her black hair was separated, knotted, and separated again into a net-like crown tied with tiny gold bands and adorned with wavering feathers. No, I corrected myself. She was not adorned with feathers—they grew in her hair, just as Miketh had said. Long and thin, they followed the lay of her hair, adding gleams of blue and purple to the black. "News of such things reached me here," she said. "One of the Aldaria is dealing with the situation. But you are not here to bring news that the culprit behind this has been found."

Cæl's voice was clear, self-assured. "The culprit and the one tasked with revealing the culprit are one and the same. Aamon Amayo revealed Iyarri to the humans, not as angels, but as what we truly are."

"That is a grave charge, Heeoa." Not an eyebrow arched, and the angle of Eleéth's head did not change, but a spill of arctic air rolled over my feet.

If my father noticed the cold, it showed neither in his posture nor his voice. "That is not the whole of my charges, Ohlera. In so doing, he falsified orders that sent nine Laidrom to their deaths at the hands of a kiaisi, including Ikkar, Idura's standing Heeoa."

"A kiaisi? I assume it's dead," she asked, inclining her head with curiosity.

"Yes, Saanire. The kiaisi was killed," Cæl answered. I bit the inside of my lip; their satisfaction at Lucien's violent death made my chest ache.

"You will need proof of these charges."

"I saw Aamon force what the humans are calling an angel through one of the stained-glass windows at the cathedral. My sister, Tiahmani, was able to catch the 'angel' before she was seen for more than a few seconds by the humans."

"And would Tiahmani back your accusations?"

"Yes."

"Why isn't she here?"

"She was too ill to travel."

Eleéth's scrutiny weighed heavy on my father, measuring the truth of his words. He swallowed and steeled himself.

"Now, Heeoa, tell me what you are leaving out." Eleéth's turned her attention to me but spoke to my father. "Tell me about her."

"She is the one Aamon threw through the cathedral window, revealing us."

Eleéth rose and stepped from her dais, her green dress a spill of fabric clasped over one luminous shoulder. She paused in front of me, and the same dark lights in her wings gleamed in her irises.

"Aurelia is my daughter. And a Linnia." My heart wrung at the shame in Cæl's voice. Shock rippled through the guards, and they traded surprised whispers. Each furtive glance cut like a paring knife.

Eleéth's eyes fell to my bare hands. "This complicates things, Heeoa," she said. Her demeanor shifted, the lines of her face tightened, and interest moved in her voice like a riptide under calm waters.

"I know."

Eleéth gestured to one of the guards. "Move her out of the way." One of the fiercely decorated Laidrom stepped between me and my father. The guard did not touch me, but tipped his spear in my direction. I stepped backward, crumpling with fear, making myself as small a target as possible. The tip gleamed, split and serrated like a napta blade.

For every step he took forward, I stepped back, until Eleéth stood halfway between my father and me, her voice as cold as the bloodstone under my feet. "Doalin, Cæl, is the Unspeakable Sin. To lay with a human." She paused, surveyed the fault lines in my father's soul, and placed the weight of his disgrace at their weakest point. "What was her mother like?" Eleéth asked.

For a moment, they locked eyes, but then my father's jaw tightened and he looked away, defeated. My heart twisted in my chest—there was no acceptable answer. None of my mother's many talents would mean anything to an Iyarri. "I am not sure I understand the question, Saanire Ohlera," he said.

Her voice rang in the stone hall, making me feel small, fragile. "She must have been an amazing creature, a human of exceptional merit, to outclass every Iyarri woman you encountered—more battle-hardened than a Laidrom, more social graces than the most refined Aldaria, a scholar of rituals beyond what any Iadnah could master. Tell me about this human who won your heart from your own people. What was it about her that turned your loyalty to unfaithfulness, our trust in you to doubt, and reduced a once-great Heeoa to something shameful and tainted?"

"I know what I did, committing Doalin, was a repulsive thing." Cæl's voice became deeper, strained. "And there is no answer that justifies my actions." I pressed arms tight against my body, trying to wall in my thoughts. Was he lying when he said he didn't regret being with my mother?

Eleéth let the silence stretch out and twine into the incense smoke before she spoke. "I have never heard words in the same breath that were both truth and a lie, Heeoa. You have tormented yourself over your own actions because you are ashamed of them, and yet you are not." Eleéth turned back toward me, the frigidness that clung to her curling around me like icy tendrils of mist. The unnatural cold cut through me in a way the bitterest of winter winds could not, and I stiffened, even my shivers constricted and fearful. Her eyes were critical, like an artist able to see through the paint, through the washes, past the canvas, and down to the wooden frame. Her scrutiny stayed on me, but she spoke to my father. "Do you love your bastard?"

A spike of fear nailed my flitting heart to my ribs. Cæl's gaze stayed fixed to the floor by Eleéth's feet. "I do."

"Look at her," Eleéth demanded. Cæl lifted his eyes to mine, the hazel fractured with pain. "Do you see the human taint to her features? She could have been Iyarri."

My heart curled in on itself as Cæl pulled in a ragged breath and averted his eyes from me. Eleéth regarded his pain with neither compassion nor pity, hate nor disdain. She stepped near to me and repeated her request. "Look at her, Cæl." She waited until he turned his eyes back to me. Eleéth slid one finger under my hair and draped it over my shoulders, exposing my back. She leaned close, silken strands of her hair falling over the scars my robe did not hide. "Linnia are not born with wings. Tell me how she got hers."

"A ritual," he said. "Aamon recruited three Iadnah to do it. He told her that, with wings, the Elonu-Dohe would accept her as Iyarri."

All I could breathe was Eleéth's scent: white sleet on frozen blossoms. Her voice was uncaring as the deepest winter. No malice, no joy, all the fairness of unbroken snow. "Do you love her more with wings?"

"You know the answer to that." His words were bitter and twisted like a napta blade in my gut.

"And yet I'd like to hear you say it. Would you love her even more if she had been born true?" she asked.

"I would. I regret my sin made her less than she could have been."

My chest tightened with a sob, and while I kept it bottled inside me, silent, hot lines of tears slid down my cheeks. So that was what he thought when he looked at me.

I peered through the veil of my hair at my father. He desperately wanted to love his clever, artistic pasahasa, but in that instant I realized how much of that was a concerted effort on his part and how effortless it might have been for him had I been Iyarri. After my wings, every effort of his—to see me fly, to master an ipuran—was equal parts generosity and selfishness. It was as much to help me find my way in my new body as it was to forge me into the Iyarri daughter his heart of hearts craved.

Eleéth's voice was impassive. "Before I hear about the crimes of another Iyarri, my advisors need to be made aware of your own, Cæl. Do you understand?"

"Yes, Saanire Ohlera."

Eleéth spoke to a guard in the back of the room. "Fetch my advisors. Be quick; accept no excuses from any of them." I blinked back tears and wiped my face clean with the sleeve of my robe. After the guard was gone, Eleéth settled onto her bench, folding and unfolding her wings in contemplation. My father stood as though he'd been carved from stone, eyes vacant. As the wait stretched on, my already dwindling confidence cratered to fear.

A few minutes later, her five Iyarri advisors entered, Maroch last. His lips were set in a serious line; today, there was no mirth to ease the ferocity of his scarred face. Eleéth nodded to her advisors. "Maroch, Anahita, Occodon, Barcus, Sisera." Eleéth gestured to me. "That is not Iyarri. Can any of you tell me what she is?" I went perfectly still, but my pulse hammered in my temples.

Confusion buckled the scars on Maroch's face, and it was Anahita who stepped forward first, slight and willowy in her Iadnah robes. With moonlit hair and pale lips, it seemed all the color had been sucked from the rest of her features and into the lucent green-blue of her eyes, wings, and the single, stunning line of Iadnah tattooing that ran down the center of her forehead. She peered at me like an oddity in a jar, then pinched the hem of my sleeve and used it as a marionette string to pull my arm upward. "What's wrong with her hands?"

Occodon stepped forward, his Aldaria robes tailored in severe lines, his steely wings pinched tight. "They're human." The sneer in his voice made me feel small, tainted.

Maroch grimaced and wiped his face with his hand. "I did not expect this when you told me she was your daughter, Cæl." My father did not move.

"A winged Linnia?" Anahita gasped as she leaned so close the hem of her Iadnah robe brushed the tops of my feet. A scholarly temper returned to her voice. "How is that possible? Linnia die after their wings are conjured forth."

Occodon's lips thinned into a fine white line, and he turned away, his wings closing like jackknives. "Kill the abomination." My body contracted in fear, but none of the guards moved toward me, although they watched Eleéth for an order.

Barcus leaned against the wall and crossed his arms and wings in a unified gesture of bored skepticism. "Was her mother a plodder?" he asked. My throat tightened—that word distilled my mother to an animal.

My father kept his face devoid of expression. "She was."

Anahita walked around me in a slow circle and threaded her fingers into my robe. "There looks to be some scarring on her back." I stiffened as the metal clasps gave way, the robe peeled forward, and the open air of the chamber caressed my back to the base of my spine.

"What do you see, Anahita?" Eleéth's voice was neutral.

"Her wings were conjured. The scarring shows where they burst forth from her back." She peered closer, her words coming slow and fascinated. "But she lived." I shivered as Anahita traced the shattered lines of my scars with her blue forefinger. "These did not mend naturally. Someone healed her—that hasn't happened since before the Rior were murdered."

Occodon's voice was tempered. "The ritual was done improperly. Kill her, remedy the situation, and let us be done with it."

"Saanire Ohlera, if I may," Sisera interjected. She, like Barcus, was Akarinu; the length of her black hair bound in bronze bands gleamed with the same hardness as her gaze. "Conventionally, this ritual ends with the death of the Linnia. I see no benefit to changing the practice now. A quick end is better for all involved."

Fear evaporated the moisture in my mouth, and I took two skittering steps sideways. Eleéth pressed one pensive finger against her lips. "The Linnia is integral to Cæl's charges against Aamon Amayo." Eleéth summarized Cæl's accusations against Aamon for her advisors. When she finished, Maroch crossed his arms over his chest and said, "True as that is, Cæl, your daughter is not Iyarri. Aamon revealing her to the humans was not in violation of the Aisaro."

Cæl cleared his throat and gathered himself. "pir-Occodon, what is the precise law regarding revealing our existence to humans?"

This Occodon recited from memory. "No Iyarri shall reveal our true nature to those that toil on the earth."

Cæl leveled his gazed at Occodon. "And do you consider yourself smarter than a plodder?"

Maroch stifled a laugh by coughing into his hand, and Occodon's face went red. "Do not insult me, Heeoa, whose seed brought forth an abomination. What is your point?"

"If you could not distinguish what Aurelia was when you walked in the room, how could a human? She has been at Lilnon for five days, and not one Iyarri has seen her for the Linnia that she is. Not even Maroch, and he both talked to her and touched her. If a human saw Aurelia and a true-blooded Iyarri side by side, could they tell the difference where you could not?"

"Of course not."

Confidence crept back into my father's voice. "Then tell me the difference between Aamon revealing a winged Linnia and a full-blooded Iyarri."

Anahita traced her fingertips over the palm of her other hand. "A winged Linnia is not an Iyarri. Aamon would have known that. Or should have."

Cæl's voice was tempered. "Aamon is counting on you to draw that distinction where the humans would not."

Eleéth turned to Cæl. "Your charges have merit, Heeoa. And yet, you have your own crimes to answer for. You are to remain at Lilnon while I investigate. I will confer with my advisors and reveal my decisions in due time." She gestured to my father. "I grant you leave. Return to your rooms, and I will send pir-Maroch with further instructions." I swayed, relief sweeping away the tension in my body.

My father cleared his throat and settled his wings behind him. "Of course, Saanire Ohlera."

I took a step toward him, and Eleéth's voice rang out: "Not you, Linnia." I froze mid-step, stealing a panicked look over my shoulder. She gestured to her guards. "Nisroc, take her to my private library so Anahita and I can examine her ourselves." A guard took me by my elbow, and I cringed away from her.

Anahita's face lit up, as though she'd been gifted all the riches in the world in one scarred package. She turned to me with a hungry smile on her pale lips. "The opportunity to see a living Linnia is so rare."

My open robe slouched over my shoulders; I pressed it to my chest with one hand and pushed my hair from my face with the other. Trembling, I beseeched Cæl with my eyes. *Don't leave me with them.* My father gave me the barest of nods, willing me strength, then bowed to Eleéth.

Essia! The scream sat trapped in my throat as they took me away.

TWENTY-EIGHT

MY GUARD MUSCLED OPEN the doors to Eleéth's chambers as dread, shame, and nausea crashed over me in a hot wave. We entered a circular receiving area; above us hung a great, suspended disc of stone, the underside enchanted like the ceilings to shine with light.

The guard gestured toward the ceiling. "Fly up."

I froze. I knew how to take off from the ground, but couldn't remember under the instant demand of the Laidrom.

The guard gave a disgusted snort, seized me around the waist, and pulled us into the air. A few wingbeats later, we cleared the edge of the disc and she dumped me onto it. I scrambled to my feet and the Laidrom led me deeper into Eleéth's suspended library. The bookcases were arcs, growing smaller as we moved toward the center of the stone. We stopped at a central table inlaid with a starburst of wood and gold leaf, a great dome of golden light far overhead. The chimes hung in the center sang the time in an entrancing, eerie requiem.

I fumbled the center flap of my robe up, twisting to do the intricate clasps. The sound of wings rustled from the far side of the library; overhead, the chimes sang louder. Eleéth wove her way through the bookcases, Anahita and a flock of three Iadnah behind her. Two women held large books, and the man cradled a tablet of drawing paper in his tattooed hands. Casting furtive glances at me, they bowed their heads and wings together and spoke in low voices. Not sure what to do, I stayed still, hoping no action would draw their attention less than a misstep.

The Iadnah settled onto saddle stools at the end of the round table, a jury in esoteric robes. Anahita's hummingbird-teal wings flicked as she stood in front of me. I inhaled, drawing the air in slowly, willing myself to stay calm.

Eleéth sat and waved her hand. "You may begin."

Anahita circled around me twice, commenting to me as she walked, the line of tattoos on her forehead pinching in concentration. "Taller than average height for a female Iyarri, perhaps average for a human." She gestured to one of the Iadnah, who produced a cloth tape measure from a pocket. The second took notes and the third drew my form in artful, efficient lines. Anahita and her assistant measured my height, the length of my limbs, and the circumference of my neck, my breasts, my waist, my hips, and my wrists; the measuring tape slithered over my body, coiling and tightening at times like a serpent. I willed myself motionless, tried to lock the unease inside me, but a thin line of sweat ran down my sternum.

"Look at me." I tilted my head down, and she peered into my face. "Red hair, gray eyes. Bone structure appears to be balanced between Iyarri and human, with eye shape and skin luminosity Iyarri, skin color paler than Iyarri." They measured the distance between my eyes, down my nose, and around my head. "Open your wings," she ordered.

I smoothed my hands over my robe, but it did little to calm my racing nerves. The muscles in my back bunched and my wings unfolded, the tips brushing some of the strange tomes ensconced in the curved bookcases. Anahita closed one hand over the top of my wing and squeezed its length, testing the bones and tissue beneath the feathers. She and her assistant pored over my wings, taking a thousand more measurements. I stifled a cry of exertion as my wings trembled. They fell closed, leaving the tape measure hanging between the assistant's lean fingers. "Linnia." Anahita's voice was sharp with disapproval.

"I'm sorry, pir-Anahita," I said. "They're still gaining strength and—"

My guard took a step forward. "Horsefeathers; she can't even fly," she said. "I had to carry her up here like an invalid."

Anahita gripped my wing and pried it open, the exhausted muscles screaming in protest. "Is that true?" she demanded.

"I can fly, but—" Anahita silenced me with a gesture and glanced from me to the far edge of the library, seeming to contemplate tossing me over the edge to see if I'd fly or crash to the stones below.

She lifted her eyes over my shoulder to the Laidrom. "Hold her wings open, since she is incapable of doing so." Strong hands clamped over my wings and wrenched them open with such force I staggered, stretched and suspended between them. My wings burned and tried to close, but the Laidrom gripped harder. I was breathing through my teeth before Anahita allowed for my release.

When the guards let go of me, I stumbled, my wings heavy and useless behind me. Eleéth's voice was like velvet: "Tell us, Linnia, about how your wings were summoned and how you survived."

That I could do. Bolstered, I pressed my lips together and gathered my thoughts, framing the Loagæth words with care. The Iadnah prodded with endless questions, and I did my best to answer. There was so much I didn't know or couldn't remember. What memories Irel's herbal draught hadn't erased had been washed away in the spill of blood on the stone altar.

"That's all you recall?" Anahita's assistant looked up from her notes and squinted at me, trying to decide if I was being deceptive or was too stupid to remember.

"That's everything, I swear."

"Summon an ipuran, if you can." I gathered my scattered concentration and focused, feeling the airy illusion settle over me. Anahita waved her hand. "Dismiss it." I did as she asked, instantly missing the feeling of protection the illusion granted me.

The Iadnah and Eleéth looked at one another, and for one hopeful second, I thought they were done. Then Anahita gestured to me and said, "Take off your robe."

I crossed my arms over my chest and took a step backward, heat flushing up my neck to my cheeks. My voice was high and strained, "Is that necessa—"

"Linnia." Anahita was patiently condescending. "I have made a request of you. Do it, or I can arrange it to be done for you." Feathers and spears shifted behind me.

We held eyes for a moment. There was no cruel glee in her expression, nor was there compassion; only the barest hints of impatience and a resolve to make good on her threat should I tarry and prove problematic. I looked down and shed my robe, trying to hide my bare breasts with my arms as I folded the fabric into a neat square and set it aside on a stool. "All of them," she demanded. Such a small scrap of fabric gave me so much comfort. I slid my underpants down, stepped out of them, and stood naked and shaking, my stomach a ball of cold lead.

Anahita circled around me again, the ends of her brilliant unalah lashing at the edges of my vision. Her voice was pitched to be clear, and I could hear pencils scratching out her words. "Dewclaws removed at some point." The edge of one of her feathers dragged across my bare calf. "Human influence on the curves of breasts and hips; hands are human-shaped and lack claws. Lack of body hair outside of head and pubis consistent with Iyarri anatomy." She paused, musing. "Turn around, Linnia." I did, a shocked murmur rippling through the gathered Iadnah at the sight of my scars. I squeezed my hands into fists as Anahita placed the tip of one claw in one of the twisted masses of sunken scar tissue and ran it upward, as though she could unzip my flesh with it. "Crude, but perhaps the best her human blood allowed."

Eleéth nodded to the Iadnah. "Map and measure the scars. I want them recorded in detail."

The smooth measuring tape settled at the topmost scar where it wrapped up the back of my neck and fell downward. It was too short.

Her claw pricked my back as she marked the end of the tape with her finger and took a second measurement.

From behind me came the chime of glasses, the crisp smell of pilzin, and the aroma of spiced food. My throat was dry and my stomach growled, but they did not offer me any, nor did I ask, not wanting to give them the opening to deny me something I desired. As time passed I grew woozy, my stomach twisting itself into empty knots.

Finally, Anahita stopped and skimmed the exhausting notes and drawings. Overhead, the ceiling waned and other lights came on, giving the room a candlelight glow. I eyed my clothes, wanting nothing more than to cover my naked, scarred body and run back to my rooms. Anahita turned back to me, her eyes scrutinizing slits. "Remind me how old you are."

I cleared my throat. "Twenty-five. I'll be twenty-six later this month."

"And do you have menses?"

My cheeks lit with color. Everyone was staring at me. "Yes."

"How often?"

My stomach rolled with anxiety and bile. "Once every several months. They aren't regular."

"And have you had any since you gained your wings?"

"Yes, once."

Anahita's brow furrowed. "You don't think she could be fertile, do you?" she asked Eleéth.

Eleéth tilted her head, pensive. "It seems possible. Many Iyarri never conceive, even with more frequent menses, but her human blood could increase her fertility."

Anahita wrapped her clawed hands around the sides of my hips, the blue of her hands vibrant against my pale skin. Every fiber of my body screamed to shy from her touch, but I locked my knees and held still. Anahita's thumbs pressed deep into my abdomen, working in circles. I tensed, uneasy with the pressure of her hands on my full bladder. "She has ovaries." The power surrounding Anahita's hands delved, thrumming beneath my skin. I shuddered. "Have you ever been pregnant?"

"No."

"Have you laid with an Iyarri?" I shook my head. "With a human?" Regret tolled in my heart, and I shook my head again. Anahita's permeating magic ceased the second her hands left my skin.

Eleéth pressed the edge of her glass to her lips in contemplation; the clear pilzin turned black with the reflection of her wings. "And she can maintain an ipuran, so a human might not realize what she really is."

"Hold her," Anahita said to the Laidrom behind me. "I want to see how Iyarri she is inside."

"No!" I cried. Blood pounded in my temples, and the Laidrom's hands reached for my bare shoulders. I twisted out of their grip and backed down one of the rows of books, my slender arms crossed over my nakedness.

Anahita's wings flared. "Linnia."

I stepped backward, deeper into the maze of books. My toes tensed in the rug, and my pinfeathers rattled against one another. Another few steps back and the bookcases narrowed my field of vision to a slice of the central area.

The Laidrom struck me from above, her body hitting mine like a star cast from the night sky. I slammed into the floor, chin cracking on the thin rug. White pain bloomed behind my eyes, and all I could hear was the chimes overhead. Clawed hands wrenched my arm behind me and hauled me to my feet. The Laidrom grabbed a fistful of my locks with her other hand and pulled my head back, each hair a pinpoint of agony atop my head. Blood slicked the inside of my mouth, and she marched me forward, back into the central opening of the library.

Anahita moved again into my vision, and the hard leather binding of a book slammed into the side of my face. White glittered like a snowstorm in my vision. "Stupid creature," Anahita spat. "This time, hold her." The other two Laidrom stepped inward, hooking my legs in theirs and holding my wings back with their bodies. The third tightened her grip, my shoulders and scalp on fire with pressure.

Anahita's voice returned to its unperturbed, scholarly tone as she gave orders to her assistants. I twisted and tried to move, but the Laidrom held me all the harder. Pain roared in my ears, warping and distorting every sound around me. It took me many moments to realize the small, pained whimpers I heard were coming from me.

Anahita pressed her stacked hands between my breasts, over my sternum. She swept her wings around my feet in a hummingbird-bright circle of feathers and chanted in the same arcane version of Loagæth that Irel, Sofiel, and Nesah used during the ritual that gave me wings. The air tingled with magical energy, like a gathering lightning strike.

Anahita's magic threaded into me like hot wires. I screamed and twisted my body, arching and contracting in the vicelike hold of the Laidrom, but to no avail. Irel's words flitted through my mind like phantoms: resisting a ritual could be disastrous. I didn't care; I wanted her power, her, out of my body with a vehemence bordering on desperation. I bit my lip and focused my will against Anahita, pushing her magic back, closer to the surface of my skin. Her chant heightened and magic plunged into me, breaking through my resistance and punishing me for my insubordination. Searing lines ripped up my center and arced down my limbs. I shrieked and convulsed, hot urine spraying my legs.

Anahita's magic broke off, and she backed away. The Laidrom released me and I buckled, crashing to my hands and knees, vomiting bile. It splashed over my hands and back onto my face, hot and acrid. I crumpled forward onto the wet, ruined rug and curled around my pained center, wrapping my wings and arms around myself. Tears and filth gleamed on my bare skin. I sobbed, wishing for the blackness of unconsciousness, but it didn't come. My head spun; the chimes rang on, their sound warped and haunting. I heard voices, but the meaning of their words was chewed away by my own humiliation.

A heavy blanket closed over me like a gladiator's net and this time, I didn't fight. The Laidrom wrapped me up enough to cover my nakedness, flew me to the floor, and marched me, stumbling, through the halls of Lilnon. The world tilted with each step I took and I swayed, knees wobbly as I tried to keep my balance. Iyarri stopped and watched, their faces contorted by shock and disgust. Whispers chased down the corridors after me, following the three-toed vomit-and-urine tracks I left behind.

A Laidrom knocked three times on a door; it was scarcely open before they shoved me through and handed a bundle of my things to my father. "Saan-Eleéth will send a messenger with further instructions. Keep your Linnia here until then." The door closed with a boom that echoed in the place where my heart had been.

My father's hands closed over my shoulders and I writhed away, holding the blanket with the other hand. It did little to hide my soiled, naked self. "How could you?" I cried, trembling with agony and shame. "You left me! You left me to them." Tears choked off my voice and I turned away.

Cæl reached for me, his face so pale it made his hazel eyes black. "What did they—"

"They wanted to know if my filthy fucking bloodline was going to end with me." My voice cracked and my heart broke with it. I struck him with one wing and turned away, wrapping my wings and the blanket around myself.

"Aurelia."

Black spots danced in my vision, and I swayed on my feet. "I'm glad Tiahmani and her pureblood baby are worth this to you." I clung to the doorframe, my entire body threatening to collapse to the floor from humiliation as much as pain.

"Pasahasa, they—" His words were hurried, desperate.

"Don't." The single word was muted, defeated. I stumbled into the bedroom, wishing I possessed the strength to slam the door. Instead I took two steps and fell against the edge of the scooped bed. My insides sagged like tattered curtains, and my wet thighs slid against one another. I tried to get my feet under me but crumpled to the floor in a tangle of wings, blankets, and indignity. Long seconds stretched thin in the darkness before my father's feet appeared in the doorway. "I don't want your help." I couldn't handle his pity, his penitence for my existence.

Cæl crouched beside me and sat me up, closing the blanket around me. I hated him. I hated him and I needed him. I let my head fall against the wooden side of the tianta. Cæl picked up one of my arms and turned it over. Bruises blossomed, purple and red, up my wrists where the guards had held me, and a trickle of blood ran from the corner of my mouth to the edge of my jaw. One eye was crimped closed on the side of my head where Anahita had struck me with the book. My gut cramped as the warm sides of his claws touched the tender side of my head.

Two booming knocks rang out on the door to our quarters. There was the sound of Cæl's footsteps and the door opening and closing. "pir-Maroch," Cæl said. Wincing and wrapping one arm around my stomach, I lurched forward and pushed the door closed with my fingertips. I didn't want him to see me.

Maroch's voice was a deep rumble. "Saan-Eleéth told me to come tell you she's summoning other Iyarri she wants to talk to, including Aamon and the Iadnah who gave your girl wings. You're both to stay at Lilnon until further notice. It should be a few days."

With a tremendous effort I hauled myself into the Iyarri bed, sinking into the fine cushions, staining them with piss and vomit.

"Word of your actions and what your daughter is have spread quickly."

"Saan-Eleéth made some sort of announcement? That isn't like her." There was a knifelike edge to Cæl's voice.

"Occodon has told anyone who will listen he advised your daughter be killed outright. It's made worse by Anahita and all her gossipy Iadnah having no idea when to shut the fuck up."

"Ah."

Maroch sighed. "I didn't come here to watch you twist in the wind, but I figured you should know."

"I appreciate it, pir-Maroch."

Cautious, I eased the blanket away from my body. Bruises like water-color autopsy lines traced in from each shoulder until they met at my sternum and ran down the center line of my body. My head spun and I wrapped myself in a bundle of copper feathers.

"Saan-Eleéth wants your sister here too. I need to know where to find her."

"Can you also deliver her a sealed message?" my father asked.

"Aye, I'll see it done."

The sound of paper tearing from one of my sketchbooks was followed by the scratching of writing.

"One more question, unofficial. Aurelia's mother—was she worth it?" Maroch asked.

Cæl's voice was low and disheartened. "Would you believe me if I said yes?"

The snowy-winged Heeoa paused, considering. "You have never been one to do rash things, and your decisions were always solid. She'd have to be something to make you impulsive. So yes, I would believe you."

"She was worth it."

"Here," Maroch said. "Take my flask. With what's in the wind, you're going to need it."

TWENTY-NINE

B Y THE TIME I forced myself out of bed and into the bathroom, the ceiling overhead reflected a midnight sky of chatoyant blues and blacks. What I needed was a soak in the baths, but I wasn't sure I was allowed to go, and didn't want to look at a single Iyarri even if I were. I buckled over in pain; one hand clutched onto clean clothes, the other on the edge of the sink. I'd been shocked once by a broken string of Christmas lights, and my body felt now like it did then: shaky, too hot, and not fully attached to my consciousness.

My father's footsteps moved through the living room. I heard the sound of the door opening and closing, then silence. I pressed the heels of my palms to my eyes, relieved he'd gone. With one hand, I fumbled on the faucet and plugged the drain in the sink. Steam rolled up the mirror, obfuscating my reflection.

I added soap to the water, swished a clean cloth through the suds, and wrung it out. I dabbed at the bruises circling my wrists like purple shackles, then worked my way up my arms, over my shoulders, and down my torso. The water in the sink went dirty as I swished the cloth around and wrung it out again, my psyche as raw as my insides. The line of bruising down my center terminated just under my navel. I hadn't ever *not* wanted children, but I hadn't exactly desired them either. The idea that, like other crossbreeds, I might be barren had been a comfort, an immutable wall I didn't need to climb. And now I was terrified I might be able to have children.

If being a Linnia made me an oddity worthy of this level of examination, I couldn't imagine what it would be like if I became pregnant. Any child of mine would be the first Linnia-spawn in perhaps centuries, perhaps ever, and my tender stomach twisted harder at the thought of what the Iyarri would think of it, would do to it.

I ran my hand over the smooth, arcing scar on my side. The first time Irel had healed me, it had been a test to see where I fell between human and Iyarri. If anyone would know what I would need to do to keep from falling pregnant, it was him. I toweled off and unplugged the sink, letting the dirty water swirl down the drain, clean, but not feeling better. I eased my body into a clean tunic and pants, pulled the filthy linens from the bed, and lowered myself back into the remaining cushions.

The door to our chambers opened and closed, and my father's form darkened the bedroom doorway a moment later. "Can we talk?" he asked.

Silence stretched out—I didn't say yes, but I also didn't say no. He stepped inside the room and set a tray of food on the side table. "I'm sorry." He sat on the edge of the bed, wings shadowing his face. "It isn't enough, and it doesn't make anything right, but I am." My father clasped his clawed hands together, glanced at me, and then bowed his head, repentant. "I thought it best for us to be cooperative, that they'd see you're more Iyarri than human. It went much further than I anticipated."

My gaze fell to my human fingers as they ran along the stiff edge of my unalah. "Why do they hate me?"

Cæl's eyes followed mine, watching the way the vane flowed under my fingertips. "Ages ago, before the Aisaro was amended to prohibit winged Linnia from joining the Elonu-Dohe, it might have been different. Now, you remind them that Iyarri and humans have more in common than they would like."

On the tray was a hot bowl of spiced porridge capped with a thin, flaky crust. I settled it atop my abdomen and ate a few tentative bites. The food quelled some of the sick feeling inside me; after finishing the rest of it, I settled back into the pillows, eyelids drooping. Cæl took my empty bowl from my hands and set it back on the tray, reached into his pocket, and took out a small tin of salve. It was pale gold with flecks of green and smelled like herbs with a medicinal bite. "Let me see your wrists?"

Cæl turned my bruised wrists over in his hands, flexing the joints. The lines of his face were fierce, but also sad and exhausted. How much doubt weighed in his heart? How badly had I damaged our chances of lenience by fighting Anahita and Eleéth's guards?

He scraped out some of the unguent with the side of his claw, spread it over my skin, and worked it into the bruises with the pads of his fingers. His eyes weren't looking at the bruises, but into them, with the same shell-shocked expression he'd worn in Eleéth's audience hall. There were many things we needed to say, but the wounds Eleéth had dealt to his heart and his pride were as raw as the ones Anahita had dealt to my body.

He set the tin aside, left the room, and returned with a blanket from his bed, a mirror to the soiled one on the floor. "Here," he said as he tucked it around me. It was brown linen, thin enough not to cause me to overheat, but heavy enough to be comforting. It smelled like his wings, of forests as old as the skies.

I maneuvered the blanket as high as I could, wishing it were large enough to hide beneath. "Thank you."

Cæl made no offers to take me from our rooms, and I made no requests to leave. Sore and exhausted, I slept late into the next day and passed the time until dusk making aimless shapes on my sketchpad. By every technical measure, Iyarri artistry was exquisite, but it made my heart hurt to draw the style I had so recently fallen in love with.

Someone knocked at the door, and my pencil stilled over the page as Cæl opened it. The latch was scarcely undone when Nesah flounced inside in a flash of golden wings and purple fabric. She peeked about the rooms for a second and gestured for someone else to come in. "She's here."

My father stepped back and swung the door wider as an unfamiliar, dark viridian–winged Iyarri entered. His robes were masculine in cut and somber brown: apprentice healer's robes. Irel followed, orange hair and blue wings like a captured summer sky. I got to my feet with a relieved smile. "It's good to see you again," I said.

Irel crossed the room and took up both my hands in his. "Look at you! I was afraid your fall through the window had damaged your wings. But they're okay, yes?"

"Yes," I said with a smile.

Nesah tittered. "I knew you'd be happy to see him." Over her long, hooded garment was a fitted vest of a paler shade that fell to her hips and closed with a woven belt.

Nesah gestured to the dark-winged Iyarri. "Aurelia, this is Hataan, Irel's apprentice. And my Semeroh." Her cheeks flushed pink. Semeroh were sometime mates of spirit, sometimes mates in body. It seemed Nesah and Hataan were the latter.

I tipped my head in greeting, unsure of the purpose of the visit. "It's nice to meet you." I recognized Hataan from the infirmary the night the Laidrom had murdered Lucien. Hataan returned the gesture, but stayed silent, his mandrake-green eyes pensive.

Nesah exclaimed over the great coppery expanses of feathers. "They turned out lovely!" Her own wings flickered like a small bird's. "Do they work?"

Her smile was contagious enough for me to reflect it. "Yes, they work."

"They were right," Hataan murmured. "She does look more Iyarri than human."

My father closed the door with more force than necessary. "Who's they?" he asked.

Nesah shrugged. "Everyone. The news from Lilnon traveled as quickly as our summons from Saan-Eleéth did. We wanted to come see you right away."

My father hesitated at the door and turned to Irel. "Do you know if Tiahmani's arrived?"

"Aye, she has. She's resting," Irel said.

Cæl frowned. "I'm going to go speak to her." He left, mouth pressed into a thin, troubled line.

Hataan took in my features. His wings shifted as he thought, the plumes not black, but a deep, iridescent green. "Are you going to ask her?" he asked Nesah.

Nesah bumped his shoulder with an encouraging smile. "You can ask her. It's your question."

Hataan tried to look annoyed with Nesah, but couldn't. There was nothing but tender adoration for her in his expression. "Is your skin color like your mother's?"

"Yes, it is."

Irel gestured to my wings. "May I?" I nodded, and he reached for my wings. Battered and sore, I tensed, the memory of Anahita's exam too recent, too raw, but Irel felt for the muscles under the feathers in a way that was both professional and compassionate. "You've gained a lot of muscle mass. Good. Much stronger." Irel extended one of my wings, testing the way the limbs moved.

"Will you be in trouble for healing her?" Hataan asked, threading his fingers into Nesah's.

The healer shrugged, unconcerned. "I've done nothing I am not willing to account for or defend." He touched the clasps on the back of my robe. "Do you mind?" I did, but shook my head. The back of the robe came down and Hataan gasped. Irel closed one reassuring hand over my shoulder and spoke to his apprentice. "Your bedside manner needs some refinement."

"But how did you keep her alive? That's . . ." Hataan struggled to find the right word. ". . . impossible."

Irel chuckled, the sound warm and reassuring. "Not quite impossible." He tested the motion of my wings again, watching how the roughly-pieced skin between my wings moved. Satisfied, he re-pinned my robe and let me turn around. "I'm relieved to see you so sound of body." He raised his eyebrows. "But how is this?" He touched over my heart with a single blue index finger. "And this?" Irel touched my forehead.

My throat tightened with words to frame my heartbroken indignity, and tears misted my eyes.

Irel's face drew together with concern. "I thought as much." He turned toward Nesah and Hataan and asked, "Might I have a minute alone with Aurelia?"

"Of course," Nesah said. "It's about time to get dinner anyway." She led Hataan by the hand, waved goodbye to me with the other, and departed.

Irel's face softened with sympathy. "Would you like to talk about what's bothering you?"

I sat on one of the benches, my wings easing around me. My teeth worried my lower lip as I sought for how to begin. Of anyone, Irel I could trust. He sat across from me, his presence comforting and unimposing. I pushed up my sleeves and held out my bruise-mottled wrists, the skin swollen and glossy with salve. With quiet words I told him about the audience with Eléeth and Anahita in the library. Color crept up my cheeks, but Irel listened with compassion.

When I finished, he took my wrists in his tattooed hands. Rare lines of vexation creased his face, aging him. An ocean of my blood had not drawn them out, but cruelty had. "I'm sorry. She never should have done that without your consent. I assume you've more injuries?" I pulled the neckline of my shirt down until Irel could see the purple, tell-tale lines of bruising from Anahita's magical dissection. Irel sighed. "As Anahita likely found out, your body is mostly Iyarri, but not quite. Her heavy-handedness made what should have been painless excruciating."

Thoughts of a would-be child swirled through me, sickening my stomach. I wrapped my arms around myself, trying to find the right words for my thoughts. "I'm afraid of her. I'm afraid of what would happen to me if Anahita was right and I can have a child." My voice buckled. "And more afraid what they might do to it."

Irel's face drew together, empathetic. "Iyarri do not take anyone by force." His words were reassuring, but didn't chase away the looming feeling of dread.

"Can't you do something anyway?" My voice was distressed, hushed.

Irel rubbed the claw of his forefinger against the pad of his thumb in a contemplative gesture, gleaming amber flashing against matte blue. "Iyarri fertility, like most of our medicine, is influenced by magic. In some cases, it's too near the wind for a couple to have children, and so the ritual influences one, the other, or both so they can't. In other cases, fertility is boosted insomuch as it can be. I can do a contraceptive ritual for you now, and reverse it whenever you'd like."

"So, the ritual doesn't last forever?" Tension eased from my shoulders. I was tired of making permanent decisions about my body.

"No, and it isn't infallible, either. It works best when applied to both parties."

I suppressed a sad, bemused snort. Whatever my mother and father used hadn't been infallible, either. "Would anyone be able to tell?" I asked, fearing the possibility Anahita could sense it and take retribution on me.

Irel shook his head. "No, and you have my confidence, you know that."

My face tightened, but I staved off grateful tears. "Thank you." I took a steadying breath. "Go ahead."

He swept his wings forward in a helio circle around me. "I'll do what I can to ease what Anahita did to you as well." Irel closed his hands over my wrists, and his eyes fluttered closed. "Relax and breathe."

I let my chest fill with the scent of Irel's wings—clean linen and herb-infused oils—then exhaled, the release of breath slow and controlled.

The healer's incantation began, the strange, arcane syllables bobbing in the air and dipping onto my skin. The place where his hands touched mine warmed, and his magic threaded into me. I stiffened, the memory of how Anahita's magic tore through my defenses and violated me still raw in my psyche. Irel kept chanting, but his magic went no further, pausing for my acceptance. I softened my face, unpinched my eyelids, and felt my resistance fall away.

The bruises warmed and tingled, their colors passing through angry purples and reds into greens and yellows, and then faded away entirely. My wings eased open, the deep ache dissipating from the delicate bones and muscles.

Irel's chant shifted, the energy concentrating under my navel as the individual threads of magic wound together, protective and warm. The healer's voice faded to silence and I sighed, sinking deeper into the bench, instantly fatigued but no longer in pain. Irel opened his eyes and smiled. "How do you feel?"

"Much better, thank you."

Irel stood, his wings refolding behind him, blue and ochre as a rain-forest butterfly. "You are welcome. I should be going. Try to get some rest." Fear and tension crept across my features as thoughts of Eleéth's verdict crowded in. Irel put a hand on my shoulder and gave me a bow of his head. "All will be well, you'll see."

"I hope so." I wished for an ounce of his confident quietude.

When he was gone, I slipped my sketchbook out from my satchel. I needed to draw, to empty my mind onto the page, to expel the pain and the confusion from my mind like infection from a wound. I pressed my fingertips to my temples and sat at the desk on the far side of the sitting room. My toes clasped the bar between the rungs of the stool. It was both soothing and unsettling to have furniture built for features I once considered deformities. I found comfort in the familiar sound of parting the book, the tooth of the page beneath my fingers, and the smell of paper and graphite.

My pencil swept across the page, the lines dark and deft. A tiny, curled infant lay sleeping in a nest of blankets, lips parted in sleep. I started to draw the hands, but faltered, suddenly not sure how thick to make the fingers or if they ended in claws. Rotating the sketchbook, I moved to the feet instead, but hesitated there, too. My pencil moved to the child's back, but I neither lowered the pencil to give it wings nor moved it away.

I set the pencil aside, took out my napta, and laced them onto my arms. Capmiali. If drawing wouldn't quiet my mind, perhaps that would.

Oi biah, the first stance. Balance, breathe. I moved into the second stance, my mind clear, strong, resolute. My napta blade flashed outward. The third stance, the extension of the second blade. The smooth metal gleamed in the light, and in the repetition, I found peace.

The lock to the door clicked open, and I sheathed my napta, the blades disappearing within the long sleeves of my robe.

Cæl returned, his face drawn. "Our audience with Saan-Eleéth is at dawn."

THIRTY

THE BLACK PREDAWN ARRIVED on tense, quiet feet. I lay in the still dark of my room and listened to Cæl toss and turn until he gave up trying to sleep and headed into the sitting area. A moment later, the sharp scent of leather polish permeated the air. Forgoing any pretense of getting rest, I rose and sat across from Cæl, but he stayed silent and buffed the blood-red leather of his gauntlet with a soft cloth.

"What's going to happen?" I hadn't spoken above a whisper, but my question seemed too loud in the strained stillness.

Cæl set his gauntlet aside, wiped off his hands, and took his hair from its ponytail. It fell midway to his shoulder blades in a mahogany curtain before he parted it with his claws and wove it into the upraised five-strand Heeoa braid. "Aamon's fate will be decided by Saan-Eleéth and her advisors. I will present my case against Aamon, and Saan-Eleéth will summon any others whose testimony she finds relevant. Then Aamon will be given an open floor to refute everything I say. Which he will." Cæl rubbed his hand over his face and sighed. "Afterward, each advisor will present either an opal for innocence, or a blade for guilt. Saan-Eleéth presents three."

Goosebumps broke out across my skin, and I rubbed my arms to dispel them. "What about us?"

"Saan-Eleéth alone decides our fate. She will decide if the ritual that summoned your wings was done as written or not and has leave to give me any punishment she feels balances my wrongdoing." Including death. Realization settled over me like a heavy gray blanket. If she decided not to spare my father, there was no line of reasoning that spared me. "As standing head of the Laidrom, if pir-Maroch decides I have earned any additional penalties, he has the right to exact those."

"Like strip your rank?" I asked.

Cæl shifted, miserable. "Aye, like stripping me of my rank." I wondered if Maroch would side with my father out of warrior kinship, or Occodon with Aamon for the same reasons. Bias, however, was not something I imagined Eleéth sought in her advisors.

"Aurelia." The lines on Cæl's face deepened with guilt and worry. He gestured to a pile of fabric on a stool by the door. "Put your hair up and dress in that."

"What is it?"

"Something Saan-Eleéth decided would be appropriate." And by the tense way he gripped one ankle with his opposite foot, not something I was going to enjoy. I went into my room and let the fabric fall open in my hands, then froze. There was no back to the dress.

A twisted length of ethereal white fabric began behind the neck, crossed the breasts and torso, and fell in sheer lengths past my knees. The open back scooped all the way to the base of my spine. My heart cowered against the wall of my chest, and I buried my face in the crumpled dress—the fabric smelled of clear skies. The other Iyarri couldn't tell I was Linnia in passing, so Eleéth wanted to frame my scars like a twisted work of art and put them on display.

I drew a dozen breaths before I moved, each one trembling with the panic twisting around my heart. There was no helping it—no amount of pleading would change the expectation, and failure to be obedient would dampen what little lenience she might give to me and my father. I shed my robe, donned the dress, and stood in the dark, wishing I could carry it with me to hide the golden lightning storm caught in my ruined flesh.

The chimes in the room sang together, but it was not the song of the hour I'd grown accustomed to. It pulsed again, the reverberation carrying through the carved stone hallways. I stilled, wondering for a delusional, desperate second what would happen if we simply did not answer the summons.

My father's silhouette appeared in the doorway behind me. "Come."

We exited our rooms and he wrapped one wing around my body, ushering me close to him. "Stay at my side and speak to no one but Saan-Eleéth and her advisors." I nodded, my voice unable to make it through the tightness in my throat.

The sound of voices grew as we wound our ways through the passages, the ceilings starting to brighten with magical dawn. The hallway broadened, terminating in an arch that opened into the audience hall. Five stories tall, it was a yawning, spiraling cylinder of arched balconies, each full of onlookers. On the ground, a sea of Iyarri stood before us, a thin path through them to the open area beyond. My father kept his focus locked on our destination. I fought the urge to stare at my feet and instead mimicked my father as we passed through a thousand pairs of wings. An ocean of whispers and the sound of feathers moving against one another gathered, swelling like a great wave ready to crash over me and sweep me away.

A skitter of clawed feet rushed up behind me an instant before pain shot up my wing. I whirled around, stifling a cry as I pulled my wing close. An Iyarri boy ran back toward three of his friends, one of my copper feathers in his hand. Blood stood out on the pale end of the quill. My father walked on, and I hurried to catch up. The whispers became words. *Linnia, abomination, her scars.* There was another tug at my wings, a third. The holes left by my feathers throbbed and a scream of pain and indignity clawed its way up my throat. I wasn't a novelty or a freak, I was a person—and those feathers were mine. But to speak was to risk Eleéth's judgement, and so I walked on, my teeth biting into my lower lip.

Eleéth presided from the largest central balcony and surveyed the gathering Iyarri. Each segment of the ternion stood together, encircled by an immense throng of Akarinu. Anxious, I searched for familiar faces. Miketh and Tiahmani stood near the front of the Laidrom, Nesah, Hataan, and Irel with the Iadnah. Nesah gave me a nervous smile of encouragement. There was no sign of Aamon's snow-white wings amongst the Aldaria.

Eleéth unfolded her wings and held them open like two banners of night sky—even the slight sound of feathers in the audience ceased. Eleéth's gaze settled on my father and me. "Cæl Heeoa, step forward with your Linnia," the Ohlera called. We walked to a circular space under the balcony on which Eleéth and her advisors stood. Droplets of my blood littered the floor behind us and murmurs nipped at our naked heels. She raised her voice to the crowd, "No matter what verdicts are spoken today, all the actions culminating in these events were disgraceful. Tribunals of such a severe nature are a rarity. Let us seek to keep them that way." Her wings, as deep as sable velvet, contracted and eased.

"Doalin, the Unspeakable Sin, has brought Cæl Heeoa before us today. Absent twenty-five years, he returned to us, Linnia in tow, to admit his transgression and to bring words of suspicion upon Aamon Amayo. Aamon is accused of using the Linnia to reveal our true nature to the humans, in direct violation of the Aisaro. Today we level judgements upon all involved. Step forward, Aamon."

I inhaled and pinched my eyes shut. Aamon had been my friend, my mentor, had done so much for me before trying to kill me. That shove through the window should have wiped away everything he'd done for me, but it hadn't. My desire that Eleéth find him guilty faltered, just as Aamon had when he'd pressed my back to the stained-glass window.

Aamon walked from a stone arch at the side of the chamber to the center of the floor. I hated him. I hated him, and yet I missed him, or at least I missed who I once thought him to be. He was dressed in flowing pants and a tunic, pale golden fabric tailored through the chest and shoulders but flared in long panels from the waist. The complement of his white wings made him seem divine, above reproach. Stupid and dangerous as it was, I wanted to speak with him about why he did the things he did. My heart said every shared moment of artful joy, every kindness he had ever shown me, was genuine, but my mind demanded doubt. Aamon bowed low before Eleéth and her advisors, descending to one knee with his wings spread parallel to the ground.

Eleéth's dark eyes glistened like pieces of jet and bore down on him. "Do you refute the charges against you?" Aamon was a practiced liar and a master of half-truths. How great Eleéth's ability was to pare truth from falsehood? Miketh said it was some power, her ohleræ, but did it unearth something in the voice, from an expression, or could she truly read the ley lines in the heart?

Aamon's voice was clear and solemn. "I do." He stood, hands clasped at his waist, confident in Eleéth's forthcoming pardon. Resentment for his composure, for his poise, for how perfectly beautiful he was built in me like a stoked fire.

The Ohlera addressed the many Iyarri in great entry hall. "Aamon Amayo stands indicted of finding a Linnia, arranging for her to both suffer the ritual of wings and be healed, and then using her to reveal our true nature to the humans, circumventing the Aisaro. In so doing, he withheld and falsified information that led to the death of nine Laidrom, including Ikkar, Idura's former Heeoa, at the hands of a kiaisi."

I closed my hand over Lucien's spiral and bowed my head. The attack in the woods seemed forever ago, and yet the memory of his last bloody kiss was so vivid I could taste it. I would have given anything to be with Lucien rather than in a hall of a thousand suffocating pairs of wings.

Eleéth gestured to my father. "Cæl Heeoa, speak your piece."

Aamon and I moved to opposite ends of the space in front of Eleéth, relinquishing the floor to my father. A thorn of worry burrowed deeper into my chest. After bowing to Eleéth and the other advisors, Cæl turned slowly, taking in those assembled. "I came to the Ohlera to admit my transgressions and to protect that which I served, and still serve: the Elonu-Dohe and the Aisaro. Should Aamon, with his half-truths and pleasant deceptions, be found innocent, these charges dropped, and I made the fool, I will not regret that I balanced both me and my child on the vane's edge of life and death in bringing these accusations forth. By my honor and by my duty I am bound to do nothing less."

Doubt rose in me like a tide in a cavern, the waves lapping at my heart. He sounded confident, but not in the way he had at our audience with Eleéth. She'd broken something in him, and it had not healed.

"To tell untruths to one another is a human failing, one which Aamon seems to have learned from them and brought to us. It cost the lives of many. He has used his position on the Council of the Four Winds to decide which truths and which lies reached your ears. The greatest asset in any battle is not blades, not a bow, not even the wind carrying us on wing into the attack. The most important thing, the crucial thing, is information. Aamon knew my daughter was in the company of a kiaisi, and yet told the Laidrom they were dispatching an unremarkable human and apprehending an unarmed young woman. Her Linnia heritage was his secret, and he paid in blood to keep it that way." He turned and gave Aamon a glare full of hazel fire. "Not in his own blood, but the blood of those sworn to protect the Aisaro, Idura, and each and every member inside of it. It is not the Iyarri way to throw others to death in place of oneself. The nine fallen Laidrom would have sacrificed their lives for any cause Idura asked of them, but for them to die for this, for Aamon's lies, smacks of pride, of cowardice. Of petty revenge."

A murmur passed through the crowd, and my father let the room fade to silence before he continued. "Before Aamon pays lip service to his adherence to tradition, to the Aisaro, let us be clear—this is about revenge. He has never stopped blaming me for Siyah's death, even though he poisoned her mind with the human art that led her to reveal herself. Aamon knew about my daughter from her birth and became a part of her life, even when she did not know what she was or know me. He used her as a means to my suffering. When he tossed her through the cathedral window, however, he went from exacting his revenge on me to putting all Iyarri in danger."

He spoke to the crowd directly. "Look at my daughter: Linnia, abomination. For any number of things you may call her, Aamon as an Aldaria recognizes the importance of using the lie of angels to protect us. Yet he saw the ritual completed, saw her healed, and wrought her into a form so close to our own that hundreds of you saw her and thought her Iyarri. My daughter has been here a week. She dined in the same hall as you, passed you in the market, and even bathed naked beside you, and not a single one of you noticed."

This was part of Cæl's plan—the realization seeped into me like hot water into tea leaves. The excursions to the market, the afternoons in the library, the way he'd insisted on going to the baths—it was all to make sure Lilnon's Iyarri saw me before they knew what I was. I wondered if the Iyarri vendor with the flying squirrel was in the crowd, and what she thought of me now.

"Even our Ohlera could not tell my daughter's true nature at a glance. If our most cherished and wise cannot see what she is, how could a human? When Aamon hand-waves and says my daughter's death would have been written off by the humans as an angel, know that in truth he revealed us as Iyarri. Aamon is counting on our hubris, on the fact that we are too prideful to call my daughter Iyarri, to avoid his accountability for hurling her to her death before a thousand humans. He may as well have tossed any one of us for all the difference the humans could have discerned. If we sacrifice the spirit of the Aisaro for the letter, if we find him innocent in this, we will have taken the first step on the path to our own destruction."

Finished, Cæl bowed to Eleéth and came and stood beside me. He was shaking. It was so slight that were he any farther away, I would have missed it. I wanted to put a reassuring hand on his arm, but couldn't, not without tipping off other Iyarri that my father was not as confident as he needed to be. The hall filled with whispers, but silenced when Eleéth spoke. "Aamon, I give the floor to you. Speak in your own defense."

Aamon bowed and turned to face the assembled Iyarri. His voice was clear, self-assured. "Our Heeoa came back to us. Were circumstances different, his return might have been something to celebrate." His white hair gleamed and his pale wings shone as though he were truly a celestial creature. "He did not go to Saan-Eleéth to save you all from me; he went to save himself, to save his Linnia daughter. She had been found out, and all her future held for her was death from the Laidrom he once called wingmates. His only hope of mercy was to go before Saan-Eleéth. Whether that speaks to his bravery or his naïveté, I cannot say." Dread closed in around me—Aamon was right, and Eleéth would know it, too.

"He speaks of honoring the Aisaro, and yet he broke it by committing Doalin. By lying with a human. By choosing her over us all every day for these twenty-five years." Aamon and my father locked eyes, and Aamon turned away from him with a pitying shake of his head. "He did not bring these accusations against me in the pursuit of justice, with the intent of honoring the Aisaro; he did it because his other option was exile and, now that his transgressions have been revealed, death.

"He speaks of his dead Laidrom. The very companions he deserted without hesitation died, not because of me, but because they were left leaderless. He left Ikkar to take up the mantle of Heeoa, but not once, in the quarter century since Cæl disappeared, did any of his men stop comparing the two and finding Ikkar lesser. Had Cæl never deserted, had Ikkar never been forced to take his post, perhaps the number of dead Laidrom would have been smaller. It was, after all, one human who killed these nine." My father's exterior stayed stoic, but I ached in sympathy at the way Aamon's words made guilt well in Cæl's eyes.

"Our Heeoa's experience with humans is limited to bedding them and killing them. My plans for putting his Linnia to death before the humans would not have had the apocalyptic consequences he fears. A thousand people saw the Linnia, and the word on their lips was 'angel,' the same word a human spoke with he saw Siyah. Interesting that Cæl thought the proper punishment, then, was death, but now he begs forgiveness.

"So, the question is why. Why did I wait so long to bring the Linnia to Idura? Why heal her rather than leave her to die?" I should have hated Aamon so much that what he called me didn't matter, but for him to call me Linnia, as if I didn't have a name, left me feeling discarded. "For as long as I have known why Cæl fled, I wanted to bring him back, see him set before Saanire Eleéth Ohlera to answer for what he had created. He can cheapen his transgressions with accusations of revenge all he wants, but the fact remains: he sired a child with a human and fled. I suspected he was alive and in hiding, and I have his sister to thank for confirming that, however inadvertently." Aamon gestured to Tiahmani, who stared straight ahead with her wings crossed in front of her body.

Eleéth gestured to her advisors. "We would like to know why you summoned Irel Li'iansa to a ritual that has not called for a healer in ages."

Aamon tipped his wings in acknowledgement. "Had the Linnia been revealed as such right away, hotter heads would have prevailed; she would have been given wings, but left to die. The additional steps I took in secrecy were needed to draw Cæl out from the shadows and into the light of justice." Aamon gestured to me, and I shrank into myself, feeling stupid and used. Aamon's voice was resonate, convincing. "Do you think if Cæl knew I'd captured his wingless Linnia and she was at Idura, he'd have stormed the gates to save her? By the time he learned of it, he'd also have been aware there was no rescuing her, and he'd have stayed hidden. To make sure Cæl came back, to make sure he'd show up and finally be held accountable for his actions, I had to give his Linnia wings." Aamon's eyes met mine with the same victorious expression he'd worn at the cathedral window. "I had to turn her into something worth saving."

A sob kicked against the inside of my chest, and my father's jaw was clenched so tight that a muscle pulsed in his cheek.

Aamon turned back to Eleéth and her advisors. "In the grand scheme of things, all went as it should. The Linnia was apprehended and put through the ritual. Then I tried to put her to death myself, in such a way that, perhaps, Cæl realizes how unnecessary Siyah's death was. I have brought Cæl's crimes to light, and now he finally faces justice."

He was right. I froze at the realization. We had played right into his hand, and every truthful word he said was a nail driving into a coffin big enough to hold both me and my father.

"She," Aamon said, unfurling one wing and pointing it at me, "is many things, but she is not Iyarri. Her week spent here at Lilnon does not make her so, and neither will any amount of Cæl's wishful thinking." Around the room, other Iyarri were nodding in agreement.

Eleéth held up one clawed hand, motioned for Aamon to stand aside, and summoned Irel to the floor. The healer gave a serene bow, and rose, pushing his tumble of marigold hair back from his face. "Tell me about this ritual," Eleéth said.

The scars on my back ached as Irel detailed each step of the rite. "As we chanted, the wings grew under her skin. We could hear bones groaning before they ruptured her flesh. When the wings finally broke free, her spine lay exposed among the ruins of her back." I shuddered under flashing memories of the pain and swallowed hard, wrapping my arms around myself. The entirety of the hall stood in rapt attention, their gazes alternating between Irel and the twisted, sunken masses of golden kintsukuroi scars on my bare back. I wanted to shrink back behind the feathers of my wings, but allowed only my arms for comfort. Irel continued, "Between giving form to the new wings and piecing her broken body together again, I was not sure she'd survive."

Eleéth's gaze was dark and even. "Why did you agree to heal the Linnia? Those parts of the ritual were stricken centuries ago, and your time and expertise could have been spent assisting Iyarri."

Many would have cowered under the weight of Eleéth's frigid presence and shifting wings, but Irel stood tranquil and contemplative. "I am a healer, Saanire Eleéth Ohlera. It is what I do. It would have been a greater affront to my talents not to use them when they were in such dire need."

"Did you know of Aamon's plans to use the Linnia to summon Cæl?"

"No, Saanire Ohlera, I did not."

Eleéth dismissed Irel back to where the other Iadnah stood. She turned to the other Iyarri on the balcony. "Advisors, before I give Cæl and his Linnia their punishments, are you ready to state your verdict on Aamon Amayo?" All five nodded. Aamon stood beneath Eleéth, patient and unshaken. The Ohlera raised one luminous hand to Occodon. "Step forward and reveal your judgment."

Occodon stepped to the edge of the balcony, the feathers of his wings gleaming like sharpened steel blades. A small table sat at the edge of the balcony, high enough for all to see. He cast a steely gaze out over the assembled Iyarri as he placed an opal the size of my fist upon the table. "The Aldaria find Aamon innocent of the charges." My stomach went cold, and the barest of smiles touched Aamon's lips.

Eleéth lifted a hand to Laidrom adviser. "State your verdict, pir-Maroch."

The spotted-winged Laidrom drew a short, ornamented blade from his belt and threw it with a snap of his wrist. "The Laidrom find you guilty." The blade stood upright and quivering in the wood.

Eleéth tipped her wings. "pir-Barcus? pir-Sisera?"

Sisera stepped forward and placed a blade on the table. "The highest-ranking of us should be held to the highest standards. The Akarinu declare Aamon has fallen short of those."

The striped-winged Akarinu advisor inclined his head in dissent, placing an opal by his counterpart's blade. "The Akarinu also feel Aamon's worth to the Elonu-Dohe is greater than the debt of his transgressions." Even verdicts. I felt thin and fragile, stretched out between them.

Eleéth dismissed them and turned to her ritualist. "pir-Anahita, state your decision."

The ritualist crossed the distance to the table and from her pocket drew a third opal. It gleamed against the blue of her tattoos. "The Iadnah find there is not enough evidence to proclaim him guilty." Anahita retook her place by Maroch and Occodon.

Three opals, two blades. Their smooth surfaces shone under Lilnon's shifting lights and twirled in my vision. Eleéth raised her arm, Aamon's fate, my fate, my father's fate resting in her hand.

THIRTY-ONE

THE WORLD BOXED IN around me, squeezing me until I couldn't expand my lungs inside the cage of my ribs. With a twist of her wrist, Eleéth's sleeve slid up the slender length of her arm and she unveiled three blades.

Guilty.

There was not a sound in the entirety of the great hall save the voice of the Ohlera. I swayed, thunderstruck with relief. She spoke to Aamon directly as he stood, shocked. "Aamon Amayo, I pronounce you guilty of the charges brought forward by Cæl Heeoa, a motion carried by the additional votes of pir-Maroch and pir-Sisera." She set the blades on the small table. Her face showed no sympathy or joy in the sentencing, only balanced judgment. "To throw the Linnia down before so many humans would have revealed us all as Iyarri, and your manipulation of the truth lead to the deaths of nine Laidrom." Aamon opened his mouth to speak, but she held up her hand and silenced him. "I do not care about your intentions. Your deceptive actions brought this upon you." Eleéth gathered herself, and the entire hall went cold as a sudden snowfall. "I sentence you to become a Naphal. If the transformation does not result in your death, you will live on in shame. Any further infraction and the Laidrom will see you summarily executed." There were shocked murmurs from the other Iyarri as the color drained from Aamon's face and guards took him by the arms.

"Linnia." The single word rang out as Eleéth gestured to the empty space in front where Aamon had stood not seconds before.

I couldn't move. The distance across the stone floor stretched out a thousand miles, and I could not bring myself to take a single step closer to Eleéth. Cæl nudged me with his shoulder. Blood roared in my ears; I floated forward until I was under Eleéth's balcony and drifted to my knees. My wings fell open, baring my back to the crowd once again. I bowed my head over shaking hands.

"pir-Anahita, detail the ritual of giving a Linnia wings," Eleéth said.

The ancient spine of Anahita's book creaked as she opened it. In a high, clear voice she summarized the ritual, time measured in the turning of dry pages. My neck ached and my knees were on fire, but I dared not move. When Anahita finished, she snapped the heavy book closed in one hand and the boom reverberated throughout the room. "The ritual ends with the summoning of the wings; the sections after are healing rites, but were stricken centuries ago." One of the guards took a step closer, raising his spear to my neck. My stomach rolled and my arms shook. I closed my eyes, not wanting to see my own blood on the floor before I died. "That said," Anahita amended, "there is nothing in here explicitly stating the Linnia must die."

I held my breath until my ribs ached, afraid to make another sound. Dizzy with relief, I pressed my hands to the stone so I didn't swoon straight to the floor.

Eleéth called to my father. "Stand before me, Cæl Heeoa."

My father took a knee beside me, his wings scooped wide and low across the floor and I trembled, fearing for him as much as I was hopeful for me.

"Wisdom is borne of suffering and time, Heeoa, and so that"—she pointed one opal-black claw at me—"is your punishment." I cringed, her words wilting me even though she spoke to my father. "Your daughter has served her own punishment as written and will live on as your penitence." My father turned and stared at me, each of Eleéth's words landing like a physical blow. "Every time you look at her, I want you to see the sin you have committed, the loyalty you lacked, and the trust you broke. Each day, until one of the two of you perishes, I want you to see your own weakness in what your blood wrought."

Cæl's shoulders sagged under the weight of her words. "Yes, Saanire Ohlera." His voice was hoarse, relief twisted with humiliation.

"She will live with you at Idura so that she does not risk revealing us to the humans. To prevent true Iyarri from mistaking her for anything but the Linnia that she is, you'll ensure her clothing reveals her scars. Upon your death, should no one else claim guardianship of your Linnia in your stead, it will be given to Anahita for as long as it survives." A smile of greed and anticipation spread across Anahita's pale lips; behind her gaze, new thoughts of the way she could study the only living Linnia bloomed and receded.

Eleéth continued, each word adding to the crushing weight on Cæl's shoulders. "Before I let you leave, Heeoa, remember that while I did not take your life, or the life of your bastard, today, I reserve the right should you fail to be anything but a picture of the most loyal Iyarri." Cæl gave the barest of nods, and she continued. "I will send further instructions within a day for how you can prove your renewed dedication to the Elonu-Dohe."

I was so weak with relief that I couldn't get to my feet, stranded in a pool of my own wings. Cæl stood, pulled me up beside him, and ushered us out from under the balcony.

Anahita stepped to the forefront of the balcony and called, "Irel Li'iansa." The healer, still at the front of his fellow Iadnah, stepped forward. "For your deviation from the written Linnia ritual, the Iadnah sentence you to death by beheading."

"No!" I screamed. My father clapped one massive hand over my mouth and yanked me against his side, but the single English word reverberated in the Iyarri hall, calling back to its own echo, over and over and over again. Eleéth's dark eyes snapped to me and every other

Iyarri followed, a thousand luminous faces, each expression scathing. I looked past them all to Irel, sentenced to death for saving my life. My heart cratered in my chest as he walked forward without even a plea to speak in his defense. Hataan buried his face in Nesah's shoulder, weeping.

Eleéth gestured to her Laidrom, ignoring my outburst and Hataan's sobs. "Their sentences will be fulfilled at nightfall. Take them away." A quartet of winged warriors led the condemned pair out of the hall.

Once they were gone, Eleéth lifted her head and called out to the audience. "This session is concluded. Go now, until the skies fall." The throngs of Iyarri dispersed, and Eleéth left the hall.

My father lifted his hand from my mouth, but I did not move away from him. Spent and overwhelmed, we held one another as Iyarri flowed around us. There were murmurs, but no taunts; curious stares, but no one pulled feathers from my wings. In a river of feathers and fine clothes the Iyarri moved back into the halls of Lilnon. I leaned against Cæl, resting my head between his collar bones, and he wrapped one scarred, protective arm around me.

Maroch called from the balcony, his voice ringing out across the expanse of stone. "Laidrom, stay—I would have a word with you." The voice shook my father from our tiny island. Maroch glided from the balcony toward the Laidrom, talons clicking on the floor as he landed, turned, and faced the assembled warriors. I was horribly out of place, but there was no way to leave the hall without drawing attention to myself. I pressed my naked back to a stone pillar as the Laidrom formed themselves into loose ranks before Maroch.

"First, I want to congratulate Cæl on the verdict against Aamon. Without his words, the traitor would have walked from here free to continue his corruption. Despite his own transgressions, Cæl came back, and risked his own life and the lives of those he holds dear to set right what was wrong. Let that be a lesson to all of us." He walked up and down the lines of feathered warriors as he talked, his voice made to carry over so many combatants. "For his courage when cowardice would have been the easier path, he will retain his rank as Heeoa. As Ikkar is dead and Idura lacks a Heeoa, Cæl will retake that—"

"The hell he will!" rang a female voice. Væries broke from the assembled Laidrom, the red blotches in her brown eyes bright with rage. She glared into Maroch's scarred face, her hands hooked and shaking. "That deserter is not fit to replace my father."

Maroch folded his arms, unimpressed. "I say he is."

Tiahmani crossed the distance to Væries in two strides and shoved her backward. "Cæl led us for years; Ikkar was never his equal."

Væries's fist was a blur of gray leather gauntlet. Tiahmani blocked the blow, the sound of leather against bare flesh loud and dull. "My father never fucked plodders," Væries growled.

A gryphon-like Laidrom with a mane of blonde waves seized me by the back of my neck and hauled me toward the center of the disagreement. "Væries is right. Look at this and tell me Cæl will be able to kill humans without remorse. He can't do the job," he yelled. With a shove of one arm he sent me stumbling in front of the Laidrom. There were shouts of agreement.

Miketh caught me by one shoulder and steadied me. Realization, cold and sharp, pierced my thoughts: Cæl held no reservations about going back to killing humans if that was what reclaiming his role demanded.

Tiahmani snarled at Væries "And what? You think you'd be a better Heeoa?"

Ikkar's daughter leaned into Tiahmani, the ends of her caramel-colored unalah red, like bloody knives. "Maybe I would be."

Miketh pushed one hand back through the tangle of black braids and waves. "Cæl can perform every duty required of him as Heeoa."

"Then he can prove it," Væries shot back. "He can earn that respect and not have it handed back to him like nothing's happened."

"Væries." My father's voice was not loud, but it was strong, commanding. The voice of a Heeoa. Everyone else fell silent, although Væries's eyes smoldered. "The things you fear are not unwarranted. I don't pretend perfection, and I have nothing but loyalty to the Laidrom, and that means to you as much as anyone else who bears our scars." Cæl paused, and though I expected Væries to interject, she stayed silent. "pir-Maroch's confidence in me is heartening, but the Laidrom cannot be led by anyone without absolute loyalty from the Vohim and the Galearii." Væries squinted, uncertain where this was going. My father came to his decision as he spoke it. "So, I challenge you, Væries Vohim, for leadership of Idura's Laidrom."

Miketh stood stunned, and even Væries was at a loss for words. Their reactions twisted doubt and anxious tension around me. After a few seconds Væries said, "I accept your challenge, Cæl Heeoa."

"Good." Maroch's voice boomed. "As the next-highest in rank outside this all, Miketh will lead Idura's Laidrom until this is resolved. I trust his fairness. I'll arrange everything and visit Idura to officiate. You are all dismissed."

Væries gave a short bow to Cæl, crossing both her scarred arms over her chest. My father returned it to a lesser degree and motioned for me to follow him out of the hall. My steps were unsteady as I hurried toward him, wanting nothing more than to cloister ourselves in our rooms. Miketh and Tiahmani fell in step beside us, but no one spoke until we were deeper into the labyrinthine passages of Lilnon, out of earshot of the rest of the Laidrom. Miketh turned to my father and asked, "Are you sure of this, Heeoa?"

"I'm not." Tiahmani scowled. "You didn't owe that little bitch anything."

Cæl's expression was serious, but there was an edge of amusement to his tone. "You two doubt I can best her? Between the two of us, I'm the one who has passed the three Heeoa Trials."

We paused outside the rooms my father and I shared. Miketh leaned against the wall and folded his wings, the effect the same as folding his arms. "I would like to say no, but you have been out of rigorous training for over twenty years."

"Væries is young and rash. This way everyone will know she had her chance to best me. When I win, those that doubt me will have less reason to do so."

Miketh tilted his head in consideration. "Aye, I suppose." His wings reflected his uneasy thoughts, the terracotta, gray, and black feathers sifting past one another.

Cæl pushed open the door. "If we're going to talk, it should be inside."

Miketh shook his head. "I'll take my leave, Heeoa, but thank you for the offer." He clasped arms with my father. "Congratulations. It will be good to have you back at Idura." He clasped arms with Tiahmani, gave me a cordial nod, and headed toward the central areas of Lilnon.

Tiahmani came inside with us. Once the door was closed she took her brother by the shoulders. "You get to come home, noromi." Her face radiated joy.

For the first time since our audience with Eleéth, my father's tense expression melted into a smile, realizing it himself. "Aye, I do."

Tiahmani threw her arms around her brother and hugged him so with such glee that for an instant, she seemed more a little sister than a deadly warrior. "Thank you. You were braver than I was."

Cæl ruffled her hair. "You're worth it."

It made me happy to see some of the uncertainty swept from our lives, but an undertow of other, darker thoughts pulled at my mind, none of which seemed to concern Cæl or Tiahmani. What would happen to my mother? What would happen to me now that my reason to exist was simply as my father's punishment? And Irel . . . Guilt and shame and sadness clouded up inside me.

Tiahmani smiled. "Of course I'm worth it. I'm also hungry. Want to come get something to eat?"

Cæl shook his head. "Go ahead."

"Aurelia?"

I blinked, surprised she'd offered. "No, but thank you."

Once Tiahmani was gone I sank onto one of the benches, the sick knot of stress in my stomach wringing silent tears from my eyes. Cæl stepped inside and closed the door behind him. He sat next to me. "It's over, pasahasa. Tears won't help it."

I leaned against his shoulder. "It isn't fair. Irel doesn't deserve the same punishment as Aamon. He didn't do anything wrong."

"I'm sure it will be little comfort to you, but Irel's punishment will be swift. Aamon's will not." His face turned grim. "Being transformed into a Naphal is reserved for those the Ohlera need to make an example of. The Iadnah pull the corruption within them to the outside. If they're lucky, they manage to live, their shame for all to see. After that, the smallest infraction means death."

I wrapped my arms around myself, and then my wings over my arms. "That's monstrous."

"That is his punishment." I arched an eyebrow, incredulous. Cæl shrugged. "Aamon knew that when he chose his path."

Iyarri leadership truly was broken. Devoid of insight, of mercy, it was just the letter of the law and its application. What was the point in punishment that removed all chance for atonement or rehabilitation? I stood up and shook my wings, trying to shake my despair away. I wanted to change, but there was nothing to change into that met Eleéth's backless requirement. Beautiful as the dress was, it rendered me exposed and hopeless, and I wished for soft jeans and a big, slouching sweater.

Lucien's spiral flashed on my braid. When we returned home I would do something in his memory. I closed my eyes, wanting to finally mourn him properly, openly.

The sound of a knock brought me back to the living area. Cæl answered it, and two of Lilnon's Laidrom stepped inside. One nodded at me. "We're here for her."

I froze at the back of the room, paralyzed by the thought that Eleéth might have decided to let Anahita have another chance to inspect me. My father took a half step between them and me. "For what?"

"At Aamon Amayo's request. He's granted one person to speak his piece to before his punishment. He chose the Linnia."

"She's not going." My father started to close the door.

"Wait." I said, my voice surprising even me. In light of the savagery of his looming punishment, I didn't want to deny him one last request. And I wanted answers. My fingers twisted into the airy fabric of the dress, my uncertainty drawing out for a single, anxious second. "I'll go." My father frowned, but acquiesced.

The guards led me downward through the cavern, deeper than even the baths. The populated areas of Lilnon fell away, the voices dimming to murmurings and then silence. The hallway rounded a bend to reveal a line of three arched, heavy doors. One of the Laidrom unlocked the last door. "I'll stand just inside. Let me know when you're done."

"I will, thank you." I stepped around his dappled-gray wing and entered the chamber, the Laidrom trailing me. The door boomed shut behind us, the sound of the lock scraping home grating my tense nerves. The prisoner's chamber was circular, peaceful, and contemplative, awash in sandstone and white linen, and capped with a dome. Soft light filtered in through an oculus.

Aamon stood beneath the circle of light, his hands folded patiently in front of him, his white wings mirroring the gesture behind him. When he spoke, it was in English. "Hello, Aurelia." His tone was calm and understanding, as if he were there to offer his condolences for my hardships.

For a moment, I was unable to respond, a tumult of conflicting emotions boiling up inside me. I hated him, resented him, but I missed him and pitied him, too. "You lied to me," I finally said. My tone held an ocean of bitterness and betrayal. All my pain, Lucien's pain, the twisted stormscape of lightning-strike scars down my back—everything could have been prevented if I hadn't trusted him. My voice shook. "And you tried to kill me."

Aamon smoothed his ponytail and sat on one of the two stone benches, his wings reflecting the lamplight like snow does fire. "Sit with me." His face was gentle, much as it had been the night Miketh brought me to him, battered and reeling from the Laidrom attack. He had reassured me, then, and tended my aching head.

I took a few steps closer and hesitated before I took the seat across from him. "Of all the people you would want to talk to, why me?" I asked.

"Two reasons. One, to apologize. Two, there are things you should know that others will not tell you."

"Apologize? For trying to kill me?"

He frowned, framing his words. "Were you any other Linnia in the world, I would have not hesitated at that window. It wasn't until I had you there, at the top of the cathedral, that I realized it meant sacrificing you, Aurelia. And I didn't want to follow through."

"But you still did it."

"I did, and, ultimately, have no regrets. Had things not transpired as they did, you would not have been pardoned and welcomed to live among Iyarri." The note of pride in his voice faded to apology. "I am sorry for using you as a tool of revenge against your father. You had no hand in Siyah's death and should have had no part in my retribution." He clasped his hands between his knees, and for a moment he wasn't the orchestrator of my pain, my scars, my near-death, but the person who had bought me paintbrushes for a gift. "So, yes, I lied to you. I lied to myself as well. But I made you as Iyarri as I could, and I do not regret that."

My wings shifted, the susurrus whisper of feathers against linen. "The best you could do was make me a living, breathing punishment?"

His laugh was a derisive exhale. "You and your father left your audience with Saan-Eleéth, and your sentencing, alive. Was the significance of her pardon lost on you? No other Linnia or her parents have been allowed to live after being discovered. Not for over two thousand years. Do you think I had nothing at all to do with that?" I folded hands, not sure what to say. "Allowing you to live as Cæl's punishment was my suggestion; I sent it to Saan-Eleéth once I learned he'd petitioned for an audience."

"Eleéth didn't say anything about that."

"Would you expect her to? Do you think her advisors would like that she knew all about you before you set foot in her hall, yet had done nothing?" I didn't want to believe him, but I did. "Once I knew you were still alive, I made every effort to see you spared and folded into the Elonu-Dohe. It may seem a small thing, but I assure you, it is not." Contrition made his voice soft.

I twisted my fingers around one another. What he'd done to me was horrible, and yet the thought of him becoming a Naphal as punishment was grossly unjust.

"Aurelia." I looked at Aamon. His face was grave. "While I've no doubt Cæl thinks he is protecting you with ignorance, there is something in the wind I suspect he's kept from you."

"What's that?" My voice was soft.

"They are going to kill your mother."

"What?" I was on my feet in a single push of wings and legs. My heart fell even as my pulse jumped. "That isn't true," I said, the words a heartbroken, rushed denial.

"Yes, it is, and yes, they are. Saan-Eleéth may have pardoned you and your father, but she did not spare your mother."

"No, they've known about her for days. If they were going to kill her they'd have done it already."

"Saan-Eleéth is keen to test your father's loyalty—"

"My father would never—"

"Yes, he would. By bringing you in front of Saan-Eleéth, Cæl ensured your lives were spared at the cost of your mother's."

"He'd never risk her." My voice was a whisper.

He arched both eyebrows. "Are you so sure?" Dread threatened to cave my chest in—I was not sure. "Your father is eager to reclaim his position as Heeoa and get back a life he lost. That cannot happen with your mother alive."

"What should I do?" I whispered.

"Leave." His voice was soft, understanding. "Take Catherine and disappear. They will not search for you as much as you might think."

My eyes searched the stone floor but found no answers. If we fled, where would we go? How would we hide? I shook my head and tried to quell my quivering, twitchy muscles. It couldn't be true, it couldn't. Aamon was not someone who chose what he said carelessly. Though he might have tended me after the Laidrom attack, it was an attack he sanctioned to remove Lucien and with him the last of my resistance to his offer of wings. A course of action that had left nine Iyarri, including their Heeoa, dead. Was it to his benefit if I disappeared before his execution? Perhaps it was a diversion. No, Aamon had a stake in this, and it was not my well-being.

I stood and turned toward the door. "You're lying," I said.

"Am I?" His words made me pause mid-step.

"You are. Everything you ever told me was to your own ends, for your own benefit. You took advantage of my naïveté once. Never again."

His voice was sincere and quiet. "Think on my words, Aurelia. I am proud to have helped you become what you are, of sculpting you into your true form; yet I regret nothing more than letting my ambition hurt you. I've given you warning and spoken my piece. Fair winds."

I squeezed my eyes shut, head reeling, and when the guard opened the door, I fled.

THIRTY-TWO

I SLAMMED THE DOOR SO hard Cæl startled to his feet. "Are they going to kill her?" I demanded. He stared at me, taken aback. "Are they going to kill my mother?" I was shouting, my hands shaking.

"Who told you that?" he asked.

"Aamon. Is she okay?"

Some of the tension left his body as he realized there was no imminent threat. "She's safe. Miketh and Tiahmani made sure she got on a plane to the Cities before they came here."

"Are they going to kill her?"

He shook his head. "No. You were with me the entire time, there was no order to kill her."

I tore through our audience and our sentencing in my mind, searching for some mention of my mother. There hadn't been one. Cæl hadn't mentioned her, and neither Eleéth nor her advisors had asked about her. My arms fell to my sides, and the tension in my chest eased.

"Now, what else did he tell you?" he asked.

"That I should leave and take Mom and let you go back to being Heeoa."

Cæl snorted and shook his head. "Your sentence requires you to live among the Iyarri and both of us to exhibit unwavering adherence to the

Asario. Don't let Aamon court you so easily into another trap for the both of us."

I bit my lip, ashamed Aamon had, again, effortlessly planted a seed of doubt. Unfortunately, it was not so easily uprooted. "I want to talk to her." Cæl's words were reassuring, but they didn't take the seasick feeling from my stomach.

My father sighed and rubbed one hand over the scars on his arm. "I do too, but it's not possible from here. We'll contact her once all this is over and we leave Lilnon."

All this. He meant Irel and Aamon's punishments, but I was glad he hadn't put it into words. "Mom isn't going to like me living at Idura." It felt better to talk about the future, even if it was an imperfect one. It eased some of the dread pressing inside me, that otherwise created a driving need to do something when there was no action to take.

"I know." He sighed, his wings folding and unfolding. "What we have after this will not be ideal, but I promise I will do the best I can for her." I nodded and sank onto one of the benches, light-headed. "You should eat," he said. "It's been a long day, and it's going to get longer."

The time until Irel and Aamon's execution drew out into a single bleak line of tension. I ate the food Cæl brought for us and mused over a hot cup of tea. For all Aamon's lies, his treachery, his deceptions, the idea of him either dying or living his life as a Naphal tied a cold knot in my stomach that the tea couldn't chase off. I hated my mind for trying to sketch the twisted thing he would become.

If I was honest with myself, it wasn't just the thought of torture, but the lingering doubt that not everything he'd said was untrue. Had he really sent word to Eleéth about my father and me to beg our forgiveness? Was he truly happy I was to now live among the Iyarri?

My dark thoughts of Aamon bordered my deeper despair for Irel. Whatever he deserved for healing me, it wasn't death. I moved the pad of my finger over the surface of the tea, rippling my reflection. The unwavering dedication the Iyarri had to the letter of the law was disgusting in its unfairness. I wished to speak to Irel, to lay a thousand apologies at his feet, but he had not chosen me to be his last visitor, and so those words were to be spoken to his corpse, if at all.

Tiahmani knocked on our door and let herself inside, her belt slung low on her hips. "Ready?" She followed my gaze to her stomach and frowned. "Can you tell?"

"Only because I know," I said.

She sighed. "That will have to do."

I hesitated at the door and cast Cæl a wary look. No matter how many times I saw his full Heeoa regalia, it unnerved me. The split napta blades, the scars, and the severe raised plait holding his hair back were all enough to summon the memories of the Laidrom who had come so close to killing me. "Do I have to go?"

His brow furrowed with sympathy. "It's best for you to be seen there. Look away in the moment if you have to."

We joined the throng of Iyarri in the halls, winged bodies all moving in the same direction. No one spoke, and no one noticed me, their thoughts focused elsewhere. Tiahmani led the way and stopped when we reached a group of Idura's Laidrom. Miketh, Væries, and Kinor were already there, and Cæl nodded as we took our places beside them. Eager to be out of Væries's red-splotched glare, I squeezed past my father and to the edge of the balcony, and promptly wished I hadn't.

I trembled as my eyes settled on where I had so recently knelt under Eleéth's balcony. A few copper feathers and smears of blood still marked the floor, and I swayed, overwhelmed with the memory. The ceiling far above us shifted with dark, ominous blues and blacks. On a balcony across from us, overlooking it all, stood Eleéth, Barcus, Sisera, and Occodon.

Miketh leaned over to my father, his voice low. "Did you hear?" My father inclined his head in question and Miketh continued. "Irel and Hataan are missing."

My heart leapt and surged with hope—Hataan had been Irel's last visitor. Had he, somehow, gotten Irel out of Lilnon? "Now what?" I asked.

Miketh shrugged. "They're going to carry on with Aamon and deal with the other two when they're caught."

The room hushed as a row of unfamiliar Iadnah entered, drifting to a circle of blue chalk symbols. They walked one way around the circle, paused in unison, then walked the other, bodies moving like tumblers in an ethereal lock. The Iadnah murmured arcane words of preparation, the syllables an eerie, esoteric chant.

Eleéth unfurled her wings and spoke, her voice empyreal. "What we are gathered here to witness has not been seen for over eight centuries. It should not have been needed then, and it should not have been needed now." Her voice echoed off the walls, whispering her words back over and over in my ears. "There is no joy in this punishment, nothing but sorrow for one of us to have fallen so low. Let this be a lesson to all—our ambitions serve the Elonu-Dohe and not our own selfish ends." She gestured toward the hallway. "Bring him forward."

A sea of Iyarri turned in one rippling motion to watch Maroch escort Aamon in. Aamon's robe was simple, heavy cloth of the purest white—no detailing, no fine needlework. The fallen Aldaria shuffled forward with his eyes on the floor. He swayed and stumbled, wings wide for balance.

Tiahmani leaned close to my father and whispered, "He looks drugged. Are you going to say anything?"

My father shook his head, his lips pressed into a thin line. "I am sure Maroch knows and just wants it done with. Whoever managed to get him something will pay when they're caught."

Maroch pushed Aamon into the Iadnah circle, walked around it himself, and stopped at the far side. Aamon wavered in the center of the circle, his wings sagging low, his hands tucked into the opposite sleeves of his robe like a monk. I leaned forward, unease lacing my chest tight as I peered over the balcony at him. This all felt wrong, off in a way I couldn't place.

Anahita walked into the room next, her hair unbound, the pale length shimmering between her hummingbird-green wings. Her blue robe was in the Iadnah style, but ornate, the gilding in gold and silver gleaming in the pale light. She paused at the edge of the circle and bowed to Eleéth. In the silence of the hall we could hear the draw of the ritualist's breath as she readied herself.

Anahita took her place at the head of the circle, and the Iadnah spread and cupped their wings so the tips touched. The chant began low in the throats of the other Iadnah, and Anahita raised her arms and tilted her head back. *"Vooan alca fifis Naphal. Vooan alca fifis Naphal."* Their cadence ebbed like the waves of the ocean. A lock of my hair wavered in front of my face, and my skin tingled.

Anahita's voice carried the melody of the rite, sailing atop the chant as a bird does the wind. The air grew thicker, charged, and scented with ozone the way it does before a lightning strike, and my scars prickled with the memory of it from my own ritual. The blue chalk symbols of the circle pulsed and grew brighter with each syllable.

Aamon lunged for the edge of the circle and stopped—the symbols, blazing aquamarine, had cast up an invisible wall. His green eyes were wide with terror, and though his mouth moved, the spell-barrier trapped the sound inside.

His eyes. Aamon's eyes were hazel, not green. I closed my hand around my father's arm. "Essia, something's wrong."

Cæl hushed me, the sound drowned out as the incantation shifted, the words harsher, stronger. Beside me, Tiahmani crossed her hands over her stomach and swallowed hard, her face illuminated with the incandescence of the symbols.

Anahita arched backward, nearly aloft, though her wings did not beat, her voice a descant to the chanting chorus. My hair stood on the back of my neck, and my arms prickled with goose bumps.

Aamon fell to his knees and crossed his arms over his chest, digging his fingers into his arms. His wings lashed like wild creatures trying to free themselves from his back, and he screamed, the cords in his neck standing out, but we still heard no sound save for the chanting. Aamon's bare feet clenched, the talons on them black and not like the curved opals I knew him to have.

I shook Cæl's arm, panic rising in my voice. "That's not Aamon."

"Quiet," he snapped.

My thoughts raced between each errant detail, from the green eyes to the black talons and back again. It was an illusion, it swirled like fog, and for a moment, I could see through it. It wasn't Aamon, but Hataan, the apprentice healer.

"Stop! Stop it!" I yelled, rushing forward. "You have to stop! That—" my voice cut off in a rush of breath as my father caught me, one muscled arm across my stomach.

I kept yelling, the words airy and distorted. Around us, Iyarri were turning to glare at me. For the second time, Cæl's hand closed over my mouth and the tips of his claws pricked my cheek. "Silence." The word was a snarling whisper.

As Anahita lifted her hand, the Iadnah shifted their chant, each taking a part like a song done in a round, their voices building, blending, summoning. I fought against Cæl, trying in vain to peel his hand off my face. I screamed my warning, the sound muffled and distorted against my father's palm. The skin on Haatan's hands split, blood seeping and spreading into the white robe. As his wings beat, feathers grew darker, shifting from white to green-black and dislodged, falling to the ground.

The Iadnah chant reached its crescendo, their wings beating together with the rhythm of their invocation. The illusion of Aamon's face shifted, the features blurring.

Anahita's voice punctuated the gathering force of the conjuration, filling the room with the sound. "*Noan yarrah balt od vooan!*" The release of power surged outward in a circular shockwave and punched into my chest. In the center of the magical circle knelt Hataan the healer's apprentice, not Aamon the traitor. The final rush of energy from the ritual dispelled the magical illusion—Aamon's face no longer, but Hataan's, his gentle face contorted by pain.

Nesah screamed, "No! Hataan! No!" But it was done, the ritual complete.

Hataan's skin split in a thousand places and blood welled forth, thick and black in the blue light. Feathers flew from his wings, taking tattered swaths of skin with them, leaving quivering muscle, naked and raw. His teeth grew fearsome and pointed, forcing their way from the bone. Blood poured from his mouth, and he slouched to the floor, writhing, transforming.

Cæl released me, his body frozen in shock, and I sagged against the balcony, queasy and brokenhearted. "Help him," I called, voice hoarse from screaming. "Someone help him!"

Maroch turned to his warriors and bellowed, "Laidrom! Split and find Aamon! Search Lilnon. I want him found, alive!" Like a murder of crows dispersing into the sky, Maroch's Laidrom took to the hunt. My father remained and watched the gruesome scene play out.

Nesah knelt beside Hataan, the invisible wall gone, the luminescence of the symbols faded to smudged chalk. The other ritualists stepped back, cringing in horror. Anahita crumpled to the floor, oblivious and spent. Kneeling in the spreading pool of Hataan's blood, Nesah cupped her golden wings over him and chanted, her face streaked with tears, her voice shaking. They were the same words Irel had spoken over me when I'd lay tattered and dying in the aftermath of my wings, but they did nothing to stop Hataan's transformation.

Hataan's screams reverberated through the hall. The wet sound of bone creaking echoed as his clawed hands contorted and became thick black talons. His wings, naked, featherless, and dribbling oily blood, snapped wide, the joints crumpling, molding into something blackened, like burnt leather twisted into tree branches.

Nesah's voice, soothing and fumbling through tears, carried on through Hataan's screams, through the sounds of his body breaking. His face became a horrific mask, cheekbones jutting upward, his brow pierced by bony spines. An open hole wept where his nose had been. He collapsed, the tension in his body dissipating. His breaths came in gurgling draws, his eyes rolling. Still chanting, Nesah knelt, eased Hataan's head into her lap, and wiped the blood from it with the sleeve of her robe.

He turned his monstrous face toward Nesah and spoke three strained words. "Kill me. Please."

Unable to speak, only to weep, Nesah shook her head and pressed her blood-streaked hand to his brow.

An Iadnah in healer's robes broke from a group of stunned Iyarri and knelt beside Nesah in the puddle of gore. Nesah clung to the healer's sleeve. "Do something, please. Help him." The healer laid her hand on Hataan, but futility consumed her expression and she tried to put the regret on her face into words. I was glad she did not. There were no words for such things.

The healer eased Nesah away from Hataan's ravaged form, looked to Maroch, and nodded. Nesah lunged back to Hataan, but the healer held her fast. The young Iadnah's golden wings flapped wildly, her blood-soaked robes twisting in the other Iyarri's grasp. "No, you have to let me help him. You can't—" Nesah's voice broke, unable to finish. "You can't." Maroch drew his okada from the back of his belt, pulled Hataan into a reassuring embrace, and carved the blade across Hataan's throat.

Okada. Mercy.

Blood spurted from Hataan's neck, and he fell forward as Maroch released him. Hataan's malformed wings thrashed, quivered, and went still. Nesah's cries filled the great chamber, and the healer handed her off to two Iadnah, who took her, struggling, from the room. Over and over she sobbed, "You can't, you just can't . . ."

Buckling under the unfairness of it all and buried by regret, I covered my face in my hands and wept, smearing hot tears over my cheeks and palms. A fire, incensed and disgusted, burned a hole in my misery. They hadn't listened because I was Linnia, and Hataan had suffered and died because of it.

Eleéth's voice cut through the hall like a winter gale. "I want to know how this happened. Iadnah, gather in the library, now. I want all of you there, no exceptions." She turned to Maroch. "I am not fool enough to think he had no allies in this. I want his guards questioned. pir-Occodon, interrogate the Aldaria. Anyone who knows anything is brought to me." Maroch nodded and barked orders at his remaining Laidrom.

Through it all, Hataan's broken body lay in a spreading pool of crimson, twisted feathers skimming the surface like dry leaves in a pond. His head lay on one cheek, eyes staring—they were the same emerald green that had gazed at Nesah with such love and adoration.

I stumbled to my feet and wrapped my arms around myself, swaying like a broken flower. Guilt, despair, and anger quarreled for my heart until, overwhelmed, I went numb.

"Cæl Heeoa," Eleéth called. I looked at her and wished I hadn't. Her wings, normally shifting like black fans, were as unmoving as carved cobalt. My father stopped and bowed. "I will call for your Linnia shortly. Confine her until then." The Ohlera's eyes gleamed dark and deadly, her question a scathing expression across her features—how had I known?

Cæl closed his hand over my shoulder to lead me back toward our chambers.

THIRTY-THREE

M Y FATHER QUESTIONED ME over and over until I faltered over my words. "Is that the entire truth?" he asked as he paced in front of our door, wings arched and claws flexed like a caged sphinx.

"Yes," I said, fingers twisting angry knots into the raw edge of my dress.

"You swear?"

"Cæl, stop," Tiahmani said without looking up. She sat curled where one of the benches met the wall, tucked into a feathery nest of wings and misery.

"This is important," he snarled. "She has to get this right when she speaks to Saan-Eleéth."

"I was right," I yelled, the instant, furious indignation of my own voice surprising me. "None of this had to happen. Hataan died because you wouldn't let me stop them."

"That isn't true—"

"Yes it is. You were so embarrassed that shutting me up was more important than hearing me out. And now you're so fucking worried about Saan-Eleéth wanting to know how I knew that you seem to have missed the fact that you kept me from yelling at the Iadnah to stop." A wavy lock of ginger hair trembled in front of my face, and I wiped my sweaty hands on the fabric of my dress. Had he just *listened* to me, Hataan might be alive.

"You have no idea—"

"Yes, I do. I might be your daughter, but I am not a child." Linnia, Iyarri, or human, it didn't matter, I had a voice, and I wouldn't let him silence me again.

My father opened his mouth to protest but was cut off by two sharp raps on the door. "Saan-Eleéth summons Tiahmani Galearii and the Linnia," called a woman's voice.

Cæl opened the door, two of Eleéth's personal guards on the other side. She gestured to Cæl. "You too. Let's go." She turned in a swirl of feathers and leather. The three of us followed without a word. We came to the Iadnah library, and a scar in the Laidrom's lip pinched as she pushed open the door. "Mind the blood," she murmured.

Tiahmani started to ask, "What bl—" and stopped. The pale stone floor in front of a crescent-shaped table was awash in red. Some if it was hours old, dried to black, but a fresher, brighter coat glistened on top. Long rivulets ran between the stones in the floor and wicked into the edges of the rug. Piled against one of the book cases were bodies, a grotesque sculpture of limbs and wings. The heads were stacked not far away, five of them. I spun, turning from them with a sharp inhale of fear and disgust, but their faces were burned into my mind: mouths agape and eyes staring, frozen in the futile struggle of their last instants of consciousness. The Laidrom grabbed me by the back of my neck and shoved me forward.

Eleéth stood at the far side of the table, wings and face taut with impatience; Occodon was beside her, gray and motionless as a graveyard angel. Anahita sat at a back table while Barcus tried to get her to drink something. Maroch stood on the bloodied edge of the nearest rug, the extended blades of his napta painted in layers of red that matched the floor. In unison Cæl, Tiahmani, and I bowed to Eleéth as our escort retook their posts by the door. Eleéth wasted neither time nor words on ceremony. "Step forward, Linnia."

Her voice made every nerve in my body seize, and I willed my limbs to motion. My feet squelched into the soaked carpet and cold blood welled up between my toes. Revulsion rolled over me like a hot, copper-scented wave. I did not look at Eleéth as she approached, but her power seeped into me, icy and penetrating. "Have you any knowledge of Aamon's escape or who may have aided him?"

"No, Saanire Ohlera." Her frigid aura chilled me until I shivered, and my words came through chattering teeth.

There was a surprised half-beat of silence before she spoke next—my words were true. "You spoke to Aamon before his escape. Detail that conversation."

I did, fumbling for the right Loagæth words and forming them with unsteady lips. I quoted Aamon's words when I could and gave summaries where I could not.

"Is there anything you've omitted?" The cold of her magic sliced through me like a gleaming dagger, filleting me to my core in its search for falsehoods. My panicked thoughts raced back and forth along my accounting, terrified I'd say one word wrong and Eleéth would read it as a lie.

Maroch's leather gauntlet creaked, and I bunched my hands into fists at my side. "No, Saanire Ohlera," I said.

"And do you have any intention to flee with your mother as Aamon suggested you do?"

My answer was defeated. "No."

Eleéth's dark feathers encroached on the edges of my vision like a coming storm. "How did you know it was Hataan and not Aamon in the center of the ritual?"

"I don't know."

"Linnia." Her voice was a thunderclap.

My words fled from my lips like frightened rabbits. "His eyes. I noticed the color of the eyes was wrong first. Aamon's eyes are hazel. Hataan's are, were, green. His jaw seemed wrong, and the talons on the feet were black, not white."

347

Eleéth's lifted her head and set a heavy gaze upon on her advisors. "And yet not a single Iadnah, not a single Laidrom guard noticed these things." Silence, thick with death, permeated the room. "Step back, Linnia."

Relief drained my strength, but I followed her order and left tacky, bloody footprints when my feet returned to the stone floor.

Eleéth summoned Tiahmani. If the blood bothered the fierce Laidrom, she gave no indication of it. "Tiahmani Galearii, did you know of Aamon's plans to escape or anyone who might have?"

"No, Saanire Ohlera." Tiahmani's voice did not shake as she answered, but she clenched one hand around the opposing wrist.

"Is there anything pertinent regarding Aamon that you know?"

"No, Saanire Ohlera."

Eleéth's dark eyes became amethyst slits. "You dare lie to me?" Eleéth crossed the distance to the headstrong Laidrom in a blur of winter-dark. Cold air rolled in front of her, as chilling and frightening as the severe lines on Eleéth's face. I closed my wings against me, though it did nothing to keep off the unnatural cold.

Tiahmani said nothing even as her skin broke out in goosebumps from the chill. Her exhale was a frosty plume in front of her face.

Eleéth spoke, her tone liquid and venomous: "Your silence will not save you any more than guilty words." She gestured to Cæl. "Don't make me test your brother's loyalty."

Cæl nodded to Tiahmani, willing her to tell her secret. Tiahmani held her silence. My heart pounded, and my eyes jumped from one to the other, willing one of them to speak.

The Ohlera snapped her wings closed and turned from Tiahmani to Cæl. "Kill her."

My father stood, thunderstruck. "Saanire Ohlera, there—"

I opened my mouth to speak, but the words froze in my throat.

"Do it, Heeoa, or I'll add you both to that pile of bodies."

Tiahmani's wings were shaking, her lips motionless with terror.

Dread and alarm flitted in my chest like panicked birds. I stepped in between my aunt and Eleéth and blurted, "Tiahmani is pregnant with Aamon's baby." Tiahmani swayed on her feet, expression stunned, terrified and grateful all at once.

Retribution swelled, inevitable and certain. I cringed, holding my arms against my chest and raising one wing in front of me as Eleéth paused and turned back around. Her face was pensive, her voice curious. "Is that true?" she asked Tiahmani, gesturing me out of the way. "You carry Aamon's child?"

Tiahmani kept her shoulders straight and her head up as she answered. "Yes, I do."

"And why withhold that you two are Nuam?"

"I was afraid it would affect the judgement he deserved and the sentence he got. Aamon doesn't know."

Eleéth tilted her head, focused on Tiahmani's abdomen. The Ohlera laid one clawed hand on Tiahmani's swelling stomach, her eyes fluttering as she tried to sense the child within. Tiahmani's face was as unmoving as stone, but a single line of sweat ran down the back of her neck. After several seconds, Eleéth waved one hand in dismissal. "The Iadnah will summon a Li'iansa who specializes in childbirth to Idura to tend you for the remainder of your pregnancy." There was a soft sigh, though I was not sure if it came from Tiahmani, my father, or all three of us. Eleéth went on, "Go now and rest. I would not have any more stress placed on you or your child."

Tiahmani bowed, face devoid of color. "Thank you, Saanire Ohlera."

Eleéth regarded me and my father. "It seems your line is most unusually fertile, Heeoa. A pity it's coupled with an equally poor choice in partners." My father's jaw tightened. "Tiahmani, Linnia, you are dismissed."

"Wait," Maroch said as he stepped forward. "I have a question for Aurelia, and I want it asked in front of Saan-Eleéth."

I looked to Cæl for an answer, but he seemed as wary and confused as I did. Acquiescing with a bow of my head, I said, "Of course."

Maroch peered at me, the scars on his face bunching around his yellow eyes. "Cæl mentioned you killed a Laidrom and have the right to our arms, but he'd had a fair few when he said it. I want to know if it's true." His breath rolled over my face, hot and smelling of darignis—of woodsmoke and scorched spices.

Keenly aware of the blood on Maroch's napta, I stammered. "Two. I technically killed two." One in the apartment and the one trapped in the windshield.

"Is that so?" Maroch's grizzled eyebrow lifted and he turned toward Eleéth.

She waved a wing, disinterested. "The Linnia speaks the truth."

Maroch seized my upper arm in one massive hand, his claws touching on either side of my bicep, and hauled me a few steps off to the side of the library. A short, double-ended blade gleamed in his other hand. Fear, cold and sharp as Maroch's knife, sliced through the little resolve I had left.

"Is this necessary, pir-Maroch?" Occodon said, his lip curling into a sneer.

Maroch pushed me backward into my father's chest—Cæl's crimson Heeoa gauntlet locked across my torso, pinning me there. "Aye, I'm going to do this myself, and I want it done in front of Saan-Eleéth so nobody questions it."

Uncertainty made my heart beat so frantically my father had to feel it right through the leather of his gauntlet. Cæl bowed his head so his lips were by my ear. "Stay still, pasahasa." His tone was quiet, reassuring, but still my body quaked with fear.

Maroch released my arm, reached into the pouch at his hip, and extracted a vial of clear liquid. He uncorked the vial, dipped the blade in, and lifted the gleaming metal to a torch. It burst into flame; Maroch let it burn for a second or two before he waved the soot-blackened blade, extinguishing the flame. A second dip in the vial returned the metal to gleaming silver.

Cæl shifted his arm so it became a bar across my torso and closed his hand around my elbow, pinning my arm to my side. The smell of curing blood and hot metal choked out the air and a scream built in my throat.

The air around Maroch's blade wavered, and heat licked my shoulder. A second later, the blade pressed downward. I stiffened and Cæl tightened his hold on me, the scream in my chest coming out as a rush of trembling air. My skin gave way and blood oozed around the metal.

Pain washed over me in a hot, red wave. The blade was keen, Maroch's hand deft, and in the space of a few smooth arcs, my arm was a sheet of blood. Out of the corner of my eye, I saw Maroch lift his hand and twirl the blade around his thick fingers, flipping it so the pointed, bloody end traded places with a squared chisel-tip blade.

He cut the skin clean off my body.

I pulled in a high, keening breath, arching my back as I clenched my hands into Cæl's clothes. Pieces of my discarded flesh tumbled down my arm, chased by blood that pattered onto stone floor and my bare feet. I clenched my jaw so tight that I feared the cords in my neck would snap and my teeth would shatter. Maroch filleted one more piece of my body away and sheathed the tiny, bloody blade. I moaned as I collapsed against Cæl, head hanging and body spent. The voids in my flesh pulsed with each beat of my heart, hot and raw, and a cold line of sweat trickled down my sternum. At my feet, curls of pale skin sat like dead worms in a bloody puddle. A wave of heat rolled through my body and my stomach heaved, but I looked away and managed not to vomit.

Maroch squeezed a small, leather waterskin above his hand. Clear, shimmering gel, like aloe mixed with sugar, puddled in his palm, and the clean aroma of fir and juniper cut through the oppressive stench of blood, hot metal, and dead bodies. He smoothed it over the weeping voids in my skin, my arm contracting as it soothed and stung in equal measure. The grizzled Laidrom shook his hand, sending a spray of bloody gel to the floor. He surveyed my arm, gave a satisfied grunt, and stepped away from me.

Cæl gave me a squeeze and, once certain I could stand on my own, released me. I swayed, the world blooming white for a moment, but held my footing.

Occodon folded his arms and silver wings in a unified gesture of disgust. "Are you quite done?"

"Aye," Maroch said, bowing to Eleéth. "Thank you for the indulgence, Saanire Ohlera."

Eleéth tilted her head in acknowledgement and gestured to the Laidrom along the walls. "Nisroc, see the Linnia and Tiahmani to their quarters." She gave my father a feline smile. "As for you, Heeoa, stay a bit longer."

Maroch tossed the waterskin of gel to Tiahmani and jerked his head toward me. "Look after her."

My aunt wrapped one dark, protective wing around me, and we walked like shell-shocked survivors back to our rooms. To my surprise, Tiahmani came inside with me. I raised one hand to my shoulder, but stopped short of touching it, indignant tears in my eyes. "Why didn't they say anything to me beforehand? Maroch didn't even ask." My voice wavered in a way I was sure Cæl wouldn't have approved of.

Tiahmani's dark eyebrows pulled together in a sympathetic gesture and hummed her agreement. She took my mangled arm in her hand and eased my shoulder toward her. "He did a fine job, though, and now nobody can say you've no right to our arms."

My chest hitched with a sob, and I sank onto a bench, peering at my deltoid. The taloned triskele design matched the one the Laidrom had, but I had no accompanying sleeve of scarring. It shone, red and glossy, like a single red star in the pale sky of my skin. Part of me was still insulted, incensed they had mutilated me against my will, but another part of me was proud to have the same marking on my arm as Tiahmani, Miketh, and my father. Like them, I had earned it. "Miketh said it also means anyone can challenge me to the Circle of Blades. They butchered my arm so the other Laidrom have an excuse to beat me up?"

Tiahmani sat beside me, her dark wing cupping around me like a hug. "They'd have to get through me first."

I sniffed, surprised she'd defend me. "Really?"

A smile spread across her face. "Aye. And, no offense, but you have no idea what the fuck you're doing yet. Anyone challenging you would look like an insecure asshole."

I wanted to smile in response, but the pulsing flesh on my shoulder burned up the expression before it formed. Tiahmani uncapped the bladder of gel and dabbed more of it onto my arm with a finger. The design itched and pulsed, the gel irritating the wound as much as it numbed the pain. "My niece took that like a Laidrom, stone-sober, and everyone there saw it." The approval in her voice shone. "Cæl was so proud of you. I know you couldn't see it, but he was."

This time the corners of my lips did lift in a smile. I could tell myself I didn't want Cæl's approval until the chimes crashed from the ceiling of the marketplace, but the warm glow in my chest wouldn't go away.

Tiahmani got to her feet, capped the waterskin, and handed it to me. "Put that on as often as you need to for the pain. It'll make it feel better, and the more you do it, the nicer the scar will raise." She pressed her lips together and gave me a grateful smile. "And thank you for telling Saan-Eleéth about this." She gestured to her stomach. "I was too afraid to say a damn word, and it almost got me and Cæl killed."

I hugged her tight, grateful she finally thought of me as family.

The ceilings in our rooms were light with dawn when my father returned. Cæl sank down across from me, cheeks hollow and feet bloody to his ankles. When he looked at my arm, though, pride lifted some of the gloom from his features. "You did well, pasahasa."

"Thank you, essia." Silence hung in the air between us like a dark cloud. "They didn't find Aamon, did they?" I finally asked.

"No. And no leads, either." He bowed his head and rubbed the back of his neck.

"What about the dead Iyarri in the library?" The images of them, mouths slack, eyes half-rolled back and glassy, rose in my mind.

"Two Aldaria got Aamon enough of the Elonu-Dohe's money to see him on his way. The others helped him escape. Before the ritual, he had to be taken to the cleansing room and the two Laidrom guarding him handed him over to the waiting Iadnah. Hataan was Irel's last visitor—they drugged Hataan, made him appear like Aamon, swapped him out. When the Iadnah handed Hataan over to the Laidrom, they said the cleansing ritual taxed Aamon and that he would be asleep for some time."

"Did you?" I nodded to his napta. The blades were the same rylene crimson as his gauntlets.

"Yes, they brought in the Iadnah who helped Aamon after you left." He fingered the lacings. "It's hard. Harder than . . ." he shook his head.

Harder than killing humans was how he'd meant to finish it. I pressed my lips together, tempted to say it for him. "They confessed?"

"Aye, they told us everything they knew. Once they finished, Saan-Eleéth ordered them executed." He pulled the laces on his gauntlet even though the leather couldn't tighten more. "None of them knew anything about his plans or where he was going. Throwaways, all of them."

"Throwaways?" My heart tore, glad Aamon had just manipulated rather than corrupted these Iadnah, but heartsick he'd caused their deaths.

"Aamon knew there would be questions, and those who helped him would be found and killed. Anyone important to him he preserved with ignorance." He lifted both eyebrows and looked at me out of the tops of his dark eyes. "Like you."

I stilled, the thought heavy and uncomfortable. "What about Irel?" I asked.

"We don't know. He went into the cleansing chambers, and that was the last time anyone saw him. At least, anyone we questioned."

Wherever Irel was, I hoped he was safe. My brow furrowed. Irel had accepted his punishment without protest, as though he planned escape all along, but he didn't seem one for subterfuge.

Cæl loosed an exhale and hung his head. "I will just be grateful that you, Tiahmani, and I were spared. We'll leave for Idura tomorrow. We're escorting Hataan's body."

THIRTY-FOUR

T HE FLIGHT HOME WAS three days on wing from dawn until moonrise. *Home*—the word undulated like the clouds we flew through, cold, formless, and shifting. My mother's house was comforting but felt like a memory from a previous life. Tiahmani's loft housed my things, but no meaningful memories, and all my time at Idura was warped with pain and soaked in blood. I closed my hand over the spiral in my hair, Lucien's pale, white fireplace rising in my thoughts. There, with him, in front of the fire—that felt like home. My fist tightened until the metal hurt my palm. While his house was there, Lucien was not.

I flapped my wings harder, catching up to the others. The belt and hip bags I wore were heavy, my wings still gaining strength, but Hataan's corpse slowed us to a pace I could manage. The healer's apprentice lay in a carrying sling, bundled in a cocoon of his own deformed wings, bound tight to his body in layer upon layer of cloth. It took four Iyarri to carry him, one holding each corner of the sling's handles in their toes.

We flew in a V, my father at the point, then the four carrying Hataan, followed by the rest of Idura's Iyarri, with me and Nesah at the rear— me because I was weakest and needed to use the updrafts coming off the wings of those ahead to keep up, and Nesah because her grief weighed her down so. No one spoke—too stressed, too exhausted, and wanting this all to be over. The beat of our wings went on, as did the unceasing lament of Nesah weeping.

We spent the nights at lucala, Iyarri waypoints that reminded me of smaller, simplified strongholds. In one of the chambers meant for resting, there was room enough for me, my father, Tiahmani, Miketh, Sofiel, Nesah, and Hataan's corpse. Exhausted, I slid down against the wall as the others carried Hataan's body in.

Nesah sat beside the ruin of her Semeroh, legs to her chest and face to her knees, golden wings shuddering. Not an inch of Hataan's leathery, blackened skin could be seen, but in places liquid, some yellow, some rusty, seeped through the outermost wrappings and the carrying sling.

The others settled in around me, but no one acknowledged Nesah's crying, not even her sister. Ignoring my screaming muscles, I stood and walked toward her. Cæl's voice stopped me. "Leave her. She needs space to mourn."

I crinkled my face and turned toward Nesah with a flick of wings. She, not Cæl, would tell me what she needed. Nesah lifted her head as I approached, her eyes glossy as lilacs after a miserable rainfall. I sat on the floor beside her. She didn't say anything, but didn't seem averse to my company, either. Two lines of fresh tears slid down the same paths on her cheeks as a thousand of their predecessors. "I'm not good at healing. I've never been good at it." Her chest hitched and her clawed hands closed into delicate fists around one green-black feather. "I tried. I tried to save him."

"You gave him comfort," I said. "That's the most anyone could have done."

She turned her face into my shoulder and cried, and though there were words, they were broken and incoherent. I eased an arm and a wing around her, trying to keep Nesah's grief from shaking her to pieces.

"But—" her voice broke and she tried again. "I would have spent my life trying to find a way to fix him." She clung to my shoulder, her claws biting into my arm. "But they killed him and then Aamon got away. He got away." Her whisper was shattered with disbelief.

I stroked her hand, unable to muster much confidence that she could have returned Hataan to his former self any more than she could have made me truly Iyarri. Aamon's capture, though, we could hope for. "They'll find him."

"Good. And I hope they kill him." She cried harder. "I've never wished harm on anything before, but I hate him. I hate him so much." Tears drowned out the rest of her words. Something innocent in her had died with Hataan, and it broke my heart to see the change in her.

After a few minutes, when her crying had diminished to a few sniffles, she asked, "Does it ever get better?"

"It does." I smoothed her hair, the ornate, braided bun she wore days-old, windblown, and frayed. "In time."

Nesah's brows knit with a silent thank-you. I shifted, and she settled against my side and put her head on my shoulder, golden tresses smelling like flowers and blood. Why she had decided I was worthy of her trust, of her friendship, I did not know, but I was grateful for it. Her breathing evened and, perhaps for the first time since Hataan's death, she slept. Her Semeroh's feather drifted from her tattooed hands to the floor, gleaming in the dim light.

I pictured the two tiny plumes woven into Miketh's braids; the way he had stared out over the white expanse of snow, his face fractured with heartbreak and loss. I watched him work thin strips of leather into a woven strap. Whatever his loss, he still carried it with him.

Careful not to wake Nesah, I took up Hataan's feather and tucked it into her hair, leaned my head against hers, and stayed with her until morning.

The river valley was full of fog as we approached Idura, the thick mist making the wooded bluffs seem like floating islands in the sky. The cool vapor soothed my tired muscles and scattered a million droplets across my feathers. The Iyarri flew faster, breaking formation, eager to be home. My father let them outpace us and dropped back by me, the yearning expression on his face tempered by contentment. As the cliff-side entrance over the river appeared, he smiled and squeezed my hand. Together, we dipped under the rock face and up into the limestone cavern.

We walked down the sloping passages until we reached the hidden stone doors. Tiahmani gave her brother a smile of pure love as her fingers found the door's trigger. "Welcome home, noromi," she said.

The pale light of Idura washed over my father's face; for a few seconds, all he did was take in the soaring cliff face and the illuminated pool. Cæl's expression was full worries and doubts, but joy and relief radiated more. "Thank you."

We flew over the water, the narrow isthmus I'd walked as a prisoner a thin stone thread below us. Idura was not home, but this time the otherworldly architecture, the Iyarri-carved arches, windows, and balconies, was beautiful rather than menacing.

Curious Iyarri waited, scattered across the balconies, and children peered around from behind their parents, who tucked them back out of sight. My father ignored them all, and I did my best to appear to do the same. We were met by an Iyarri woman with burgundy hair and wings, eyes the color of trapped blue morpho butterflies. The bronze cuffs on her wrists and ankles flashed as she gave my father a bow and introduced herself. "Kahaviel Akarinu, I've been waiting to show you and your daughter to your quarters."

"Of course," my father said. "Lead on."

Kahaviel gestured down one of the hallways with willowy grace. "We'll go to your daughter's rooms first."

We threaded through several passages until we reached a large spiral staircase in the back of the first floor. The steps were pale limestone with a polished silver railing, but napta blades bridged the gap between the rail and the stairs instead of spindles. Down the spiral we walked, hundreds of still-sharp blades glinting. "Fallen Laidrom," my father said with reverence. "A reminder of what is given to keep the rest of us protected."

As we neared the base of the staircase, the spaces we passed were empty, waiting to be filled with the weapons of the dead. I pictured the blades of the Iyarri Lucien had killed in the voids. Near the end of a hallway, Kahaviel stopped at a door and opened it for me. "Here you are. It should meet your needs."

The suite was similar to those at Lilnon, but with a single bedroom. I set my bags down and thanked her. She gestured for us to follow her again; the next door we stopped at was not far from the base of the napta-studded staircase. Though it was the same dark wood as the others, the stone around it was carved with severe patterns reminiscent of the swirling designs of my father's scars. Kahaviel spoke to Cæl: "Maroch decided you will resume residency in the Heeoa quarters until the challenge with Væries is resolved."

Kahaviel nodded, and my father pushed open the door.

The room inside was massive, the ceiling two stories above us. The door opened into a large central sitting room, and a wide, blade-lined staircase ascended at the back of the quarters, forking halfway up. These blades were more elaborate than those on the other staircase; made from the napta of fallen Heeoa, then.

My father looked around the room, a stranger in a familiar place. Reaching down, he laid a hand on the most recent napta blade on the staircase. "Thank you," he said.

Kahaviel took her leave and my father unshouldered his bags. The weight that lifted from his frame was far greater than what he set down. One leaden thought rested in the bottom of my mind. "Essia? Can I go visit Mom? To make sure she's okay?"

I thought he'd say no, that it risked too much, but instead he opened the door for me. "Go on. Be quick and don't draw attention to yourself."

The windows of my mother's house were aglow when I landed among the trees in the backyard, but I paused after two quick steps toward the house—she wasn't alone. She and Aunt Erin were in the kitchen, laughing over glasses of wine.

It made me smile, and it made my heart ache.

She was alive and home and happy, but there was no way for me to join her. Seeing the white house under the weeping willows from an unfamiliar vantage was strange, as though it'd changed in my absence. I traced the line of one of my feathers with my fingertips. The house hadn't changed, my mother hadn't changed, but I had, in ways that ran deeper than wings and scars.

Their laughter rang out, familiar and joyful, and I turned from the house. To go in would invite questions neither my mom nor I could answer in front of Erin, and I'd ruin a rare evening for them both. I took two steps and leapt into the sky, thinking a silent promise: *I'll come back, Mom, another time.*

Idura was northeast of my mother's house, but I flew northwest instead. There was one more place to visit.

THIRTY-FIVE

T HE NIGHT GREW FRIGID and damp, and my silhouette blotted out puddles of starry water in the snow-streaked ground. I alighted to the top of a broken tree at the edge of Lucien's property and bowed my head, heart as heavy as my exhausted wings. The same color palette painted the earth and the sky: pewter silver, blueblack, and Payne's gray. A reverent stillness held sway, the slate roof of Lucien's house tomblike. I clasped my hands and pressed them to my trembling lips, exhaling a mournful breath that plumed in the night air and faded.

A crypt needed remains, but his house felt close enough. It twisted my insides to imagine the disregard the Iyarri would have shown his body—no respectful interment or final words, whatever the Laidrom had done to him so bad Aamon said I shouldn't see. The need to say something for him swelled, but the words wouldn't come, and my inhale hitched with a sob.

A wall of storm clouds loomed on the horizon, dark and oppressive as the guilt around my heart. I turned my face skyward and blinked back tears, the clear patch of the heavens over me dotted with stars. He hadn't deserved any of this. And yet, I couldn't have pictured him acting differently—Lucien's resignation that he would meet death at the claws of the Iyarri was too strong. I knew the secrets he hid from the rest of humanity. I could have shared that life with him.

Grief invaded each crevice of my heart like freezing water, expanding until it threatened to break the whole of it into pieces. I closed my hand around the spiral he'd given me, the thoughts of him maddening: his smile, the ferocity with which he'd risked his life to save my own, the tender way he'd tended my wounds, and the desperate restraint when we'd kissed. I'd loved him. I clenched my fist around the spiral until my fingers hurt. I still loved him.

Far below and on the opposite side of Lucien's house, golden light sputtered to life against the trees. Fire. Its intensity grew, and I scrambled to my feet, talons digging into the wet bark and my heart thudding in my chest. Not a fire, but firelight, from a window. It was impossible—it was stupid to dream he was there, alive—but for a second hope incinerated every shadow of doubt around my heart.

I swooped over the house in a blur and hit the shadowy ground hard enough to stumble. The windows in the living room and bedroom waxed brighter with firelight, and there, one arm resting on the mantel, staring into the flames, stood Lucien.

Relief sapped me and my knees buckled. My hands fluttered to my face, a cry of disbelief escaping between my fingers. I stared, trembling, not trusting what I was seeing. The flickering light cast warm licks of red and orange into Lucien's hair and made the whisky glass in his other hand shine like an amber star.

"Lucien." I exhaled his name, took two hurried steps toward him, and hit a wall of realization at the tree line. He lived, a miracle in of itself, and perhaps, with the Iyarri thinking him dead, had moved on and built a normal life for himself. What right did I have to undo that? To put him back at risk? I sagged against the trunk of a tree, the bark damp and cold under my hands. He could have his life, his human life, and maybe find someone and have the family he desired.

Selfish, I took a step forward, but the ache in my heart and the lead weight of my stomach stopped me. He thought I was dead. My bare feet dug into the wet earth and I wrapped my wings around me in a miserable shroud. The girl he loved might as well be dead. If he'd mentally buried me as someone he'd cared for, I'd destroy that the second he saw what I truly was.

In the distance, lightning flashed in the approaching cloud bank and thunder rumbled. Lucien moved away from the fireplace, out of my line of vision.

The memory of the two of us in front of the fire surfaced, the tenderness of my hand in his when he'd told me about his past and I'd expressed remorse for his hardships. *Don't be. It's better than living a lie*, he'd said. He might hate that I was Linnia, but he would hate not knowing what happened to me more. Reconsidering my decision every step of the way, I donned my ipuran, shook the water from my wings, and walked to the door. I felt like a stranger, wrapped in my lie of an illusion and standing on his porch—we'd never come in the front door. Hope and heartache warred in my chest; I unballed my fists, steadied my ipuran, and knocked.

Frigid water dripped from the trees and slapped onto the wet ground, measuring time, but then came the sound of footsteps, the cadence made imperfect by a limp. Golden light spilled out around me as Lucien opened the door.

He stared at me, stunned, and I froze, waiting for his reaction. "Lia?" He breathed my name and took a step forward, reaching with one hand as if he expected it to pass right through me. Instead, his fingertips touched my cheek and the surprise in his face buckled to poignant relief. After all the pain, the indignities, the suffering, I'd weathered under the Iyarri, the tenderness in Lucien's touch was so overwhelming I swayed on my feet. My eyes fluttered as his touch turned into a caress, his thumb sliding along my cheekbone.

I closed my hand over his and smiled, my face crumpling to contain the tears welling up in my voice. "Hello, Lucien."

His embrace was instant and fierce. Lucien spoke against my temple.

"You're alive." He held me as though I'd disappear if he let me out of the circle of his arms. "Oh my god, you're *alive*."

I tightened my arms around him, the cool scent of his cologne enveloping me, and tried to ignore the way his arms wrapped across my back but missed my wings. "I missed you," I murmured into the soft fabric of his shirt.

He held me, fingers threading into my hair. "I missed you too." Lucien put one hand under my chin and tilted it upward so my face was in the light. There were too many questions, but none of them mattered, each of us needing the reassurance of the other's safety, of the simple fact that the other was alive. There was the shadow of stubble on Lucien's face, a day or two old. I reached up and ran my hand down his cheek; he turned his face into my palm and whispered, "I can't believe you're here." He lifted my hand away from his face and we kissed, all the longing and fear of our time apart mixed with the joy of our reunion.

Lucien leaned against the wall of the house and drew my body against his; for a moment there was nothing to tell him, no heart laden with secrets, just bliss, love, and reunion. His lips were wanting and one hand cupped around my ribs, over where the napta scar lay on my skin.

When we released one another, he took me by one hand. "Let's get you inside." His eyes flickered to the night sky. "Were you followed?"

"No, we're safe."

He ushered me into the living room and shut the door behind us.

"Lucien, a lot happened and . . ." I tried to find a way to get to the truth right away, but it crawled deeper inside me, out of reach. I gave up, my words dissolving into ones I wanted to say instead. "I was so afraid. I thought you were dead."

"I know." He pushed my windblown hair back from my face. "I thought you were dead too, as soon as they took you." Lucien pressed his hands to either side of my face and lowered his forehead to mine. "I thought I'd lost you." His voice was taut with emotion.

My eyes flitted closed and I savored his skin against mine, the way his hair fell forward against my cheeks. "I thought I'd lost you too," I whispered.

Lucien pressed his lips to my forehead, then my lips. "You have to be freezing. Go sit by the fire, and I'll get you something to drink." Even after he said it we stood, still holding one another, until he eased away to make good on his promise.

The pale marble fireplace blazed with a crackling fire; I settled on the love seat, angling myself so my wings hung over the edge. My father's house, Lilnon, and Idura made me forget the human world wasn't built for wings, and I hated the way they turned the familiar foreign. On the coffee table, bathed in the dancing light of the fire, was the tiny statue of Eros and Psyche I hadn't had a chance to give Lucien. I covered my mouth with my hand and leaned forward, one wavy lock of hair falling in my face. Eros's wings were chipped at the ends, and there was a crack in the base, but it had survived the crash. The text around the base was still readable.

Why should you wish to behold me? Have you any doubt of my love? If you saw me, perhaps you would fear me, perhaps adore me, but all I ask of you is to love me.

Lucien gave me a steaming cup of coffee and eased down beside me, favoring one leg. He followed my gaze to the statue and said, "It's a miracle that survived. I expected to find it in pieces."

I put a hand on his thigh, enjoying each line of him under my fingertips. "That's not the only thing I expected to have been in pieces," I said, leaning against his side. "How did you get away?"

"Got far enough away to fall down a steep ditch and then crawled into a culvert. I flagged down a truck on the other side of the woods." He ran his hand back through his hair. "Woke up in the ER." He put his bare foot on the coffee table, pulled up the leg of his black drawstring pants, and showed me the crumpled starburst scar on the back of his calf. He quirked a sideways smile at me. "A little lower and I'd have been Achilles."

Stars and feathers, I had missed that smile. I returned it with an ease that I hadn't felt in months. "Is it bad?"

"Tore a bunch of muscle and almost severed a tendon, but could have been worse." He relaxed his leg, the exit scar on his shin a messier twin to the one on the calf. "I'm supposed to take it easy for another few weeks yet."

"What about your shoulder?"

He snorted. "Which one?" He turned toward me and pulled the neck of his heather-gray shirt to one side. A similar scar punctuated where his collarbone ended and his shoulder began. "If my stitched-up shoulder and the leg weren't enough to put me off work, this was. It's taken me forever to be able to lift anything again."

I traced the outline of the scar with my fingertip; my touch made Lucien's blue eyes glaciers afire, his pupils dark and dilated. I leaned forward, my palm flattening over the scar, and kissed him to chase off the inevitable. He eased me onto his lap, his mouth burning mine with the fiery taste of his nightcap. Warmth flushed along my skin as I pressed myself to him, the curves of my hips molding into the angles of his.

His heartbeat hammered under my hand, our desire so scorching it burned away my ipuran where we touched, but Lucien, his eyes half-lidded, hadn't seen. I lifted myself from his lap and stood with my arms and wings wrapped around myself, steadying my ipuran with a deep, shaky breath.

Lucien's expression shifted, worry hiding in the shadows on his face. "What's wrong?"

He deserved to know who he was kissing, who he thought he loved. I tried to talk around the knot in my throat, but pressed my lips together and shook my head.

Lucien took my human hand, his fingers reassuring and tender. "Lia, whatever it is, you can tell me."

I didn't know what would be worse, telling him or showing him.

My vision swam with tears and I blinked them back, dread a cold knot in my chest. My voice was quiet. "Just before Thanksgiving I met my father. My mother kept who he was from me until then."

Confusion washed across his handsome features. "I don't understand."

"I know." I fumbled for the right words, but no explanation existed but the truth. "I'm not human."

Lucien went still. "What?" I held his hand tighter than I should have. The crackling of the fire became a forest fire in my ears. He looked at my feet, three-toed and clawed. He saw shoes, maybe boots.

"My father is Iyarri." My ribs boxed in and I couldn't breathe.

His hand tensed in mine, but he didn't lift it away. "And your mother hid that from you?"

"Yes." My head hung forward. "I don't even know where to start, I am so sorry."

He glanced at the entwined marble figures. "That's what you were trying to tell me." After a moment's pause he exhaled, long and slow. "But you can't help that, Lia."

My heart both wanted to burst and sink into a hole in my chest. He accepted it, accepted what I was. I should have told him ages ago. I should have trusted him to understand. My voice was failing me, and it cracked when I spoke. "Look at me." I couldn't do it. I couldn't bring myself to drop my ipuran.

He looked at the statue on the table to me, confused. "I am looking at you."

Tears spilled from my eyes and down my cheeks. "No, *look* at me."

He understood then, I think. It was in the way the confusion left his face even before he focused enough to see through my ipuran. The moment he pierced it, the blue in his eyes grew so cold it extinguished the reflected firelight in them.

He pulled his hands away and stood in one motion. His glare not enough to put distance between us, he backed away a few steps, too. "How? How the fuck did they do that to you?" He glared at my wings.

My stomach turned to ice, and I clasped my hands to my chest. "A ritual, something they do to all the Linnia, all the half-breeds. It's supposed to kill them. Us." Lucien just stood there, staring at the way the firelight danced across the copper feathers and lit the golden teardrops in my unalah.

"How, though?" His voice was hoarse.

"I'm trying to explain, Lucien. I'm so sorry." My thoughts whirled like the motes over the flames.

He covered his face with his hands and sat down, though it was on the far end of the couch rather than near me. Lucien dropped his hands to his lap. "Okay, explain." His eyes were hard, but he was listening.

I told him everything.

Lucien's expression grew darker and colder as I unraveled the story. I came to the attack, how I was carried off by Miketh. "They lied to me. They told me you were dead." A chill went through me as I wondered if Aamon knew of Lucien's escape and had lied to me about that too. Had I not been so broken, so hopeless, I might not have agreed to wings, at least not right then.

His voice was dark. "And you believed them?"

"Shouldn't I have? You thought I was dead, too." He went silent and after a moment I continued, voice weak with shame, telling him how I had accepted Aamon's offer of wings. Lucien was stone-still. More words spilled out of me until, heart aching, I finished my tale, clenched my hands together, and waited.

Lucien stared at the statue on the table, his body as still as the tiny marble figures. When he looked at me, his eyes brimmed with the things my father had seen in my mother: fear, rejection, anger. "So, if I understand this right," he said, voice icy, "after you thought I was dead, any reservations you had about becoming one of them just disappeared?"

"No." I shook my head, my heart thudding in my chest. "Aamon lied to me and—"

"Not nearly as much as you have to me."

"Lucien, I—"

His voice was cruel, twisted by pain. "You what? You lied to me. This entire time you knew, and you didn't say a goddamned thing."

"I didn't think you'd listen."

"And that's some sort of excuse?"

"No, I was going to tell you, that's what the statue was for."

He shoved his hand back through his hair. "And after that? You figured you'd let me go on risking my own ass to save you?" He paced, his hands shaking. "I almost died to save a goddamned Iyarri."

"I am not Iyarri," I snapped.

"Jesus, Lia, look at you!"

"And how I look is the only thing that changed! You'd see that if you looked past these." I flared my wings; the force made the dying flames flare and tossed specks of spiraling light up the flue.

"So, you would rather I just pretend you aren't . . . whatever the fuck you are." My face crumpled and he glared into the darkness, his voice dripping with scorn. "I mean, why not? You were happy enough to pretend to be human to get through the door."

"Would you have listened to me if I hadn't?" Unshed tears made my voice waver.

"That isn't the point," he snapped.

"Then what is the point? I can't change who my parents are or what I am."

He scowled. "How was I so stupid?" He looked up at me, his beautiful face twisted by hate and rage and heartbreak. "My faith was a lie, and now you are too." His anguished words buckled to a choked sob.

I stood and reached out to him. "Lucien, please."

He pulled away as though my fingers would scald him. "Don't touch me."

"I didn't know how to tell you the truth."

"Of course you didn't. You're an Iyarri, all they know how to do is lie." He brought his fist to his lips, eyes bright with unshed tears.

"Lucien, I love you."

An eternity passed before he spoke. When he did, his voice was so low and strained I barely heard him, even with my damnable Iyarri ears. "Get out."

I stood frozen, heart fractured, unable to move. Lucien could have forced me to leave, but he would not touch me, not even to throw me from his home. He grabbed the tiny statue and hurled it against the far wall. It burst into a million pieces that rained upon the wood floor. "Get out!" he yelled.

I bolted, my chest twisting with a sob as I ran over the marble, the broken pieces biting into my feet. I stumbled but my wings kept me balanced; I hated myself, then. Half-blinded by tears, I fled out the door. Stinging, icy rain pelted my skin, and the rolling thunder drowned out the sounds of my feet splashing through puddles. Wrenching my wings open with a sob, I leapt into the thunderstorm-tossed sky.

THIRTY-
SIX

I LIMPED DOWN THE NAPTA staircase, my bare feet cut and bruised. At the bottom I paused and looked over my shoulder, tight with dread that someone would see me, hear my quiet, choked sobs. Miserable relief coursed through me—a trail of water droplets and smeared, wet footprints were the only things behind me.

Pulling the door to my chambers closed after me, I pressed my back to it and slid downward until I was sitting on the stone tiles. My sodden wings sagged on either side, and I folded forward and wrapped my arms around my knees. My heart ached, my stomach twisted with nausea, and my ribs were full of dull pain from the force of my sobs. I bowed my head under the weight of my anguish. *I inflict no other punishment on you than to leave you forever. Love cannot dwell with suspicion.*

I wanted him back.

His anger I had expected. The tears standing in his eyes and the wrenching sob I had not, and I should have. My selfishness gnawed at me until my gut was a hollow pit of despair.

Eventually, I changed into dry clothes and crawled into the tianta, settling my wings over me. My feet ached, my chest ached, and my heart ached.

The night passed in fits of sleep; I would wake nauseated, guilt-wracked, and forlorn, then curl back up and hope for sleep to take me again. My head was full to bursting with images: Lucien's look of revulsion when he peered through my ipuran, the way tears shone in his eyes, the hail of shattered marble. My thoughts chased through my mind, poltergeists in darkened hallways. Not human enough for Lucien, not Iyarri enough for the rest of them. I didn't belong at Idura any more than I belonged anywhere else, but I couldn't go back and change the choices I'd made. Even if I could, I didn't know if, or what, I'd have chosen differently.

By the time I finally gave up on sleep and got out of bed to wash my face, the ceilings were starting to brighten. As I waited for the water to warm, the mirror reflected back dried lines of tears on my cheeks. My eyes were bloodshot, the skin around them red and puffy. My feet and legs were spattered with dried mud, and my skin itched with the grittiness of it. I made do with the small sink and a washcloth, not in any hurry to go to the baths.

Someone knocked on my door, and I wiped my cheeks with my sleeves. "Come in."

Nesah cracked the door and poked her head inside. "You are here." She crept in like a timid cat and fussed with her belt. "I came to see if you were coming."

My mind fumbled through fog. This morning was Hataan's burning rites. "I'm not sure if people want me to go."

Nesah's voice was small and wilted by pain. "I want you there."

Her heartbreak reflected my own. "I'll be there."

She picked up my two hands and smiled. "Thank you. I have to go help prepare, but thank you." She gave my hands a squeeze and was gone.

I paused at the large double doors to the Iadnah library even though they were propped open. The library was stories tall, capped by a dome of glass, and its walls were lined to the ceiling with bookshelves carved into the stone. There were no ladders, just a stone runner for perching along the bottom of each shelf.

A large, crescent-shaped table dominated the center of the room, the floor around it encircled by blue marks similar to those that had sealed Hataan to Aamon's fate. Tiahmani gestured me to her side; I walked around the table on which Hataan's body rested.

Nothing had been done to mask his brutalized form, no artfully draped cloth to hide the error that cost him his life. Instead, someone had cleaned Hataan's body, dressed him in his Iadnah robes, and arranged his nearly severed head in line with his neck. Even with the blood washed away, what skin remained was blotched and bruised. His hands were crossed over his stomach, the thick black claws gleaming like sharpened onyx. Hataan's feet bore frightening talons, far longer and sharper than a normal Iyarri set. His wings, featherless, black, and leathery, were folded at his sides.

Much of Idura was present, and the Iadnah library was large enough to hold everyone. Some stood on the floor, others perched on the bookshelf railings.

What stunned me most were the children. Absent at the execution ritual, they were here for this. They stood near their parents, as solemn as the adults. There was fear at Hataan's contorted body, but also respect.

I scanned faces, looking at the myriad of emotions pressed into them: rage, sympathy, and regret, but mostly sorrow and shock.

A female Iyarri stepped forward, wings all shades of gold-red and ochre, like a phoenix not yet burst aflame. She was older, her hair done in a complex looped bun, the strands a mix of silver, copper, and gold. Tiahmani whispered in my ear. "That's Denôé, head of the Idura's Iadnah."

If Denôé were human, I would have guessed her to be in her sixties—though she walked to the center of the library with the straight-backed grace of royalty. Her voice was clear. "My brothers and sisters, we gather here to pay tribute to Hataan Li'iansa, an aspiring healer of great skill, whose life was wrongly taken in the place of a traitor's." She gestured to his mangled form. "This hull is all that remains of a gentle soul, one who spent great amounts of his energy setting right the wounds of others with compassion. Hataan pulled Iyarri back from the brink of the emptiness he was cast into. He did it without seeking thanks or recognition because it was in his nature to make whole and preserve life.

"This, his only life, was taken from him ruthlessly and senselessly. In the end, he cursed none of us for our error, for our lack of vigilance, for not finding out the truth. He held no malice toward us, his last request simply for an end to his suffering. It was all we could do to oblige him." Denôé went on, though the words blurred together in one requiem of sadness and loss. I swallowed around the lump in my throat, my eyes stinging with fresh tears. Hataan was dead, the spectacle of his body twisting and transforming caught behind the eyes of every Iyarri who had witnessed it, like a mirror that would not give up a reflection.

Denôé offered no solace that Hataan or any of the other recent dead would be reunited with those who mourned them in some chimerical afterlife, where his broken body would be made whole again and the point of his horrific misfortune revealed. She did not speak of gods or of souls that endured beyond this mortal plane, no allaying words about a time for healing and a time for dying.

Denôé raised her wings in two great feathered fans as her eulogy reached its dénouement, her voice stoic but her heart weary. "And so, we send Hataan into the flames, that they will consume his body, and pass the responsibility of carrying his memories to each of us."

The leader of the Iadnah bowed her head to signal the end of her speech. She turned and six other Iadnah, Nesah among them, stepped out and stood on the outer rim of the blue symbols that circled the table. They extended and cupped their wings so they stood wingtip to wingtip. Every other Iyarri near to the circle drew away. There was a resolve, a new depth to the pale lavender of Nesah's eyes, carved by pain, loss, and appalling injustice.

The Iadnah's chant began with Denôé, the syllables soothing and compelling as she raised her hands above her head, mimicking the extension of wings. On the floor beneath their bare, three-toed feet, the blue chalk symbols pulsed with light and sank into the stone floor. The chant repeated itself, and Denôé was joined by the Iyarri to her left, who raised his hands in the same fashion. Two voices became three, became four, became five and then six, Nesah's voice as the seventh adding the highest and sweetest notes.

The incantation shifted, and blue flames appeared on Hataan's body, licking at the corpse. There was no tinder or source of ignition, nothing but a cold, dead body to feed upon, and yet the flames grew. The blue flames consumed him, blocking out all but a distorted silhouette. Waves of shimmering heat moved upward, contained within the circle so that not a hair, not a fold of an Iadnah robe fluttered.

The chanting became a hum, low and deep, and pulsed with the flames. Within the space of the Iadnah's mystical song, Hataan's grotesque shell was reduced to ash. As the humming quelled to silence, the flames died, sinking into the pile of blackened cinders.

The Iadnah let down their arms, and Nesah's tears finally spilled down her cheeks, leaving two bright lines. She was not alone. Many faces, including my own, were damp with tears. Denôé turned to those assembled. "Go, and remember, until the skies fall."

Read on for a sneak peek at the second book in
The Iyarri Chronicles, *Mourning's Dawn.*

ONE

FEATHERS FLASHED AND THE split blades of napta rang like silver tuning forks. Two Laidrom warriors battled in the center of the great hall, their bare three-toed, taloned feet quick and light inside the braid of silver metal embedded in the stone floor. Around them, a second, frightful circle formed, this one made from the wings and weapons of spectating Iyarri. My father stood among them, watching for the strike that would decide the victor of the contest.

I drew a wary breath, even though I was far across the hall, with a heavy table between me and the fighting Laidrom. This might have been sport for them, but my body remembered the way similar blades had once parted my skin.

Each combatant was light as a sparrow but formidable as a gladiator. They circled one another, grinning, their luminous, scarred skin gleaming with sweat, blades extended from the gauntlets on their forearms. Mihr lunged forward, her wings arching, the long swallowtail feathers comets behind her.

Ralceor darted aside and parried her blow. His black hair rippled with the motion, the smooth curtain broken by small braids twined with strings of beads and feathers. Bare-chested, his body was sinewy and powerful.

With a cry of exertion, Mihr slammed her wing into Ralceor and sent him staggering. I sucked my breath in as she lunged forward, leading with her napta blade. The Laidrom cheered, raising cups and sloshing liquor, the droplets of red darignis pattering to the floor like blood. Ralceor recovered his footing, gold and black wings flashing as he gathered himself for a block—but at the last moment, he lashed out with a bladed gauntlet, the feint low and fast. A single, shallow red line appeared on Mihr's thigh.

"First blood—Ralceor wins!" boomed Cæl's voice.

Mihr and Ralceor retracted their blades, clasped forearms in a warrior's handshake, and traded smiles of a contest well-fought.

With a sound like a sail cracking in the wind, the watching Iyarri snapped their wings upward in unison and then parted to allow Ralceor out of the Circle of Blades first. Laidrom clapped him on the shoulders and music kicked up, thrumming drums and lilting wood flutes. The sound reverberated inside the carved stone heart of the bluff—perhaps it was meant to sound celebratory, but to me it sounded like they readied for war.

It was the summer solstice and the third night of Micali, the peak of the five-day Fête of Hands, and the air was thick with the smell of sweat, feathers, and darignis. Ralceor waved one clawed hand to his father, Bahram, who stood not far away from me, flicking his wings in time to Miketh's flute. Bahram gave his son a nod, the lines of his smile creased deep with pride.

I pressed my human hand to my chest, my sigh falling to rest against my lonely, envious heart; Ralceor was new to Idura, recently sent from Lilnon. Everyone had loved him instantly while, half a year later, they still hated me.

The differences between me and the Iyarri were so slight that, by hiding my hands in my sleeves, I'd made sure no one at Lilnon had known what I was. I had the same three-toed feet, the same fey-lithe build, and even the same keen senses, all traits inherited from my father. My ginger hair was unremarkable, and the ritual that had summoned the great copper wings from my back had also drawn other Iyarri qualities from my blood: a higher body temperature and luminous skin. But these similarities brought no kinship; instead the Iyarri treated them as things I'd stolen, things that weren't rightfully mine. Hatred honed their scrutiny. While all Iyarri had luminous golden skin, some were lighter, others darker—they'd only thought my paleness freakish once they knew my human mother was the source of it, and so I stood out like a wisp of moonlight in a searing ray of sunlight.

A Laidrom pulled me from my uneasy thoughts as she stumbled past my table and doubled over a trash barrel, retching.

The hard swell of my aunt's pregnant belly pressed into me as Tiahmani leaned close and shouted over the din. "I told you the Micali hangover would last as long as the fête itself. I might miss darignis, but I sure as hell won't miss the headache this year."

My temples pulsed, but my headache and dry eyes weren't from alcohol. The clamor of the fête made me crave the escape others had taken hours ago; although the holiday and its celebration were not limited to the warrior sect, most other Iyarri had long since left for their beds. I longed for mine. In the six months I'd been at Idura, I'd spent as much time as I could cloistered in my rooms. Cæl and Tiahmani had wheedled a promise out of me that I'd stay until the twenty-second chime, hoping that with exposure, the Iyarri would accept me more.

I wasn't holding my breath.

They blamed me for the death of Ikkar, Væries's father and Heeoa, leader of the Laidrom, even though it had been Aamon's lies and Lucien's guns that ended him. They blamed me for my father's transgressions with my human mother, as if I were the cause rather than the result of their relationship. They blamed me for existing among them, even though it was by the decree of Saan-Eleéth Ohlera, their highest law-speaker, that I do so as a reminder, as a punishment, for my father siring a child with a human.

A Laidrom scowled at my back as he passed behind me, deliberately clipping my shoulder with a wing. The wide neckline of my finely embroidered, backless dress slipped down my shoulder, and I pushed it back up. The dress, too, was a reminder and a punishment. I was the first Linnia in two thousand years, and Eleéth had ordered me into clothes that framed my scars like a twisted work of art and put them on display for all of Lilnon to see.

I pushed my hair back over my shoulder, the long tumble of waves a futile attempt to veil my scars. More golden and luminous than my skin, they shone like the metallic veins of a kintsukuroi cup, each line a place where my body had torn apart as my wings ripped free.

Unable to maintain my anger anymore, I was simply weary of it; of the underlying ridicule in even the smallest statements, of the intolerance, of the fact that none of my artistic talents would ever outweigh the fact that my mother was human.

For the last two days, the Iyarri at the fête had ignored me and I them, drawing to pass the time and stealing away whenever I could. Now, I stared at the time-telling chimes in the corner, willing the stone shard hanging in the center of a spiral of metal tubes to pulse with enchanted light and chime the hour when it stayed dark.

I pressed my hand to my aching forehead and looked back down at my drawing, trying to block out the pounding drums and shouting Laidrom. My own napta gauntlets hugged my arms, dark and severe. In contrast, the pair I was drawing on paper were lighter, more feminine, and had metal detailing that looked like sprays of feathers and vines.

Suddenly, a glass slammed down next to my drawing with such ferocity, I jumped. Kinor leaned over me, his tawny wings flashing gold in the light, like he was a griffin given human form. "Hey, Linnia, how about a drinking contest?" A cruel smile carved its way across his face as he savored the way I was frozen still with terror. "You're not drinking straight out of my flask, though. I don't want any half-breed backwash."

I dropped my gaze with a shake of my head and tightened the grip on my pencil. Inwardly, I cringed at the memory of the way Kinor had thrown me in front of the other Laidrom as proof my father shouldn't be Heeoa. It was Kinor's criticism that had forced Cæl to challenge

Væries for leadership of the Laidrom. Now, with the contest only a week away, Kinor had grown bold in his disdain.

He unscrewed the top of his flask and poured, the darignis hitting the bottom of my empty water glass and rolling in a wave before it filled the vessel in earnest. The darignis was aphotic red with bright flecks of copper and heavy swirls of black. The aroma of scorched spices and woodsmoke wafted upward, a searing reminder of why its name meant hellfire.

Tiahmani pushed herself up on one arm and arched both eyebrows at Kinor. "Back off. She said no."

"She didn't say shit." Kinor's breath rolled over my face in a reeking wave of stale liquor.

"I said back off." Tiahmani snapped the words and backhanded the flask from Kinor's hand, one of her wings clipping the edge of the table as she moved. The heavy wood jumped and the glass of darignis tipped onto my drawing. I lunged forward and snatched the paper up with a cry, too late to save it from the tidal wave of red. It hung in my hand, dripping wet and ruined—the paper stained mottled garnet, the graphite feathering and blurring.

Kinor's hardened leather flask clattered across the floor. The rabble quieted. Drinks stopped midway to mouths and hands hovered over now-silent drums. My chest cratered with humiliation and my heart shrank back against my spine as I lowered the drawing to the soaked table, pinned by a growing circle of eyes.

Across the room, Væries picked up the fallen flask, approached, and pushed it against Kinor's chest, but kept her eyes trained on me. Her delicate features were crinkled into a glare, the red splotches in her brown irises contracting to hot, angry pinpricks in brown velvet. My gut twisted at the sight of her—many Laidrom favored her to win over Cæl and, once again, I regretted that my father had challenged Væries to prove himself and quell the dissension.

Her bloodshot gaze dropped to the scar on my deltoid, the mark that gave me the right to bear napta. The honor I got because I killed not one but two Laidrom "How about a challenge you can't say no to, Linnia? You and me, Circle of Blades, first blood." Her voice was slurred and her lips parted in a vicious, feline smile; I cringed and stepped back from her. "And when I win, I'm going to peel that mark off your arm and give it to your father as a consolation prize once I beat him too."

I clapped my hand over the scar and heat flushed through me. The memory of Maroch carving the talon-ended triskele into my deltoid rose in my mind, the way a hot sheet of blood had covered my arm and pattered around my bare feet. "Everyone knows you can beat me." My voice sounded far away as I took another step backward and toward the door.

Tiahmani put a quelling hand on Væries's shoulder. Ikkar had been Tiahmani's Heeoa once too. "You're drunk. Leave off."

Væries shrugged off Tiahmani's hand. "I know I'm drunk, but it's not like I need to be sober to beat her."

Tiahmani arched one dark eyebrow. "You need to prove yourself against a Linnia? Ikkar—"

"It's justice for him," Væries snarled. I recalled Aamon's words: *Lucien killed Ikkar, the Laidrom Heeoa. There is a great cry for retribution, and the only person left for them to exact it from is you.* Much had changed since Aamon spoke those words to me, but the sentiment had not. The memory of Væries cradling her father's corpse surfaced. Shattered by Lucien's gunshot, one eye socket had been empty, and there was an open void where the side of his head had been—months had not dimmed a single grisly detail. I knew it was pride and grief that drove Væries, but the way they manifested in such rage sent my heart quavering against my ribs in fear. She was frightfully capable of meting out equal destruction in a single strike, and she didn't need more than one to kill me.

Væries grabbed the front of my dress and shoved me so hard I staggered. "Get in the ring, bitch." I trembled as Væries stalked into the ring. Her dark hair was pulled up in a messy bun held with silver tines. Loose tendrils brushed the scarring on each arm that marked her as Vohim, a higher and deadlier rank than even Tiahmani's.

Bahram leaned near to Tiahmani, dropping his voice to a low, critical rumble. "And Væries aspires to lead the Laidrom?"

"Væries's always been . . ." Tiahmani searched for a word and pushed a hand back through her dark hair. "Challenging." I frowned at the understatement. "After the kiaisi killed Ikkar, it's been impossible to convince her that what's best for us is Cæl's leadership."

Desperate and stalling for time, I bit my lip and cast a pleading look across the great hall to my father. Cæl looked fierce in his Heeoa garb: wide-legged pants, mahogany hair pulled back in an upraised five-strand plait, and gauntlets the color of dried blood on his arms. He could get me out of this. He could distract Væries, call for his Laidrom to gather, something, anything to derail this train of events. Cæl met my eyes but stood motionless, his redwood wings crossed, his lips pressed into a thin, stressed line. Realization cut through me: there was nothing he would do. There was nothing he *could* do. For my father to step in, to protect me when none of his Laidrom would have warranted such sheltering, was out of the question. His rule as Heeoa was tenuous, and that his challenger was now my combatant rendered intervention out of the question.

The other Laidrom pounded tables like war drums in encouragement, and I shook my head and wiped my sweaty hands on my dress. "No, I'm not going to—"

Tiahmani pulled me close, her voice a hissing whisper. "Doesn't matter. She challenged you, and that mark on your shoulder means you can't refuse." She gave my arm a reassuring squeeze and pushed me through the packed circle of bodies and into the circle with Væries. "Just remember what we taught you, and block her strikes as best you can."

Laidrom gathered like a murder of crows around us, the ones closest standing with their taloned feet on the floor, those behind perching on tabletops.

With shaking fingers, I cuffed the sleeves of my dress up over the hardened leather of my napta. The formed leather gauntlets, the intricate lacing, and the metal framework holding the blade were forged with equal eye to form and function, but the oak-brown leather and arcing silver accents were unique to this pair, to the Iyarri I had killed. Judging by the blazing hate in the eyes of the Laidrom around me, they recognized them and remembered their fallen wingmate.

My heartbeat sped up as the crowd quieted down, and I returned my eyes to Væries. My damnable artistic eye noted every difference between us. I was taller, but slender; Væries was luminously tan, lean, and muscled. She had better than a century of training with her blades; I'd had less than a year. My stomach rolled with dread.

Cæl approached the edge of the ring and gave me a nod of reassurance, but the tightness in his neck and shoulders mirrored itself in my own body.

In a moment of still terror I wondered what would happen if Væries killed me. If she did, my father would care, at least for a while . . . but he'd only known me, really known me, for a year. After grief would come gratitude; he could reclaim his previous life in a way that was impossible while I lived as a reminder of his failing. It might even strengthen his resolve to be the most loyal Iyarri the Elonu-Dohe had ever counted amongst its ranks.

Kinor held out a flask to Væries and winked. "To victory?"

Væries scooped the molded leather from his hand and drained it in a single motion. She grimaced and shook her head, eyes bright with drink. "To victory."

My father stepped into the circle and turned around once, taking in the spectators with an even gaze. The planes of Cæl's face were strong, his eyes intelligent. "The contest is until first blood. No one interferes with the combatants." He stepped to the edge of the circle and waited for Væries and me to nod that we were ready.

I wasn't. I wasn't sure I ever would be.

Væries unsheathed her napta with a flash of silver metal and an equally frightening grin. My heart hammered against my ribs, and I fought to clear the memories of the way other napta blades had carved into my skin, but every arcing scar on my body seemed to tingle.

I drew a deep, steading breath and centered myself. With a flick of my arms I unsheathed the deadly split blades, looked to my father, and nodded.

"Begin!" Cæl's voice boomed out across the banquet hall.

Væries's blade whistled toward my face, and I threw myself backward with a terrified inhale.

LOAGÆTH WORDS

ahasa /ah-HA-sa/: Mother.

Aisaro /AI-sa-ro/: The code of Iyarri law.

Akarinu /A-kah-REE-nu/: Iyarri who are not in the ternion, literally "praiseworthy," because those within ternion could not do their jobs without the support of the Akarinu. Akarinu are the merchants, educators, artisans, farmers, architects, and infrastructure management of Iyarri society.

Aldaria /al-DAR-ee-ah/: Part of the ternion, this group focuses its efforts in hiding Iyarri from the human world. Ranks, lowest to highest: Orcanin (resource management), Pothnir (Iyarri and human finances), Amayo (keeping the Iyarri undiscovered through direct human manipulation).

Amayo /ah-MAI-oh/: The highest rank in the Aldaria, specializing in the direct manipulation of humans to hide Iyarri. Rank designated by three borders on their otherwise plain clothing.

biah /BI-ah/: A single stance in Capmiali.

Capmiali /CAP-me-AH-lee/: Iyarri style of fighting practiced by the Laidrom, sometimes trained by moving through each of seventy-seven stances.

darignis /dar-RIG-nis/: A very potent Iyarri liquor favored by the Laidrom. Deep red in color with flecks of copper and smoky black swirls, it smells like scorched spices, woodsmoke, and ash.

Doalin /do-AH-lin/: The "Unspeakable Sin" of an Iyarri mating with a human and producing a child.

Elonu-Dohe /EY-lon-noo-DOH/: The overarching term for Iyarri society.

essia /ESS-ee-ya/: Father.

Galearii /gale-AHR-ree/: The lowest rank in the Laidrom. General warriors and scouts. Rank designated by scarring on the right arm.

gephna /GEF-na/: A flexible expletive not fit for polite company.

Heeoa /HEE-oh-ah/: The highest rank in the Laidrom. There is one Heeoa per stronghold who acts as a general to all Laidrom there. Rank designated by scarring on both arms and down the back and chest.

Iadnah /EE-ahd-nuh/: This mystical and esoteric group is the most specialized and selective of all the Iyarri in the ternion, also making them the fewest in number. They are regarded as somewhat reclusive in an already highly insular society. Each title has three ranks within it, but broadly denotes the specific type of magic specialized in: Vadali (enchanting magic), Sondn (transformative magic), Li'iansa (healing magic). Rank markings begin with blue tattooing on the hands at first rank, up the arms at second, and a draped circle of symbols across the chest and over the wings at third.

Idura /EYE-dur-RA/: Iyarri stronghold located in the bluffs over the Mississippi River near the Twin Cities, Minnesota.

ipuran /EYE-pur-an/: A mentally projected mask that makes Iyarri appear human on the ground or as a winged bird in flight.

Iyarri /EE-yar-ee/: Name of the winged raced that used to live alongside humans, but has since withdrawn their influence from.

kiaisi /kee-EYE-see/: Iyarri-killer. Formerly a term used for those humans that lived with Iyarri, they turned on and murdered the Rior, fracturing the Saanir.

Laiad / LAY-add/: The Fête of Knowledge, which occurs in the fall and is overseen by the Iadnah. This Luah focuses on a reverence for the truth, learning, and rituals. This fête is held in the Iadnah library, which is filled with music and soft lights.

Laidrom /LEE-ay-drom/: The military branch and internal police of Iyarri society. When capital punishments are decreed the Laidrom often take the role of executioners. Their primary role, however, is killing humans who have learned the truth about Iyarri. Ranks, lowest to highest: Galearii, Vohim, Heeoa.

Li'iansa/LEE-eye-AN-sa/: Iadnah who specialize in healing magic.

Lilnon /LIL-non/: Iyarri stronghold in New York.

Linnia /LIN-ni-ah/: A half-breed cross between an Iyarri and a human, called Nephilim by humans.

Loagæth /lo-AH-gay-eth/: The Iyarri language.

Luah /LOO-ah/: An Iyarri Fête or festival. There are four per year: Odecrin in the spring, Micali in the summer, Laiad in the fall, and Nalvage in the winter.

lucala /LOO-ca-la/: Meaning "waypoint," it is a place for traveling Iyarri to rest when flying the distance between two strongholds.

Micali /ME-kuh-lee/: The Fête of Hands, it takes place over the summer solstice and is presided over by the Laidrom. This Luah focuses on things wrought with the hands: buildings, victorious battles, and other fruits of manual labor.

Na-hath /NA-hath/: An ancient

form of Loagæth used by the Iadnah for arcane ritual work.

Nalvage /NAL-vazh /: The Fête of Remembrance, is held across the winter solstice on the longest night of the year. During this Luah Iyarri reflect on what separates them from the humans and are mindful of what it takes to maintain that position.

Naphal /na-PHAL/: A "fallen" Iyarri, one transformed into a featherless, twisted monstrosity as punishment. Reserved for the most heinous of crimes/traitors.

napta /NAP-tah/: The favored weapon of the Laidrom. Each napta is comprised of two parts, a gauntlet and a blade, and are worn in pairs.

Nisroc /NIS-rok/: Laidrom who serve as formal guards to the Saanir.

noro /nor-roh/: Sister.

noromi /nor-OH-me/: Brother.

Nuam /NOO-ahm/: An Iyarri mate that is the mother or father of a couple's child.

ohleræ /OH-ler-rae/: The innate power that enables an Ohlera to tell truth from a lie.

Ohlera /OH-ler-ra/: High Iyarri law-speaker, able to flawlessly tell truth from a lie. One half of a Saanir.

okada /oh-KA-da/: A shorter Laidrom throwing blade often worn as a pair at the back of the belt. Standard issue is a plain pair, but fancier versions are often given as a gift to Laidrom to commemorate an important event. Means 'mercy,' with the implication of mercy-killing.

Orcanin /OAR-kan-in/: The lowest rank in the Aldaria. Rank designated by a single line of bordering on the edges of their otherwise plain clothing. Focuses on resource management, such as redirecting human supplies to an Iyarri stronghold, or maintaining the land around strongholds as either protected wildlands or private (Iyarri-owned) property.

pasahasa /PAS-ah-ha-SA/: Daughter.

pilzin /PIL-zin/: A thick, crisp non-alcoholic drink that tastes of juniper berries and is served extremely cold.

pir- /peer/: An honorific given to the advisors to an Ohlera.

Pothnir /POTH-en-IR/: This middle rank in the Aldaria focuses on both Iyarri and human finances. They ensure that Iyarri currency is minted and that the Elonu-Dohe have as much money as they need to keep themselves hidden from humans. Rank designated two borders of embroidery on the edges of their otherwise plain clothes.

Rior /REE-or /: High Iyarri empath, able to gain supernatural insight into a situation. Murdered by the kiaisi, breaking the Saanir.

Saan- /san/: An honorific used when speaking about a member of the Saanir.

Saanir /SA-near/: A ruling pair over a segment of Iyarri society comprised of an Ohlera and a Rior.

Saanire /SA-near-ee/: The full honorific used when addressing an Ohlera or a Rior directly.

Semeroh /SEM-er-oh/: An Iyarri mate in the spiritual, sexual, or companionship sense. It is not uncommon for an Iyarri to have multiple Semeroh, each sharing a specific passion.

solpeth /SOL-peth/: An innate Iyarri ability that makes them supernaturally persuasive to humans.

Sondn /SON-din/: Iadnah who specialize in transformative magic, such as giving a Linnia wings, turning an Iyarri into a Naphal, or magically cremating a corpse.

ternion /ter-NEE-on/: Composed of the three groups of specialized Iyarri: Laidrom, Aldaria, and Iadnah.

tianta /TEE-an-ta/: Iyarri bed; a large oval scooped out of carved wood, like a shallow nest that keeps wings inside while sleeping.

unalah /oo-NAH-lah/: The long, trailing feathers on an Iyarri's wings. Decorative rather than functional, those with eye-spots and ocellate markings are considered highly attractive.

Vadali /vah-DAH-lee/: Iadnah who practice enchanting magic that imbues an inanimate object with specific properties at the will of the caster. Common uses include making the ceilings of a stronghold glow with magical light, chimes that toll time markers or summons, and sending messages between magic circles.

viruden /VIE-rue-den/: Beautiful.

Vohim /VOH-him/: The middle rank in the Laidrom. Act as lieutenants. Rank designated by scarring on both arms.

CAST

Aamon /AH-mon/: Iyarri; Aldaria Amayo

Anahita /AH-na-hi-ta/: Iyarri; Iadnah Sondn and advisor to Saan-Eleéth

Aurelia /or-REEL-ee-yuh/: Linnia; daughter of Cæl and Catherine

Barcus / BAR-cuss/: Iyarri; Akarinu advisor to Saan-Eleéth

Cæl /KAYL/: Iyarri; Laidrom Heeoa; Aurelia's father

Catherine /KATH-rinn/: Human; Aurelia's mother

Denôé /den-OH-ay/: Iyarri; Iadnah Vadali and Council of Four Winds member at Idura

Eleéth /eh-LEE-eth/: Iyarri; Saanire Ohlera

Hataan /HA-taan/: Iyarri; Iadnah Li'iansa; Semeroh to Nesah

Ikkar /ICK-kar/: Iyarri; deceased; Laidrom Heeoa of Idura; father of Væries

Irel /IR-rel/: Iyarri; Iadnah Li'iansa

Isaiah /ay-ZEY-ah/: Lucien's birth name

Khaviel / KAH-vee-ell/: Iyarri; Akarinu and Council of Four Winds member at Idura

Kinor /KIN-or/: Iyarri; Laidrom Galearii

Lucien /LUW-siy-ahn/: Human; kiaisi

Maroch / MA-roc/: Iyarri; Laidrom Heeoa; advisor to Saan-Eleéth

Miketh / MEH-keth/: Iyarri; Laidrom Vohim

Nesah /NEE-sa/: Iyarri; Iadnah Sondn; sister to Sofiel

Occodon /OCK-co-don/: Iyarri; Aldaria Amayo; advisor to Saan-Eleéth

Siyah /SEE-yuh/: Iyarri–deceased; Akarinu; Aamon's Semeroh

Sisera /SIS-sur-uh/: Iyarri; Akarinu advisor to Saan-Eleéth

Sofiel /soph-EYE-el/: Iyarri; Iadnah Sondn; sister to Nesah

Stephen Keller /STEF-en/: Human–deceased; painted *Angels Unseen*

Tiahmani /TEE-ah-MA-nee/: Iyarri; Laidrom Galearii; sister to Cæl

Væries /VAIR-ees/: Iyarri; Laidrom Galearii; daughter to Ikkar

Acknowledgments

You must gather your party before venturing forth—those that lent their support on this journey made it possible for me to make it to the end of this first book, and, skies willing, many more after.

I am eternally grateful for my husband David, for his unerring belief in me, for how he understands the work and the struggle like no one else, and for being the singular best thing that has ever happened to me.

To my friends who have known these characters for years: Jessica Bauer, who deserves a medal for dealing with my persnickety Libra sensibilities when it came to both writing and web design, and Nicola Hastings for our angst sessions because writing is hard, and who offered support and suggestions across endless edits and iterations.

Thank you to my mom, for encouraging my love of reading and books from an early age and to Andrew, Jeremiah, and Sarah, for making me feel like the coolest big sister in the entire world. Karin and Max, thank you for an incredible photo shoot weekend and making me look like a Real Author™.

I'm humbled by the tireless work and expertise I received from everyone at Wise Ink, but especially Laura Zats, who could make me laugh at my own flawed writing and knew how to challenge me to make it better.

My deepest thanks to the insanely talented Carlos Quevedo, who pulled the cover image from my head and gave it form—without him this book would have been far less lovely.

And to my Patrons, who not only believe my creative endeavors enough to extend their support, but also remind me that, when I'm deep in the weeds, that this is all something to be very excited about.